After the Fall

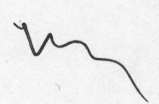

Also by Julie Cohen

Dear Thing
Where Love Lies

After the Fall

JULIE COHEN

 St. Martin's Griffin 🞄 New York

AFTER THE FALL. Copyright © 2016 by Julie Cohen. All rights reserved. Printed in the United States of America. For information, address St. Martin's Press, 175 Fifth Avenue, New York, N.Y. 10010.

www.stmartins.com

The Library of Congress Cataloging-in-Publication Data is available upon request.

ISBN 978-1-250-12742-6 (trade paperback)
ISBN 978-1-250-12743-3 (e-book)

Our books may be purchased in bulk for promotional, educational, or business use. Please contact your local bookseller or the Macmillan Corporate and Premium Sales Department at 1-800-221-7945, extension 5442, or by e-mail at Macmillan SpecialMarkets@macmillan.com.

First published in Great Britain under the title *Falling* by Black Swan, an imprint of Transworld Publishers, a Penguin Random House company.

First U.S. Edition: May 2017

10 9 8 7 6 5 4 3 2 1

For Lillian Cohen: grandmother, card player, one-eyed driver, crosshatch doodler, *kneidlach* maker; always remembered, always missed

And we, who have always thought
of happiness as rising, would feel
the emotion that almost overwhelms us
whenever a happy thing falls.

Rainer Marie Rilke, 'Tenth Elegy',
translated by Stephen Mitchell

Chapter One

Honor

The last stage of Honor Levinson's life began at the top of the stairs in her home in North London.

The windows had been cleaned two days before by the young man who came every spring with his bucket and ladder. The sun shone through the glass, warming a stripe of carpet and wall, stroking against Honor's cheek as she passed through it on the way to the stairs, carrying a basket of laundry to be washed.

She was thinking of the laundry she used to have to do: the weight of PE kits and trousers caked with mud at the knees. School uniforms and gardening clothes, shirts that needed ironing, knickers and pants and handkerchiefs. So many loads every week, one after the other, unrelenting, just for one child and one woman. Sometimes it had felt as if her home were festooned with dripping clothes. She had to negotiate a jungle of drying socks and tights just to get into the bath. For something that took up so much time and effort, washing clothes was under-represented in literature.

This afternoon her basket contained two blouses, a vest, a

skirt, and three pairs of knickers. None of them dirty, really; what did she do to make her clothes dirty these days? Those days of sweat and soil and spills were over. Now her basket was light, as light as the sunshine in the side of her vision.

Honor balanced the basket on her hip and put her hand on the banister. The wood was warm, too, from the sun. Downstairs on the ground floor, the phone rang. She stepped forward to go down the first stair and she missed it.

The shock wasn't that she was falling. It was that she had missed the step, that her body had forgotten the language of the house, how to do this thing she had done every day for most of the years of her life. Honor put out her hands to stop herself but the banister slipped from her grip and she hit the riser hard with her hip and kept falling, slithering down the wooden stairs on her back.

'Stephen!' she cried to the empty air.

No pain, not yet, just thuds as she slid down the rest of the stairs, with no one to catch her. The back of her head bounced off a step and she saw stars. They were clearer than anything she had seen in a long time.

She knew this feeling, as if she had played this out in her mind many times before. The last moment, familiar as a child or a lover.

She came to rest at the bottom, splayed on the floor. The phone rang for the second time. *Two rings*, Honor thought. *It all happened in the space between two rings of the telephone.*

Now she felt it, or some of it: the back of her head, her hip, her back, her bottom, her elbows – impact rather than pain. Her head was resting on the last step. She lay in another pool of sunlight and dazzle. But she was alive. When she called out, she had been certain she wouldn't survive.

10

Honor touched the back of her head. It was warm and wet, and her hand, when she saw it, was shaking and covered with blood.

Seeing it, the pain came.

'Stephen,' she said again and her voice came from someone else, someone old and weak.

Honor sat up, ignoring the screaming from her back and hip, the pounding in her head. She sucked in a breath and, holding on to the banister, tried to pull herself up.

She immediately fell back down, squealing aloud with pain from her hip.

The phone rang for a third time, or perhaps it was the fourth. Broken hip, old woman living alone, what a cliché she was. All these years of struggling, and she was a cliché. Carefully, gasping, Honor turned herself so she was lying on her left side, the side where her hip wasn't broken. Using her arms and her left foot, pushing herself across the wooden floor, she crawled towards the phone.

There was a telephone on each storey of her house: one in her bedroom, one in the kitchen in the basement, and one here on the ground floor, in the living room. Her mobile was upstairs in her bedroom. Honor crawled through the doorway, slipping on her wet hands, her weak foot, to the Persian rug. She rested for a moment there, the wool scratchy against her cheek. Blood dripped from the back of her head, down her face. *Cold water to wash that out*, she thought, and the phone rang again, for the sixth time? Tenth?

It had been ringing for as long as she could remember and she still had a metre to crawl.

She drew in a deep breath tasting of dust and wool, and pushed herself forward once again. It was more difficult across

11

the carpet. As soon as she was better she was going to put this carpet in the nearest skip, bloodstain and all.

The phone was on a low table by the sofa. She wriggled the last few inches, using her shoulder to propel herself forward. Honor hooked her arm around the table leg, pulled as hard as she could and the table toppled over. Thank God for flimsy furniture.

Luckily the phone landed beside her, the receiver off its cradle. She snatched for it with her good hand. 'Hello?' she said. 'Hello, I need help.'

A pause. Her hair had come loose and was hanging in her face, dark with blood. She could feel sweat on her upper lip. It had been some time since she had last sweated.

'Yes, madam,' said a voice on the line at last, heavily accented. 'Good day, this is Edward from Computer Access Services. I am calling about trouble with your Windows computer?'

'Piss off,' she told him clearly, and pushed the button to hang up the phone. She dialled 999. 'I require an ambulance,' she told the operator, and waited the million hours until she was put through.

'Ambulance service, what's the nature and location of the emergency, please?'

'I've fallen down the stairs and I have broken my hip and I am bleeding from my head.' She gave the calm-sounding woman her address.

'All right, ma'am, I've alerted the dispatcher, and I'm going to stay on the line now and try to help you while you're waiting. You say you've hit your head and broken your hip? Are you having any difficulty breathing?'

'That's about the only thing I'm not having difficulty doing.'

'Good girl.'

'Don't patronize me, I'm old enough to be your grand-mother. My name is Honor.'

'Yes, Honor,' said the dispatcher, a hint of humour in her voice. 'If you don't mind me saying, your telling me off is a good sign. Is there anyone with you?'

'I'm alone.'

'Is your head still bleeding?'

'Yes.'

'OK, Honor, is there anything you can use to press against it and stop the bleeding?'

She groped upward. A cushion, squashed nearly flat from use, lay near the edge of the sofa. Honor pulled it off. She pressed the cushion against the back of her head, gritting her teeth at the stab of pain. She held the phone to her ear with her other hand. It was slippery with blood.

'I've done it,' she said to the woman on the other end of the line.

'That's good to hear.' She sounded young and chirpy. Like Jo. Honor closed her eyes and pictured wavy hair, a pink-lipped smile.

'Honor? Are you still with us?'

She shook her head, trying to clear it. *Still with us*, another cliché, trying to make this whole incident sound inclusive, when she was more alone than she had ever been before.

'I can't walk to the door to let the paramedics in but there is a key under the blue plant pot holding a geranium.' There was a buzz in her ears; blackness grew from the centre of her world. 'I'm going to pass out now, so I hope they come quickly.'

★ ★ ★

13

She is at the top of the stairs, noise from the party swelling around her. She leans on the banister and sees the top of a man's head below her. He has dark hair, glossy and thick, and is wearing a brown tweed suit. He is taller than the people standing around him. He holds a drink in one hand, whisky, and the other one is resting on the newel post of the banister, on the round ball that crowns it. His hand is slender; even from here she can see the nails are clean, cut short. He wears a watch with a thick black leather strap.

Every detail so clear. Sharp.

'What's his name?' she asks Cissy, standing next to her.

'What, you haven't met him yet? That's Paul.' Cissy turns to someone else, and Honor keeps on looking.

There are people around him but he is alone. Somewhere, someone laughs loudly and instead of looking for the source he turns his head and looks up, straight into Honor's eyes.

For the first time, she feels as if she is falling.

'Hello, love? Can you hear me?'

Honor opened her eyes, tilted her head. A blur above her, two blurs, wearing green and yellow. 'Paul?'

'No, my name's Derek, this is Sanjay, and we're paramedics. Can you squeeze my hand for me? Fell down the stairs, did we?'

'*I* fell down the stairs. I don't know about you.' Her mouth was dry. How much blood, how much time? One of the paramedics was messing about with her head, with any luck stopping the bleeding. She heard the rip of packets opening, the rustle of bandages. She tried to struggle up, get some of her dignity back. She'd called him Paul. How embarrassing.

'What's your name, love?'

'Honor Levinson.'

'Can you tell me what day it is, Mrs Levinson?'

'Tuesday the eleventh of April. You shall have to ask me something more difficult than that.' Her voice was raspy and hard.

'I'll get these questions out of the way and then I'll start with the *Pointless* questions, shall I? Are you taking any medication?'

'I'm eighty years old, of course I'm taking medication. It's in the bathroom cabinet.'

'Blood pressure eighty over fifty, Sanjay. Are you feeling dizzy, Mrs Levinson?'

'Yes.'

'Are you alone here?'

'Do you think I would have left my underwear on the stairs, otherwise?' She closed her eyes and gritted her teeth as the paramedics shifted her, placed a restraint on her head to stabilize it.

'She must have pulled herself all the way from the bottom of the stairs to the phone,' said one of the medics. 'Pretty impressive.'

'Morphine,' she gasped.

'Don't worry, we've got gas and air in the ambulance and we'll have you to hospital in a tick. Do you have anyone you'd like us to ring for you, Mrs Levinson?'

'Doctor. Doctor Levinson.'

'Is that your husband?'

'No, it bloody is not. It's me. I don't have anyone to call.'

They lifted her, more delicately than she could have thought possible, onto the stretcher and out through the door where the ambulance was waiting. Honor kept her eyes closed, unwilling to see the pedestrians who would be pausing to gape at the helpless old lady carried out of her home, frail as a bundle of twigs. Once she'd known all these people, everyone in the houses all around. The outside air cooled the tears on her cheeks.

'No one,' she whispered as they slid her safely into the back of the ambulance, and she repeated their names in her head like a song, the names of no one.

Paul, and Stephen. Stephen, and Paul.

Chapter Two

Jo

'Hey, man, wait for me!' The teenager pushed past Jo, who was pressing all her weight down on the back of the pushchair so the front of it would lift up onto the bus. He flashed his pass and was up the stairs, yelling to his mates, before she could say anything.

'He was in a hurry,' Jo said to Oscar, sucking his thumb beside her. Iris yelled out 'No!' and threw her beaker out of the pushchair. It landed in the space between the bus and the kerb, and rolled out of sight.

'Oh God. Sorry. Hold on to the pushchair, Oscar. Step up. That's right. Stay there.' She shoved the pushchair up into the bus and dropped to her hands and knees outside. The person behind her in the queue tutted. 'I'll just be a minute!' she called cheerfully, reaching under the bus. The beaker had rolled almost all the way to the front wheel. She retrieved it and stood up, red-faced, her hair escaping from its clip, just another forty-year-old mother getting in everyone's way.

'Mummy, the bus is going to go without you!' Oscar's forehead was wrinkled, his eyes panicked, ready to cry.

'No, no, sweetie, it's fine.' Jo scrambled up into the bus, bumping against the shopping bags hanging from the handles of her pushchair. She wiped dirt from the beaker with her skirt and gave it to Iris. 'Hold on to that now, darling. Sorry,' she said to the bus driver, and the people behind her, and everyone. 'My purse is . . .'

It was on the pushchair, wedged into the folded canopy. She found it and unzipped the top. 'Sorry, I've only got a five-pound note.'

'No change,' said the bus driver. Jo looked back at the other people behind her in the queue. Some gazed back blankly; some averted their eyes.

'OK,' she said. 'Just take it. It's still less expensive than paying for parking.' She pushed it under the glass barrier with a self-conscious laugh.

'Can we sit upstairs, Mummy? In the front seat?' Oscar pulled at her jacket.

'Not with the pushchair, sweetheart. Go ahead and find a seat, I'll park Iris.'

There was only one seat, near the back. Oscar scampered to it while Jo manoeuvred the pushchair to the space near the front. Thankfully, there were no other pushchairs this time. A woman in an overcoat buttoned up to her neck was in the fold-out priority seat and she gave Jo's loaded pushchair a dirty look.

'Sorry,' said Jo. 'We've done rather a lot of shopping.' She glanced from Iris, strapped in, to Oscar in the back, alone.

'Mummy!' he yelled.

'You forgot your ticket!' called the bus driver.

Jo went back for it. As she took it, her phone rang in her pocket. She shoved the ticket in her pocket along with her ringing phone and returned to Iris. The little girl grinned, holding out her hands to her mother. Chocolate stained all round her mouth, even though Jo had wiped it with a napkin after they'd been to the café. It always came back. How?

'I'll just get you out, sweetheart,' she said, smiling down at her daughter, and the bus pulled away with a lurch. She caught herself on the post and heard Oscar calling for her, the beginning of panic in his voice.

'Oscie,' Iris told her.

'Just a minute.' She unbuckled Iris, the little girl's sticky hands going round her neck, into her hair, sweet breath on her cheek. The pushchair, without the weight of Iris to keep it steady, tipped backwards under the weight of the shopping. Jo righted it with one arm, the other around her daughter. The woman in the priority seat sighed.

Have you forgotten what it's like to have children, you old bat? Jo thought, but instead she smiled and said, 'Sorry,' and carried Iris up the aisle to where her brother was sitting. She passed another group of teenagers in their school uniforms, earphones in, talking loudly to each other, long legs sprawled over seats they had no intention of giving up. In her pocket, her phone stopped ringing. She picked up Oscar with her other arm, settled both children on her lap, though Oscar was hanging half off, trying to peer out of the window past the man sitting next to him.

The pushchair fell over again. The woman gave it an even filthier look, and moved her handbag conspicuously six inches to the right.

I will tell this story to Sara tomorrow, Jo thought, *and we'll laugh.*

'Mummy.' Oscar squirmed on her. 'I'm hungry.'

'It's not far now, sweetheart. And you just had a muffin at the café.'

'I'm *really* hungry.'

Jo snaked her arm round so she could reach into her other pocket, the one with her keys instead of her phone, and found a small plastic container. 'Cheerios,' she said, producing it, grateful that there was something in it other than a used wet-wipe. She packed these small pots every morning, hiding them in various places, to be apparated like a bunny in a magician's hat at vital moments when distraction was needed. Sometimes she forgot. Sometimes she found pots she'd left there days before.

'No!' said Iris, and filled her chubby hand with the cereal. Little Os dropped onto Jo's lap, onto the seat and the floor. The man sitting next to the window stared straight ahead.

'Save some for your brother,' Jo said.

'I don't like Cheerios. What does this button do?' Oscar pressed the big red button on the post in front of him. It dinged. Delighted, he pressed it again.

'Ten minutes till we get home!' said Jo, though it would be more like twenty until they passed out of the cramped streets of Brickham town centre and into the broader leafy suburb. And then a walk through the park and down the street before they reached their house. Under her jacket, her armpits were damp, and her hair was bound to be a mess. 'Not far now! Do you want to sing a song?'

'The wheels on the bus,' sang Iris through wet Cheerios.

'If you don't stop that bloody kid pressing that bloody button I'm going to stop this bloody bus right now!' The driver's voice came via a microphone and blared through the bus. The teenagers laughed.

'Sorry,' said Jo, her words lost, catching Oscar's hand and holding it. He struggled to free himself. 'You can't press the button, Oscar, the man asked you not to.'

'That man is rude,' said Oscar.

'Oscar loves riding on the bus,' Jo said to the man sitting next to them. 'And he loves pressing buttons. Any button at all. He keeps on changing the television settings. I'm hoping he's going to be a computer programmer or an engineer.'

The man grunted and continued to look out of the window. They passed by the end of Jo's old street, the one she'd used to live in with Stephen and Lydia. If she craned her head, she could see the brick front of their old house. And then up the hill, down the road, trundling into the suburbs, stopping to let more people on and off with a hiss and a sigh.

'I'm really hungry, Mummy,' said Oscar. 'And I'm bored.'

'Do you want to play with my phone?' Oscar nodded vehemently and Jo let his hands go to reach in her pocket for it. 'Oh, I missed that call. Do you think it was Lydia?'

'No,' agreed Iris, bouncing up and down on Jo's lap and reaching for the phone, too. Iris loved talking to her big sister on the telephone. Jo held it up, squinting at the missed call number on the screen. A London code, unfamiliar number, message left.

'Just a second, sweetheart, I need to listen to this first.' Unease twiddled in her belly as she dialled the voicemail number.

'Hello, Mrs Merrifield, this is Ilsa Kwong at the Homerton University Hospital. I wonder if you could return my call as soon as possible, on this number. Thank you.'

It's Lydia. It's Lydia. Taken the train into London, hit by a bus. Hit by a car. Assaulted by strangers. Why didn't she call me herself, why did she go without telling me, my little girl, oh Stephen—

'Mummy, I want to play Angry Birds.'

'Just a second, Oscar,' she said, disconnecting from voice-mail. 'Mummy has to make a quick phone call.'

It couldn't be Lydia. Why would it be Lydia? School had only just finished for the day. Lydia would be walking home with Avril, pausing in the park to hang out and trade banter with the boys, but not too much, because she had to study. Jo was being silly, being a crazy mother hen. Still, she checked her phone to make sure there were no missed calls or messages from Lyddie.

'But I want to play Angry Birds!'

'As soon as I return this call, sweetie.' Her fingers were shaking as she dialled. She squeezed Iris to her, smelling chocolate and child, remembering Lydia at that age, not quite two, sticky and precious.

The phone rang several times before it was answered – long enough for Jo to run through the entire scenario in her head: Lydia stepping off the kerb, in front of a bus, in hospital in a coma . . .

'Thomas Audley Ward, Ilsa Kwong speaking.'

'Oh hello,' Jo said into the phone, falsely bright, feeling the man next to them twisting with irritation in his seat. 'This is Joanne Merrifield, I'm just returning your call?'

'Joanne Merrifield . . . Joanne Merrifield. Just a moment, let me find my notes.'

Jo gripped the phone and held her youngest daughter tighter.

'Mummy, *owie*,' whined Iris.

'Why do people feel they have to use their mobile phones on public transport?' said the person sitting in front of Jo, one of the people who hadn't offered her and her two young children a seat. 'As if we all want to hear what they have to say.'

'You just rang me five minutes ago?' prompted Jo, for the first time thinking of Richard, driving too fast, talking on his phone in traffic. But they wouldn't ring her if Richard was hurt.

'Oh yes, here we are. Mrs Merrifield, we have your mother here, admitted earlier this afternoon.'

'*My* mother? My mother is . . . oh, do you mean Honor?'

'Honor Levinson, that's right. She had a fall at home. She gave us your number to ring as her next of kin.'

'I'm her daughter-in-law.' Jo sagged in her seat with relief. Of course it was Honor. 'Is she all right?'

'She's been admitted and she will probably need to stay in for several days, but she's stable. She's resting comfortably.'

'Good. She'll need— I'll—' Jo paused, thinking ahead, planning as she always seemed to be doing. Her mind reshuffled circumstances and responsibilities.

'Hungry, Mummy!'

Oscar was squished up against her, plucking at her sleeve. They weren't at their stop yet, but they were close enough to get off the bus and walk. Jo punched the red button.

'I want to press!' Iris cried in her ear.

The nurse, or whoever she was at the end of the phone, was silent. Jo pictured her rolling her eyes, writing on paperwork. Multi-tasking.

She held Iris up so she could press the button, which she did with a little shout of glee. 'You press it too, Oscar, it's OK,' she whispered, then said into the phone, 'I'm so sorry, I'm on a bus with my children and we're at our stop. Thank you for

23

ringing; please tell Honor I'll be in to see her today, as soon as I can get there.' As she ended the call, Oscar was pressing the red button over and over. 'OK, time to go, sweetie!'

Oscar hopped off her lap and trotted to the front of the bus, his ginger head bobbing. Jo carried Iris after him. The bus braked just as she leaned over to pick up the toppled push-chair and she staggered, banging her hip against the luggage rack.

'Just a minute!' she called, and for speed's sake wheeled the pushchair towards the bus door without strapping Iris into it.

'Thank you,' Oscar trilled to the driver as he opened the door.

'Thankoo!' Iris trilled, being carried past.

Jo thought this more than sufficient, actually. She shoved the pushchair out onto the pavement, took Oscar's hand, and stepped off the bus, balancing Iris on her hip. The bus hissed at her and moved off almost before they'd fully disembarked.

The pushchair fell over backwards.

'Next time we are taking the car,' said Jo, heaving it upright yet again and settling Iris more securely on her hip. 'There are adventures, and then there are *adventures*. Shall we run?'

Oscar squealed and scampered off down the broad pave-ment, lined by neat gardens, towards the park. Jo ran after him, steering the pushchair with one hand. Lyddie would be home already, or in a minute, or maybe she'd see her in the park, and Jo could settle the children and take something out of the freezer, iron Lyddie's uniform for tomorrow quickly, put away the shopping, brush her hair and teeth and jump into the car. With any luck she could be on a train to London before five o'clock. It would be rush hour on the Tube – would it be better to drive? What would the North Circular be like?

Her mind went to Honor as they ran. A fall. She couldn't picture Honor ever falling. She could only picture Honor standing straight.

Chapter Three

Lydia

*I*t started with yoghurt.

   Does that sound dramatic, or dumb? The How To Write book I'm reading says that you should open your stories with a dramatic line, something to pull the reader in. The problem is, of course, what sort of dramatic line do you choose, when nothing really dramatic happens to you ever? Just a series of little events that cause way more worry than you would think, if you observed them from the outside?

   Well, there was the one dramatic thing that happened to Dad. But I wasn't there.

   Anyway, it did start with yoghurt, so that's how I'll begin my story. I was in the lunch queue trying to decide between a strawberry and an apricot yoghurt. Apricot is vile, but it was low-fat, and the strawberry was full-fat. Personally, I do not give a flying monkey about whether a yoghurt is low-fat or not, but Avril is doing this thing where you check the package of everything you eat for how many grams of fat and sugar and carbs it has, and then you enter it into some app on your phone. Erin and Sophie and Olivia are doing it because they are the eating disorder girls, and for some reason Avril has taken it up too because of some imaginary cellulite on her thighs. It won't last. She can't resist Maltesers.

But right now they're obsessed, and I knew that if I came back to the table with a full-fat yoghurt after eating my entire packed lunch, they would all watch every mouthful I took, imagining it appearing directly on my hips. Not that I care about what the Bulimia Buddies think. I eat when I'm hungry like a normal person.

But Avril. So I reached for the apricot.

'Hey, lezza, move your fat arse.'

It was Darren Raymond, standing ahead of me in the queue — I recognized the spots on the back of his neck, which are my pleasant view every Maths lesson. He was talking to someone standing in front of the service area. Tall, lumpy, holding her empty tray in front of her. That new girl, the one with the funny name.

'Yeah, get moving, you're holding up the whole queue,' said another boy.

'Some of us are hungry for something other than pussy.'

The queue erupted into laughter. The new girl's face was bright red. Her eyes were searching for a grown-up, someone to say something, to tell the boys off for swearing, but the dinner ladies had disappeared.

'I'm — I'm waiting for my lunch,' she stammered. 'I'm — it's a special lunch, gluten free.'

'It's a special lunch, gluten free,' mocked one of the boys, I couldn't see which one. But I could see the girl's hands on her tray: white-knuckled, and shaking. I didn't know her name, but anyone could see how she felt.

'And pussy-flavoured,' said Darren, the wit.

'Oh, grow up,' I called at him. 'You're never going to know what pussy tastes like, Darren, except in your dreams.'

Roaring laughter. Darren Raymond's spotty neck went pink. On the other side of the service hatch, a dinner lady showed up with a single plate of food, looking around, half-smiling, to try to discover what the joke was about. I squeezed up the side of the queue and went to pay for my yoghurt (and just for the record, £1.40 is way too much for a small pot of fruit-flavoured bacteria).

At the table, Avril was folding her napkin into a little crane. She perched it on my palm when I sat next to her: it was so light it barely weighed anything. Something about the tilt of its head reminded me of her.

'That's your best yet,' I told her.

'It's for you. A little gift to celebrate your return.'

'Why, thank you, darling.' We traded a complicit look. It's you and me against all the rest of these idiots.

Darling.

Erin was twisting a plastic straw into a gnarled shape. 'I have no idea how you eat so much and stay so slim, Lyds.'

'Witchcraft,' I said, peeling the top off my yoghurt, though Erin didn't mean it as a question. It doesn't take a genius to know that I can eat a lot and stay slim because I run about a million miles every week. She just wanted to make me feel self-conscious, because that's the way she'd feel if she ate anything more than a single apple at lunchtime. As if we didn't all know that she ate her own body weight in Doritos every evening before chucking it all up in the toilet.

Anyway, I was taking the top of my yoghurt off and dipping my plastic spoon into it because they don't trust us with proper cutlery — Mr Graham is always banging on about ecology, he should have a word with the school meals service and their plastic everything — when I noticed there was someone standing next to me.

It was that new girl, whatever her name was, something beginning with B. Her tray had a plate with some orange-ish mess on it; her cheeks were still flushed red. Or maybe that was the way she always

28

looked. Her hair was short but it flopped into her eyes, because her fringe was long.

'I just – I just wanted to say,' said the new girl. 'You know. Thank you.'

All of the other girls at the table were looking at us. I could actually feel them counting the seats, making a calculation: five chairs filled with people, one heaped with books and pencil cases and jumpers. The new girl's parting was pale against her dark hair. Her jumper was too new and her skirt was too long, above white folded ankle socks.

I shrugged. 'The boys were being stupid, and I wanted to get my lunch.'

The new girl nodded and paused for a moment, as if she were considering asking us to move the jumpers so she could sit down. But then she carried on walking. She found an empty table at the far end of the room.

'What happened?' Avril asked. 'Why was she thanking you?'

I told them about it. Avril laughed, and the other girls giggled and glanced at Darren Raymond and his table, who were all throwing bits of bread roll at each other. Darren is a straight-up geek, Maths and computer nerd, and spotty to boot. The type of person who needs someone to pick on to hide how socially inadequate they really are.

'God, they are so ignorant,' said Erin, sighing elaborately. 'Anyone can see that she's not gay.'

'Really?' I said, licking yoghurt off my spoon. I couldn't really taste it. 'How can you tell?'

'She doesn't look anything like Georgie and Whitney.'

'I'm not really an expert, but I don't think that all gay girls look exactly like each other,' said Avril.

'It's a weird name, though,' said Sophie. 'It's a boy's name.'

'And that haircut,' said Olivia. 'She could do with some make-up.'

'And losing a couple of stone.'

'Just because she's ugly, it doesn't mean she's a lesbo,' said Erin. 'Georgie and Whitney aren't ugly. Well, Whitney isn't.'

'Ooh, you fancy Whitney,' tittered Sophie.

'Shut up.'

'I would hate to be called a lesbo,' said Avril. 'I'm still hungry, Lyds, can I have some of your yoghurt?'

I slid the container over to her. 'Have the rest of it. I'm not hungry any more.' I picked up the paper crane she had made.

The new girl sat alone, eating her gloppy lunch. I didn't look in her direction but I knew she was there. I could feel her, and I've kept on thinking about her, for the rest of today, which is why I'm writing about her now.

It was a stupid thing to do. I've forged a connection between us, and now I'm going to notice her everywhere, when up till now I've been blissfully ignorant. I'm going to notice how the new girl doesn't have any friends; how her white socks look nearly the same colour as her legs; how people whisper and turn their backs. I'm going to notice the sniggers when teachers say her weird boy-name. Which isn't even that weird, it turns out. Someone told me after; her name is Bailey. Girls have boys' names all the time. Nobody picks on Tyler, or Billie. If the new girl were cooler, she could totally pull it off.

But she's not. She lugs that name around with her like she lugs her extra weight, her make-up-free face, her gluten-free lunch. And those little-girl socks.

God, if you could just tell these people. Blend in. Watch, and copy. It's so much easier. People are looking at you all the time. They're making up their minds about you. It's better to decide yourself what they're going to see.

But you can't say that. Not to someone who doesn't know it instinctively. Not to someone with no sense of self-preservation.

I sat at that lunch table today, twirling the crane in my hand, feeling Avril beside me eating from my spoon, feeling the others surrounding me with their chatter and security. A bubble, as fragile as a paper crane.

I stroked my finger against the crane's wings, slowly, one carefully folded wing then the other, watching them bend under my touch.

I still have it. It's sitting on my desk right now, looking at me. Does that sound dramatic, or dumb?

'Go on, Lyds, give us a picture,' said Harry Carter. He was lounging against the wall as if he were posing for the cover of a boy-band album.

Lydia would have kept on walking, but the corridor was narrower there and she had to slow down because of the Harry Carter effect on passing traffic. She stopped and struck a pose. 'Sure, take one now,' she said.

He pouted. 'You know that's not the kind of picture I mean.'

'Oh hi, Harry,' said Avril.

'I know exactly what kind of picture you mean,' Lydia told him. 'Do I look like the stupid kind of girl who would give you a picture to share on the internet with all of your pathetic friends?'

Harry's smile got wider. He had very white teeth, straight and even like a pop star's, and a dimple that half of the upper school were desperate to touch. Sophie had written his name at least a thousand times in the back of her notebook.

'I heard what you said at lunchtime,' he said. 'You told Darren Raymond all about your pussy.'

'What I said was that he wouldn't get near mine, or anyone else's, in a thousand years.'

31

'I think you're hot.'

'Think all you like, thinking is free.'

Blend in, watch and copy. Although in this case, Lydia was mostly copying from television, because nobody knocked back Harry Carter in real life.

He leaned forward and whispered, 'Take one in the bathroom after school and text it to me. I won't share it with anyone else, promise.'

'In your dreams,' she said, and winked at him, before turning away.

'Just like Darren Raymond!' yelled Harry after them, turning to his friends and laughing.

She linked her arm with Avril's. 'Come on, or we'll be late and we won't get to sit together.'

'Will you?' Avril asked as they reached the English block.

'Will I what?'

'Send Harry a picture.'

'God, why would I do something like that?'

They reached the classroom early enough for there still to be seats together at the back. 'He's fit,' said Avril. 'And I think he likes you.'

'Not my type.'

'He might send you a picture back.'

'Bleugh.'

'Do you really not like him? Oh, do you have a pencil?'

Lydia gave Avril a pencil. 'Why are you going on about Harry? You don't like him, do you?'

'No, I wasn't saying I *liked* Harry – I was wondering about him for you.'

'Because I thought you liked Zane.'

Avril shrugged. 'He's a little – I don't know, boring.'

'How do you know he's boring? He never says anything.'

Zane was, in fact, way too thick for Avril. He was totally safe.

'We Facebooked last night,' said Avril.

'Zane can type? That's a surprise.'

'He can't spell.'

Lydia laughed in relief. 'You need a speller?'

'I just want someone who has something to say, you know?'

'Like Harry?'

'I wasn't saying that.'

'How bad was his spelling?'

Avril took her phone out of her bag to show her; Lydia hung over her desk.

'Miss Toller? Miss Levinson?' said Miss Drayton, walking into the room, and Lydia instantly launched herself back into her seat. 'Is that your phone, Avril? Could I trouble you to turn it off and hand it to me for the duration of the lesson? We only have a few weeks until your exams, and I would like all of your attention, please. Then get out your copy of *Far From the Madding Crowd* and read to us from page 115. Start from the beginning of the chapter.'

Avril shot Lydia a wry look and gave her phone into Miss Drayton's hand. She dug out her dog-eared, annotated paperback copy of the novel as Miss Drayton placed her confiscated booty on the top of her desk, a reminder to anyone else who might think of texting or tweeting during English. '*The Hollow Amid the Ferns,*' she began.

Lydia put her finger in her paperback to hold the place and she watched Avril.

When you spent most of your time with someone, you

hardly ever got to really look at them. You were too busy looking at other things together. Even when you were talking to each other, you never actually stared at someone. You only glanced, glanced away, looked at other things.

Looking at her now was like a stolen square of chocolate, melting over Lydia's tongue in the secrecy of her closed mouth.

Avril had rich dark hair, almost brown enough to be black, straightened today and spilling over her shoulders. She always tucked it behind her ears. Her fingernails were bitten short. She wore a tiny silver shell ring that Lydia brought back for her from Naxos when she'd gone on holiday there, before Mum and Richard had split up.

Her lashes were long and darker than her hair. There was a mole on her cheekbone, and freckles that came out with the sunshine. There were two holes in each of her earlobes — Avril's mother hadn't discovered the second one yet. They matched the holes in Lydia's ears. They'd had them done over half-term. The piercing gun got stuck in Avril's left ear and the hole bled. They went to McDonald's afterwards and Lydia held a cube of ice from her Coke against Avril's small intentional wound. The melting ice ran down her bare arm and Avril wiped it off with her finger.

'*He had kissed her,*' read Avril, clearly and not loudly, but in a voice that carried. Avril's voice always carried. She used to stand in front of their class in Year Seven and read her book reports, back in those days when she wore her hair in plaits and Lydia asked Mum to do her hair the same way, though Lydia's always slipped out and got ragged. They used to wear identical Mary Jane shoes. Even then, when Avril would read, Lydia would close her eyes to listen to the sound.

They had made each other who they were. Avril's hair, Lydia's laugh; Lydia's holiday, Avril's finger. They bought the same clothes at the same time, though the items looked different on each of them. Their histories were written on each other's bodies.

That would never change.

'Lydia Levinson?'

Laughter brought her back to the present. She was at her desk in the back of Miss Drayton's room and everyone in the room had turned around to stare at her.

'I know that Avril's very pretty,' said Miss Drayton, 'but it's your turn to read now, please.'

Avril smiled. She rolled her eyes and twirled her finger around her ear. Someone sniggered. From the front of the room, Lydia heard the name, 'Bailey.'

The blush that she hated raced up her neck.

'The next chapter? *Particulars of a Twilight Walk*?' suggested Miss Drayton. Lydia flipped pages and, clearing her throat, she began to read.

Chapter Four

Jo

Jo had CBeebies on the telly and a fish pie in the oven by the time Lydia came home, Avril beside her. Both girls had shirts untucked, school jumper sleeves rolled up, coltish legs bare between skirt and socks. As always, they were taller than she expected, their long hair shoved into sloppy ponytails.

This past autumn, on the morning of the first day of school, Jo had suggested a brush. Lydia's hair was so lovely when it was brushed smooth, falling in shiny coppery waves around her face and down her back. She'd given up any hope of the brush when she'd seen Lydia's best friend at the door, come to pick her up for school. Avril's hair was in a messy bun, and therefore Lydia's would have to be, too. The two girls had dressed alike, talked alike, loved the same music and television shows, from the moment they'd met.

Lydia slammed the door and Avril sniffed the air and said, 'It smells great in here, Mrs Merrifield.'

Jo looked up from the sink, where she was washing cherry tomatoes. 'Fish pie. I made extra last week and froze it. You're welcome to stay for tea, Avril.'

'Can't,' said Lydia, heading out of the kitchen. 'I just came in to get changed, then I'm going out.'

Avril gave Jo an apologetic smile. 'We're meeting some friends at Starbucks to revise. I hope that's OK.'

'No, I have to— Lydia!' Lydia had started for her room, but she came back reluctantly. She leaned against the door frame, ready to be gone again.

'I've got to go into London to see your grandmother,' said Jo, wiping her hands on a tea towel. 'I need you to give Oscar and Iris their tea. I should be back by nine or ten at the latest.'

'I can't,' said Lydia. 'I've got plans.'

'I'm sorry, but this is more important.'

'It's schoolwork. We've got exams coming up.' She recited it as if she were reading it off a sheet. 'GCSEs can determine your entire future career, both academic and professional.'

'I know, and that's true – but Honor needs me, and it's urgent.'

'Why can't Oscar and Iris come with you?'

'I told you, I won't get back till after their bedtime. I can't drag them to London. Why don't you stay here and revise? There's plenty of fish pie, and Avril can stay here and have some, too.'

'I arranged for us to meet Erin and Sophie at the café,' Avril said. 'They're waiting for me there. Sorry, Mrs M.'

'What about Richard?' asked Lydia. 'It's about time he looked after his own kids for a change.'

'Lydia!'

Avril looked down at her shoes, but Lydia stared right at Jo.

'I'm not calling Richard,' said Jo, hearing the edge in her

37

voice. 'There's no time for him to get here anyway. I'm asking you, as a responsible near-adult, to look after your brother and sister for one evening while I go to see your grandmother, who needs me. And in fact, I'm not asking you – I'm telling you. I'm sorry, but you're going to have to stay at home.'

'That is so unfair!' Lydia turned around and stormed across the kitchen. Jo heard the door of her room slam, and sighed.

'I've got to go. Sorry, Mrs M. I hope Lydia's gran is OK.' Avril slipped out.

Jo counted to ten, and went to Lydia's bedroom. It was on the ground floor, across the short corridor near the front door that was always clogged with wellies and raincoats. She rapped on the door. There was no answer, so she said through the door, 'I'm going to dish up tea before I go, but you'll have to sit with them, even if you don't want anything to eat yourself. And you'll have to clear up afterwards. Don't forget to brush their teeth.'

No reply. Jo tipped her head back and looked at the ceiling.

'Honor has had a fall. She's in hospital. I'm going to bring her some things from home.'

A stirring behind the door, but no answer.

'She's all right,' added Jo. 'In case you were wondering.'

She waited for several minutes, and then went to the kitchen to take the pie out of the cooker and spoon out two portions on plates to cool. Jo was about to call Lydia again when the girl came into the kitchen. She'd changed into low-slung tracksuit bottoms and a T-shirt that skimmed her flat stomach. She scraped a chair against the floor and sat down at the table. Jo opened her mouth to say something, then closed it again and went to fetch her handbag and car keys.

★ ★ ★

She was still seething, still rehearsing what she should have said, the perfect words to make her teenage daughter collapse instantly into the correct contrition, when she walked through the glass doors into Homerton University Hospital reception. It wasn't until she entered the ward that the antiseptic smell of the hospital filtered through her awareness, and Jo closed her eyes and thought, *Stephen*.

The telephone call, ten years ago. Ten years ago, this June. The words from a stranger. Strapping Lydia, aged six, in the back seat where she immediately fell asleep. The drive to the hospital with her hands shaking on the wheel, Jo afraid she was going to crash until the moment she turned off the ignition. Carrying her daughter into the hospital, long legs dangling, and holding her in the lift, on their way up to see Jo's husband, Lydia's father, where he lay in a bed with a machine breathing for him. The chemical smell of fear and the little girl, asleep and trusting in her arms.

The lift dinged and Jo opened her eyes. Her flat soft-soled boots made no sound on the polished tile floor. Outside, the light was fading, but inside the hospital it was bright midday. She pumped sanitizer on her hands and went through to the ward reception desk. 'Hi, I'm here to see Honor Levinson?' she said, and the nurse set off to show her the way.

The ward was full of old people in beds. Some were asleep, some watching television; one or two had relatives sitting in plastic chairs. One man was lying on his side rapidly texting into an iPhone. Honor was sleeping in a bed at the far end. Her head was wrapped in bandages.

'My God,' said Jo, 'she really had a fall, didn't she?'

'She's sleeping, bless her,' said the nurse. 'She's only been awake for a little while since I've been on shift, when I took her obs. Best thing for her. The bandages make it look worse than it is – she only has a few stitches on the back of her head. I'll see if I can get a doctor to speak with you.'

Left alone, Jo pulled a chair up to the side of Honor's bed and looked at her. She had never seen her mother-in-law sleeping before. Awake and upright, Honor was slender and tall, but under the blanket she seemed nothing more than bones. Her skin was waxy, her cheeks sunken over her glorious cheekbones. Her mouth was half-open, showing fillings in her teeth. She had a line going into her right arm. Her breathing was soft but audible.

Jo couldn't believe Honor had named her as next of kin. Honor would never want Jo, of all people, to see her this way.

She looked old. Her long silver hair was untidy. Not unlike Lydia's style, thought Jo, and she reached over to neaten it, when a voice said, 'Hello, I'm Dr Mukhtar.'

Jo straightened up almost guiltily and shook the doctor's hand. He looked incredibly young, smooth-cheeked as if he hadn't yet started shaving. Was that a sign of getting older, when the doctors looked like children?

'I'm Honor's daughter-in-law,' she explained. 'I came as soon as I heard she'd had a fall, as quickly as I could.'

'Yes, a fall at home, down the stairs I think. Concussion and a head wound. The most serious injury was her hip.'

'She broke her hip?'

'Yes. She's had surgery this afternoon to repair it; luckily, we were able to operate quickly. There's some osteoporosis, which isn't uncommon at her age, of course, but from all accounts it was quite a fall.'

'She must have been terrified,' Jo said.

'Well, it says on her notes that Mrs Levinson was—'

'Dr Levinson. She's got a PhD; maybe two. She gets ever so cross if she's called Mrs.'

'Is that so,' said the doctor politely. 'Well, Dr Levinson was conscious when she was admitted – she rang 999 herself – but she was confused.'

'I can't imagine Honor confused.'

'She was in a great deal of pain, and there was the concussion. We've been monitoring her carefully. At her age, a broken hip is no laughing matter. Does she live by herself?'

'Yes.'

'Well, we'll be keeping her in for several days whilst she recovers from the surgery, and she'll need to talk with an Occupational Therapist to make some plan for her care when she gets out of hospital. She'll have to have physiotherapy to restore as much mobility as possible, and she's going to require a lot of help with day-to-day living.'

'Of course. We'll sort something out.' Jo looked back down at Honor. *Poor Honor*, she thought, and was instantly surprised that she could ever think such a thing of her mother-in-law. She was certain that her mother-in-law had never thought such a thing of her.

Honor's home was a tall, narrow brick house in Stoke Newington, raised from the pavement by a flight of stone stairs, which were slippery with the light falling rain. The key to the front door had been with the few belongings that had been taken with Honor into hospital. Jo let herself in and wiped her feet on the doormat, looking around.

It felt empty, inhabited by silence and the papery smell of

41

books and dust. Jo turned on the light and saw the blood on the floor. It was a trail, crossing the hallway from the bottom of the stairs to the lounge. There was a larger patch of it near the stairs, where a laundry basket lay upside down.

'Oh, Honor,' Jo said. She stepped over it and went down to the kitchen to get a cloth. The teapot sat near the kettle; a tea towel was discarded on the table next to an open-spined book, but that was the only clutter – a huge contrast to the way Jo had left her own kitchen. She found paper towels and cleaning spray, rags under the sink and some carpet cleaner, and brought them upstairs.

Jo took a moment before she began cleaning, regarding the blood warily. Was it going to make her sick? She wasn't good with bodily fluids, with vomit or wee or blood. She gagged changing Iris's nappy sometimes, still. In the end she got down on her knees and sprayed the fluid on the stains. The scent of fake lemons covered up any smell that the blood might have had, and the stains on the floorboards came up easily enough with the spray. It was surprisingly bright red on the paper towels. It looked as though Honor had lost quite a bit of blood.

Jo's stomach hitched and she put the back of her hand to her mouth, thinking of lemons. Round and yellow, sharp and dimpled and fresh. Lemons on trees, growing. She swallowed and bent back to her task.

The floor itself wasn't all that clean. Dust and dirt came up with the blood; there were dust bunnies near the skirting boards. Jo worked her way across towards the stairs and nudged the laundry basket out of the way. There was something small and white crumpled underneath. Jo picked it up: a pair of knickers. She gazed up the staircase and saw another pair, and a vest, and some other things.

Honor Levinson would never leave her knickers in public view. The sight of these, lying where they'd fallen, was somehow more horrible than the sight of Honor's blood.

Jo stood and quickly gathered the clothes together, putting them in the righted basket. She couldn't tell if they were clean or dirty, and she wasn't about to inspect them closely to find out. She'd take them home to wash them.

She had to stop again and put her hand to her mouth when she went into the lounge and turned on the light. It was like something out of a horror film. There was blood on the carpet here, and a large dark stain near the sagging chintz sofa. A table was overturned and the phone lay beside it. Jo righted the table, wiped blood from the phone, checked for messages. None.

Jo attacked the rug with carpet-cleaning spray and wet rags, and managed to get most of the blood out, but there was still a brown stain in the Persian weave. She double-checked the room to make sure she hadn't missed any spots of blood, keeping her gaze trained carefully on the floor, knowing the danger in looking too carefully at the photographs on the wall. Once she was satisfied, she carried the cleaning stuff downstairs, her arms aching from the scrubbing, and threw all the rags and the paper towels in the bin. Then she washed her hands and arms with washing-up liquid and, sighing, put on the kettle for a cup of tea. She hadn't had anything since the coffee in the café with the children this afternoon.

She'd never made so much as a cup of tea in this kitchen, in the many years she'd known Honor – she had never been allowed to – so she had to look around a bit to find the canister. She noticed, as she did, that the kitchen was tidy, but rather dirty. There were cup rings on the counter, breadcrumbs near the toaster. The cabinet doors had splashes of tea and a few fingerprints on them. The white top of the cooker was splattered with nearly-invisible grease.

This was not how she remembered Honor's kitchen. The house, every inch of it, had always been scrupulously clean – books dusted, candlesticks polished, mirrors clear; so much so that Jo had always gone into a frenzy of cleaning of her own house before Honor's visits. Stephen had thought she was being ridiculous. 'My mother doesn't care whether you dust underneath the refrigerator,' he'd told her, but Jo was certain that she did. She knew Honor's high standards. She knew she was wanting in Honor's eyes.

In the end, Stephen had always taken a duster and joined in. Honor had taught him how to clean, after all, and he was good at it. He had a scientist's methodical mind. He'd moved furniture, reorganized kitchen cabinets, reached on top of wardrobes. He'd given little Lydia her own toy broom, so she could help 'when Granny came'.

Jo's second husband, Richard, had thought it was funny. He laughed at her and went back to watching the football while she hoovered around him with Oscar and then, the next year, Iris strapped to her body in a baby sling. 'She's not even your mother-in-law any more – who cares what she thinks?' he'd say. 'You don't work so hard to please *my* mum.'

That was because Richard's mum, Frances, had a cleaner and never lifted a finger to wipe or polish, whereas Honor did everything, in between reading every book that had ever been written, writing articles, picking apart theories and arguments. Honor cleaned and polished that entire tall house filled with the furniture her parents had bought, listening to Tchaikovsky. And that was why Jo had refused when Richard had said he'd hire a cleaner, although Honor's visits were few and far between. She wished she'd put up more of a fight against hiring an au pair.

When was the last time Jo had seen Honor? She'd sent a card at Mother's Day ... had it been Christmas?

Christmas. Or rather the week before Christmas, when Lydia's school had finished for the holiday. When Jo had bundled Lydia and Oscar and Iris into the car and paid the congestion charge and driven into London so that she could spend two hours trying to keep her small children's sticky hands off the books, explaining to Oscar that Granny Honor didn't have a Christmas tree because she was Jewish, stumbling over the explanation as Honor sat, straight-backed, watching her as if waiting for her to make a mistake. They had gone as soon as they could leave, obligation honoured.

So: nearly four months ago. It wasn't good enough. Honor was Lydia's only living relative except for distant great-aunts on Jo's side of the family. Jo should have made more of an effort.

Jo drank her tea quickly, scalding hot. The milk was near its use-by date; Jo poured it down the sink and threw a tub of coleslaw and a bag of salad in the bin. There were eggs and yoghurts and bananas with a few days left in them, and a small block of cheese, which she put in a plastic bag to take home along with the laundry. She gave the entire kitchen a quick wipe-down, unplugged the kettle and the toaster, emptied the bin and took the bag outside. Then she went upstairs to pack some things for Honor in the hospital.

This is me riding to the rescue, Jo thought. *Not on a white horse or with superpowers. I remove stains and save bananas from certain death.*

45

She moved quietly through the house like a ghost, past the towering bookshelves and the dark furniture, being careful not to notice that she wasn't in any of the silver- and gold-framed photographs.

Chapter Five

Lydia

'Some things about Granny Honor'

I *can't actually picture Granny Honor in hospital, lying down in a bed. She's always standing up. She barely sits down long enough to drink a cup of tea. She reads books whilst pacing – I've watched her, a novel raised to her face, walking back and forth across the rug in her living room. She keeps a pencil behind her ear and sometimes she pauses to scribble in this notebook that she keeps open on a side table. Then back and forth again, frowning at the book in her hands, her bony nose pointed at the pages. Every now and then she mutters.*

There is an actual path worn in the rug, where Granny Honor has paced back and forth, reading hundreds of books.

Granny Honor is not a relaxing person. She's angular and hard, not the way you think of a grandmother being. Mum has photos of her mum, my Nanny Carole who died before I was born, and she looks soft and huggy, even in her wheelchair, with a smile on her face in every picture. Granny Honor isn't like that. She has this way of looking at you the same way that she looked at that book, as if she's scrutinizing you, analysing you for what you're really trying to say.

She's an expert in Russian literature, pretty much a genius. There's a whole shelf in her study upstairs filled with books she's written or contributed to, all with stiff, upright spines and titles that have colons in them. She gave me my first lesson on First Wave Feminism when I was like three years old.

I always feel like an idiot next to her. I'm sure about 98 per cent of the population would. But she's the reason I want to be a writer, I think, and definitely the reason why I want to read English when (if) I go to Cambridge, instead of Physics like my dad. She's so passionate about books, believes they really matter. Those have been the best conversations we've had: about books we've both read. They're probably the only real conversations we've ever had, actually. I feel a little bit too stupid to talk to her about anything else.

She sends me books for my birthday, and then when I visit her or when she visits here, she takes me to a café and we both order cake, coffee for her, hot chocolate for me, and we talk about the books. And those conversations are wonderful. Sort of like the stories really happened, but then you can take a step back and look at them almost from above, talking about how they were written, or why the author had made this choice and that one. Why they'd chosen a wardrobe as a magic portal, or why you even needed Lockwood in the first place, or what it meant that Manderley had burned.

It's like zooming a powerful camera lens on all of these stories, so that you understand them better than anyone else. And as an added bonus I am much better at English than anyone else in my year; in fact, Miss Drayton wanted me to take my GCSEs early and do an AS this year like I did with French, but I didn't because I wanted to stay with Avril.

But when we're not talking about books, I'm not really sure what I should say to Granny Honor. I hope she's all right.

★ ★ ★

Snakes and Ladders, some naughty biscuits before bedtime, a good round of *Thomas the Tank Engine* and a pillow fight. Lydia got OscanIrie into bed, came downstairs, heard Oscar calling and went back upstairs to get him another drink of water, and then she came downstairs again and collapsed on the sofa, automatically turning on the telly.

She should revise. But her head felt heavy, her limbs weighted. She got so tired. All the time, every day, from pretending so hard. Watching what she said, how long she looked, whether she touched. Watching other people watching her, wondering what was in their heads. Sometimes when she came home from school she felt like she could barely stand up and talk. Not that she could really relax at home, either, unless she was in her room alone, but at least OscanIrie didn't care what she was like or what she was hiding. And Mum was too busy to notice her, to really *notice* her.

Sometimes that made it harder, when no one was paying attention. Sometimes, when she was comfortable, she almost forgot to keep up the walls.

On the way home from school, Avril had been talking about maybe going to her dad's for the summer holidays, after their exams were over. Her dad lived in Birmingham, and when Avril had gone there two years ago for the whole Easter holiday, Lydia had been more lonely than she'd ever been in her life.

She reached for her phone. She had five messages.

Avril, 15.40: Sorry you couldn't come, thx 4 top!
Avril, 17.25: It was OK. Call me. x
Mum, 18.06: Hi sweetie. Granny H OK. Going to pick up some things to make her more comfortable. Will try not to be

late. All OK with O & I? Cake in tin if you are hungry.
Xxx

Avril, 19.00: OMG r u watching Top Model? This is
VILE, ring me.

<unknown number> 19.11: now u send me 1

The last text had a picture attached. It was taken in the
mirror so that the phone covered up most of his face, but she
could still tell it was Harry. Chest bare, briefs pushed down to
expose himself.

She deleted it. Didn't even think; thumb working by itself.
She deleted it and then held her phone, furious and
much more shocked than she should be, considering she'd
seen much worse. Much worse, just Googling kitten
pictures.

But never directed at her. Never sent right to her, for her
to look at, not able to avoid it because it was on her phone.

Lydia's hands shook. What was he playing at? Did he think
she'd *like* that? Did he think his dick was so mighty and
powerful that she'd immediately melt, rip her clothes off at
the mere sight of it, send him a photo screaming please, please,
objectify me, wank over my digital tits, *please*?

Her phone chimed with another message.

<unknown number> 19.26: or evn betta 1 of u an Avril 2geva!

Lydia threw her phone across the living room. It hit Oscar's
plastic toy garage and clattered to the floor.

She stared after it, wide-eyed, breathing hard.

He knew.

Harry Carter knew. And if Harry knew, then his friends
knew, then Erin knew, then Avril . . .

She clenched her fists. No. He couldn't possibly know. She

was too good at hiding. Harry Carter wasn't clever enough to see inside her head.

Harry Carter was the sort of perv who thought that girls owed him naked selfies. Who thought that if a girl and a girl got together, it was only so that a boy could watch them. Who thought the only thing better than two tits was four. Who didn't understand real longing, real love.

Who didn't understand that his misspelled, barely literate text had pushed its way into thoughts she only allowed herself at night, alone with the doors closed. It had left greasy fingersmears, the odour of sweat, on her dreams.

Her phone chimed.

She forced herself to breathe slowly. Deeply. She walked over to the toy garage and picked her phone up, ready to block Harry's number, delete the texts.

It was from Avril.

Have you seen this photoshoot on TM? They are crying! Skype me when kiddies in bed, cannot watch this alone!

Lydia pressed the phone to her pounding heart. Avril didn't know. Harry couldn't know. Her mask hadn't slipped. She would never have let it.

Chapter Six

Jo

'I don't know how she's going to stay in that house by her-self,' said Jo, putting two more mugs of coffee on the table.

'Get a carer in?' suggested Sara. She took another biscuit. 'I shouldn't have this, but I love your shortbread. I'm going to start a diet on Saturday, so I don't look like a whale in Tenerife.'

'You don't look like a whale, you have a lovely figure,' said Jo automatically.

'Thanks, but you're lying. My arse needs its own postcode.' She dunked the biscuit. 'Bob makes fun of me when I start diets.'

'That's because he knows you don't need one.'

'That's because he never notices me any more. I swear, he doesn't even see me. If I ask him if I look good in something, he just says "yes" without even glancing up from his phone. The only reason we don't bump into each other when we're walking around the house is because we're rarely in the same room.'

'Well, you're both busy.'

'The children, he looks at.'

'He's a great father.'

Billy, Sara's eldest at age four, wandered over to the table. 'More biscuits?' he said hopefully, and Jo put some on a plastic plate.

'Don't forget to share them with the others,' Jo told him. 'Offer them round, like a waiter.' Billy trotted to the other side of the open-plan family room.

'That should give us another five minutes' quiet,' said Sara. 'At least until he starts arguing with Oscar again about who gets more cars.' It was a punctuation of every play date, breaking up a fight between Billy and Oscar. Fortunately Iris and Polly, both under two, could sit side by side playing and happily ignoring each other for hours. They were in a shaft of sunlight now by the front window, making separate meals at Iris's toy kitchen. 'Do they grow out of the fighting and into the sharing? I ask you as a more experienced mother.'

'There's a wonderful stage when they're five, and it lasts through till about age eleven. They're sweet and loving and funny.'

'And then at age eleven?'

Jo rolled her eyes in imitation of a teenager.

'Lydia?' said Sara.

'She's a wonderful girl. She really is. She's had so much to cope with, without a dad, and she works so hard at school, and she's so good with her brother and sister.'

'But . . . ?'

Jo tried to resist complaining, but it was too much. 'She's impossible at the moment. Yesterday I asked her to stay home and babysit while I went to London to see Honor, and you would have thought I'd proposed handcuffing her to the kitchen table.'

'I was the same as a teenager. I thought I was so cool, and I made my mother's life hell. I feel sorry for it now. That's one consolation. I haven't told Mum, of course. Do you feel sorry for what you put your mother through?'

'I didn't put her through anything. Mum and I always really got along. And I was always a good girl, maybe too good. I liked pleasing people. Of course my mum had multiple sclerosis, and she was unwell a lot of the time, so I had to grow up fast.' Jo propped her chin on her hand, leaning on the table. 'I think I was more like Lydia's friend Avril. She's always cheerful, always has a polite word for everyone.'

'Isn't she the one whose mother—'

Jo nodded. 'It hasn't affected her, though. She's a lovely girl. I wish Lyddie would take a leaf out of her book. Lyddie's so negative. Sometimes it seems that there's no trace of that sweet little girl any more.'

'She's still in there.'

'I remember exactly when it happened. It was age eleven, actually. All the girls at her school were going crazy for these woven bracelet things they were making for each other. So I bought her some materials, which was fine, but then I made the mistake of looking some patterns up on the internet. I made her a bracelet after she'd gone to bed. It turned out quite well. The next morning, when I gave it to her, she was *horrified.*'

'You were trying too hard to be cool?'

'I thought I was just making her a bracelet. We used to do all those things together, before. When it was just the two of us.' She sighed. 'That's another thing she's had to cope with

– a stepfather, and our divorce, and other children taking up my time.'

'You've raised her right,' said Sara. 'She's bound to become a human being sooner or later.'

'I hope so. She wouldn't even say goodbye this morning on the way to school. It's as if she has a whole world inside her that she can't bear to share with me.' Jo felt again the small stab of hurt at seeing her first born daughter slam out of the house, head down, mouth pressed shut. 'Or she's angry with me about something.'

'What could she possibly have to be angry with you about? You're a great mum. You'd never do anything to upset your children.'

Jo felt a pang of guilt. She'd never told Sara about her visits to Adam, nor how furious Lydia would be if she knew about them.

'On the other hand,' she said quickly, 'Oscar and Iris were fed and happy and put down to bed safely last night, so she was serious about looking after them.'

'She's a good kid underneath.'

Jo raised her mug to her mouth. The things our friends tell us because of loyalty; the things that they don't even allow out into conversation. Sara would never consider saying that Lydia was turning into a stroppy little cow, no more than Jo would confirm aloud that Sara actually had put on an extra half a stone since she'd stopped breastfeeding. Female friendship required building each other up, denying each other's faults, unhesitatingly taking each other's side, listening to problems and saying that they were really not that bad. Not digging too deeply for secrets that wanted to stay hidden.

Friendship was a small miracle, something Jo appreciated

even more these days. Her friends in the centre of town, the other young mums she'd got to know during her first marriage when Lydia was a little girl, had all melted away after Stephen's death. She could understand it; they'd felt awkward, with their happy marriages and their living husbands. Jo was a widow, a tragic person, a reminder of all the things that could go wrong, all the things that could destroy your happiness in a split second. And of course, as a single mother trying to hold down a job, she'd not had much time for a social life.

Then she'd married Richard and moved out to the suburbs, where it was harder to talk with people, and she was busy having babies. Living in a beautiful house that felt like an island, her husband becoming more and more distant, until he left.

She'd only known Sara for just over a year. They'd met in the park one day, a sunny spring mid-morning when the playpark was full of toddlers and preschoolers. Oscar was climbing up the slide and sliding down, again and again, letting out a whoop of joy each time. Jo was sitting on a bench at the side and six-month-old Iris was nestled in her arms, fast asleep in the sunshine. Spring had always been difficult for her, since Stephen, but it was a perfect day.

Jo had gazed at her beautiful boy, so active and happy, and then down at her precious girl, asleep and rosy-cheeked and trusting. She listened to the shouts of children playing and to her horror, felt tears gather in her eyes.

She couldn't cry in the park. Everyone would see her. They would talk about her. *That's the woman whose husband ran off with the twenty-one-year-old au pair. Yes, apparently they were carrying on the entire time right under her nose. They live in one of those big new-builds, so there was plenty of room for them to do it in.*

And her first husband, he was that man — you remember, don't you remember how he died?

The tears had poured out of her, endless, refusing to wait until night-time when it was safe to cry, after the children had gone to sleep. Jo tried to blot them with Iris's blanket, but it was difficult to do without waking the baby. And she didn't want to wake the baby. A baby shouldn't spend the first months of her life surrounded by sadness and anger.

A tear fell on Iris's face and Jo wiped it off, as gently as she could with her shaking hands. She bowed her head and felt a bead of mucus hovering at the tip of her nose. She swiped at it with her hand, but it kept on coming, more and more of it, like the tears. She had tissues in her bag, but she couldn't reach them without disturbing Iris. Annoyance poked at her despair and anger. Why didn't anyone say something to her? If she saw someone crying in the park, anyone, she'd go up to them and offer them a tissue at least. She'd ask if they were all right.

But no one came. It was the same as after Stephen's death, when the phone stopped ringing.

It was a confirmation that from now on, Jo was on her own. Everything was down to her, only to her. The thought made her cry even harder.

'Whoever he is, he's a bastard,' said a voice in front of her. Jo had wiped her nose, though it was useless, and looked up to see a woman standing with a baby on her hip. Her curly hair was like a black halo around her head. 'Or is it post-natal depression? I had that with my first one, it sucks.'

'Do you — don't you know?'

Sara peered at her. 'No. Should I? Are you famous or something? Here, have a tissue.'

57

Jo took it gratefully. 'I thought everyone would be talking about me.'

'Mate, haven't you noticed? Everyone in this park is too busy taking selfies with darling Hugo or Eugenie to spare a glance for anyone else. Rich people, they drive me crazy. People are much nicer over at Palmer Park. Last time I had a crying fit over there a nice little old lady came over and offered me some homemade curry in a plastic container. I only come to this park for the sandpit. You want a wet-wipe?'

Now, a year later, months of coffee and confidences behind them, Jo said, 'I don't mean to be negative. I think it's seeing Honor like that. I thought she was a force of nature, Sara. I thought nothing could ever happen to her.'

'Well, I only met her that one time, and she was terrifying. How old is she?'

'In her mid-seventies, at least. And she looked every year of it in that hospital bed. She didn't wake up once.'

'It's going to happen to all of us eventually, no matter how scary we are.'

'She's a very intelligent woman,' said Jo. 'She raised Stephen all by herself, you know, while she was working as a university lecturer, and this was in the seventies and eighties. She's very admirable. She's just . . . outspoken. And she likes having her own way.'

Sara shook her head. 'It's amazing about you, Jo. You never say anything bad about anyone.'

'Well, there's nothing bad to say. We've had our difficult moments in the past, but I feel sorry for Honor. She's so alone. Imagine putting me down as next of kin. It just shows how few people she has to help her.'

'She has money though, right? Wasn't she some sort of doctor?'

'Not a medical doctor; she's got a PhD. She's an academic.'

'So she should be able to afford to get someone in. She's probably saved up for something like this.'

'I don't know. Academics aren't rich. I think she's living on her pension. I don't like to ask, of course. I'd offer to hire a nurse for her, but . . .' Jo trailed off. Sara knew her financial situation already: how she was more or less completely dependent on her ex-husband for support while the children were small. 'It's not the sort of thing I can ask Richard to do.'

'Well, the local authority will get someone for her, to help her out.'

'The house is completely impractical, though. The kitchen's in the basement. That wouldn't be such a problem if she had someone bringing her meals, but even if she put a bed in her lounge, the ground floor doesn't have a bathroom. You have to go downstairs to the little toilet off the kitchen, or upstairs to the proper bathroom on the first floor.'

'Time to install a stairlift?'

'I don't think Honor would hear of that; they're so ugly and slow. And anyway, the entire house is up a flight of steps from the road. If she stays there, even if she can get around inside, she'd be housebound most of the time. I think it would drive her crazy. She rides her bicycle everywhere normally. At her age – can you imagine?'

'So, what you do then is find a big, burly hunk of a carer who can look after her and carry her in his lovely muscular arms down the stairs and then push her in a wheelchair around the park every morning. Honor can have her fresh air, and a hot man to look at. Simples.'

Jo laughed. 'And where should we find this hunky male carer? Hunky Male Carers R Us?'

'There must be some somewhere. There are millions of little old ladies who would welcome a scheme like this. In fact, I'm tempted to break my leg myself.'

'The thing is, Honor is so independent. She's always done everything for herself. I can't see her being happy about being looked after by strangers.'

'Well, nobody's a stranger once you've—'

'Mummy! Billy took my car!'

'There it goes,' said Sara, getting up from her chair. 'I'll sort it.'

While she squatted down between the boys and tried the delicate art of convincing preschoolers to share, Jo wiped down the table, rinsed out her mug, and put the kettle on again.

The house in Stoke Newington, crowded with books and memories, was far too big for Honor on her own. In Jo's mind, it was difficult to separate Honor from her house. They were both tall and thin, crammed with knowledge and obscure references to a religion Jo didn't know much about; they shared a scent of paper and old wool. Whereas Jo didn't think that this big airy house here in suburban Woodley reflected her at all. A house that reflected Jo would be crooked, full of cushions and textiles, pretty teacups and an antique dresser in the kitchen, painted floorboards and pastel walls. Roaring fireplace, worn leather sofas, windows of old glass that distorted the view outside and made it magical.

This house was too new, a cube of brick with faux white pillars in the front. Inside, the angles were all perfect, the windows draught-proof. Richard had insisted on choosing most of the furniture, and though it was tasteful and comfortable, it was too modern. When they'd moved in, Jo had tried displaying her collection of flowery teacups on an open shelf in the kitchen, but they didn't look right amongst all the stainless steel and granite. She'd put them back in their tissue wrappers, meaning to find another place for them, but then she'd had Oscar and she was too busy, and then Iris, and then it wasn't wise to have teacups around when you had two toddlers. The cups were at the back of a cabinet, in a box.

Jo had lived here for nearly four years, since Richard had bought the house and they'd married, and aside from the clutter, she'd left hardly any trace on it. She'd meant to paint the walls, hang pictures, but the walls were still their original white — aside from the little handprints, the flecks of flung Weetabix.

Maybe that was what Jo was made of, after all: smeary fingerprints and old cereal.

Stephen and she had been saving up for an old cottage where her teacups would have looked perfect. Where every object was precious and full of happy memories. But then Stephen had died, and that was the end of that dream.

She reached for the biscuit tin to refresh the plate and saw movement outside the window. The hedge on the side facing the kitchen was low; Richard had planned to put up a fence to block the view of the cluster of chocolate-box faux Victorian brick houses built there after they'd moved in. He'd been furious when they'd started building. 'Too many people,' he'd said. 'It crowds the schools, and puts more traffic on the roads.' But what he'd meant was that the houses weren't expensive enough. That they brought down the tone of the neighbourhood. Every time Richard had looked out of

61

the kitchen window and seen the builders at work, he'd flushed with anger and ranted about the council, building permissions, a fence.

But then he'd never put the fence up. Knowing what she knew now, Jo supposed he'd been too distracted by Tatiana.

There was someone on the other side of the hedge. From here, Jo could see him from the waist up. It looked like he was raking up grass clippings: a young man, in his twenties maybe. He had sunglasses pushed up into brown curly hair, and an unshaven face.

Stop it, filthy middle-aged lady, she thought, and smiled to herself. But she kept on looking, just for a moment, with the top of the biscuit tin in her hand in case she needed to look away and appear busy suddenly. Because a tug of attraction, no matter how inappropriate and one-sided, was better than thinking about the house she'd never had and the husbands she'd lost.

Focus on the positive, focus on the future. Her mother had always told her that, and set Jo a good example. The MS that had eventually killed her had crippled her first. But despite her pain, she'd always kept cheerful. Her advice was what had kept Jo going after Stephen had died, in those colourless days that stretched on and on and felt as if they would never end. It was what had helped her over the past year since Richard had left. She had three beautiful children, and a comfortable house, and a good friend, and a body that wasn't so worn out that it couldn't respond to the sight of a good-looking man.

'Whoa, who is *that*?'

Sara had come up behind her and was staring out of the window, close enough to brush against Jo. Jo's cheeks heated.

'Don't – he'll see us.'

'But who is it?'

'He must be one of the people in the new houses.'

Sara sighed. 'Do you remember what it was like, sleeping with a bloke in his twenties? Bob could do it all night.'

The wistful, lustful expression on Sara's face made Jo laugh, despite her embarrassment. 'Stephen used to—'

She stopped herself. She turned back to the biscuit tin and loaded up the plate again, with the last of her homemade shortbread. Dusted with sugar, cut into squares, crumbling at the edges. This was reality, this was now. Too many calories in the kitchen with the children playing nearby. It was a good life. It should be enough.

'Anyway,' she said, 'I think that Honor should move in here with us for a little while.'

Chapter Seven

Lydia

I don't have to write about the first time I met Avril. I'll never forget it. But it makes me feel good to think about it. It's hard to believe it was only a bit more than five years ago.

Mum married Richard in August and I was the only bridesmaid. I probably should have put up more of a fuss, but I couldn't really believe it was happening. Mum made it into this whole bonding opportunity for us: trying on dresses, choosing music and flowers. We went for coffee a lot, and we spent a lot of time talking about Dad — not in a heavy way, just in a nice way, remembering him. We talked about the things we'd done together as a family, just the three of us. We looked at pictures of when I was a baby, and our holidays on the beach in Lowestoft. She reminded me of how he used to read me a story every single night, and how he named my favourite teddy bear Galileo. I think she wanted to reassure me that she wouldn't forget about him, even though she was getting remarried.

Looking back at it, she was trying to reassure me, too, that I was still important to her. She let me choose almost all the music for the ceremony, and she let me choose her dress. Which in retrospect, looking back at the photos, was a mistake, because at eleven, I had this thing for big fluffy princess skirts and lots and lots of sequins. I'd never been to a wedding before and it was all pretty exciting for me. I got to invite all my friends to the reception and we all drank litres of Coke and stayed up ridiculously late. Then I went on honeymoon with them to Thailand, which was brilliant in a way, but in another way it was awful, because Richard wasn't happy that I had come along. He tried to hide it, and he bought me lots of things to make up for it, but I got the impression that all of this had been Mum's idea, and he'd have rather been alone with her. Every morning I got up early and I saw how many lengths of the pool I could swim before they emerged from their room. I tried not to think about what they were doing in there, but I knew anyway.

One night in one of those fancy outdoor restaurants by the sea, where there were all these candles and fairy lights and impossibly beautiful people serving you your dinner, I tried to bring up one of the memories we'd talked about. 'Remember how Dad always wanted to build the highest tower made out of sand? All those different techniques he'd try to stop it from crumbling?'

I expected my mother to laugh, like she usually did, and counter with the story of the one time he'd used the beach umbrella and it had opened up and flown away, but she didn't. She glanced at Richard, whose mouth had narrowed, and who was reaching for his wine. 'Isn't it a beautiful sunset?' she'd said instead. 'What is it, do you think, that makes them so much more colourful here than in England? It's the same sun, isn't it?'

It's exactly the sort of inane thing Mum says when she wants everyone to be happy. And I got the message loud and clear. Of course a man on honeymoon wouldn't want to talk about his wife's first husband. Of course not. But the real message I got was that every-thing had changed now, and everything that had been, was over. And within a week of us returning from Thailand we'd moved out of our own house in the centre of Brickham near my primary school, to this new house, and then Mum was pregnant with Oscar, and everything had changed.

On top of starting secondary school, I was totally new in town as well. My new summer uniform was too big and it was scratchy, and I was scared. The summer was over and I had to stop pretending I was special and start to think about coping with how I was different.

I already knew I was different; I'd known for a long time, as long as I can remember, maybe even before Dad died. But I never really figured it out properly, never really thought it through, until that autumn, when everything was new.

Sometimes I used to pretend that I had a superpower that nobody had noticed yet except for me. For example, that I had eyes that saw too much, that could see beyond the visible spectrum, beyond ultra-violet and infrared. I used to tell myself that I had to wear sunglasses in order to fit in with normal human beings.

But that wasn't it. The sunglasses were just pretend. I didn't have superpowers; I don't. I have to hide in a much more obvious way than wearing sunglasses. At age eleven, about to start secondary school, I was learning about it.

Mum walked me to school on my first day. She wore a blue dress that was nearly the same colour as my new scratchy school uniform, and though that was naff beyond words, I was sort of grateful for it. I suppose it was meant to be a sign of solidarity. After a few weeks of feeling increasingly like I was in the way in Richard's house, I felt that I needed all the help I could get.

'I'm so proud of you,' said Mum. She is always saying things like that. She is proud of every little thing that I do, which is nice and I know it's meant to build self-esteem, but when you get to a certain age, you begin to realize that tying your own shoe-laces or starting secondary school or even getting top marks in your year isn't really

66

such a big thing to be proud of. We were getting near the school gates now, and I was looking for someone I knew, anyone, maybe someone who'd miraculously also moved here from my old primary school. I wanted someone to shield me. If I walked into the playground by myself, I would be too open, too visible.

But all of the kids walking in were strangers. I couldn't even see anyone else new, like me, with their parents. They all looked hopelessly grown up, tall and confident, knowing exactly where they were going.

'I've got this for you,' Mum said. She'd stopped, so I stopped too to see what she was talking about. She took something out of the pocket of her dress. It was a man's wristwatch: gold, with a brown leather strap.

I knew this watch. Mum kept it in her jewellery box, right at the back. I got it out and looked at it sometimes. It was engraved on the back: From J to S, with love forever. *It was the watch my mother had bought my father for their wedding. She had saved up her earnings at the café for nearly a year to afford it.*

The gold plating was a little scratched, but the glass was uncracked.

'I can't wear it,' I told her. 'It's not part of the uniform.'

'Put it in your pocket. No one will know.'

I slipped it into my own pocket, feeling the weight of it. 'Thank you.'

'Daddy would be proud of you, too,' Mum said. 'So proud to see his little girl grown up.'

And that was not what I needed to hear, not right now, not with my dead father's watch in my pocket, and a whole ocean of children I didn't know waiting to look at me. I bit the inside of my lip hard enough to hurt, so that I wouldn't cry. I turned away from Mum and her soft green eyes, and it was that exact minute that I saw a girl walking towards us. She had a summer uniform on too, but it looked less stiff than mine, as if she'd been wearing it for longer. Her dark hair was brushed back into a neat ponytail, she had brown eyes and a small mole by the side of her mouth, and she had a blue X-Men backpack slung over one shoulder.

She was the most beautiful girl I'd ever seen.

She was a total stranger, but she walked right up to me and Mum and she said, with a smile, 'Hi, my name is Avril. I'm new and I don't have anyone to walk in with and I wondered if you would walk in with me?'

I couldn't help but stare. This beautiful girl, with her X-Men backpack and her easy, confident walk, dared to go right up to a stranger and ask something like that. I never would have dared that in a million years. What kind of girl was this? Was she even safe? Why would she choose me, of all people?

'Oh, that's so kind, Avril,' said Mum in her gentle voice. 'Lydia doesn't know anyone either.'

I elbowed Mum, who was making me look bad in front of this girl. But the girl just smiled at Mum, and then she smiled at me. 'That would be really great,' she said.

There was a little waver in Avril's voice as she spoke. A little tiny waver, that maybe she was hoping no one else would even notice.

I noticed it.

'OK,' I said.

Mum went to hug me, and I stepped back a little, wanting a hug maybe but also knowing it wasn't really cool, and Mum took the hint (for a miracle) and put her hands back into her pockets. 'Have a wonderful day, Lyddie. Tell me all about it afterwards.'

'All right,' I said, and the beautiful girl Avril and I walked through the school gates together. We walked, not saying anything, shoulder to *shoulder, and all I could think was,* I am walking next to the most beautiful girl in the school.

When we got into the middle of the playground, I risked a glance backwards, but Mum was gone. She would be walking quickly back home, and she would have that smile on her face that she got when she was trying not to cry. I was glad I didn't have to see it.

'*Do you like X-Men?' asked Avril. 'It's my favourite film.'*

'*I like it, too.'*

'*What would be your mutant power?'*

'*I'd be able to see everything.'*

'*I'd be invisible. But if you could see everything, you would be able to see me!'*

I could look at you for ever, *I thought. My heart pounding, I said, 'We'd have to work together.'*

'*Thank you,' said Avril. 'I was a little bit scared back there, but as soon as I saw you and your mum I knew you would help me.'*

'*There's no need to be scared,' I said, and at that moment, I knew I was saying the truth. 'It's all going to be fine. You can hold this for a little while, if you want.' I took out Daddy's watch and put it into her hand. 'It's a magic watch. It can make you feel brave, because my daddy was brave, and it was his.'*

She took it, and turned it over in her hands, and she nodded. 'I feel better already,' she said.

And that was the beginning of everything.

Chapter Eight

Honor

'No,' said Honor. 'That is not a good idea.'

She felt rather than saw the hurt on Jo's face, and heard the recoil of her body. It was literally as if she'd been slapped.

Jo never could hide anything. From the first time Stephen had brought her home, his new and beautiful girlfriend, Jo's face had been open and childlike, every emotion written on it plain to see. The emotion had been worse, more exposing, than her cheap dress and bad shoes, the books she hadn't read. Everything about her screamed, *Will you be my mother, too, my new mother, to replace the one I've lost?*

Honor had winced in embarrassment for her.

'But it's the best thing,' Jo insisted. 'You wouldn't have to worry about meals, or company, or getting around. There won't be any stairs for you at all, not like at home.'

'The key word,' said Honor, 'being *home*. I have no desire to leave my home, where I have lived nearly all of my life. The home my father bought and furnished.'

'Mrs Levinson, you've had a serious accident.' Honor didn't

70

know the consultant, and she didn't remember his name. He was a strip of a thing with a high-pitched voice.

'Don't talk down to me. I know what you're trying to say: I'm old. And yes, I am old, but that's not the problem. The problem is that I fell down the stairs. Anyone could fall down the stairs, no matter what their age. I don't plan to do it again.'

'Nobody's saying you're old,' said Jo. 'In fact, I think you're in amazing shape, Honor. You rode your bicycle every day, didn't you, up until you fell?'

Honor pressed her lips together. This was the worst of it, worse than the pain: the condescension. From everyone, not only from Jo, but from Jo it was worse. Jo, who no longer wore cheap clothes or bad shoes but who otherwise hadn't changed at all. A beautiful blur of bouncing auburn hair, flowery dress, cheery voice. She wore rose-scented perfume and a necklace made out of string threaded through pieces of dried pasta, which clicked together as she moved and advertised *I am a mother of small children.*

'What we're saying,' Jo continued, 'is that you should be somewhere that you can be looked after, while you recover.'

'Nonsense. I'll hire a nurse.'

'You should be with people who care about you.'

'And that is you, is it?'

'Well . . . yes. Of course.' But the slight hesitation gave her away.

'You don't like me,' Honor said. 'We have never liked each other, and Stephen's death has set us free from each other. You don't want me in your home; you don't like visiting me. You're offering out of guilt.'

'I'm offering because you're Stephen's mother, and Lydia's

71

grandmother, and you need help, and I'm happy to give it. And of *course* I like you in my home, Honor. You are always welcome there.'

How did she manage to say things like that, and sound so sincere? It was a skill that Honor had never possessed.

'No,' she said.

'As I'm sure you know, Mrs Levinson, we aren't happy about discharging elderly patients unless there is a homecare plan in place.'

'Dr Levinson,' she told him. 'My name is Dr Levinson. It is not Mrs Levinson. If you don't like calling me "doctor", since I'm not a medical person like you, perhaps you will be so kind as to call me "Honor".'

The doctor shuffled his notes.

'We have a bedroom on the ground floor with an en-suite bathroom,' said Jo.

'That's Lydia's, isn't it?'

'Lydia will be happy to let you use it. We'll repaint the room and hang new curtains. My friend Sara's husband Bob says he'll drive his van up to London and fetch any of your furniture you'd like to have with you, so you can sleep in your own bed, if that makes you more comfortable. And Dr Chin says he's happy to refer you to the Royal Berks if you need any follow-up care.'

'You seem to have this all arranged,' said Honor drily.

'The children would love to have you, too,' said Jo.

Honor grunted.

'They'd be excited,' insisted Jo. 'Lydia was going to make you a card – she really wanted to – but she had homework. It's her exam year, you know.'

Honor had five cards. One made by Oscar, a finger painting

that had been labelled in Jo's neat handwriting as 'a dinosaur'. Two made by Iris, with the same fingerpaints but no discernible subject. One from Jo, with a picture of hyacinths. One from her neighbour Charvi, who was in her fifties and complained about her sciatica every time she walked up the front stairs. The cards jostled for space on the tiny bedside cabinet, along with a plastic jug of water and a cardboard kidney dish containing Honor's toothbrush and toothpaste. They fell down whenever a doctor or nurse drew the curtains around the bed of the snoring woman who was next to her in the ward, and Honor had given up trying to keep them upright.

She also had one balloon. This was new; Jo had brought it today, along with grapes, a novel that Honor would never read, and a plastic box of homemade brownies, 'to keep your strength up!' Jo had bounced in, smelling of roses, her shoes whispering on the floor, and the balloon trailing behind her. It had taken Honor a few moments to work out what it was. It was silver and yellow, round, with a streaming yellow ribbon, and it said GET WELL SOON on it.

'What is that?' Honor had said, looking up from the book she wasn't reading.

'I thought it might cheer you up!' said Jo, as bright as the balloon, even though Honor could see that her flat question had hit home. Jo tied it to the railing at the foot of the bed and said, 'There – that looks jolly.'

It was ridiculous. It would get in the way of the nurses when they changed the bed linen. It would lose its gas within a day and droop. It made her appear to be a child. Honor planned to ask a nurse to remove it as soon as Jo left.

But Jo did not seem eager to leave. She was eager, instead, to have Honor moving in with her.

'No,' Honor said again. 'I'd rather have a nurse.'

Jo turned to the doctor. 'Maybe Honor and I need some time to—'

'I'll let you talk it over,' he said, and left them. Jo sat down in the chair next to the bed.

'Honor,' she said softly, so bloody kindly, 'I understand that you want to stay in your own home, but this is just a temporary measure. Nurses are expensive, and although I'm sure the council can help you, with us you wouldn't have to—'

'I am perfectly able to take care of myself. You needn't worry. I'll be up and on my feet in no time.'

'But all those stairs—'

'I,' she said firmly, 'will be fine.'

'You must have put me down as your next of kin for *some* reason, Honor.'

Honor was gratified to hear the exasperation in Jo's voice. It was better than this cheeriness and this patience that must be false, that she must be putting on for the doctor's benefit, for her benefit.

'I didn't have anyone else,' she said. 'And I don't need anyone else, either. I am absolutely fine on my own.'

The mattress underneath the sheet was lined with plastic. It rustled every time Honor moved; it kept moisture on the surface so that at night her body felt steamed, like a slice of fish.

Until now, she had never spent a single night in hospital. Even when she'd had Stephen, she'd insisted on going home the same day, before dark. The woman across from her had dementia and spent every morning from two o'clock to four o'clock calling for someone called Twisty. The woman next to her snored. When Honor did get to sleep, nurses woke her up to take observations, and she would lie awake afterwards, staring into the half-light, waiting for the pain to begin again.

The medication they gave her helped, but it wore off. First there was a dull throbbing, then a slow knife through her hip. By the time the nurse came with her pills, she was on fire. This evening she had caught herself nearly snatching at the pills, wanting to cram them into her mouth and down her throat, under the steady gaze of the nurse.

She had carefully returned them to the paper cups. 'I don't think I need them today,' she had said.

And now it was three in the morning, not that you would know it, with the lights on and the nurses wandering back and forth on their crepe soles, talking in low murmurs. The balloon bobbed at the end of her bed and made crinkling sounds every time someone passed.

She had not read her bank statements for some time, but her memory was good. She knew her expenditure, her income. Her only asset was her house, the house her father had bought, which she would not sell. The Occupational Therapist who had come to see her this afternoon after Jo left had told her what a private nurse would cost. It was more than she could afford. And what would the council be likely to provide?

'We would move you to a rehabilitation centre,' said the OT, who was brisk and smelled of mint gum and cigarettes. 'You would stay there until you were able to cope on your own, perhaps with someone to pop in once a day to help you.

75

The benefit of this would be that you would be in the system, if you need more help in the future.'

In the system. The system that led to trading your home for an institution, losing your life to dependency. The system that crunched up old people who were past their use, and shoved them into strange bare rooms and the condescending voices of strangers.

Honor lay back on her pillow, took a deep breath of air that smelled of hospital laundry and disinfectant, and closed her eyes. She thought about Stephen, as she always did. First thing upon waking, last thing upon falling asleep. Stephen's hair slicked to his head when he was born, and the way his squashed-up face turned to hers. Stephen running in the sunshine in Clissold Park, his knees covered in scabs and grass stains. Stephen after a nightmare, climbing into bed with her, pushing his sweat-dampened head under her chin, against her neck, sighing into that heavy childish sleep. Her one precious boy. She thought about Stephen until the pain swam away somewhere else, and she was able to sleep.

She is in the synagogue, her father's synagogue, in a little room to the side, waiting to be called to her son's funeral. She wears a black dress; a torn ribbon is pinned to her breast. She is alone, the only mourner, as she was at her father's funeral. But this is her son's.

This is a dream, and she knows it even as she's dreaming. Stephen's funeral wasn't like this; his funeral was in the Brickham crematorium and it was crowded with flowers and people. She sat in the front row and Jo was there beside her, her arms around Lydia. The air was hot and June-heavy. There were no ribbons to tear, no way to show grief but crying.

In the dream, the door opens by itself, into the main body of the synagogue, and Honor walks to the front, painfully, as if moving through a forest of knives. She expects a closed coffin, simple blank pine, but this one is open. Stephen lies inside in his black suit. His face is peaceful and unmarked. He could be asleep, except that he is lying flat on his back with his hands folded on his stomach, and Stephen always slept on his side, curled up.

There is no one else in the synagogue but her and her dead son. No rabbi, no congregation. Wife and child of the deceased are also official mourners, but Jo and Lydia are not there. Honor's footsteps echo in the room. She lays her hand on Stephen's.

'You shouldn't have done it,' she whispers to his handsome, still face. 'You should have kept on running.'

Stephen does not stir. But behind her, she hears a muffled footstep, and she turns and Stephen is standing at the back of the synagogue, in the light shining through the tall windows. He wears his running clothes: T-shirt, shorts with a hole in the hem, battered trainers.

'Why did you never tell me?' he says to her, across the distance of pews and time.

His voice sounds exactly as it did in life. Exactly as it did when he asked her those questions. She did not reply then. She cannot reply now. She wants to run to him, to take him in her arms, to breathe him in deep, but the anger in his eyes roots her to the spot, her hand still on the hands of her dead son.

'Why did you keep him a secret from me?' he says. 'All my life, why did you never tell?'

Honor woke up suddenly and completely. Her hip screamed with pain, but she had only made a gasp. It echoed in her ears, along with the pounding of her heart.

Her dream had been bright and clear, every colour sharp, but now the half-darkness of the ward pressed on her eyes and on her chest. It was silent, as it never was in a hospital, and the curtains were drawn around her bed and she was alone. Alone always and for ever, with all of the choices that had left her alone.

She groped for the call button and before she could press it she knew that she would go to her daughter-in-law's house. She would go. She would have no choice, if only to hear the noises of other people in the middle of the night, to feel their gravitational pull, when it was dark, when she was alone and in pain, unable to stop hearing the questions, remembering the omissions she had made, the people she had lost, the prayers – that mourner's Kaddish by the graveside, familiar as the rhythm of her heart – that she had never said.

Chapter Nine

Lydia

*E*very day I run through a hundred scenarios of where it could happen. On the top of a bus, in the back of a classroom, on our walk to school. On a wind-blasted moor. In the back row of the cinema. On a sleepover in my bed.

In every single one of those fantasies, I'm blushing and stammering. I wish I could imagine myself eloquent and passionate, but I can't. I'm blushing and stammering and I look like I'm terrified.

And in every single one of those fantasies, Avril takes my hand and pulls me close. 'Me too,' she says. Or even better, she whispers it.

It could happen. It is possible. Maybe Avril's been hiding how she really feels, all of this time. Or maybe she just doesn't realize it, but when I confess, her eyes will widen. Everything will click into place. The world will make sense at last and we will be exactly who we are meant to be.

And the world will explode into flowers and unicorns and happy-happy-joy-joy balloons and streamers and confetti, and wars will cease and there will always be rainbows.

It isn't possible. I know it isn't.

It's not like I'm afraid of being gay. It's the twenty-first century. Being gay is all right. The gay kids at school stick together like a tribe. Georgie and Whitney are practically the couple of the year, though sometimes I wonder if they're mainly together because they're the only out lesbians in the entire school. So they don't have a lot of choice but each other.

If you can stick it out, if you're popular enough and weird in the right kind of way, if you can laugh off the insults and the teasing and not mind being defined by this one thing about you instead of by all the myriad other things that you also are. If you can live your life as a caricature of yourself and fit in with what people expect of you – if you can adapt from one kind of pretending to an entirely different type of pretending – it's all right. It's survivable. You can even be proud of it, if it makes sense to be proud of something that you've had about as much choice in as the colour of your eyes or the shape of your nose.

If you're brave enough – and also if you don't happen to be in love with your best friend.

Teachers thought they knew what went on in the classroom, but they really didn't have a clue. As Mr Singh droned on and on about quadratic equations at the front of the room, doing all the whiz-bang stuff on the interactive whiteboard that he thought made up for the fact that his lessons were boring on a galactic scale, a piece of folded paper was being passed from desk to desk around the classroom. When it got to someone, they unfolded it, sniggered, and wrote something down before folding it up again.

Lydia was doodling in her notebook, big swirls and flourishes. It helped her think, especially since Harry Carter had plonked himself down right next to her in the lesson and was trying his best to get her attention. He might have scraped himself into top set Maths by the skin of his teeth, but he was an idiot of the first degree, who could not take a hint.

Avril was in a different Maths set, so Lydia couldn't even glance at her and roll her eyes. She'd chatted with Avril for hours last night, as usual. They'd watched *Top Model* together on Skype, and then from the beginning on +1, and then they'd just hung out, talking about nothing, like they always did.

The tip of Lydia's pen swirled into a spiral, round and round inwards towards a small centre point. She knew absolutely everything about Avril, and Avril knew everything about her, except for this one thing. It was the one question she could never ask. So she sifted through the information she had about her best friend, all the secrets and the confidences, like one of those oracles they'd learned about when they read *Julius Caesar*, poking through entrails to find out the future. Avril was a virgin, the same as Lydia. She'd never had a serious boy-friend, just some snogs – the same as Lydia. They'd snogged the same boy, Lucius Arnsworthy, in Year Nine and they'd both agreed he was fish-lipped, but did that even mean any-thing? If a boy was fish-lipped, you didn't exactly have to be gay to work it out.

'Pssst!'

It was Harry hissing at her. She kept her eyes on her spiral, going over and over the middle point so that her pen dug a hole in the centre.

'Pssst!' This time he reached over towards her. Lydia leaned back, but he didn't try to grab her; he put the folded piece of paper that was making the rounds on her desk, on top of her notebook. Then he smirked at her.

Lydia waited until Mr Singh's back was turned at the white-board to open it, under the cover of her desk.

BAILEY SWINDON IS A CARPET MUNCHER PUT YOUR INITIALS BELOW IF YOU AGREE AND PASS IT ON!

There were a dozen sets of initials below it in different colours of pen and pencil.

She turned to glance back at Bailey. The other girl was bent over her notebook, writing something – presumably the equations that Mr Singh was babbling on about. With the other hand, she was scratching her nose. She didn't have the slightest idea that this primary-school trick was going on around her, poor cow.

Lydia held up the note and ripped it in half. Then she tore it into strips, then shreds. She collected the bits of paper in her hand and walked up to the front of the room, where the bin was.

'Lydia?' said Mr Singh, who miraculously noticed that she was out of her seat. 'What are you doing?'

'Getting rid of rubbish, sir,' she said, and dumped the paper into the bin. Sniggers. Harry made a goofy face at her.

Bailey kept on writing.

When the bell rang for break, Harry was over at her desk like a shot. 'Did you like what I sent you last night?'

'Not much.' Lydia put her books in her bag and tried to look the perfect mixture of disdainful and uncaring. As if she had nothing at all to hide; as if she hadn't thought of Harry's text once since he'd sent it. 'I didn't like your note just now either.'

'That wasn't my note. I didn't sign it. Anyway, you owe me a picture now. Don't forget.'

'I don't owe you anything, Harry.' She picked up her bag and went for the door.

'I think you're really pretty. And you're clever, too.'

'Well, that's nice.'

She didn't miss the jealous gazes of the group of Year Nine girls they passed. Ideally, she would tell him to piss off. But she couldn't shake off the niggling fear that he might know something.

'Did you like my idea of you and Avril together? She's hot, too.'

'Don't be gross.'

'I'll send you something again tonight. Maybe that will change your mind. Or maybe you'd rather see it in person?' He bent closer to her to say it and his breath warmed her ear. His hand rested on her hip. That was enough. Lydia stopped and glared at him.

'Can't you take a hint, or do I need to spell it out for you? I'm not interested in you. I think you're an immature tosser with a head as big as a football pitch and the sense of humour of a flea. I don't want to see any selfies of your tiny dick, or any other part of you. Got it?'

Harry stepped back. His eyes narrowed, and to Lydia, he looked more intelligent than he ever had before. She was aware of the people around them, quiet now.

He was going to say it, say what he knew. He was going to strike back at her because she'd rejected him in public.

He shrugged. 'See you later,' he said, and turned and loped away, leaving Lydia feeling weak and sick.

Later, they were in Lydia's room. Avril was lying on the bed, painting her nails with Lydia's purple varnish, and Lydia was sitting with her back against the bed, choosing music on her iPod. Every time Avril shifted, Lydia could feel it against her back.

'I think you were a little bit harsh on Harry,' Avril said.

She hadn't mentioned it to Avril. 'Who told you?'

Avril shrugged. 'A few people were talking about it. Why did you do it?'

'Well, for one thing, he was passing round this stupid note about the new girl in my Maths lesson. It's like something a ten year old would do. And for another thing, he keeps on asking for pictures of my tits.'

'Oh, all the boys do that. They don't mean anything by it.' Avril rolled over onto her back, fingers held high in the air. 'Are you sure you don't fancy him?'

'Fancy him? God, no. Why would I tell him where to get off if I fancied him?'

'I don't know. You're weird like that sometimes, Lyds. You like telling people off.'

'I don't.'

'You do. Like with Darren Raymond. And your mum. You're always arguing with her.'

'That's not because I *like* it.'

'I just ... you know. Sometimes people like to argue with the people they fancy. It's like an attraction love/hate thing.'

'I do not love Harry Carter.'

'OK.'

'I don't. I don't even like him as a person.'

'He's not that bad. He seems OK actually.'

Her voice was elaborately nonchalant. Lydia twisted round.

'*You* don't fancy him, do you?'

'He's fit. Everyone thinks so.'

'Maybe he's fit, but I've got to tell you, Avril, he's a twat.'

Avril waved her hands in the air, like two purple-tipped starfish. Lydia snagged the bottle of varnish before she knocked it over.

'But he is so gorgeous, Lyds,' confessed Avril. 'So incredibly, wonderfully, astoundingly, epically gorgeous. Those dimples! Oh my God I just want to lick them.'

'You do?'

'I didn't want to say anything before because I thought you might like him. But if you're sure you don't . . .'

'I'm really sure. But Avril, you can't like him.'

'Why not? I can like whoever I want.'

'But he's . . .' Lydia struggled to put it into words. The thing was, Avril was right. Harry wasn't any worse than a lot of the other boys. The real problem with Harry was that he wasn't Lydia. 'You deserve a lot better than him.'

'Everyone fancies him. Absolutely everyone. When I – when I thought he liked you, I was sort of jealous.'

'He doesn't like me. He doesn't even know me.'

'So you don't mind if I ring him?'

Lydia began painting her own nails, turning her face away from Avril's.

'I won't ring him if you mind,' Avril added quickly.

Lydia bit her lip and concentrated on filling in her thumb-nail. 'I don't – you can ring whoever you want, Av. But I really do think you deserve better.'

'Better than the most popular boy in the school?'

'Girl, you should be holding out for Harry Styles. That's what I'm doing.'

Avril giggled. 'Well, same name. And I think he's as

good-looking. I wonder what he looks like naked. All that luscious skin, like chocolate ice cream.'

The picture Harry had sent to Lydia swam in front of her eyes, making her paint her skin instead of her nail. She shook her head slightly to try to dispel the image, but the problem was, once you saw something like that, you couldn't unsee it. You kept on thinking about it: whenever Harry's name was mentioned, you automatically thought about Harry's dick. Maybe that was what Harry had intended. But why? Why would anyone want someone to think that way about them? It seemed so dirty, so animal, so far removed from love.

She wondered if she should have kept the photo instead of deleting it. She could have shown it to Avril now, like a treat that only Lydia could share, and been rewarded with her squeal of delight, or even better, disgust. It could have been an object of complicity between them.

But even if they giggled about it, laughed and mocked him, burst into snorts of laughter whenever they saw him in the hallway, Lydia would still know that Avril had that image in her head for ever.

And what if Avril liked it? What if that was what Avril wanted?

'You wouldn't believe—' she began, but then she thought better of it and shut her mouth. She'd wanted to tell Avril about the photo now that it was gone, share the experience in some way, because the last thing that Lydia needed was to keep any more secrets from her best friend. And because they could still have the giggling, still have the complicity, without the actual photo around to pollute them.

But if Avril actually liked Harry, really liked him, maybe she would be jealous that Harry had sent Lydia a photo. She'd been jealous when she'd thought Harry liked her. Avril would probably be happier if she didn't know.

'Wouldn't believe what?'

'How I have completely messed up this manicure.' Lydia drew a purple line down her entire hand with the nail-varnish brush, and held it up for Avril to laugh at.

A knock on the bedroom door. Two quick ones, not a volley of toddler banging, so it was Mum. The door opened almost immediately and Jo poked her head in. 'Hello, girls! Hello, Avril, I didn't know you were here. Do you want to stay for tea? It's lasagne.'

'Yes, please, Mrs M, that would be great.'

'Mum, do you mind waiting for me to answer before you come barging in?'

'Oh. Sorry.' Her mother didn't take the hint, though. She opened the door all the way and stood in the doorway, twisting a lock of hair in her hand, as if she were purposely trying to look like a nervous schoolgirl. 'Are you revising?'

'Yes,' said Lydia, though any fool could see they weren't.

'I need to talk to you about Granny Honor.'

Lydia nodded. She knew what was coming: her mother was going to ask her to make a handmade Get Well card, as if she were a little kid like OscanIrie. 'I'll ring her,' she said quickly, before Mum could suggest it. 'I did try to ring her yesterday, but she didn't pick up, so I sent her a text.'

'Does Honor even know how to do texting?' Mum asked.

'She never answers. I'm glad she's better,' Lydia added, because she was.

'She's agreed to come and stay with us for a little while. Isn't that great? It will be good for you to spend some more time with your grandmother, more than just an afternoon visit every now and then. And Oscar and Iris hardly know her.'

'She doesn't like little kids,' said Lydia. 'She told me one time that Dad was the only baby she'd ever liked. She said she had little or no desire to spend time with a creature who couldn't engage in rational discourse and that she vastly preferred children after the age of seven.'

'Well, she won't be able to hold out for long against Oscar and Iris. They're so much fun.'

'They're sweet little kids,' Avril agreed loyally.

Mum took a deep breath. 'There's only one thing. Honor won't be able to get up flights of stairs. So she'll need to take over this room for a little while.'

'But the guest room is tiny! Where am I going to put all my stuff? And I'm doing my GCSEs, I need somewhere quiet to study. There's no room in there for a desk, even.'

'Well, I was thinking that you might want to move up to the top floor. It's about time we did something with all that space, anyway.'

The finished loft space was where Tatiana had slept until she ran off with Richard the Sleazeball. They'd been using it as a junk room ever since, shoving all of Richard's stuff up there that they didn't want to deal with. It was bigger than her current bedroom, though because it was under the eaves, there were parts of it where the sloped ceiling was too low to stand up under.

'You'd have your own en-suite up there,' Mum added, 'and it would be quieter for you to study in, right at the top of the house. We can clear out all the junk and maybe give it a fresh coat of paint on Saturday.'

Lydia looked around at her bedroom, painted her favourite

shade of purple, with her posters exactly where she liked them, all of her stuff arranged just so. This room was the only good thing about moving to this house. Aside from Avril, of course. The French doors out to the garden that she opened on warm days to fill the room with fresh air. At night she heard hedgehogs snuffling in the garden; a few times she had heard the bark of a fox. When she couldn't sleep, she slipped out of the house and gazed at the stars. Their faraway brilliance made her think, for a little while, that her own problems weren't that big after all.

'I'd love to have a room like that,' said Avril, 'tucked up away at the top of the house. It's so romantic.' Her eyes were wistful.

'All right then,' said Lydia, with enough resignation in her voice to make her mother understand the weight of what she was asking. How Lydia, once again, was the one who shouldered the changes her mother had decided to make.

'Wonderful!' Mum stood up, beaming. 'I think this room will be perfect for Honor. She'll be right at the heart of the house, where we can look after her. Anyway, dinner will be ready in a few minutes, girls. I'll call you when it's on the table.' She went to the door, and paused. 'You know what would be really nice, Lyddie? If you made Granny Honor a lovely handmade Get Well card. After you've finished revising for your manicure exam.'

As soon as Mum left, Avril flopped back down on the bed full-length. 'That room is huge! What colour are you going to paint it?'

'I don't know. Also, have you thought that it's the same room where Richard was shagging Tatiana?'

'Yuck.'

'I know.'

'Your poor mum. She didn't deserve that.' Avril sighed.

'Honestly, I have no idea why Mum is so mad keen to have my grandmother move in. They hate each other.'

'I can't imagine your mum hating anyone.'

'It's not hate so much as this awful tension between them. Mum gets all chirpy whenever she's around, a little bit manic. And Granny Honor just looks down her nose at her. It's really awkward. And she's like my only living relative besides Mum, so Mum feels we have to spend time together. It's easier when I just go and visit Granny Honor in London. We don't have to talk much.'

'Do you want to know something secret?'

Lydia climbed up on the bed too and lay down so they were side by side. Their legs aligned, heads close, shoulders touching, hands clasped the same way. Avril was warm and her hair smelled of grapefruit shampoo.

'What?' Lydia said.

'Sometimes I wish your mum was my mum. Wouldn't that be great? Then we could be sisters, real sisters.'

Her voice was sad. Avril hardly ever talked about her life at home, but Lydia knew, of course. She'd been there often enough when the bedroom door was shut and they had to creep around the house, making as little noise as possible. She put her arm around Avril and hugged her.

'I wish that, too,' she lied.

Chapter Ten

Jo

'Where's Daddy?' Oscar jumped up so that he could see better out of the window.

'He should be here any minute, sweetheart.' Jo shifted Iris on her lap and adjusted one of the slides in her thick dark curls. 'I know he can't wait to see you.'

'He's late again?' Lydia appeared in the doorway, in skinny jeans and a stomach-skimming T-shirt, her hair artfully messy and her eyes lined with too much black. 'Jesus Christ, that man is pathetic.'

'He's their father,' Jo reminded her. She heard the tartness in her own voice and softened it. 'Where are you going?'

'Out.'

'I thought you might want to help me with the painting?'

'Oh, *Mum*. I thought you were going to do Granny Honor's room and I was going to do mine?'

'Well, yes, but I could do with a hand. Or you could paint upstairs and I could paint downstairs, and we could meet for lunch. It would be like a painting party.'

'Party!' said Iris, clapping her hands.

'I've told Avril I would meet her.'

'Avril could help.'

Lydia gave Jo a look that clearly said *Are you mad?* Jo wondered where teenagers learned these things from.

'I'm doing revision, remember? I'll do it tomorrow.'

'Tomorrow is when we have to go and pick up Granny Honor.'

'I'll do it tonight, then.'

'Don't forget to text me.'

'Whatever.' Lydia headed for the front door. 'I'll be back later.'

'Don't you want to say hello to Richard?'

'What for?' She banged the door after her.

Charming. But Jo had to admit, Lydia did slightly have a point. Even though Jo believed that Richard had tried his best to be pleasant to Lydia, the two of them had never clicked. It had been the subject of many discussions between Jo and Richard when they were still married. Jo had said that maybe it was because Lydia, who'd been eleven when Jo and Richard married, was too old to accept a new parent figure in her life. Richard would snort and say, 'Nonsense. She remembers her own father and I can't compare.'

Jo would deny it. But in this particular thing, out of all the things that Jo and Richard discussed during their marriage, Richard had been right. Jo had known it even as she denied it. Richard couldn't compare to Stephen.

Maybe that was even why she'd married Richard. *Probably* that was why she'd married him. It was easier to accept something lesser.

'Daddy!' cried Oscar, and Iris launched herself off Jo's lap to toddle over to Oscar at the window. Jo saw Richard's Jaguar parked on the drive behind her own Range Rover. There were two people getting out of it.

Her stomach sank, but she said brightly, 'Here he is! Look, Iris, it's Daddy's car. He's come to take you out for the weekend.'

'Daddy!' Oscar yelled again and he scampered to the front door, Jo following with Iris in her arms. He was just tall enough to reach the doorknob and open the door before Richard could knock.

His father stood on the doorstep. He wore an open-necked shirt, white to suit his tanned complexion. His black hair was casually styled. He looked not one day older than the day he'd come into the estate agent she'd been working at as a receptionist, and made a beeline for her, told her his property requirements and then asked her out for dinner.

'Hey, Oscar,' he said, holding out his arms to his son. His expensive watch glinted in the sun. Oscar ran to him and was scooped up.

Iris hid her face in Jo's neck.

'Hello, Richard,' said Jo. 'Hello, Tatiana.'

Richard's new girlfriend – the person whom Jo had hired, at Richard's insistence, when Iris was born, to help her with the children – stood slightly behind Richard, and had the grace to look self-conscious. She was tall and willowy, with long straight dark hair and the casual posture of youth. Her face was as tanned as Richard's; she wore an effortlessly chic outfit of white linen trousers and a black sleeveless top. 'Hi, Jo,' she said in her Russian accent, all fur hats and sexiness.

Richard kissed his son and held out his other hand for his daughter, but Iris shrank away from him. 'Honey, it's your daddy.'

'She's feeling a little shy today,' said Jo, smiling. She did not say *She barely remembers you*. She did not say *You didn't come to see them last week when you said you would*. She did not say *You ran off with Tatiana before Iris had the chance to know who you were and deep down, I'm glad that she's shy with you*.

'It's Daddy, darling,' she crooned to Iris instead. 'He's going to take you out somewhere nice.'

'No,' said Iris against her neck.

'We're going to ride in Daddy's car!' crowed Oscar, who had not forgotten his daddy. Who had a photograph of Daddy beside his bed and spoke about his daddy most evenings before he went to sleep and whose questions about why Daddy hadn't come today occasionally forced Jo to lie about Daddy's important job which kept him busy and far away.

'It's such a sunny day that we thought we'd go to the seaside,' Richard told him, and Oscar wriggled and crowed again.

'The seaside?' said Jo. 'That's lovely, of course, but I didn't pack—'

'Don't worry, just to Bournemouth. We can buy sunscreen and all the extra things they'll need. And ice cream,' added Richard, and Oscar bounced up and down in his arms.

'Chocolate ice cream!' he yelled.

'Any flavour you want, my boy.'

'Did you hear that?' Jo said to Iris, who was breathing hot into the hollow of her collarbone. 'Ice cream!'

'And fish and chips for tea,' said Richard. 'What do you say, Irie? Wanna come?'

'No.' Iris's voice was muffled in Jo's hair. She clasped her hands more tightly. 'Mummy.'

'Oh, sweetie,' murmured Jo, cradling the precious little body. 'It's your daddy. He wants to spend time with you. He'll bring you back on Sunday afternoon.'

'No.'

'It's her favourite word at the moment,' Jo explained to Richard. 'She doesn't always mean it.'

'Iris? Do you want to come with me, darlink?' Tatiana held out her arms.

'No,' said Iris, but she lifted her head and looked at Tatiana. Then she unclasped Jo's neck and reached out for Tatiana. Jo relinquished her, still feeling the trace of the warm little body pressed against hers.

'So what's your plan with your glorious free weekend?' asked Richard. 'Ladies of leisure who lunch?'

'I don't know any ladies of leisure.'

'Yummy mummies, then. Oh well, you're not dressed for it anyway.' He nodded at her old jeans, her well-worn T-shirt and trainers. 'Gardening?'

'Painting Lyddie's room. Honor's coming to stay with us for a little while.'

'What, that old bat?'

'Old bat!' repeated Oscar, and giggled.

'She broke her hip and needs a bedroom on the ground floor until she's back on her feet.'

'Rather you than me. Listen, Jo, we've got something to tell you, a date to put in your diary.'

'Let's go to the seaside!' commanded Oscar.

'One minute, mate, I have to talk to your mother.' But he paused, playing with the Velcro strip on Oscar's shoe. Rip open, close, rip.

'A date?' said Jo, trying to keep the impatience out of her

voice. 'Are you going on holiday again?' Yet another week or two when Richard couldn't see his children.

'Well, yes. Eventually.' Rip. Rip. 'Two weeks in the Cayman Islands, actually.' Rip. The fastening was coming loose from the shoe. 'But before that, we're getting married.'

Jo stared at Oscar's shoe, felt like she was falling.

'Twenty-fourth July,' said Tatiana. 'It is a Sunday.'

Jo gathered herself and smiled up at Richard and at Tatiana. Now, she noticed the ring on Tatiana's left hand, on prominent display as she held Jo's daughter. It was a large and sparkly diamond, of course; bigger than the stone Jo had chosen for her own ring when she'd become engaged to Richard.

'Congratulations,' she said. 'Lovely ring, it's so pretty.'

'Richard asked me to marry him on my birthday in Nice,' said Tatiana.

Richard had also asked Jo to marry him in April, but in Paris.

'Well, Happy Birthday as well,' Jo said. 'That's great news, I'm so happy for you. Should I buy a hat?'

Richard had the slight good grace to look uncomfortable. 'Well, you're invited of course, Jo. It's all amicable, isn't it, mate? But we wanted to tell you right away because Tatiana would like Oscar as a ring bearer and Iris as a flower girl.'

'My mother is making the dresses,' said Tatiana. 'She is making a pink one with silver sparkles for Iris. Just like a princess.'

'Lovely,' said Jo. 'Well, of course, they'll be thrilled. I'll put it in the diary.'

'You don't have to come if you don't want to,' Richard said. 'Mum's happy to look after the children.'

'I'll think about it.' Jo picked up the changing bag and the overnight bag she'd packed and left ready by the door, and handed them to Richard, who took them with a comedy wince.

'Oof! What's this full of, rocks?'

'Wipes and nappies, mostly.' Though to her knowledge, Richard had never changed a single nappy in his life. Tatiana was perfectly conversant with nappies, of course.

They'd be having children of their own before long, and where would Oscar and Iris be?

'We'll have them back by lunchtime tomorrow,' said Richard. He leaned forward to give her a peck on the cheek, and she was enveloped by his aftershave. He hadn't changed it; it was the same sandalwood and lime that he'd been wearing when he'd first asked her out; the same kind she'd bought him for Christmases. That was Tatiana's job now, too.

Jo kissed Oscar and Iris. 'Be good for Daddy and Tatiana. Have fun.'

'No!' said Iris.

Tatiana laughed. 'She is more adorable by the day.' Richard started for the car with Oscar, and she paused. 'Thank you, Jo. You are being very civilized.'

'Oh, well, I just want everyone to be happy.'

'You are special woman.'

Jo shrugged, her smile frozen.

'And you should come to wedding. My mother is also making seventeen kinds of cake.'

'Seventeen! Fancy that.' She gave Iris an extra kiss on her round cheek, and breathed in the baby smell to last her until tomorrow.

She stood and waved to the car as they left, but neither

97

Oscar nor Iris noticed, as far as she could tell. Then she allowed herself to slump, and go back inside.

The mirror in the hallway told her what she already knew. Her hair was scraped back, her face naked of make-up. She had a spot starting on her chin. Her T-shirt didn't quite hide the softness of her middle, the post-breastfeeding flatness of her boobs. Her jeans bagged around her backside.

Was she really surprised that Richard had been attracted to the young, lithe, beautiful woman who'd been living in their attic room?

'Just wait until she has children,' Jo said to her reflection, but she didn't like her expression as she said it. And besides, who knew if that would even be true? Tatiana might be one of those women who kept their figure after pregnancy. Maybe Richard would spend more time at home with Tatiana and her children. Maybe they would make the perfect family, one that Richard had never been able to manage with Jo.

Or maybe it had nothing to do with natural beauty at all. Maybe it was all about making an effort.

Jo snorted and went off to her bedroom. Fifteen minutes later she was wearing a top that had a small hole in the hem but which fitted her properly. She was also wearing foundation, powder, blusher, eyeliner, eye shadow, mascara and lip gloss, and though she hadn't taken the time to wash her hair, at least she'd brushed it and put it up neatly into a bun on the top of her head. She looked better, and even though no one was going to see her, why shouldn't she paint her mother-in-law's bedroom in full slap? If she wanted to, just to make herself feel good?

Because it made her feel foolish. But not quite foolish enough to wash it off.

She played music loud enough to shake the walls and painted Honor's room a pale blue, the colour of a washed-out sky. The colour was fresh and lovely, much prettier than the violent purple that Lydia had painted her walls when they'd moved into this house.

Jo loved painting. She remembered how she'd painted every room of the tiny terraced house she and Stephen had rented when they'd moved to Brickham so he could take up a lectureship post. Every room a different colour. Her favourite was their bedroom, a soft moss green that made her feel as if she were a cosy nesting bird.

And she'd painted, too, when her mother passed away, in the house where she'd grown up in Cambridge. She'd scrubbed down the woodchip with sugar soap and she'd coated everything with fresh, pure white, to chase away the memories of her mother's laboured breaths, the reality that she was no longer there to clasp Jo's hand.

It was supposed to be a new beginning. As much of a new beginning as there could ever be, in this life.

Jo finished the first coat and surveyed her work. The purple wasn't going down without a fight; she'd need to do another coat at least. Still, the room was much brighter than it had been. It would be lovely and cheerful for Honor once it was finished.

While she was waiting for the paint to dry she made herself a cup of tea and a sandwich, deliberately not scrubbing the paint speckles from her hands first. They'd only get messy all over again, and she had no one to set a good example of handwashing. She took her lunch outside to the back garden, where there was a sunlounger still left out from last summer.

Oscar liked to bring his teddies out here on fine days and pretend to put them to bed.

It was a beautiful spring day – a perfect day to go to the seaside, actually, though she hoped Richard would remember to buy sunscreen and put it on the children. With the children gone and Lydia out, she was glad she had a project to keep her busy. Spring was her least favourite season. Even now, in April, she could feel what was coming later: the visit to Adam in May that she would have to conceal from Lydia – and Honor, too, this year. The anniversary of Stephen's death in June. The sleepless nights.

She had used to love spring. Loved the world coming to life around her. But now even the cheerful flowers and the new leaves gave her a sense of dread. After ten years, you would think she would have learned to love spring again. Time was supposed to work magic, smooth things over, and it had been a long time. She should try to love spring again.

Jo ate her sandwich and lay back, cradling her cup of tea on her stomach, letting the sunshine warm her face and arms, making herself relax. The grass needed mowing, and the beds needed weeding, and there were toys strewn everywhere waiting to be tidied away, but that wasn't Jo's job, not today. Today she was painting, and only painting. It was so rare that she had time to do only one thing, that it felt like an unbelievable luxury.

It was even rarer that she had five minutes to sit still in the middle of the day, doing nothing, by herself. To listen to the birds singing in the trees, listen to the breeze rustling the leaves. The distant sound of traffic, a jet somewhere far over-head, going somewhere she did not know.

She closed her eyes and willed herself to love spring again.

New grass, new leaves, the birds singing. The scent of green and soil. All the life uncurling from the earth. She thought about the delight it caused in Oscar and Iris. A new beginning, like a room painted white.

But could painting a room erase everything that had happened in it?

A tear slid down her cheek.

'Nice day, isn't it?'

Jo sat up so quickly that her tea slopped onto her shirt. The man who had spoken was on the other side of the hedge, only about a metre away. He was leaning on something, a rake maybe, and the sun was behind his head, caught in his curly brown hair. It took her a second to recognize him as the man that she and Sara had ogled through the window last week.

'Sorry,' he said immediately. 'I didn't mean to startle you. Did it burn you?'

'Oh, no, I'm fine, thank you, sorry.' Jo wiped her cheek, and then her top. 'The tea's gone cold,' she said inanely.

'Your top, though – it's stained. I'm sorry, it's my fault.' He grinned at her; one side of his mouth tilted up higher than the other and there were smile lines in his cheeks – more like dimples, really, because he was too young to have wrinkles. He had a bit of beard stubble on his face and it somehow made him look even younger.

'If you let me know where you bought it, I'll happily replace it,' he was saying. 'Or I can have it cleaned for you.'

'No, no, of course not. It's a really old top. I've been painting in it.' She held up her paint-spattered hands to show him.

'Nice colour.' He extended his hand over the hedge, and Jo scrambled up to shake hands with him. His palm was warm.

'I'm Marcus. New neighbour who can't resist peering through hedges.'

'I'm Jo. And it's fine, absolutely fine. Lovely to meet you.'

'Likewise.'

He didn't say anything immediately, just looked at her and smiled, and Jo's pulse hammered. Had he seen her crying? Had he seen her a few days before, when she'd been watching him out of her kitchen window?

His smile was open and friendly. His eyes were greyish-blue. He had some freckles on his nose from the sun.

'Well,' he said. He cleared his throat. 'I suppose . . .'

'When did you move in?' Jo blurted out. And immediately blushed.

But he didn't seem to mind. He put his hands in the back pockets of his faded jeans and said, 'About a month ago? No, three weeks. I've never had a new house before, and I feel I should keep everything about it perfect, you know?'

'I know. I felt the same way when we started living here. Did you . . . did you move far?'

'Just from the other side of town. I've got a new job and this is closer. And it's definitely a nicer neighbourhood. Have you been here long?'

'Three years, nearly four.'

'Seriously, how long does it take before you stop feeling guilty about leaving smudges on the skirting boards?'

'It depends whether or not you have children.'

'Ah. That makes sense.' He nodded at the clutter of toys in Jo's garden. 'Are yours helping you with the painting?'

'They're with their father for the weekend.'

'Blessed peace and quiet. And I've interrupted it.'

'It's a pleasure. I mean, I wouldn't know what to do with

peace and quiet anyway. It gives you too much time to think.'

'It's a pleasure for me, too,' he said quietly, and for a split second Jo allowed herself to fantasize that this lovely young man actually meant what he said, that he was actually talking to her as an attractive woman and not a harried, paint-spattered neighbour who really should take better care of her side of the hedge.

'Well,' she said. 'I think it's safe for me to put a second coat on.'

'Happy painting. Nice talking with you, Jo.'

'You, too.' She picked up her mug from beside the sun-lounger and headed back towards the house. It was ridiculous, but she swore she could feel him still looking at her; a warmth on the back of her neck.

'Jo?'

She turned. He *was* still looking at her.

'If you – if you really don't want me to replace your top that I ruined, maybe I can replace your cup of tea. Sometime?'

'Um.' What was this? 'Yes, of course. I mean, yes! That would be great. Thank you.'

'See you later, then.' He bent down to pick up something, and a minute later Jo heard the sound of hedge clippers. She hurried into the house.

She caught a glimpse of her reflection in the stainless steel refrigerator door. Her hair had come loose in tendrils; her eyes were bright and her cheeks flushed. For a moment she thought she saw someone much younger. Someone that she used to be.

Chapter Eleven

Lydia

*W*here's Daddy?
It was Oscar's voice she'd heard as she came out of her room, Oscar's little plea, but for a moment she'd thought it was her own. High and innocent, with a childish lisp, asking the same thing.

Where's Daddy?

Daddy's gone, darling. He's gone.

Lydia ran. She rarely walked anywhere when she was alone; she liked going fast. And besides, Avril's text had sounded . . . worried.

And Mum had sounded disappointed when Lydia hadn't stayed to have a painting party with her. Like she was trying to make Lydia feel guilty for wanting to have a life of her own. And Lydia did feel guilty, a little bit, because it was true that she and Mum hardly had any time together any more, but why did it always have to be on Mum's terms, something Mum wanted them to do?

Anyway, Mum enjoyed stuff like painting. Within five minutes of the kids being picked up by Richard (when he got there, finally, the jerk), she would be humming along with the radio, in that way she had of being slightly behind the beat, and opening all the windows and twirling around with a big grin on her face because it was a beautiful day.

Her mother did things like that. She made daisy chains and danced in parks. She thought eating an extra cupcake was the height of naughty fun. Lydia used to think it was really cool. OscanIrie still did, and they were lucky, she supposed.

Mum's view of the world just didn't encompass being sixteen and gay and in love with your best friend. Even in the worst times, Mum was cheerful. Smiling. Looking for silver linings, trying to stay happy. She acted as if she was a rubber duck, able to bob over all the troubling things in life, saying you had to accept them and move on, when anyone could see that if Dad hadn't died, if Mum hadn't married Richard, everything would have been much better.

Avril lived nearly a mile away, in an estate of one-and-two-bedroom flats, built too close together around a courtyard of a car park about ten years ago and starting to wear. It was a different world to Lydia's neighbourhood with wide lawns and high fences; here the grass was studded with dandelions, and someone's bin had overturned into the street. Lydia skirted the spilled rubbish, which looked as if foxes or dogs had been into it, and went through the car park to Avril's block.

Avril was sitting outside the door on the step. Her chin was resting on the knees of her curled-up legs, her arms around herself; she was looking out for Lydia. She looked fragile and pale and Lydia's heart made a great thump.

'What's up?' She was breathless.

'I need you to . . .' Avril swallowed. Her voice was hoarse, and she was wearing the T-shirt she usually slept in. 'I can't lift her myself.'

Lydia's eyes widened. Avril got up, hugging her chest now. They went inside and up the stairs to the flat where Avril and her mum lived. Their footsteps echoed.

The flat was dark, and there was a sour smell in the air. Shoes cluttered the floor of the narrow corridor leading into the flat. The curtains in the living room beyond had all been closed, but there was sunlight filtering through the open bathroom door, and in it Lydia could see something on the floor, something coming out of the doorway to the bathroom.

'I found her this morning,' Avril whispered. 'I don't know how long she's been there. She wasn't in when I went to bed last night.'

Avril stayed, hovering near the closed front door, still hugging herself. Lydia went forward and saw, as she got closer, that the shape on the floor was a pair of feet, shoes still on. Dread pooled in her stomach.

When she looked through the door of the bathroom, she saw Avril's mum lying on the tiled floor. She lay on her side, her mouth open, her face grey. A pink fluffy blanket had been draped over her and tucked beneath her body. A string of saliva dangled from her mouth and pooled on the floor near the toilet.

'Oh my God.' Lydia took a step back. 'Av, is she . . .'

Mrs Toller answered the question Lydia couldn't ask by taking in a great shuddering breath, and letting it out with a long moan.

'She's passed out,' said Avril over Lydia's shoulder. 'I put the blanket on her because I didn't want her to get cold. But I can't leave her here, and I can't lift her myself.'

'Have you tried waking her up?'

'Of course I have! When I found her, she'd been sick all over the floor. I cleaned her up and put her on her side like they said in that First Aid course we did at school. Yelling in her ear the whole time.'

Avril's voice was high-pitched and hysterical. Lydia reached back and took her hand. It was cold.

'I just . . . I just need you to help me lift her up and put her into bed.'

'OK. Of course. Do you think we need an ambulance?'

'No. No, no ambulance. The neighbours would all see. I did that once and she . . .' Avril scrunched her face together as if she were trying to stop from crying. 'No, she's just had too much. She'll be all right in a few hours when she's slept it off.'

'But what if she banged her head, or hurt herself falling?'

Granny Honor had broken her hip, just falling down a few stairs. Older women had fragile bones, especially older women who didn't look after themselves, like Mrs Toller. She was skinny and slack under the blanket. Lydia had never seen her eating anything. Avril often made herself a sandwich or got some crisps from the garage, on the nights when she wasn't eating at Lydia's house. Lydia wasn't sure if she was supposed to know that, but she did.

'She's just drunk,' said Avril, and now her voice was no longer hysterical. It was angry, with a brittle edge to it. 'She went to the pub and she drank too much and she came home and passed out in the bathroom. She promised she wouldn't do it, but she did. Just . . . help me move her.'

Lydia nodded. Carefully, she went into the bathroom, stepping over Mrs Toller's legs. 'Mrs Toller?' she called loudly.

107

She bent down and shook her shoulder. Mrs Toller's eyelids fluttered, but they stayed closed, and she took in one of those shuddering breaths again and let it out with another moan.

'I'll get her shoulders, and you get her legs, all right?'

'OK.'

Lydia pushed at Mrs Toller's shoulder so that she was on her back, and she put her hands under her armpits. She had no idea of the best way to lift a person. That might have been on the First Aid course she'd taken with Avril, too, but she hadn't remembered it. All she remembered was giving CPR to a plastic dummy that smelled like stale Barbie dolls.

'On three?' she said, hoping she'd be strong enough to lift Mrs Toller, hoping they wouldn't drop her halfway to the bedroom. Hoping she wouldn't puke again. Hoping, though it was a betrayal of Avril, that a grown-up would walk through the door and take charge. That someone had already called an ambulance.

'One . . . two . . . *three.*' She heaved upwards, and Mrs Toller was heavier than she'd expected, a dead weight, but to her surprise, she and Avril managed to lift her. Her midsection hung down, dangling the blanket, just over the floor.

Avril shuffled backwards into the corridor and Lydia moved forwards, Mrs Toller slung like a sack of potatoes between them. She moaned and muttered something.

'Just taking you to bed, Mum,' said Avril, trying to sound bright and failing, breathless. Lydia had a split second to worry that they wouldn't be able to bend Mrs Toller's body enough to get her into the corridor, but since she was so limp, they were able to manoeuvre her by bending her at the middle. They carried her the few feet down the corridor and into her bedroom; Avril bumped open the door with her hip.

Mrs Toller was heavy enough that she'd slipped down quite a bit, so it was a struggle to lift her enough to put her on the bed, which was unmade, the duvet a tangled heap at the bottom. Lydia heaved, but her arms lacked the strength to get Mrs Toller up. In the end she climbed onto the bed herself, with her shoes on, taking Mrs Toller with her, crawling backwards on her knees and sliding the woman across the bottom sheet so that her head was more or less near the pillow.

Panting, she watched Avril take off her mother's shoes and push her legs onto the bed. She pulled up the duvet over her, and Mrs Toller groaned again, turned on her side, and curled up. The curtain was already drawn, and Avril and Lydia tiptoed out of the room. Avril went straight to the kitchen, found a large bowl and poured a glass of water, and brought them into her mother's room.

Lydia waited for her in the corridor. 'Are you sure it's OK?' she whispered. 'Doesn't bumping your head make you throw up, too? If she's got a concussion, shouldn't she go to A and E?'

Avril shook her head. 'It's not concussion, it's gin. I checked her head for bumps and there aren't any that I could tell. I think she just lay down and went to sleep in the bathroom. It wouldn't be the first time, though usually I can wake her up.'

Her face was still white, and she was beginning to shiver. Lydia put her hand on her cold arm and stroked it to warm it up.

'I could call my mum,' she suggested.

Avril shook her head again, so hard this time that her hair nearly whipped Lydia's face. 'Don't do that. I don't want your mum to know. She'll be all right. She'll just have a hangover.'

Avril's teeth were chattering now.

'Do you – do you want a cup of tea?' Lydia asked. The question sounded like something her mum would ask. 'Or something else to drink? I know – a Coke.' Avril started for the kitchen, but Lydia stopped her.

'Go and sit on the sofa. I'll bring it in.'

The fridge had cans of both full-fat and Diet Coke in it; Lydia took the red can, because even though Avril usually drank Diet, she could do with the sugar. She put some bread in the toaster, too, and while it was toasting, went to get a blanket from Avril's room. She brought both to Avril, then went back to the kitchen to spread the toast thickly with butter and jam.

This was also something her mum would do: feeding. It drove her crazy, sometimes – as if real problems could be solved with carbs. But Lydia couldn't think of anything else to do, any other way to help. She brought the plate through with another two cans of Coke. Avril was staring into space on the sofa, with the blanket wrapped around her. Lydia balanced the plate on the arm of the sofa next to Avril and sat down next to her, popping her own can.

'She just had one too many in the pub,' said Avril.

It was more than that. Lydia heard the pain in her friend's voice, all the other times that Avril had never told her about, all the times that Avril had had to deal with by herself, and she wanted to hug her, kiss her, hold her close. Curl around and into her, surround her. Kiss her forehead, her eyebrows, her cheek. Stroke her hair and tell her it didn't matter, she loved her, she would look after her. That the two of them could be happy. They didn't need anyone else.

'What can I do?' she asked helplessly.

'Just . . . stay here. Can you hang out for a while? I don't want to leave her, and I don't want to be by myself.'

'Yeah.'

Avril reached for the remote and turned the telly on. They sat there side by side, in the blue light, looking at the television without seeing it. Lydia felt every breath Avril took; slowly, minute by minute, she felt her shivering subside, and her body quieten.

She could not reach out her hand.

What felt like much later, after Avril's mum had woken up and slumped into the kitchen, feet dragging, to put the kettle on, Lydia went home. She was astonished by the sunshine.

At home, the entire downstairs smelled of paint. In what used to be Lydia's bedroom, Mum was reaching up, rolling a second coat of light blue paint on the walls. The purple underneath still showed through in patches. She turned around when Lydia entered, putting her free hand on the small of her back.

'Oh, hello,' she said. 'Is Avril with you?'

Lydia saw that Mum's cheeks were flushed; she appeared to be wearing make-up, though she was wearing a lot of paint on her face and hair as well. The top of her chest was pink, and her eyes bright, as if Lydia had caught her doing something naughty, instead of putting a second coat of paint on the walls.

She looked younger and prettier. More like the Mum she remembered of a long time ago, when Lydia was little, when they had done all those things together. When Dad was still alive. She was the Mum who fed her, who bought her Disney DVDs, who insisted on painting the toenails on both of their feet pink and who loved to fly kites and dance in fields. Who always told her things were going to be all right, when Lydia was young enough to believe her.

All in a rush, Lydia wanted to go across the room and snuggle up into her mother's arms. She wanted to tuck her head under Mum's chin and let her stroke her back and make 'there there' noises like she used to when Lydia had a bad dream in the middle of the night.

But that would require explanation. It had been too long. And she knew that it wouldn't change anything, not really.

Instead, she picked up a paintbrush. 'Where do you need help?'

Mum's eyes widened in surprise. 'Well – if you wanted to go along the skirting boards for a second coat, that would be great. Thank you.'

Lydia nodded, and the two of them worked together in silence for a while. It wasn't a painting party, but it was sort of peaceful.

Chapter Twelve

Jo

Lydia was plugged into her phone, staring out through the windscreen as they negotiated the North Circular on the way to the hospital. Above the sound of the car engine, Jo could hear the flimsy drum and bass sound escaping through the headphones. It was as if yesterday hadn't happened. Not that they'd said much to each other yesterday. Sometimes it was like living with a stranger.

She reached over and tapped Lydia on the arm. Lyddie sighed and took one of her earbuds out. 'What?'

'I thought maybe we could have a chat while we were driving to get Granny Honor.'

Lydia sighed again and took the other earbud out.

'We don't seem to spend much time together these days,' said Jo. 'When you were little, we spent every day together.'

'Well, I have a life now, you know.'

'I know. And it's natural that you're growing up. And I'm really busy, too, with your brother and sister. I'm sorry that I don't have as much time for you as I used to.'

Jo waited, hoping for some response, an apology in kind, but Lydia only fiddled with her phone.

'How's school?'

She shrugged.

'Are you worried about your exams? Not that you should be; you're a very clever girl. But I know they put the pressure on these days.'

'It's OK.'

'I thought we could work on a revision timetable together. You know, with coloured pens and stickers. With treats built in, so that you have something to aim for. That would be fun, wouldn't it?'

'Mm.' Lydia stared out of the window.

She was losing her. Her little girl, her firstborn, was slipping away all the time. Jo couldn't gather her up into her arms any more; couldn't tickle her until she laughed so hard she was squealing. Couldn't play dress-up and paint her nails, couldn't make it better with biscuits and warm milk, couldn't tuck her into bed and kiss her on the forehead.

When she was little, Lydia would laugh easily, and cry easily, too. Her emotions were so clear on her face. She was soft-hearted and tender. When she was seven, a skinny little girl with no father, she'd saved up all of her pocket money and asked Jo to donate it to the plaque they were putting up on the bridge for Stephen.

Lydia's phone played a musical note, the special note she had for texts from Avril. Jo heard it all over the house at least twenty times a day. Lydia read the message, and stuffed the phone into her pocket. When Jo glanced at her, her face was screwed up, as if she'd just received some sort of a blow.

'Lyddie? Are you all right?'

'I'm fine.'

'Was it some bad news from Avril?'

She couldn't look at Lydia properly because she was driving, couldn't study her face for pain or evasion. 'Avril's fine,' said Lydia, but her voice was angry.

Jo swallowed her questions and tried to concentrate on her driving, and on giving her daughter some space. The Range Rover was much too big for driving around London. It was much too big in general; Jo felt silly driving around so tall, as if she were looking down on everyone else. Richard had bought it, as Richard had bought everything.

'How did you know that Dad was in love with you?' Lydia said abruptly.

Jo signalled left and negotiated the bend before she answered. 'I knew from the very beginning. You know the story, right? How I was working in that café in Cambridge to save up some money so I could go to uni?'

'And how he came in every day with all these big thick books to study and drink tea, and how he never even looked up from his books for the first three weeks and then suddenly one day he did?'

Jo smiled, pleased that Lydia was talking at last. 'I looked forward to him coming in every day. I even had a cup ready for him and I would save him one of his favourite scones, even though he never noticed that I did it. You probably don't remember the way he had, of being so fully absorbed in what he was thinking of that it was as if nothing else existed. I thought he was adorable. He needed a haircut and he was tall and gangly and he wore glasses. He looked like a young mad professor.' Jo grinned. 'The other girls in the café teased me that I was falling for a nerd.'

115

'You used that word back then? *Nerd?*'

'Not everything was invented by your generation, Lyddie. Anyway, one day, he looked up when I brought him his tea – I don't know why he did so that day. He told me later that he'd had a feeling that something important was going to happen, from the moment he'd woken up that morning. I put his cup of tea and his scone down on the table and he looked up from his book and our eyes met.'

'And it was exactly as it's described in the books.' Lydia said it like the often-repeated phrase that it was. They had gone through this story many times before, the story of the moment when her mother and her father had fallen in love.

'It was,' Jo said. 'Exactly. He had the most beautiful hazel eyes, just the same colour as yours, Lydia. We stood there staring at each other in that café for what felt like for ever but I suppose it was only a few seconds. I don't think I breathed for the entire time. And then he cleared his throat and asked me if we could see each other after I finished work, and the rest is history. Instead of going to uni, I married him, and then you came along.'

'But how did you know he loved you? I mean, how did you *know*?'

'Your father had a wonderful gift of concentration,' said Jo. 'I'd seen it already with the way he studied his books, which was part of why I was attracted to him, I think. But it wasn't just Physics. When he loved something or someone, he threw himself wholly into his feelings. I never doubted that he loved me. It was in everything he said, everything he did. The way he touched me, and looked at me. And you know, he shouldn't have fallen in love with me. He was about to get a First in Physics at Cambridge, he had a brilliant career in front of him, and I was a waitress in a café with no university education. But your dad didn't care about any of that. He loved me, and that was enough for him. He was exactly the same way with you, when you were born. You were his world.'

'If it was like that, why did you settle for someone like Richard? Doesn't that cheapen what you had?'

'My marriage to Richard wasn't the same as my marriage to your dad,' said Jo carefully, 'and it didn't end well, but that doesn't mean it was cheap. We have Oscar and Iris now. I wouldn't change anything for the world, if it meant losing them. Just like how I wouldn't change a thing that happened with your dad, even though we lost him. All the pain was worth it, because of the good things, because I loved him.'

'But you didn't love Richard.'

'Why do you say that?'

Lydia let out a huff of exasperation. 'All that stuff you just said. Richard never treated you that way. And you were never happy with him, not really.'

'Lydia, when you're grown up, you'll realize that there are lots of different kinds of—'

'Bullshit.'

Jo blinked. 'Pardon?'

'*Bullshit*. There's only one kind of love, and that's the kind of love that you feel for ever. Even if you can't have it, you still feel it. You never let the person you love go, and you never stop missing them.'

She was so vehement that Jo risked a glance at her, even though the traffic was getting heavier.

'Yes,' she said. 'You're right. You deserve honesty. I married . . . I married Richard because he was – he *seemed* steady. It wasn't easy, Lydia, working full-time as a single mother. He

117

seemed like a good choice. I thought he would look after us. And I cared for him. I really did care for him.'

. 'But you didn't love him.'

'I . . . he swept me off my feet. You know what Richard is like. I thought at the time that it was the right thing to do.'

And it was springtime. Springtime and I didn't want to remember. I wanted something else to think about when I lay awake at night.

'I thought it was right,' she said again, hearing the weakness in her own voice.

'Don't do it again, Mum. Don't go with some guy just because he's good-looking and you fancy him, and because you think it might be a good idea, or because you need a man to make you feel better about yourself.'

Jo gripped the steering wheel and tried to ignore the insult. She tried to hear what Lydia was really saying, underneath the accusations and the anger. The hurt, and what had caused it.

'Is that what you felt it was when I married Richard? Did you feel that I was betraying your father?'

'Just don't. *Don't.* Please?'

'All right.'

'Promise me.' Lydia leaned forward in her seat, straining against the seatbelt, her arm braced against the dashboard, trying to look into her mother's face. Full of the same intensity that her father used to have, the same hazel eyes. 'Promise me you won't.'

'I promise.'

When they arrived at the hospital, Honor was sitting in a chair next to the main entrance, her belongings beside her in a neat pile.

'Hello!' said Jo, as usual wondering whether she should

118

offer to shake hands or kiss, and deciding on neither. 'I hope you haven't been waiting long?'

Honor only shrugged, which Jo took as meaning that yes, she'd been waiting for ages. She stood up by herself and walked slowly with her cane out of the sliding doors towards the car, which Jo had left on double yellow lines, hazard lights flashing, with Lydia in the back seat to guard it. After their conversation, with that oddly intense bit, Lydia had plugged herself back into her phone and put her music back on, as if she'd said all she intended to say and now the topic was closed. And Jo hadn't pushed it, too busy concentrating on the directions from the satnav.

'Looks as if you're getting on well with that cane,' Jo said, opening the car door for her.

'Irritating thing.' Honor handed Jo the cane. She winced, and Jo hurried to take her arm.

'Let me help you up into the car.'

She supported Honor's arm, kept her steady as she stepped up into the Range Rover. Honor let out a little huff of breath as she pulled herself up, which was her only betrayal of pain.

'Can I help you with—'

'I can buckle a seatbelt,' snapped Honor, though by the time Jo had put Honor's belongings in the boot, then come round to her own side of the car, Honor was only just clicking the belt closed. She stared ahead through the windscreen, her face unsmiling. Lydia had greeted her grandmother when she'd climbed in, but now she was firmly plugged back into her headphones.

'Well,' Jo said cheerfully, 'let's get going!'

Honor said little as they drove. Jo tried asking about the hospital food, and the doctors and nurses she'd met, about

Honor's physical therapy sessions, but it was as hard as trying small talk with Lydia, so she gave up and listened to the sat-nav's pleasant voice instead.

She pulled up on the double yellow lines in front of Honor's house and put on the hazard lights again. 'I'll just write a little note for the windscreen, and hopefully we won't get a ticket,' she said, and then looked at Honor, whose face was inscrutable. 'It must be good to see your house again.'

'For the last time in a while,' Honor said sourly and unbuckled herself. She got out of the car more easily than she'd got in, by sort of sliding off the seat. She stood on the pavement looking up at the flight of stairs to her front door. To Jo, it looked more or less like Everest.

'So, we can help you up these, no problem. Right, Lyddie?' Lydia, who had at last taken her earphones out, nodded.

'I can climb these stairs. I don't need help.'

'But we're happy to—'

Honor turned to Jo. 'This is all going to work out a lot better,' she said, 'if you stop offering me help. If I need help, I will ask for it.'

It felt like a slap. 'Oh. Oh, well, all right then, that is good to know. How about – how about Lydia stays here to keep you company and I'll go on ahead and put the kettle on.'

She flew up the stairs, opened the door and retreated to the kitchen. It was probably unfair to leave Lydia in charge of Honor, but Jo felt a sharp reply hovering on her tongue and she knew she couldn't. They had to get off on the right foot. They *had* to.

Honor was an old lady, in a lot of pain, facing a lot of changes. She was bound to be tetchy for a while.

She has been tetchy since I've known her. And she has never, ever liked me. Jo tried to suppress the thought, and filled the kettle with fresh water.

The house felt abandoned. The fresh scent of cleaning fluid had dissipated and it smelled like old linoleum and damp. Dust lay in a film over everything. It was best Honor wasn't coming back here to live right away; she'd never be able to keep on top of it, and she wouldn't like a stranger in her house.

Is it going to be any better with her in my house?

Jo found a fresh cloth and wiped down the kitchen surfaces, listening for signs of life upstairs. It was going to be a struggle for Honor to get up those stairs; she wouldn't want more of an audience than necessary. The kettle had boiled and she had wiped down everything, swept the kitchen floor, opened the window to let a bit of air in, and set out a tea tray with pot, cups, spoons, strainer, sugar and milk jug, before she heard voices. She rinsed and folded the cloth, hung it to dry, and put the kettle on to re-boil before she went upstairs.

Lydia had brought a chair for her grandmother from the living room, and was standing beside her taking instructions about what Honor wanted. She was smiling, nodding patiently, and Jo felt a wave of love for her daughter.

Honor, on the other hand, was pale and her face was shiny with sweat. Jo bit back an exclamation of concern, knowing it wouldn't be welcome, and went to the car to get the flask of milk and the biscuits. It took her fewer than ten seconds to climb the stairs to the front door. It had taken Honor nearly twenty minutes.

We are doing the right thing, she told herself again.

'Just sit there and relax,' she said to Honor, as chirpily as she could, 'and Lydia and I will have everything packed in no time.' She held up a flask. 'I brought some milk; I'll make you a lovely cup of tea while you wait. You've probably been dying for a decent cuppa.'

'Tea is just about the only palatable thing that the NHS can make.'

'I'll be back in a tick!'

She made the tea properly, warming the pot, measuring from Honor's canister of loose tea. At home, she dunked a tea bag. But she was going to have to make an effort now. She put the canister on the table in a prominent place, to remember to take with them; it would be a comfort to Honor to have the tea she was used to.

When she brought the tray up, Honor looked a bit better. 'My father bought this house,' she said to Jo. 'I've lived here for most of my life, except for my time at Oxford. I don't like to think of it empty.'

'Well, it's not for long.' She put the tray on the hall table and poured the tea. 'As soon as you're healed you'll be back home. Now, what do you need us to pack?'

'I've written lists.' Honor gave her a folded piece of A4. 'This is what I need from my bedroom. Lydia is doing my study.'

'No problem at all.'

'Where . . .' Honor began, and then she paused. Jo, who had never witnessed Honor lost for words, put the milk jug down.

'What happened . . . to the blood?' Honor gestured at the floor in front of her chair, the path into the living room. Her hand, lined with veins, was shaking slightly.

'Oh, I cleaned it up when I came to fetch some things for you for the hospital.'

'You shouldn't have done that.'

'Of course I should! You wouldn't have wanted to come home to that mess.'

'I still see it,' Honor muttered. 'Like I still see Stephen.'

She was gazing fixedly at the floor, the way she'd stared out of the windscreen of the car earlier. Jo had the distinct impression that those words had not been said for her to hear.

'I'll just push this table closer so you can reach the tea tray,' Jo said, 'and I'll make a start.' She fled upstairs, as she'd fled downstairs before.

The list was long and comprehensive. It was written in a round, smooth handwriting – not Honor's, so Jo assumed a nurse had helped her. She began to take clothes out of the chest of drawers and wardrobe, folding them neatly on the bed, ready to be packed into a suitcase once she'd fetched one from the loft.

It was when she was holding up two blouses, wondering which one was the 'white with short sleeves' one that Honor meant, and deciding to pack both of them, that she saw it.

It had been there all along, of course. It just happened to be framed between the two blouses as she held them up, and her eyes, tricked into looking in that direction when she'd been training them not to, caught on it, and held.

It was a photograph of Stephen.

He was wearing his academic gown on a summer's day. The sunlight shone into his eyes and he was squinting, smiling, wrinkling up his nose in the way he had. He was twenty-one years old and it was after his university graduation ceremony, where he had accepted a first-class degree in Physics.

Jo had been there. She'd been standing to one side, out of

shot, as Honor took the photo. She'd been holding a bottle of champagne. As she stood here, now, in Honor's room, she could feel the cold neck of the bottle, the drops of condensation on her hand. The sunshine on the top of her head, her new shoes rubbing on her foot, bringing up a blister on the heel.

I still see Stephen, Honor had said.

After that photograph had been taken, after Honor had gone home, Jo and Stephen had walked from Cambridge station back to Jo's house and they had had the first argument of their relationship, and one of the worst. Jo had burst into tears, saying over and over again, 'She hates me. She hates me, and I don't know what to do to make her not hate me.'

'She doesn't hate you,' Stephen said, but he had to know it wasn't true.

'She thinks I'm stupid and not good enough for you.'

'Well, we know you're not stupid, and you're more than good enough for me.'

'I can't do it. I can't see her any more. It makes me feel—'

'She's the only person I've got, Jo.'

'You've got me.'

'She's my mother. And she's not a bad person, she's just . . .'

Jo had pushed his arm away from her waist. She remembered the day she'd first met Honor. She'd been so excited to meet Stephen's mother, the woman he spoke of so highly. She'd even thought, naively, that Stephen's mother might be some sort of replacement for her own, who had died the year before.

'Have you seen the way she looks at me?' Jo accused. 'She looks at me as if I'm a piece of dirt. And you've never said anything, not once.'

'You're trying too hard, it makes you seem—'

'Stupid? Stupid standing there among all your clever friends and your genius mother, me, the waitress girlfriend, the townie? If you think that, too, then maybe we should—'

'I don't think that, but she's only trying to protect me.'

'Protect you?'

'Jo, I love my mother. She's had a very difficult—'

'She's had a difficult time? *She* has?'

'I'm sorry you feel this way but I can't take sides.'

'And if you can't take sides, I'll always lose.'

Now, in Honor's bedroom, Jo blinked her eyes hard. She lowered the shirts and sat on the bed, heedless of the clothes she'd folded, and she stared at the photograph of her first husband when he had been young and alive and not her husband yet. In her memory she heard her own voice, tear-choked and hysterical, the angry words she hardly ever spoke. She had desperately hoped that their love would make her his equal, that if she just loved well enough and deeply, that everything would turn out for the best. That they would all be a happy family. Humiliation had crushed her when Honor, raising her camera, had asked her to step out of the shot, please.

She rubbed the fourth finger of her left hand with her thumb. Bare now.

That was twenty years ago, a lifetime.

And now here she was, with Stephen gone, and her packing Honor's things so that she could take her home with her.

They had lived through that photographed moment together, the three of them, Stephen and Jo and Honor, and they all had different memories of it, and now it was frozen and nearly all of it was gone. A husband lost, and a son. Only Jo and Honor were left.

Perhaps they had more in common than Jo had thought.

'I still see you, too,' Jo murmured to the photograph. She got up from the bed and she touched it, her finger sliding across cool glass. She took in the details of Stephen's face, not the things he shared with Lydia that she saw every day – the wrinkled-nose smile, the hazel eyes, the attached earlobes – but Stephen. How he looked, the facts of his face. She thought about him almost every day, but it was easy to forget the reality of him. How he had once been here, the most important person in her life. They had been so young. They had learned how to love together, and Stephen had never taken sides no matter how many times she asked him to, and Lydia was right: for all its obstacles and shadows, for all of the secrets she'd kept, it was real love. The kind of love you only found once.

She traced his hair, his chin, his neck, and then she went back to packing Honor's clothes.

Chapter Thirteen

Honor

Her former daughter-in-law lived with her three children in an ugly new house on an ugly commuter estate where all the roads, in some unfathomable quest for intellectual cachet, had been named after English poets. The house on Keats Way was brick and ostentatious, faux-Georgian on the exterior but entirely modern inside, the kind of house that had two cars parked in the drive, one of them invariably a Range Rover, one an Audi or BMW or Mercedes. The neighbours were all white and there were no churches or mosques or synagogues or libraries but there was a Waitrose and several chic coffee shops and florists and even a cupcake bakery in the specially-built shopping precinct.

Honor did not come here often, and when she did, she could not help inwardly reciting Keats's *Ode on a Grecian Urn*. The people who built this estate had very little, if any, sense of beauty, or truth, or irony.

'Here we are,' said Jo cheerily. 'Home at last!'

It wasn't home for her. Nothing would be where she could find it. Her belongings would be sparse and few. There would be children underfoot and unexpected clutter, and she would be dependent on Jo. Every move would be subject to scrutiny. She wouldn't be able to hide.

Pain flared in her hip as she lowered herself from the car onto the drive. Jo hurried to supply her cane. Lydia started unloading the boxes of books she'd packed, going ahead of them into the house. Honor's feet crunched on the gravel and her cane shifted as she moved. Her foot caught on the doorjamb and she stumbled, catching herself on the door frame.

'Honor, are you all right?' Jo was, of course, right behind her.

'I am fine.' She lifted her foot, exaggeratedly, over the small obstacle. Inside, the air was cool and there was a strong scent of paint.

'Your room is straight through there, but why don't you relax in the family room for a little bit while Lydia and I unpack for you?'

'I can unpack,' Honor said quickly.

'But we're happy to do it, and you must be tired?'

'I want to be able to find things.' She remembered the house well enough from her rare previous visits to know that the door to the room she had been given was straight across the hallway, past the stairs. Jo accompanied her there, talking the entire time.

'It's got its own ensuite, and its own door to the garden. Hopefully it will be quiet for you, not too noisy from the children.'

'You can hear everything going on in the kitchen,' Lydia told her, passing by, presumably on her way back out to the car. 'I've been woken up every morning for the past four years by Mum putting the kettle on. Sorry.'

'It's not that noisy, is it, surely? Oh, I'm sure Lydia is exaggerating. Anyway, we'll try to be quiet. It's certainly quiet now, with Oscar and Iris with their father.'

It might be quiet if you would stop babbling, thought Honor.

'Why don't you have a seat here and I'll fetch you some tea, and then we can bring things in and you can tell us where to put them.'

Honor stretched out her hand to the back of the chair Jo had pulled out for her. 'I don't require yet more tea. Just leave the boxes and bags by the door. I'll manage.'

'But—'

'I will manage.'

She sat, waiting, her face turned towards the window while Jo and Lydia brought in her belongings and deposited them on the floor. 'Well, that's the last one,' said Jo at last, slightly out of breath, her voice not as chirpy as it had been fifteen minutes before. 'Are you sure that—'

'I'll be fine,' said Honor, getting up from the chair and waiting by the door for Jo to go away.

'I'll make the lunch then,' said Jo. 'We'll have it after Richard brings the children back. Meanwhile I'll leave you to get settled in.'

'Please do.' Then Honor shut the door firmly, turned to this new room, and took a deep breath.

The scents were unfamiliar, the sounds. The chair didn't know her body, as her chair did at home. The bed would feel strange. How long would it take her to be able to move around this house as she did her own, knowing where things were, reaching for them without having to think? Would she ever be able to do it?

It was foolish to have come here. But what was her other choice?

Honor sighed. She found a box of books and dragged it across the carpet to one of the bookcases.

Lydia had been correct: from this room, you could hear everything that was going on downstairs. Most of the ground floor was taken up by an open-plan kitchen/diner with a family room attached. Honor heard Jo pottering around it, moving saucepans, running the tap. She heard Lydia going upstairs. Slowly, Honor began to unpack her belongings, arranging them as much as possible to mirror the way she had them at home.

Her books were her friends. She felt each of them, weighed them in her hands as if she could absorb their much-read contents through touch, and then shelved them according to author. That done, she hung up her clothes, put underwear into drawers.

Shoved back in one of the drawers, she touched folded paper. She drew it out and held it up to the light: a paper crane, carefully folded. She balanced it on the top of the chest and carried on unpacking.

When she was finished, her hip and head were throbbing, so she lay down on the bed. She had a white NHS bag of pain medication in her handbag, which she tried not to think about.

The doorbell rang and she heard the deep, arrogant tones of Jo's second husband, Richard, along with the Russian accent of his new tramp girlfriend, and the high-pitched voices of the children. Their footsteps scampered all around, accompanied by squeals and bangs and laughter, and Honor thought about toys left on the floor, messes she would not be able to see, little bodies careering into her healing bone. She squeezed her eyes shut tight.

Jo knocked on Honor's door. 'Lunchtime!' she trilled as only Jo could trill, as if Lunch were some great occasion the likes of which no one had seen before. Honor raised herself from her bed, retrieved her cane, and made her way into the hall and towards the main room, the source of all the noise and also of the scent of roasted chicken and potatoes.

Her stomach rumbled. The food at the hospital had not been good. And she rarely cooked for herself, lately.

The cane slipped on the polished wooden floor. Honor tightened her grip on it and walked in shuffling steps towards the table at the far end of the room, near the doors to the garden. Her foot struck something hard, plastic-sounding, and she recoiled, fighting for balance, anticipating pain. Against her will, she let out a small sound of fright before she managed to use her cane to stop herself falling.

'Are you all right?' Jo called, evidently from the kitchen area. 'Oh God, it's toys on the floor.' She rushed over and picked something up. 'Oscar, honey, you need to put your toys away, it's dangerous for Granny Honor. Honor, I'm so sorry.'

Aside from the stairs, this was considerably more hazardous than the home that Honor was not allowed to live in. She made her way to the table and took the nearest seat, the one with the light from the window full on it, but when she sat on it, it was too high.

'That's my chair!' cried Oscar, the one who was three. And it was his chair; it was a wooden contraption, presumably adjustable. Honor manoeuvred herself out of it.

'Honor, I've put you next to Oscar.' Jo pulled out a chair for her. On her way, Honor collided with Iris, who was chasing

131

her brother around the table. Honor had to grab the back of the chair to stop herself falling over.

'Iris!' said Jo. 'Oscar! Get into your chairs now, no running around. We have to be careful of Granny Honor.'

There was no trace of anger or censure in her voice; it was as cheerful as normal. The children resumed running around, paying no attention to the mild rebuke. Honor took the opportunity to sit down safely, the toddler rushing past her again, giggling.

'Lydia!' Jo yelled up the stairs, and resumed her clattering of pans and utensils. The smell of roasted chicken and hot fat was almost overwhelming here in the kitchen. Jo placed a platter in front of Honor; she could feel the heat on her face, hear the sizzle. Water sprang in her mouth and she had to press her lips together.

'Lydia!' Jo yelled again, and then, closer, 'Shall I carve, Honor, or would you like to?'

'I don't think I can be trusted with knives,' Honor muttered, and winced as one of the children knocked against her chair again.

'Oscar!' A small grunt, as Jo picked up the little boy and deposited him in the chair that Honor had vacated. Another as she did the same to Iris. 'Lydia! Honestly, that girl never hears me. I will have to—'

'Just a *minute*!' came Lydia's voice from somewhere in the vicinity of the stairs.

'Well, we might as well start. Breast or leg, Honor?'

'Breast.'

'I want the wing, I want the wing, I want the wing, I want—'

'Wing for you, Oscar. And Iris, some peas?'

'No!'

'You have to eat your vegetables, darling, to make you big and strong. Two potatoes or three, Honor?'

'One.'

A scrape of chair, and Lydia sat across from Honor. She was strawberry lip gloss and easy-moving limbs, hair a lighter shade of red than her mother's. 'How's it going, Granny H?' she asked, reaching across the table to grab a serving dish. 'Settled in?'

'Lydia, don't reach. Honor, can I get you anything else? Would you like some gravy? What about a glass of wine? I have a bottle of white chilled.'

'I am fine, thank you.'

'Oscar, use a fork, please. Iris, can you try some of those peas? Everyone, let's have a toast! To welcome Honor.'

They raised their glasses and beakers. Lydia leaned right across to clunk her glass with Oscar's.

'You are really very welcome, Honor. We're pleased to have you here.'

'With any luck, it won't be for long.' She speared food with her fork, took a bite, and chewed, hot crackling potato, soft inside. She wondered how on earth she was going to get through all the mealtimes in this house.

'Yes, my name is Iggle Piggle,' shrilled Iris, loud enough for Honor to wince.

'Iggle Wiggle Iggle Iggle Piggle,' joined in Oscar.

'Have you done your homework yet, Lyddie?'

'I'll do it later.' Lydia's phone chimed a musical note, and she pulled it out of her pocket to answer.

'Do you have to at the table?' said Jo, and Lydia responded by getting up noisily and stomping to the other end of the room.

'Iggle Wiggle Iggle Wiggle Woo!'

Something wet and soft struck Honor's hand. She raised it: a lump of potato, a smear of gravy.

'Iris, don't throw your food! I'm so sorry, Honor.' Jo reached over with a napkin, and Honor pulled her hand away.

'I can do it myself,' she said, in a voice that was meant to convey what she thought of small children out of control and singing gibberish during mealtimes, of teenagers leaving the table to answer telephone calls, of mothers who were ineffectual and who lived in houses strewn haphazardly with toys.

'Lydia, come back to the table, please,' said Jo.

'No, I'm going out.'

'Lydia!'

The door slammed.

'I want dessert, Mummy!' Oscar said.

Honor thought of Stephen. She wondered what Stephen would make of this new family. Of the way his daughter was growing up. Of the way his wife fluttered and fussed.

She raised her fork to her lips but it was empty.

Chapter Fourteen

Lydia

I *can't believe she's got off with him.*
I shouldn't have gone to pick up Granny H with Mum. I should have stayed behind, so that I could have seen Avril, because if I'd been with her we'd have gone out together, and if we ran into Harry in Costa we would have just chatted to him or whatever and he would have gone away.

But Mum insisted and so I was in the car with her on the way to London when I got the text that Avril had met up with Harry. And then practically minute-by-minute updates of how they were having a coffee, and how Harry likes lemon and poppyseed muffins like she does, and how they were going to hang out in the park. And then no texts at all, for the rest of the morning. She didn't answer any of mine. Which was even worse, because then I was imagining what they were doing.

And then the awfulness of bringing Granny H back here! She was in a right strop, especially because we had to carry her back down the front stairs of her house to the car. She didn't want us to, and she tried really hard to get down the stairs, but you could see it in her face that she was in so much pain. She looked older than she ever has, like a skeleton practically.

I've been looking at my own face in the mirror trying to imagine what I will look like when I get that old. I don't even know if I want to get that old. It must be sort of horrible to feel your flesh almost melting off your bones, and have your skin go all slack and wrinkly. I wonder what she sees when she looks in the mirror – if she sees what I see when I look at her, with the wrinkles and the sunken lips and the coarse hairs on either side of her mouth that she hasn't noticed to pluck. Just like two or three of them, but still. I wonder if she sees that – what she's really like now, or if she sees a version of herself from when she was young. Because Granny H was good-looking when she was young, I've seen the pictures. Not pretty like Mum used to be and still is in a way – she was more dignified-looking. Handsome.

And now she's hardly anything more than a collection of bones. I know because Mum and I had to put her into this sort of chair-lift hold to get her down the stairs. Granny H was livid about it, but it wasn't a problem for us, she hardly weighs anything. But she held her head up, not looking at us, not looking at anything, her hands in fists, and it felt sort of embarrassing. Like she was naked, or that we'd caught her on the toilet. Her cheek was brushing against mine as I carried her, and Granny H is wrinkly but she does have really lovely soft skin, and always smells of Chanel No. 5, but I couldn't turn my head to smile at her or say something nice, because I was too embarrassed. I just helped Mum carry her down to the car and helped her in and I got in the back and listened to my music all the way home, which didn't make much difference as Granny H and Mum weren't really speaking anyway, except for those inane chirpy comments Mum kept making so that she could pretend that everyone was happy. And no text from Avril.

On Monday she had to sit next to Harry Smug Carter in Maths, trying to ignore his smirks in her direction. Lydia bent her head and concentrated more on Maths than she ever had before.

She'd listened to it all the way to school: what an amazing kisser Harry Carter was, what beautiful eyes Harry Carter had, how Avril and Harry Carter had got Ellie Jacobs who was in the sixth form to buy them cans of cider and how they'd held hands while they were drinking them. How Harry Carter liked The Clash which was so cool, and how they both really loved the Transformers films which was an incredible coincidence. Also, *again*, what an amazing kisser Harry Carter was and how he'd asked to meet up after school, too.

Lydia didn't get a word in. She didn't dare to get a word in. But Avril didn't seem to notice; she skipped on her long legs with the rolled-down socks and the rolled-up skirt, everything about her so familiar it made Lydia's entire body ache.

On Saturday when Lydia had left her, she'd been curled up in a chair staring at the telly, drawn and worried about her mum. And now she was lighter than air, about to burst with excitement, and Lydia had nothing to do with it.

She felt something strike her arm and looked over. 'Jealous?' Harry mouthed to her, raising his eyebrows.

Jealous enough to kill you with a stare, you son of a bitch. She rolled her eyes at him and went back to her equations, calculating instead what he had meant.

She didn't trust him. Harry Carter was a snake. He couldn't possibly love Avril, not someone like him.

The next lesson was Geography, and they had a mock which meant they had to write quietly for the entire time whilst Mr Graham walked between their desks. She didn't have any time to speak to Avril before he passed the papers out. Avril used to have a bit of a crush on Mr Graham but she hardly even glanced at him today. When Lydia looked over, she was staring into space with this silly expression on her face, as if she were on some sort of drug. When Lydia tried to force herself to write, nonsense flowed out of her pen onto the page.

Mr Graham made them write right up to the bell. Avril was so slow, ridiculously slow, getting her things together. 'How's your mum?' Lydia whispered to her, and Avril shook her head.

'Was she OK yesterday?' Lydia continued anyway, in a low voice when they got out into the corridor, because even though Avril didn't want to talk about it, Lydia did. She wanted to remind Avril that they had secrets together. That Lydia was the person she trusted, the one she could turn to when things went wrong. 'Did she tell you what happened?'

'It was nothing, all right? No big deal.'

'You say that, but I know you were worried.'

Avril turned on her angrily. 'I said, no big deal.' Her phone went off in her handbag and she dug it out, walking faster than Lydia. Lydia caught up with her in time to see Avril's delight when she read the text.

At lunchtime, for once, Lydia picked at her food as much as Erin and Sophie. Avril wasn't eating either. The only consolation was that she'd not yet told the other girls about her and Harry. But was that worse, that Avril was keeping it a happy secret? She kept sneaking glances to the other end of the dining hall, where Harry was sitting with his mates, laughing. Probably about Avril. How easily Harry had bagged her.

A ball of misery rose into Lydia's throat.

And this was only the start of it. Only the start of a lifetime when Lydia would have to swallow her silly dreams and watch Avril with other people whom she loved more than she loved Lydia. This wasn't what love was supposed to be like. You weren't supposed to lose everyone.

Harry glanced up from his conversation with his mates, searching out Avril. He raised his hand and Avril came to life. She jumped up and scurried over to join him.

Erin's mouth was open. 'What's going on with Avril and Harry?'

'Nothing,' said Lydia.

'Clearly it's something. Don't you know? Aren't you two like joined at the hip?'

Lydia screwed up her sandwich wrapper and began tearing it into pieces.

'Wow, she's like his lapdog,' said Olivia, and for once, Lydia agreed with her.

'Did they get off with each other?' Erin asked. 'You must know.'

'I don't want to talk about it,' Lydia snapped before she could think, before she could plan what wouldn't give her away.

'Oooh,' tittered Sophie. 'You're jealous, aren't you? Wishing you hadn't blown your chance with him?'

'Is it all right if I sit here?'

It was Bailey, the new girl, addressing herself to Lydia. The other girls stopped talking and stared. Bailey's hair was still naff, and she still wore the ankle socks, but at least this time her lunch consisted of a salad and a yoghurt, instead of the glop she'd had before.

'What I mean is,' said Bailey, 'is this seat taken?'

It was Avril's seat.

'I won't talk to you or anything if you don't want me to,' Bailey added. 'I just need somewhere to sit and eat.'

It was that, the offer not to talk, the straight-out acknowledgement that she didn't fit in and that she was resigned to it, that got Lydia. She moved Avril's books to one side, clearing the table space for Bailey. 'Knock yourself out,' she said.

Erin leaned over. 'She's got a crush on youuu,' she crooned into Lydia's ear. Lydia rolled her eyes.

Across the dining hall, she heard the silvery sound of Avril's laughter.

Chapter Fifteen

Jo

'I spy, with my little eye, something that is green.'
   'Tree!'
'No.'
'Flower!' Oscar hung onto the side of the buggy, jumping up and down. Iris was asleep and had been for twenty minutes, having exhausted herself with a tantrum in Waitrose. Oscar was still full of beans, and Jo was hopeful that maybe she'd actually get the shopping done without another meltdown from him, too.

She hadn't slept much last night. Mostly she was worrying about Honor, but around three o'clock, the old thoughts had started coming back, the same ones she'd had for ten years now in the middle of the night. It was always worse in the spring. In the end, she'd got up and made herself a cup of chamomile tea and read her book until nearly dawn.

She suppressed a yawn. 'Flowers aren't green, Oscar.'
'That one's green!' He pointed at one of the planters in the middle of the shopping precinct.
'That's not a flower, sweetie, that's a fern.'
'Fern!'

'Nope. Keep looking.'

'Apple!'

Jo looked around. 'Where's an apple?'

'In my mind!'

'Things that are in your mind don't count, sweetie. They have to be things that you can really see.'

'Grass!'

'You're getting warmer.' Oscar looked confused, so Jo explained, 'It means that the thing you're looking for is really near the grass.'

Oscar stopped walking, peering hard at the patch of grass beside the fabric shop. Jo mentally ticked off her list: Waitrose done; key cutters next to get a set made for Honor, which would be fine because Oscar liked poking at all the keys on display; library last because Iris might have woken up by then and even though she woke up cranky, Oscar would look at books so that Jo could give Iris a cuddle. The library had a toilet too, and baby-changing facilities.

Her shopping trips these days were always zig-zags around the precinct, visiting the shops in the optimal order to keep the children happy and interested. She always had to do the supermarket first, whilst the children were still fresh, because that's where tempers would fray: where Oscar would ask for sweets he couldn't have, and Iris would decide it was fun to grab items off the shelf at toddler pushchair height and throw them onto the floor. If the kids were relatively happy and not bored yet, they could get through those hurdles without too much trouble.

Of course this meant that if she wanted anything frozen, she'd have to come back at the end of her shopping trip, too, so it wouldn't melt whilst she ran her other errands. She hadn't quite worked out a way around this yet, other than getting Lydia to look after her siblings whilst Jo went to do the shopping on her own. Even without children, Jo caught herself planning her route to avoid the rows of sweets, positioning her trolley more than a small arm's reach away from the heavy cans.

Sometimes she saw couples doing their weekly shop together with their children. They ran interference for each other, one distracting the children whilst the other found items on the shelves. She remembered doing this with Stephen. He used to make illustrated lists for Lydia, so she could tick off items as they went into the trolley.

'Bin!' cried Oscar.

'The bins are black,' said Jo, looking at the nearest bin to make sure, and seeing Marcus from next door walking across the precinct. He wore a white shirt and a green tie, sleeves rolled up, and he was holding a canvas shopping bag. He smiled when he spotted her, raised his hand, and changed his course to approach her. Jo scrubbed at her eyes quickly, as if she could get rid of the shadows under them.

'Hello!' he called. 'How are you doing, neighbour?'

'Fine,' answered Jo, irrationally pleased that he'd gone out of his way to greet her, irrationally disappointed that he'd evidently forgotten her name. 'How are you, Marcus?'

He held up his canvas bag. 'On a lunch break from work. I've been sent out to replenish the tea bags and the biscuits. Don't judge me because of the bag.'

It was pink, with daisies on it. 'I wouldn't dream of it.'

'That's a relief.' He squatted down to eye-level with Oscar. 'Hello there, I live next door to you. I think I've seen your trucks in your garden.'

143

'I love trucks,' said Oscar. 'I have eighty million of them.'

'That is impressive.'

'This is Oscar,' said Jo, 'and the one asleep in the pushchair is Iris. Oscar, this is our neighbour, Mr . . . ?'

'Marcus is fine. Nice to meet you, Oscar.' Marcus held out his hand solemnly and Oscar shook it, up and down, one-two.

'I didn't know he knew how to do that,' Jo said.

'A nice, firm handshake. A good thing to have.' Marcus straightened up, smiling. Even though he wore more formal clothes than when she'd seen him before, his hair was still dishevelled, as if he'd forgotten to brush it before he went to work, or as if he'd been running his fingers through it. 'What's your mission, then, Jo?' he asked, and Jo felt a burst of joy that he had remembered her name, after all. This young man who probably wasn't ten years older than her own daughter.

'I have a very exciting schedule of the key cutter and then the library. We've already been to Waitrose to try to find something that will tempt my mother-in-law to eat.'

'Ah. Mother-in-laws are tricky, I hear. Haven't got one, myself.'

His face was clean-shaven today, and there was a small mole on his cheek, the only flaw in his smooth skin. Jo tried to bring herself back to the moment.

'Honor's staying with us for a bit whilst she recovers. She's had to have hip replacement surgery. She's not the easiest person to live with.'

This was an understatement. Honor had barely said a word since she'd been installed in Lydia's former room the day before. She ate nearly none of the Sunday roast that Jo had cooked and went to her room before the children were in bed, refusing all offers of hot drinks or help. Jo had heard her still shuffling around behind the closed door at eleven, when she'd gone up herself.

This morning, Honor had been up before Jo had come downstairs with the children. Jo had found the kettle hot and a plate with toast crumbs in the sink.

'She doesn't really want to spend any time with us,' Jo heard herself saying. 'She stays shut up in her room. She doesn't even look at you directly – she sort of stares over your shoulder all the time, even when she's speaking to you. As if eye-contact is too much trouble.'

'Sounds like most teenagers I know.'

Jo laughed, as much because of his sunny grin as what he'd said. 'I don't know what to think,' she confessed. 'On the one hand, it's great that Honor's settled in so quickly and that she feels confident enough in the house to look after herself. On the other hand ... I'd sort of hoped that we'd be behaving like a family.'

'What does your husband say?'

'Oh, he's— Honor is the mother of my first husband, who passed away.'

'I'm sorry.'

'Don't be, it was a long time ago.' Jo thought about her moment in Honor's room yesterday, looking at the photograph; the moment in Waitrose just now, watching the couple. Lying in bed awake last night. She hurried on. 'I had Oscar and Iris with my second husband.'

'He must be very special to put up with a mother-in-law who isn't even his.'

'He doesn't have to put up with her. We're divorced.'

'Oh.'

145

He didn't add anything, or do anything, just stood there politely. Because she'd been stupid enough to basically tell him in the middle of the shopping precinct, with her two kids in tow, for heaven's sake, that she was single and available.

'So about . . .' he began at last.

'Anyway,' she interrupted, before he could say he needed to get going, make his excuses and embarrass her further, 'I'm sure that you don't want to hear my entire history in the—'

'Streetlamp!' yelled Oscar.

They both looked at the little boy, who was jumping up and down and pointing at a streetlamp in the middle of the patch of grass as if it were the most exciting thing in the world.

'What's that, mate?' said Marcus.

'Streetlamp! The streetlamp is green, Mummy, is that it?'

'Yes, it is, darling! I Spy,' she explained to Marcus.

'Your turn!' said Oscar, turning to Marcus. 'You guess!'

'All right.'

'Don't you – I mean, please don't feel that you have to play a game with him. I know you're on your lunch break.'

'Already had my lunch,' said Marcus. 'And the world won't collapse if people don't get their tea and biscuits in the next five minutes. Lay it on me, Oscar.'

'I spy with my little eye, something that is brown!'

'Hmm.' Marcus put his finger on his chin and gazed around them. 'The ground?'

'No!'

'The bank?'

'No!'

'The sky?'

'The sky is *blue*!' Oscar was beaming, his shoulders thrown back in the way he did when he was being bossy.

'So it is. Your mummy's hair?' Marcus caught Jo's eye for a second. 'No, your mummy's hair isn't brown. It's more . . . auburn.'

'Ginger,' said Jo.

'Auburn,' affirmed Marcus. 'Hmm. Let me see, then. Not the ground, or the bank, or the sky which is blue, or Mummy's hair. How about . . . my shoes?'

'Yes!' cried Oscar. 'Brown shoes!'

'Good work! You nearly got me there, mate.' He exchanged a high five with Oscar, and straightened up.

'You're good with children,' she said.

'I've got a nephew about his age.'

He hesitated, and Jo jumped in. 'Well, we've got to get these keys cut before Iris wakes up. Nice to see you again, Marcus.'

'Nice to see you, too. And nice to meet you, Oscar. I'll make Iris's acquaintance later. Jo, I was . . .' He ran his free hand through his curly hair, making it stand up a bit more. 'I still owe you that cup of tea.'

'Oh. Yes, that would be' *another opportunity for me to gawp at you and make a fool of myself* 'nice.'

'Great. Come by any time you're free. I'm number thirty-six.' He glanced at his watch. 'I'm sorry, I really have to go, or I'll be late.' He walked away, backwards, holding up the pink daisy bag. 'I'll even throw in a biscuit!' he called, and turned and loped off at half a run. Jo watched his easy stride, his graceful body, until he was out of sight.

Chapter Sixteen

Honor

When the house was deserted, it was much quieter than her house in Stoke Newington. Traffic was sparse; the passing cars were well-serviced and full of children.

Honor had nothing to do. No household task, no research to complete, no errands she was able to run. Before she had gone out, Jo had brought her a flask of tea, a plate of biscuits and another plate of sandwiches, covered with cling film, accompanied by an apple and a banana. They all sat, untouched, on the small table near the comfortable yet not too soft armchair that Jo had also arranged for her specially. She had also arranged a grabber – a sort of pincer at the end of a stick, controlled by a handle. It was to allow Honor to pick up things without getting out of her chair, or bending down.

This was the radius of her world: what she could see from the edges of her eyes, what she could reach with the end of a stick.

Honor stood and walked with her cane out of her bedroom into the empty house. She had carefully flushed all of her pain medication down the toilet in the ensuite. The pain was bearable, or she would make herself bear it; the doctor had assured her that it would abate, day by day, as her wounds healed. He had also told her to be as active as possible. 'You want to use that joint to strengthen it, even though it will be hard at first. Only be careful – we don't want you falling again!'

The condescending 'we'. At least Jo didn't use that particular construction. Honor was more grateful for that than the room, or the grabber, or the carefully prepared food.

She made her way across the slippery floor, using the cane, across the kitchen to the door leading to the garage. Here in the semi-darkness, in the scent of oil and concrete, in the open space abandoned by the too-large car, was something else she was presumably meant to be grateful for. In the shadows it hunkered like a large clumsy insect, a misshapen beetle perhaps.

It had arrived this morning, in the back of a van that beeped as it reversed into the gravel drive, and Jo and the children had harried Honor outside to marvel at it.

'Scooter!' Oscar had cried, jumping up and down, running with that never-ending supply of energy. 'It's a scooter, Ganny H! And it's purple!'

The sunshine was dazzling; Honor could see squat wheels, a flash of purple. 'You got me a mobility scooter?'

'I thought it would be useful, and it would give you more independence,' said Jo. 'You can go to the shopping precinct, run your own errands. I mean I can drive you, of course, but if you wanted to do it yourself.'

'How much does one of these cost?'

'I rented it. You can have them by the week. It's not as good as your bicycle, but . . .'

'I'm not certain that this is—' Honor was surprised to feel a small cool hand slip into hers. Oscar tugged her towards the scooter. 'Come and ride it, Ganny H!' At a loss as to what else to do, she went with him. 'This is the seat here,' he told her, pointing. 'And this is the start button. Can I press it?'

'No, Oscar, it's Granny Honor's scooter, not for little boys,' said Jo.

Honor could not see the start button, but Oscar, impatiently, put her hand on it. 'Press it!' he insisted, so she did. The scooter came to buzzing, vibrating life. Oscar whooped in delight. 'I want a ride!' he cried.

She shut it off. Oscar made a disappointed noise.

'I'll put it in the garage for now,' said Jo, cheerfully, but Honor could hear her disappointment. Yet another thing Jo had done that Honor was meant to appreciate, and did not.

Now, hours later and alone, Honor approached it. She put her hand on its smooth carapace. For a moment she thought about getting on it, pressing the button. Trundling out onto the pavements of Woodley and somehow, guided by intuition perhaps, making her way at four miles per hour, metre by metre, down Keats Way, across Tennyson Street, out of the regimented blocks of suburbia to the jumbled streets of London, back to her home. There had been a film about that, hadn't there? An elderly person taking their destiny into their own hands.

She snorted. She was not an inspirational film. She was a woman. Once she had been a daughter, an academic, a lover, a reader, a mother. Object of pity, object of desire, subject of scorn.

Now none of those. Only a woman. Another old lady. Useless, irrelevant and invisible. This scooter did not give her freedom; it represented her limits.

It also meant that Jo had not guessed her secret.

It had started nearly a year ago, when the words began to jump.

She had been reading a sentence and it shifted on the page. A word leaped, changed position, suddenly higher than it had been before.

She retraced her reading – back to the beginning of the sentence, reassuringly solid and black next to the white margin, and started again. And in the same place, the sentence bucked up, as if it had become detached from the page, as if it had become capricious.

And then the word after, and the word after, until the tail end, the right margin, when the words lay still again. She tried the next line, which lay still near the margin, and then jumped in the middle, mid-phrase. Again, on the next line, the next paragraph, the next page.

She put down her book and rested her eyes, rubbing her forehead. It was evening and she was lying in her bed with the reading lamp on. It was a hardback edition of *Anna Karenina*. The pages were soft from the touch of her fingers. With her eyes closed she could visualize the page she had just tried to read. She could see the sentence that had moved, as it should be, rock-solid and reassuring. If she opened the book on her lap, she would be able to put her finger on it without even looking, because words did not move. Their meanings might shift with time and experience, translation and context, literary theory and fashion.

But words themselves did not judder on the page like clumsy dancers.

For her entire life she had read whilst walking. Physical movement helped her think. She enjoyed reading as a passenger in a car or a train or an aeroplane. She had occasionally opened a book and snatched phrases from it whilst she was riding her bicycle, steering with her knees, listening for obstacles.

She liked the feeling of the world moving around her whilst her words stayed solid and safe and true.

Honor thought of the sentence she had been reading: *They have no conception of what happiness is, and they do not know that without love there is no happiness or unhappiness for us, for there would be no life.* She opened the book and put her finger on it by feel, without looking. She pictured the sentence in her mind.

When she opened her eyes, the words danced.

After this first tremor she carried on reading for several months, regardless. With a book she knew well, it was less of a problem; the words at the edges around the margin stayed obediently still, ranks of reliable soldiers, and she could predict the meaning of the dancing middle, even if she couldn't quite catch the words. But a new book was impossible to understand. Meaning became slippery, syntax distorted. Distracted by movement, she couldn't follow a sentence she had started.

Honor knew what was causing it. Thirty-five years before, she had seen her father put down his newspaper and rub his forehead; she had noticed him, a man who'd always taken the greatest care with his appearance, missing spots when he shaved, tying his tie askance. She had suggested a change in the prescription of his glasses, and she and Stephen had walked with him to the optometrist – to help him choose new frames, she said. Really it was because she knew that her father wouldn't pass on what he'd been told. Levinsons were not fond of doctors.

So she was there to hear her father's description of what he saw: *It's all hazy in the middle, and sometimes it jumps.*

She was also there to watch the optometrist administer tests, and to hear the diagnosis. Thirty-five years had not dulled her memory of the horror, for a man who had worked with his hands, who had recognized faces, lived in the same community, gone to the same *shul* for all of his life, who measured rope and chain and nails and screws by eye, who knew everyone by sight.

And now here Honor was, thirty-five years later, older than her father had been when he had begun to go blind. And her world was all hazy in the middle, and it jumped.

A computer screen was no better than a book, but she had Googled it anyway and though the text seemed to scroll itself, she found out everything she needed to know. Macular degeneration, a progressive destroying of the pigments of the retina, which manifested as a haziness in the centre of vision, followed by eventual blackness that destroyed everything directly in front of you.

Incurable, inevitable, inherited.

The words jumped because her peripheral vision was better than her direct vision, and she was moving her head to catch them. They weren't shifting; she was. The centre of her sight was melting away, like a piece of paper held over a candle.

There was nothing she could do to slow it or to prevent it. So she chained up her bicycle and shelved her books and put away all the parts of herself that relied on seeing. Except for her years at Oxford, she had lived in her house since she was a child and she knew it by feel and touch, smell and hearing.

But then she'd mis-stepped. She'd fallen.

And now here she was in a house she did not know, and she had to hide the hole in her seeing.

Chapter Seventeen

Jo

She woke hearing Stephen's scream.

Eyes snapped open into darkness. Jo sat up, shaking. She wiped sweat from her forehead. The glowing clock said 03.14. She was here, in her house, in the king-sized bed alone, with her children sleeping around her, Stephen's mother sleeping downstairs. The scream had only been in her mind.

She still heard it.

She pushed off the duvet and swung her feet out of bed. It was still only April; this was early. The anniversary wasn't till June. Jo knew from experience that she had to get up, make herself a hot drink, find a book to read or a television programme to watch, or else she would keep thinking about it. About Stephen's last moments, about what he had seen, how he had felt. The fear that must have ripped through him, his most secret feelings coming to life as he died.

His hands, scrabbling at nothing. His glasses falling off his face. The police hadn't returned them to her; they must have been smashed. She had given the undertakers his spare ones, even though the casket was closed, even though he had no use for them.

What had Stephen seen?

Jo bowed her head into her hands. She knew she would not sleep again tonight, and she would have to put a bright face on everything tomorrow.

It was only April.

Jo knocked on Honor's door. 'Yes?' she answered from inside, and Jo tentatively opened it. Honor was sitting in her armchair with a thick book in her lap. She seemed to do very little else.

'Oscar and I have made some green fairy cakes. I've brought you one with a cup of tea.'

She brought the plate and cup over. Honor glanced at the fairy cake – green sponge with a green splodge of icing – nodded once and turned her attention back to her book. It was huge and heavy, with Russian writing on the cover. How could Honor make Jo feel small simply by holding a book?

'Oscar's very fond of green food colouring,' Jo explained. 'Which is ironic, really, because he refuses to eat any green vegetables except for avocado.'

Honor grunted. She turned a page.

'Also,' Jo ventured, 'I wanted to talk with you about a calendar. I thought we could have one that we kept in the kitchen, and we could all write our appointments and things in it, so that we'll be able to coordinate better.'

'A calendar.'

'Yes, you know. To write down things like Lydia's exams and Oscar's nursery, and the various bits and pieces I have to do, and then of course your appointments. It'll help me, so I know when I'll have to drive you to the hospital, and so on.'

'I'll take a taxi to the hospital.'

'Well, there's no need, if I can drive you. I'm very happy to, and that's why you moved in here, after all.'

Honor looked at Jo, in that odd way she had, of actually looking over Jo's shoulder instead of meeting her gaze. It was an extra slap in the face.

'I thought it would be easiest, and central, if we put it up on the cupboard door near the fridge, for example,' Jo added. Also, it would save awkward conversations like this. She held out the calendar, which she'd had underneath her arm. Iris had chosen it; it had photographs of kittens dressed in little outfits.

'All right,' said Honor. 'If that's what you want.' She took the calendar and Jo retreated.

In the living room, Iris and Oscar had brought all of their cuddly animals downstairs. Both of the children had green faces and fingers, and there were suspicious smudges on the pelts of the toys.

'Are you ready to go outside for the tea party?' Jo asked them.

'No!' Iris agreed, squeezing Irving, her pink elephant who she slept with every night.

'Underneath the tree, Mummy,' ordered Oscar.

'Underneath the tree sounds perfect. You bring Irving and Mr Diddy outside and choose the spot, and bring the others outside too, and as soon as I've hung out the sheets I'll be right along with some more cake.'

She brought the laundry basket of bed linen outside, where she could watch the children arranging their animals in a wonky circle amidst the fallen blossom, whilst she hung the

157

sheets on the line. Sunshine and children were the perfect antidote to a sleepless night. Oscar and Iris trotted back and forth from the house to the tree, fully absorbed in the task. She watched Oscar's surefooted, sturdy tread, arms and legs pumping; Iris's springy wobble, curls bobbing. When did they lose that childish way of walking and settle into a grown-up stride? She tried to think back to Lydia, and couldn't remember. She remembered how Lydia used to walk – fast, recklessly, heading hell-for-leather for the nearest obstacle and only veering aside at the last minute. And she knew how Lydia walked now, with her long legs and her unconscious grace, as if any moment she would break into her effortless run.

But she couldn't remember the transition from child to woman. She'd been too busy carrying on with life to take notice. It was sad. She must remember not to miss it with Iris and Oscar.

Sheets hung, she brought out a fresh plate of cakes and a teapot full of squash and settled herself on the grass next to Irving.

'Tea, Mummy,' said Iris. She lifted the teapot and dribbled squash down her front.

'I'll do it,' said Oscar, taking the teapot and carefully pouring a plastic cup full of squash. He handed it to his sister, who said, 'No,' and slopped more squash on herself, taking a drink.

'Good pouring, Oscar. Will you pour some for me, too, and all the animals? And Iris, do you want to make sure everyone has a cake?'

Jo brushed a petal from her hair and watched her children busy and happy in the sunshine. She had memories like this of her own mother. In fact, if her mother were still here today, she'd be out on the grass too, drinking from a teacup full of squash. She wouldn't let her pain stop her from spending time with her grandchildren. Like Jo, she knew that these moments didn't last for ever.

Jo took a bite of green cake and held up the rest of the cake to Irving the elephant's mouth so he could take a bite. She looked up just as Honor came out of the back door. Jo got up and hurried over to her, so she wouldn't have to walk across the garden.

'Here you are.' Honor held up the kitten calendar.

'That was quick.' Jo took the calendar and glanced at it. Honor had written on it in her bold, spiky handwriting. 'Oh. There's something already in for today.'

'It's my appointment.'

'Two o'clock?' It was nearly one thirty; she'd been looking forward to half an hour or so of playing, and a relaxing afternoon of not having to haul the kids anywhere. Now she'd have to clean up the kids and herself, and get them all into the car in the next ten minutes if she was going to get there in time, especially with Honor's current slow pace. And Iris usually started her nap at two; she'd been hoping to get Oscar down then, too, because he'd been running around all morning. She'd tentatively planned an hour with the kids asleep, to catch up on the laundry. Or maybe even a cup of tea and a book, if she got another load of bed linen hung out quickly. She could use the dryer, of course, but she was trying to save electricity. The bills.

'Yes,' Honor said. 'It's at two.'

'But you never told me, Honor.'

'I was going to take a taxi. As I said. I'll ring one now.'

'No, no no, of course not. Iris, Oscar, we have to get cleaned up and go for a trip in the car.'

159

'No!' said Iris, stamping her foot. Oscar's face fell; tears were imminent. Honor had taken her own phone out of her pocket.

'You can't call a cab,' Jo told her, 'it'll never get here in time. It's not like London where you can grab a passing one; they take a little while to turn up.'

'No,' muttered Honor, 'it's nothing like London.'

'I'll drive you, it's not a problem.' Maybe Iris and Oscar would fall asleep in the car, and Jo could read her book in the car park while she waited for Honor to be finished.

But the sugar in the cakes and squash took its toll. Oscar and Iris sang 'Old MacDonald' at the top of their lungs all the way to the hospital, while Honor gazed stoically out of the window. Jo wanted to join in; she loved singing with the children, making all the animal noises, but Honor's expression stopped her, and then she was angry at herself. Why shouldn't she sing with her children?

There was no place to park near the entrance, so Jo had to drop Honor off. 'I'll find somewhere to park and take the children to a café or a playground,' she said to Honor, through the rolled-down window. 'Just text me when you're finished and I'll pick you up right here.' Honor nodded and started off. 'And get someone to give you a lift to Orthopaedics in a wheelchair!' Jo called after her. 'Or one of those golf-cart things!'

Honor appeared to take no notice. Jo sighed and drove around the car park looking for a space, whilst her children quack-quacked here and there behind her. She had to drive right to the top level in the end, squeezing her car in beside a large black Lexus.

'Hide and seek in the park!' Jo told the children, unbuckling them.

'No!' said Iris. 'Want to sing.'

'You can sing in the park, darling.'

Oscar scrambled out of the car at a run, straight towards the path of traffic. Jo only managed to snag him by the hood of his top. She held on to it and carried Iris on her hip, till they got to the bank of lifts, where Oscar immediately pressed all the buttons, so they stopped at every floor on the way down.

There was a park across a busy street from the hospital. Oscar pressed the button for the traffic lights, too, and Iris screamed and held out her hands because she wanted to press the button. 'Quickly, then, sweetheart,' said Jo, putting her down as the light went green. Iris stabbed the button with her chubby finger; by the time she'd finished the light was red again and the two children had to press the button over and over again until it was green.

The park was quiet aside from a few people on benches having their lunch. 'I'm counting first!' cried Oscar, and he squeezed his eyes shut. 'One, two, three, four, six, nine, five . . .'

Iris squealed. Jo took her hand and they scampered over to a bush. 'Hide behind it, Iris,' whispered Jo, but Iris said 'No' and hid her face in her hands, obviously following the dictum that if she couldn't see Oscar, he couldn't see her. Jo crouched beside her.

'Fourteen, fifteen, twenty! Ready or not, here I come!' Oscar opened his eyes and yelled, 'I found you! It's too easy, Mummy!'

'Why don't you hide, and Iris and I will try to find you,' Jo suggested.

'Hide with Oscie!'

Oscar pouted. 'I don't want to hide with Iris. She's rubbish.'

'Hide with Oscie!'

There was a glob of greenish snot in each of Iris's nostrils. Jo didn't have a tissue, so she wiped Iris's nose with her hand and wiped her fingers on the grass.

'Please, Oscar, take your little sister this time. Then next time, you can hide and Iris and I will look for you. Stay in the park, though, OK?'

Reluctantly, he took her hand. Jo sank onto the grass, glad of the moment's quiet. Half an hour ago, she'd been tired, but looking forward to a day with her children. What had happened?

Oh well, at least they'd have fun in the park, and maybe the naps could happen later. And the laundry...well, she'd get that done somehow. With any luck, she'd be worn out enough to sleep tonight.

'Count!' Oscar ordered her.

She closed her eyes. 'One, two, three . . .'

They toddled off. Jo opened her eyes halfway and watched them as they headed for some bushes, then changed their mind and went towards some trees.

Her stomach rumbled. She hadn't managed lunch; she'd had half a green fairy cake since breakfast at seven this morning, which had been one of Oscar's Petit Filous and a satsuma. Her bag had raisins in it, and some crackers, but she'd forgotten it at home in the rush. Also her book. And the tissues for Iris's nose.

So many things were necessary for children. How did people do it, before the days of plastic pots of snacks and disposable tissues and nappies? Was it easier, because you didn't expect those things? In some societies, women carried children for years, didn't they? And breastfed till the age of five? There

162

were some advantages to that, she supposed, in that it saved you carrying the world's largest nappy bag everywhere.

A wail from the clump of trees. Jo jumped up and sprinted for her children. The part of her mother's brain that knew each of her children's cries and instantly catalogued them into varying categories of pain, fear, dismay, temper, knew that this wasn't life-threatening, but her body reacted instantly nevertheless. Because it could be, this time. Because disaster happened when you weren't expecting it, when you were happy.

Oscar stood looking down at himself and crying. Brown gunk was smeared on the knees of his trousers and on his T-shirt. Jo thought he must have found the only muddy puddle in the park and knelt in it, until she got close enough to smell it.

'Oscie dog poo,' Iris told her, solemnly, eyes wide.

Shit. Damn. Bollocks. And she had no bag, no wet-wipes, no spare clothing. She saw the dog mess he'd knelt in: it was fresh and enormous, like something deposited by a bear. It had two dents in it, exactly the shape of Oscar's knees.

'I didn't see it, Mummy! I was trying to hide!'

'It's OK, Oscar, it was a mistake,' she soothed. She rolled up his T-shirt on the bottom so she could get it off him without getting dog mess in his hair. Then she removed his shoes and checked their soles – thankfully, clean – and took off his trousers. Oscar kept on crying. His tears dripped on Jo's head whilst she undressed him.

She took him onto her lap for a cuddle and to put his shoes back on him. 'Here, sweetie, you can wear my cardigan to play in. See.' She put it on him, and rolled up the sleeves; it came down nearly to his ankles.

'Don't want to play,' said Oscar, sniffling. 'Everything's stinky.'

'Did you get any on your hands?'

'No,' said Oscar, though Jo had a quick sniff and she thought he probably had. Of course he did; Oscar touched everything. It was a symptom of being bright and curious, she reminded herself. Not a lack of common sense.

'Don't put them in your mouth, all right? We'll have to go back to the hospital and find somewhere to wash.' She rolled the dirty clothes up so that the worst of the mess was inside, stood up, reached for Oscar's hand, thought twice of it, and then gritted her teeth and took it. 'Come on, Iris, we're going.'

'No!' said Iris, but after the third time Jo asked her, she came along. Jo checked her over for dog poo, too, but mercifully, she'd stayed clear. To hold both their hands, she had to stuff Oscar's clothes under her arm. The whiff of dog shit accompanied them through the park, across the street, and into hospital Reception.

'Is there a toilet we can use?' she asked the lady at the greeting desk. She wrinkled her nose and pointed down the corridor.

Jo made both Iris and Oscar wash their hands twice, and use the hand sanitizer too. She used toilet paper to clean their faces – Oscar had some suspicious smudges. She'd hoped for paper towels to wrap Oscar's clothes in, but there were only hand-driers so she rolled the clothes more tightly into an inconspicuous-looking package. It still smelled, though.

'I'm hungry,' announced Oscar. Jo looked at him, swamped in her purple cardigan, and at Iris, who, she just noticed, had green icing in her hair. She put her hand in her pocket and was relieved to find a ten-pound note.

'Let's go to the café, shall we?' she said cheerfully, and steered them down the corridor towards the enticing aroma of coffee.

She stowed the dirty clothes under the table and settled them all with chocolate muffins and drinks, including a double-shot mocha with whipped cream on top for herself. She refused to think about her soft middle when she ordered it; there were only so many ways to cope with such intimate contact with dog poo, and it was too early in the day for gin. Jo was about to raise her drink to her mouth when she saw the telltale expression of intense concentration on Iris's face.

'Oh no, Iris, not now,' she said. But the little girl's face had gone red and her lips puffed out.

'Iris done a poo in her nappy,' announced Oscar, tucking into his muffin.

Jo felt the attention of the people around them, who were only trying to enjoy a coffee during what was probably a stressful time in hospital. 'Sorry,' she murmured to the café as a whole.

'It's stinky, Mummy, you have to change her,' said Oscar.

'I know, and I'm sorry, Iris honey, but I have no nappies with me.' She looked around; they had shops in hospitals these days. But she had only a few coins left, after buying the muffins and coffee. Maybe another mother nearby, one who was better prepared than she was . . . ?

Her phone rang whilst she was searching pensioners' faces desperately for a fellow young parent. 'Where are you?' Honor asked her.

'We're in the café,' Jo said as Iris grunted with effort, and the woman sitting at the next table tsked. 'Are you finished with your appointment?'

165

'I've been at the front door for the past ten minutes.'

'Right. Fine, we'll come and get you in the car.' She stood up. Somehow her mocha, sprinkled with brown chocolate, looked infinitely less appealing. 'Come on, darlings, we've got to pick up Granny. You can bring your muffins with you.'

She tried not to think about the trail of brown crumbs they left on the polished hospital floors. And she really tried not to think of the whiff trailing behind them, either. She didn't dare use the lift, for fear of someone else getting in with them, and for pity of the people who came after them, so she carried Iris up four flights of stairs, holding her breath for as much of that as possible. Oscar whined at climbing the stairs, so she carried him for the last flight too. Iris squirmed in her car seat, and Jo tried to say brightly, 'I'm sorry, Iris, I know it's uncomfortable, sweetie, but we'll change you as soon as we get home and put you in a nice bath, all right?'

She hoped it wasn't one of those poos that would leak out of the sides and onto the car seat.

Honor was waiting outside the door, as she'd said. She was looking paler than she had before, and more drawn. Jo hopped out to help her up into the car, but she pulled her arm away. 'I can manage.'

'How did it go?'

'It's humiliating, what do you think?' Honor snapped. 'The doctors treat you like a half-wit. It's not like relaxing in a café.'

Jo didn't say anything back. She did not trust herself.

'What on earth is that smell?' said Honor.

Jo pressed the 'window down' buttons for the front and back and drove off. Iris was snivelling, clearly overtired. Oscar was smearing his chocolate-caked fingers on the inside of the car door. Honor glanced into the back seat, shuddered ostentatiously, and positioned herself so that her nose was pointing out of the window.

Honor was an old woman who was in pain (though Jo's own mother had been in constant pain for years, and even when she was dying, she had never taken it out on others). Honor was not used to dealing with poo of various sorts (though who ever got used to it, even after three children?).

Jo breathed through her mouth and when Iris's snivelling became full-scale crying, and when Oscar joined in, she kept her cool. She kept it right up until they pulled into her driveway at home and she turned to Honor and said, 'Can I help you getting out of the car?' and Honor replied, 'I'm not one of your children, thank God.'

'Do it yourself then,' Jo said crossly. 'I've got enough to deal with without you being rude to me as well.'

She opened the back door and scooped Oscar out, and then went to the other side to get Iris. She carried them both inside, leaving the front door open for Honor, for when she finally made it to the house. How she managed that, was evidently not Jo's problem.

Lydia was in the kitchen with a girl Jo didn't recognize. They had spread their schoolwork out on the table and had ripped open a packet of biscuits from the centre, spilling crumbs everywhere. Jo carried the children straight through and up the stairs to run them a bath.

Her children were fine. They were normal children. Normal children stank sometimes, they got messy, and they cried. Maybe Honor had never seen it before; maybe Stephen had been perfect, but she didn't think that he had. Maybe Honor had conveniently forgotten.

And next time, Honor could get a taxi and be late.

'I don't want a bath,' wailed Oscar, and Jo, cleaning Iris's bottom with a wet-wipe, snapped, 'Stop it, Oscar. Just *stop it*. I have had *enough*!'

His eyes went wide and his lip wobbled. But he swallowed, and was silent. Iris and he got into the bath without any of their usual playing. Jo scrubbed them briskly, efficiently, and lifted them out one at a time to towel them dry.

'Do you want to put the powder on?' she asked Oscar, holding out the talcum, but he just shook his head. Jo bit her lip.

I am a terrible mother. And I left Honor in the car alone.

She put fresh clothes on both of them and brought them downstairs to watch television under a blanket. The front door, which she'd left open, was shut, and when she peered through the front window, the car was empty. When she went into the kitchen, Lydia's friend was gone.

'Did Granny Honor come in?' Jo asked her. Lydia shrugged. 'Didn't you hear her?'

'I wasn't listening.'

'Could you do me a favour, Lyddie? Could you knock on your grandmother's door and make sure she's OK? Bring her a cup of tea?'

'Why can't you do it?'

'Because Granny Honor isn't all that pleased with me right now, and I'm not all that pleased with myself, either. And also, I think it would come better from you.' She sank into the chair that Lydia's friend had vacated, with a sigh. Her head throbbed, her arms hurt from hauling several stones' weight of children around, her clothes were damp, and she still smelled vaguely of dog shit.

'I'm trying to do my homework.'

'Please, Lyddie. And a biscuit, if you haven't eaten them all. Who was that here, just now? I've never met her.'

'Just someone I'm revising with. Maths.'

'I thought you were revising with Avril.'

Lydia stood up. 'Avril isn't in my Maths set. Keep up.'

'Lydia, I don't like being talked to as if I'm stupid.'

'Well, now you know how I feel.'

From outside the open window, a rumble of thunder. And almost immediately afterwards, a patter of rainfall.

'I've got washing outside,' Jo moaned. 'Lydia, could you help me—'

'I'm making Granny Honor her tea, like you asked,' said Lydia, crossing to the kettle.

Jo hauled herself to her feet again and went out of the back door. The rain was cold and fell in heavy drops. At the bottom of the garden, she saw Oscar and Iris's abandoned animals, mid-tea party. She ran to them and began to pick them up, muttering to herself out here where no one could hear her, about her daughter, her mother-in-law, about how sometimes she wanted another adult around just to share things with, someone who could see the funny side of her close encounters with poo, and how she had left a disabled elderly woman in a car alone.

'Someone left the cake out in the rain?'

Jo started, her arms filled with damp fur. Marcus was standing on the other side of the hedge, pointing at the plate of green cakes left on the grass. He was wearing a blue shirt this time, the sleeves rolled up, and no tie. The rain spotted his shirt and landed in his hair.

'Sorry,' he said. 'I've always wanted to say that. Can I give you a hand?'

She thought of trying to make an excuse, so he wouldn't feel obliged, but he was already stepping through the gap in the hedge and scooping up animals. 'Thank you,' she said. 'We were having a tea party, but we had to abandon it.'

'No problem at all,' he said. 'Do you want me to do this, and you can get the sheets in?'

The rain was falling harder now. 'Thank you,' she said again, and she ran for the washing line.

She unpegged one sheet, which she flung over her shoulder, and started on another. Marcus ducked under the line, his arms full of animals. 'Put the sheet on top here,' he said, gesturing with his chin. 'I'm guessing the animals are more precious than the sheets.'

'And harder to dry,' Jo agreed, pulling a second sheet down and piling it on top of the animals to protect them from the rain. 'Thanks again. This is really beyond the call of neighbourly duty.'

'Hey, you let me say my horrible "MacArthur Park" line. That's made my day a lot better.'

'I thought you'd be too young to know about disco.'

'You're never too young for disco.'

She pulled down another sheet, putting the pegs in her pocket with the others, and he followed her so she could put that one on top of the first. 'You've had a tough day too?' she asked.

'One of those days where nothing goes quite right. Overslept, mouldy bread in my sandwich, colleagues in foul moods. I escaped early. You?'

'No mouldy bread, but mine hasn't been much better, and has had *way* too much poo in it.'

'Want to tell me about it?'

His question should make her feel embarrassed, patronized. It didn't. It made a lump come up in her throat, and her eyes burn.

'I just – sometimes I just get tired of dealing with it all myself. You know? Sometimes I wish someone else would do something without my asking, or that someone would say thank you, or that the fairies would come and do the washing and the cooking and the bedtimes and the shopping.'

'I'd love those fairies too.'

'I know, it's ridiculous. I shouldn't complain. I've got this beautiful house, and my wonderful children, and everything. I'm lucky.'

'Even if you're lucky, that doesn't mean you can't have bad days.'

'I know. But I get so . . . tired, Marcus. Stupidly tired. Trying to please everyone, who won't be pleased.' She ripped down a pillowcase. They were damp now; the rain was beading on her bare arms, dripping down her neck.

'Sometimes you just have to please yourself.'

'You know what I would like? It's nothing difficult. Once, just once, I'd like someone else to make me a cup of tea, and I could sit down and drink it all the way to the bottom of the cup, without it going cold.'

She'd pulled down another sheet. They were piled up in Marcus's arms, nearly up to his neck, a heap of snowy white. There were petals in his hair, she noticed, from the tree.

'The offer's still open,' he said. 'I'll make you a cup of tea whenever you like.'

Jo had no idea why she did it. It was the simple offer, or it was the petals in his hair, or the raindrop rolling down his cheek. It was his blue eyes, the same colour as the sky before

171

it was covered with clouds, or his arms full of animals and the sheets that she slept in.

She stepped forward, on her tiptoes, put her hands on either side of his face, and kissed him on the mouth.

He was warm. There were drops of water on his lips and his cheeks were slightly rough under her palms. She heard him breathe in a sharp breath of surprise through his nose and for a moment she did nothing but take in the shock and pleasure of it. A kiss on the lips with a man, the sort of touch she hadn't had in what felt like a very long time. An intimate connection with a stranger. She could feel his pulse in his lips, his clasped hands pressing against her belly, smell the rain and the scent of the washing and the faint citrus of his shaving lotion.

All that in a single moment, no more than a few seconds.

And then Jo realized that he wasn't kissing her back.

She stumbled backwards, mortification flooding her. 'I'm so, so sorry.'

He looked stunned. Well, he would, being attacked by his neighbour.

'It's OK, Jo.'

'You were just being nice and I – I don't know what got into me.'

'It's fine. Really, it is.'

Marcus held the pile of toys and laundry. He wouldn't have been able to fend her off, even if he were the type to be cruel to a desperate older woman.

'I like you a lot,' he added.

Jo choked back a sob. Now he was letting her down gently.

'It was a mistake,' she said, 'it was a horrible mistake. I don't do things like this. I'm really sorry. Here, let me take these.'

She began grabbing the sheets from his arms, bundling them into damp tangles, avoiding his gaze.

'I'll do it,' he said gently.

She couldn't take his kindness. 'No, I'll get it, it's fine, I'll just put all the animals into this sheet here like a big bag, see? It's fine. Everything's fine.' She dropped a fitted sheet onto the grass and tugged the animals into it, conscious of his hands near hers, his eyes watching her, the rain in his hair, the dampness of his lips, the scent of him, oh God.

'Jo . . .'

'Thank you for your help, I really appreciate it, and I'm so sorry, again.' She put Irving on top of the heap and pulled the sheet together into a sack. She would have to wash the sheet again. She would have to start all over on everything.

'I really don't—'

'Bye,' she choked, and ran into the house, the wet sheets bumping against her legs.

Chapter Eighteen

Lydia

Lydia ran.

When she ran, things made more sense. The world slowed down around her. Her body with all of its errant desires and needs concentrated solely on putting one foot in front of the other, arms pumping, breath easy, smooth-gaited and covering the miles.

She used to run with her father, when she was little. They'd go running through the park, round and round the perimeter in a circle. Her father bought her proper running shoes, in blue and red and silver, and they both wore matching Superman T-shirts. Her little legs would get tired but it seemed like her father could run for ever. He used to run marathons. When she got a stitch he would scoop her up onto his shoulders and she would laugh, holding her arms up to try to touch the leaves of the trees.

That was one of the ways she remembered him best.

Lydia ran without looking at her surroundings. The pavements were smooth and wet after the rain and the air was cool on the sweat that filmed her forehead and her neck and legs.

One house after another, street after street, Tennyson after Yeats after Coleridge after Browning. Her English teacher in Year Nine had made a map of the estate with little pictures of the actual poets and samples of their poems next to the streets named after them. They were all men.

If she could tell her father about how she felt, he would know what to say. He would know what to do. Her father would understand; he wouldn't try to pretend that everything was happy or ask for reassurance that she was OK and everyone was normal. He would take her running and he would lift her up to brush the leaves.

And she was not looking at her surroundings, but her legs knew she was thinking of her father. They carried her past the houses into a tunnel of trees. The road inclined upwards slightly, and the air was hushed and cool. And then there was the bridge.

She liked running here sometimes. Her mother avoided it, didn't even drive over it, would go miles out of her way. But Lydia thought it was peaceful. She stopped, breathing fast, and took her earbuds out.

The bridge went over a railway cutting. The sides were steep and covered with green, sloping down to the gravel bottom, where four sets of tracks pointed in either direction. In the distance was a bridge just like this one: an arch of red brick with black iron railings.

It was quiet here; something about how the cutting was made, or maybe the trees around it, meant that the normal neighbourhood sounds didn't penetrate. Lydia put her hand on the railing and stretched, holding one leg bent behind her with her hand to ease out tightness in her quadriceps. She read the metal plaque attached to the bridge.

IN MEMORY OF

DR STEPHEN LEVINSON

3.9.1970–10.6.2005

The plaque was going slightly green at the edges. She stretched her other leg and ran her fingers over the words. She'd done it so often, over the years, that she could read it with her eyes closed.

'I love her, Dad,' she whispered. 'I don't know how to let her go.'

Lydia brushed her palm over the plaque again. Looked out over the open air, the empty space between one bridge and the other, waiting for an answer that didn't come.

She thought about the book she had borrowed from Granny Honor's room this afternoon, the familiarity of the writing in it. Was it, as she suspected, a part of her father's story? Was it something that could help her understand what to do?

Lydia lingered on the bridge, rubbing the words, until a train rushed by below her and disturbed the silence, and then she turned and started running again.

She ran fast enough so that her lungs burned and she didn't have to feel her heart.

Chapter Nineteen

Honor

'Turn it, Ganny Honor, look.' Oscar reached over and pushed her plate around. The lasagne appeared in the bottom of her field of vision.

'Oscar, keep your hands to yourself at the table, please,' said Jo. Honor merely nodded at the child, tacit thanks, and began to eat.

'I'm going out right after tea,' announced Jo. 'It's your parents' evening, Lydia, so I'll need you to stay in to look after Oscar and Iris.'

There was a challenge in Jo's voice, as if she were anticipating an argument from her daughter. It was the first time Honor had heard her stating a demand to one of her children, rather than pleading a request.

She felt herself nodding involuntarily.

She would never have suspected that Jo had a temper. In the twenty years she had known her, she had never once raised her voice. She had been a beautiful blank: kind, polite, cheerful, letting people like Honor walk all over her. Even at Stephen's funeral, she had been quiet, absorbed in Lydia's welfare rather than her own grief. She had barely cried. At that moment, Honor had hated her for that.

But it seemed that there was a spark inside her son's wife, after all. However small, however weak – she had enough spirit to battle against Honor.

'More lasagne, Honor?' Jo asked her, and the woman laid down her knife and fork.

'I believe I will,' she said.

She went back to her room after the meal, as she usually did, and sat in her armchair. She covered her mouth to suppress a burp. Jo, whatever her faults, was a very good cook, especially of comfort food. A few minutes later there was a knock on her door.

'Granny H?' said Lydia, poking her head in. 'I wondered if you were bored?'

Boredom is for people without inner resources, she was about to reply, but something about Lydia's voice stopped her. 'I am not. But I would be glad to have a conversation.'

'I have to watch OscanIrie. Do you want to come out and sit on the sofa with me for a while?'

Lydia wanted something, but Honor couldn't tell what. She nodded and came out to the living area, walking slowly to avoid the toys on the floor. She perched on a sofa. The two younger children were sitting on a beanbag on the floor, watching television. Lydia sat down beside her, jiggling her foot. Honor could feel the vibrations through the sofa.

'What's on your mind?' Honor asked.

'I wish Dad were here,' said Lydia. 'I really wish he were here. I'd like to talk with him. I could talk with Mum, but she's so . . . I don't know if she'd really understand. She thinks that if you're nice, then everything will work out for you.'

'That seems like rather a lot to expect from mere niceness,' said Honor. 'In my experience, that is not how the world works.'

They were silent, listening to the television. The programme appeared to be about some sort of creatures who could do yoga but not speak English. It was a wonder that children learned any language skills these days.

They had never been close, she and Lydia. As a very young child she had been boisterous, too full of energy, never settling. And then once Stephen died, Honor could not look at her without seeing Stephen.

Jo had brought her to visit not long after the funeral, and when Lydia had walked into the house, even at age six, the light had caught her face in exactly the same way as it had used to catch Stephen's when he returned home from school. The hair was different, the clothes were different, but the expressions were exactly the same, and Honor had been struck with longing so sharp it was like a knife. She wanted to grab this little girl and hold her and never let her go. She wanted to stare at her for hours, tracing the resemblance to her father, to Honor's dead son. She wanted to cry and to kiss Lydia, over and over, and spend every waking moment with her, shutting out everyone else in the world. Reliving her son's childhood through her granddaughter's.

And of course none of that was possible. It was irrational and frightening. It was unreasoned love, far too close to loss, the same way she had loved Stephen and, at one time, Paul.

So Honor withdrew. She loved Lydia too much and therefore she could not love her unrestrainedly. They were careful with each other, with much unspoken.

This girl was Honor's only living relative. Honor had no idea how to make small talk with her, or how to talk about their lives. They had never done it. The only thing they had ever discussed at length were books.

'What have you been reading?' she asked now.

Lydia stopped jiggling. 'I borrowed your copy of *Hamlet*. I hope you don't mind. You were out taking a walk.'

She had gone for a walk up Keats Way. Carefully, step by step up the wide pavement, returning exhausted.

'Of course I don't mind. You are welcome to any of my books, you know that. *Hamlet* is a wonderful play. Have you read it yet?'

'I started. I . . .' Lydia shifted on the sofa so that she was facing Honor. 'Actually I wanted to ask you about what's written in the front of your copy.'

'Oh. I see.'

Honor knew what was written inside it; knew the shop it had come from in Oxford, knew the high shelves and the smell of paper and binding. She knew the moment it had been bought. She could see his hands selecting it, handing over the money. The smooth motion of his writing, with his favourite gold fountain pen, on the flyleaf. She knew the moment he had passed it over to her, at a corner table in a café where they would not be seen, and she had opened it to read what he had inscribed within.

'It says *H. I think of you always*,' said Lydia. 'And it's signed *P*.'

'Yes,' said Honor.

'Was that . . . were you . . .'

'It was written by your grandfather. Yes.'

On the television, she heard the strange creatures crying

out in nonsensical joy as they floated into the air. How strange to call Paul 'your grandfather'. How strange to be speaking about him at all.

'I . . . don't know anything about him,' said Lydia. 'Is he . . . is he still alive?'

'I don't know. He wasn't much older than I, so it's possible.'

'You're not in touch?'

Honor folded her hands in her lap. 'Paul Honeywell was my professor. I was a junior lecturer, newly appointed. And he was married.'

'Your professor? So — like your teacher?'

'No, the Head of the department where I worked.'

'And you were in love with him? Did he leave his wife?'

'Yes, I was. And he with me; at least then. And no, he didn't.'

'Did you think he would leave her? I mean, you must have hoped, right?'

'He never told me that he would leave his wife for me.'

'So what happened?'

Honor closed her eyes. The falling moments replayed themselves.

The stolen glances, the accidental brushing of hands. The awkward pauses, full of things unsaid, at the end of departmental drinks. The time he called her back, saying 'Honor', her name in his voice meaning more than her name.

And she had gone back to him. She had touched his face, in the shadows, before they heard someone coming and sprang apart. The impression of his skin stayed on her fingers for days.

The first time had been that weekend in Copenhagen at

the convention. They'd had too much wine at dinner, knowing what was going to happen, both afraid of it even though they both wanted it so much. And then the unimaginable luxury of his hotel room: that bare hotel room, with an unshaded light bulb and scratchy sheets, a smeared glass of cloudy water. All that time together. All those hours till morning. She touched him from the crown of his head to the soles of his feet, drinking in every part. She had not known she could be so greedy. She had never suspected it of herself, before then.

'I loved him anyway,' she said to her granddaughter. 'I loved him without hope.'

She felt Lydia's gaze on her face. She knew what she was thinking: she was wondering how such an old lady, dried out and hobbling, could have been capable of a passion so strong that it had made her forget reason.

One day, you will be eighty, and you will feel thirty-five. Some days, you will feel twenty, or ten, or six. You will stretch out your hand for people long dead. You will feel a shock when you touch your own papery cheek.

There was no point in saying that to someone Lydia's age, of course. She would never believe it. The young think they will be young for ever. Honor certainly had.

She felt a fierce stab of protectiveness for this girl with her coltlike limbs and her careless hair and her smell of fruit-flavoured sweets.

'Anyway,' she began briskly, 'you'll enjoy *Hamlet*. It's all about death, of course, and Hamlet is a fool, but that's rather the point.'

'But . . . if he never left his wife, how did you manage with having a baby? My dad, I mean?'

'I went to live with my father in the house in Stoke

Newington. My mother had died some time before, but he took me in. I was grateful. I was a grown woman, in my thirties, and old enough to know better. Not all parents would have been so accepting.'

'And didn't he want to know where the father was?'

'We didn't discuss it.'

They didn't discuss much, Honor and her father. Shimon Levinson had been a man of few words. Not an affectionate man, either. As a child she had never received kisses or cuddles from him; would have considered it unthinkable. Honor's mother had been the one to soothe hurts and give kisses at night. Her father had been a constant solid source, not of love, but of presence. Reliability. Even after he sold his hardware shops and had retired, you could set your watch by his habits.

But when Stephen was born, he had come to the hospital and held the baby, his grandson, with a tenderness that brought tears to Honor's eyes. He kissed Stephen's downy head.

'It's a new beginning,' he said to her, his voice hoarse with emotion.

And Honor suspected for the first time that her father's lack of affection had not been because of a lack of feeling. That perhaps it was precisely the opposite. He felt too much to express it easily in caresses or words.

Even though he was gone, she understood him more as the years passed. She saw his own nature in hers.

Now, Honor reached out. She touched Lydia's hand and she took it into her own. The soft, unblemished skin, halfway between a child's and a woman's.

'We have perhaps not talked enough, you and I,' she said.

'Was it worth it, to love him?' Lydia asked her. 'Even

knowing what you know now? Would you still have done it?'

Honor rubbed her thumb against the back of Lydia's hand. She remembered other hands in hers. Paul's, and Stephen's. Her father's, at the end.

'I would not have changed anything for the world,' she said.

Lydia went upstairs to put the children to bed and Honor stayed on the sofa, thinking about what they had said. She never spoke of Paul to anyone. This was perhaps the first time she had mentioned his name on purpose in forty-five years. It was not easy to say aloud.

But there was a thread, running from Paul through her, to Stephen, to Lydia. Honor had been raised in a religious family and although she had discarded those traditions, they had tethered her to the past in a way that she imagined Lydia did not have.

Perhaps it was time to speak of him. Perhaps she should have spoken of him long ago, but she had done her best not to think about that.

Why did you never tell me? Stephen had asked. Honor swallowed, hard.

Lydia re-entered the room; Honor could tell by her tread before she saw the movement. 'I . . . I have these,' the girl said, sitting down beside Honor. She put something in her grand-mother's hands. A bundle of paper, perhaps envelopes. Letters.

'The handwriting is the same as in your book,' Lydia said. 'That's what made me think, but I couldn't remember where I'd put them.'

Honor sifted them in her hands. She moved them and held them to the light. She could see Paul's handwriting on them, every one of them, firm thick black strokes writing out Stephen's name and address. The address in Brickham, the house Stephen and Jo had lived in when he was lecturing at the university here.

'They haven't been opened,' Honor said.

'No,' said Lydia. 'I didn't – I never. I didn't know who they were from. Are they from his father, do you think? My grandfather? The return address is in California.'

'Yes.' How strange, to touch something else that Paul had touched, now, so much later. The envelopes were heavy, good quality: greeting cards rather than letters.

She had had a letter like this, before Stephen died. Before she had argued with her son. It had the same handwriting, the same stamp.

Lydia drew in a breath. 'I . . . I used to wait for the post. When I was a little girl. I got into the habit of it. I liked to get it first thing. After Dad died, I collected anything that had his name on it and I kept it. I put it in a special drawer. I think I thought . . . I thought that if I kept them, he might come back for them. That's silly, isn't it?'

'It is silly, but understandable,' said Honor, who had some recent experience in denying reality.

'I have all sorts of things in there – mostly junk mail and bank statements, I think. I never opened them or read them. But these ones came every Christmas. I suppose I thought they were Christmas cards.'

'Perhaps they are.'

'I don't know if we have any from before Dad died. Mum threw away all his letters and things. She said they were too painful to read. She only kept a few of his books and his wristwatch.'

The stamps were American. There were eight letters. 'Have they stopped arriving?'

'I think so. I mean, this was all I could find. They're all addressed to our old house before we moved here, so maybe they just haven't been forwarded. He must have ...'

'He must have thought Stephen was still alive.'

'Yeah,' said Lydia. 'Did you know he was writing to Dad?'

'No.' Stephen had never told her about the letters. Was that her fault, too?

'Should we – do you think that we should read them?'

Eight letters from her lover to his son, unread. Honor closed her eyes and she battled with herself. But she was old, now, and who would it hurt, to touch the thread, to let it spill through her fingers?

'You read them,' Honor said. 'You read them to me. One at a time. Please.'

Chapter Twenty

Jo

Parents' evenings would be easier if not for the other parents.

The ones she didn't know well weren't hard; they were mostly very nice people, and Jo enjoyed exchanging a few pleasantries over the plastic cups of orange squash that the school put out for them in the gym whilst they waited between appointments. They might know the old gossip about her and Richard, but they wouldn't say anything. They would pretend not to know. Politeness and small talk gave you a screen, and the subject in common of the school, and exams. And there were plenty of single parents around, or parents there without their partners, so Jo didn't feel conspicuous being by herself.

It was the people like Helen and Logan Travers who you had to watch out for.

'Jo!' Helen came rushing up to her from the gym entrance, Logan at her heels. Their daughter, Erin, lagged behind. 'How are you?' She kissed Jo on either cheek.

'I'm great, how are you?'

'We saw Richard, and heard he'd proposed to Tatiana.'

Helen's face was the picture of sympathy and concern.

'I'm absolutely fine with it. Iris is excited about being a bridesmaid.'

'And how is Lydia coping?'

Lydia probably thinks good riddance, and I can't much blame her.
'Lydia's coping really well, thanks.'

'It must be so hard, to lose two father figures like that.'

'Lydia misses her father, of course. We both do.'

'And you must be lonely!'

'I don't really have a chance to get lonely, with the children, and Lydia's grandmother is staying with us for the moment, too, while she recovers from surgery.'

'Her grandmother? You are a saint! I think of you often, Jo. I'm so sorry I've been so busy.'

'We must get together for dinner soon,' said Logan. 'We have a friend or two you might like to meet.'

They'd used to have dinner parties together, before Richard left; sometimes their daughter Erin and Lydia would have a sleepover, too. Jo pictured what it would be like now, sitting next to one of Logan's friends, a divorcé or confirmed bachelor who would be no more interested in matchmaking than she herself would be. He would, of course, have been prepped by Logan and Helen about the sad breakdown of her marriage.

'Yes,' she said, 'we must. Hello, Erin, how are you?'

'Fine,' said Erin loudly. She was wearing tracksuit bottoms, slung low enough to show the top of her pants, and she was staring straight at Jo with a strange smile on her face. At least it was good to know that Lydia wasn't the only teenager who acted weird sometimes.

'Erin's doing ever so well,' Helen said. 'We were thrilled

with her predicted grades. Lydia's must be wonderful too – so much to live up to! Isn't she with you?'

'She's looking after her brother and sister. I've only seen the English and French teachers, but so far, so good.'

'Come along, darling,' Helen said, 'we've got Mr Treadbull now. I have no idea why we have to have conferences with the PE teachers! Lovely to see you, Jo, let's set a date for dinner, yes?'

'Of course,' Jo said, making a mental resolution not to answer the phone if Helen rang.

But she wouldn't ring. And if she did, Jo would answer.

She checked the slip of paper with her appointments on it. The school ran their parent-teacher evenings like a pro-duction line, with the teachers arranged in the gym and the dining hall behind rows of desks, and a bell ringing to signal the end of each appointment. She had Geography next, with Mr Graham, who was also Lydia's new tutor since Miss Wheeler had left at Christmas; according to the little map she had, he was sitting in the back right corner of the dining hall. She headed over, so she'd be on time.

She looked around for Avril's mum, but as usual, she didn't see her. Mrs Toller had only come to one or two parents' evenings in their secondary-school career so far; in fact, that was one of the few times that Jo had actually met her. Often Avril helped Lydia babysit while Jo went to the school, but tonight she hadn't turned up, and Lydia had snapped Jo's head off when she'd commented on it. Jo had thought maybe that Avril was with her mum instead. It was an important parents' evening, the last one before the girls started their GCSE exams.

But there was no sign of her.

Jo frowned. There was something wrong there. All the

meals Avril had at their house; all the time she spent with them. Not that Jo minded, at all. She loved Avril; she was like another daughter – at times distinctly more pleasant to her than her own daughter was. But Jo worried about her. It was clear she wasn't getting what she needed at home, if she spent so much time at their house. And yet she couldn't broach the subject. Avril deflected it, and so did Lydia.

She resolved to try again, when she had the chance. She respected Avril's boundaries, but Avril was still a child. She needed someone looking after her.

Geography was over by the serving hatches. The air smelled of cabbage and chip fat, the same smell Jo remembered from her own school dining hall. Teenagers these days seemed so complicated, so much more sophisticated than Jo had been, but some things, at least, never changed. Chips for school dinners.

The bell rang, and Jo made her way towards the back of the room, where a couple were just leaving a desk occupied by a man in a blue suit, with glasses and curly brown hair.

It was Marcus.

He hadn't looked up yet. He was writing something down on one of the papers that littered his desk. He had a plastic cup of the same orange squash she'd just been drinking; his tie was loosened, and the glasses she'd never seen him wearing before were horn-rimmed, round. Sexy.

She couldn't breathe.

The bell stopped ringing. Had it been going all this time? It echoed in her ears, and at that moment, Marcus looked up and saw her.

He had half a smile on his face, but it melted away. His eyes widened.

Around her, other parents were moving, going to desks,

shaking hands, sitting down. Keeping their appointments, like she needed to keep hers. Feeling like a robot, she carried on forward.

It couldn't be him. He might teach here – he'd never mentioned what job he did – but he couldn't be Lydia's teacher. Her tutor.

But the name label on his desk said MR GRAHAM – GEOGRAPHY.

He stood as she approached. The scrape of his chair on the wooden floor seemed very loud.

'You're . . .' He cleared his throat and checked the list on his desk. 'You're Lydia's mother?'

She nodded. He started to hold out his hand, but then he seemed to think better of it.

'Why . . . don't you sit down?'

There was a patch of pink on each of his cheeks. Jo took a seat, her limbs stiff, and he sat down across from her. They looked at each other.

Petals in his hair, and she'd reached across and kissed him. *Yesterday.*

'It's good to see you again,' he said.

'How—' she began, and needed to swallow. 'How is Lydia doing in Geography?'

'She's fine.' He ran his hand through his hair. 'Lydia Levinson. Yes, she's a very bright girl. Doing French A level early, top sets in everything. Obviously I . . . obviously I haven't been teaching her for long. But she shows definite aptitude for the subject, and she's doing well across the board. Wants to go to Cambridge, she says.'

'Yes, like her father did.'

'Jo, I didn't know you were her mother.'

'I didn't know you worked here.'

'Yes. Since . . . I started here at Christmas.'

The taste of his lips, damp with rain.

'So . . . is there anything I can do to support Lydia at home?' She had already asked the same question of the English and French teachers.

'Well, with the exams coming up, obviously she needs to revise. And she . . . she could do with a bit more focus, especially lately.'

'I'm not surprised, if Avril's in the class with her. The two of them chat constantly. They're best friends.'

'That might be it. Yes, maybe. You . . . um, are you all right, Jo?'

'Fine, thank you.'

'Because yesterday I didn't mean . . .' He glanced around the room, seemingly remembering their surroundings. 'Ah. Would you like to see her mock results?' He shuffled papers. She looked at the page he passed over to her, but couldn't understand the figures on it.

'She . . . what are you predicting for her in Geography?'

'We're hoping for an A-star, if she keeps her focus.' He met her eyes again, and then looked back down at the paper. 'Of course, that's easier said than done.'

'I understand.' Where was the bell? Jo twisted her damp hands together.

'Jo—'

The bell went. She stood. 'Well, thank you. I'll talk to Lydia about paying more attention in lessons.'

He scrambled to his feet as well. 'Yes. Right, thank you. I'll, um . . . see you.'

She nodded again and fled.

* * *

She was still a wreck when she got home. Oscar and Iris were watching *Rastamouse* in their pyjamas and Lydia and Honor were sitting on the sofa together, apparently looking at Christmas cards. Normally this bit of family harmony would please her, but she felt shaky inside and desperately humiliated, and wanted nothing more than a very large glass of wine.

Lydia jumped up as soon as Jo came in. 'I'm going out,' she said.

Honor stood and began to make her way back to her room, the cards under her arm.

The wine would have to wait. Jo sat on the carpet, pulled Iris onto her lap and watched *Rastamouse* with her and Oscar. The storyline about missing cheese did nothing to distract her from her thoughts. Nor did bedtime stories, or tucking in, or kisses. She did it all on autopilot. By the time she had come downstairs to the kitchen and poured a large glass of pinot grigio, she had resolved two things. No, three.

First, she would be friendly and breezy with Marcus. He was her neighbour, and Lydia's teacher, so she couldn't ignore him completely, but she would be distant. She would not linger in the garden or gaze out of her kitchen window or take him up on his offer of a cup of tea, if he were polite enough to make it again, which was unlikely to say the least.

Second, she would not refer to what had happened between them in the garden.

And third, she would never ever kiss another man ever again. Ever.

She gulped her wine to cement her decision and laid her forehead on the table.

She jumped when there was a knock at the back door. Lydia had returned already and forgotten her keys, she thought, but when she opened the door it was Marcus. He'd taken off his suit jacket and his tie, but he still had his glasses on. Her heart and stomach did a massive leap.

'Hi,' he said. 'Can we talk?'

'Come in.' Resolution one out the window, then.

He hesitated. 'Is Lydia here? Because . . .'

'She went out.'

'Right. OK.' He stepped in and Jo shut the door after him. 'It's . . . you've got a nice house. I like how it's open-plan.'

'Thanks. Cup of tea?'

'Please. I've been – it's been a lot of talking. Parents' evening, I mean.'

She put on the kettle and he stood in her kitchen. He was nervous. He kept rubbing his thumb against his index finger, as if he wanted to wear away the skin.

'The kids?' he said.

'They're in bed. And my mother-in-law is in her room, doing whatever she does in there.'

'I'm sorry about earlier. I couldn't . . . there were too many people. Jo, I honestly had no idea that you were the mother of one of my students. I didn't even know you had any children other than Oscar and Iris.'

'I didn't know that you were a teacher.'

'It's my fault. I should have mentioned it. I suppose I just think that everyone can tell anyway, since that's what I look like. Chalk on the fingers. Ink on the tie.' He tried a self-deprecating smile, but it melted away as soon as he'd done it.

'You don't look like a teacher. You look like . . .' Jo threw away resolution number two. 'Well, you can probably tell from what I did in the garden yesterday, that I think you look good.'

He leaned back on the kitchen island, gripping the granite worktop in both of his hands. 'Listen, I mucked that up yesterday. I'm sorry about that, too.'

'No, I mucked it up. It was totally out of order.'

'It wasn't out of order. It was wonderful.'

She stared at him.

'I was surprised, that was all. I didn't expect it. I hadn't thought you were interested. So I . . .' He gestured, grimacing. 'I'm not always the most articulate person. I mean sometimes I am, but other times, not. You can probably tell.'

'You're articulate enough.' *It was wonderful?* 'You didn't think I was interested in *you?*'

'Well, you know, you're busy, you have a life. And you're beautiful. And you've probably had your fair share of random blokes coming on to you, and the lecherous neighbour is such a cliché, so . . .' He shrugged. 'And then you kissed me out of the blue, and I was surprised, and I blew it. I'm sorry.'

She couldn't quite process this. '*You* blew it? Wait, are you saying you're attracted to me?'

'Yeah. Of course I am. And also, I like you a lot.'

The kettle boiled. She ignored it. Marcus Graham, Geography teacher, adorable in glasses and a shirt that could do with an iron. Liked her.

Was standing in her kitchen, looking at her, liking her.

'But you can't,' she said helplessly. 'How old are you – twenty-five? You can't have been teaching for very long.'

'I'm twenty-nine, I've been teaching for seven years, this is my second school, I'm Head of Department. Does that even matter?'

'I'm forty, Marcus. I have three children.'

'So?'

'So? It's impossible. I could practically be your mother.'

'No, believe me, you couldn't.'

His smile this time was slightly crooked. Sexy.

She found it quite difficult to breathe.

'But you're my daughter's teacher.'

Marcus took a deep breath. His hands tightened on the granite. 'Yes. That's a problem.'

'I mean, could you get sacked for that?'

'For fancying you rotten? I don't think I can get in trouble for inappropriate thoughts about a student's mother. Pending further legislation.'

'No, I mean if we . . . did anything.'

Her heart was pounding like crazy. Basically she'd just confirmed to Marcus that she wanted to do something with him. She'd practically propositioned him, in theory at least. If he'd been in any doubt after she'd kissed him in the garden.

And he fancied her rotten.

'I . . . don't know,' he said at last. 'I don't think it's a good idea.'

'No,' she said hastily. 'It's definitely not a good idea.'

'I was wondering, do you know if Lydia's planning on doing A level Geography?'

She blinked. 'What? No, I don't . . . I mean I don't know, but it's unlikely. She only took it to make up her subjects; she likes English and languages. No offence.'

'None taken.'

'Though you might change her mind.' Yes, having an incredibly good-looking teacher might make Lydia reconsider

196

her A level choices. It would have made Jo reconsider, at Lydia's age.

No. She couldn't think about her daughter having a crush on the same man that she did.

'But if she doesn't change her mind,' said Marcus, 'if she wants to continue on with languages, like you say – not that I would discourage her from doing a subject that she enjoyed, of course.'

'Of course.' Why were they talking about Lydia?

Because Lydia was pretty much the only thing that was keeping her from doing something insane, right now.

'But if she *doesn't* take A level Geography,' continued Marcus, 'I'll only be her teacher for another few months. They change tutor groups for A level as well.'

'So you mean – we could wait.'

'We could wait and see.'

'Until you're not her teacher any more. And then, if we still feel the same way ...'

'We could spend some time together before that. As friends.'

'That would probably be the best thing to do.'

'We could get to know each other better.'

'And definitely not do anything,' Jo said. 'Because it's not a good idea.'

'It's not a good idea.'

'So we're agreed.'

'Yes. Right.'

She'd leaned back against the worktop, too, across the kitchen from him. She held onto the counter in an echo of his posture.

She remembered the feeling of his face in her hands. The

197

scent of him. He looked steadily across at her, his eyes blue and intent, a faint flush on his cheekbones. She couldn't look away.

Definitely not breaking any more resolutions or promises tonight. Definitely.

They met each other halfway across the kitchen. His hands in her hair, hers on his face, their mouths pressing together. She'd been remembering his taste since yesterday but he tasted better, his mouth was hotter, and he held her to him and kissed her as if he couldn't get enough. He felt so alive, his kisses full of a passion she barely remembered as being possible. His tongue touched hers and she moaned without meaning to.

She didn't know they were walking backwards until she came up against the kitchen cabinets. He could get closer this way; her breasts pressed against his chest, and his groin fitted into her. Marcus took one hand out of her hair to unbutton the top of her blouse, still kissing. She felt him shaking.

She had no idea how this was happening; how they had crossed this barrier so quickly, from hesitant words to no words being needed. She pulled his shirt out of his trousers and put her hand on his back, stroked up his skin. He made a sound deep in his throat and dipped his head to her chest, kissed her bare skin on her collarbone. She tilted her head back. He licked her neck and she shivered.

'It's a bad idea,' he whispered against her. She could feel her pulse on his lips.

Honor, in the next room. Oscar and Iris, asleep upstairs.

'Not here,' she said and he paused. Retreated half a step from her. They stared each other in the face. His eyes were wide, unfocused, glasses crooked, his mouth open, breath coming fast. He looked shaken, as if he had been given news of some calamity.

The front door opened.

'Lydia,' she whispered.

'Shit.' He released her and frantically began tucking in his shirt.

'Out the back door.' She pushed him. He went.

Jo straightened her skirt, buttoned her blouse, ran her fingers through her hair. Rubbed the back of her mouth with her hand. She felt his hands on her, his lips on her skin. She turned to the sink and washed her hands, listening.

Lydia's footsteps went upstairs and faded to the top of the house.

Jo's legs were trembling. She could taste Marcus on her tongue.

What had she done?

He was gone, now, and she could think. This was not the sort of thing she did. It wasn't the sort of thing she ever had done. Kissing a stranger, with the children in the house, with her mother-in-law in the next room, with her daughter about to come in. Kissing her daughter's teacher.

She was going insane.

And what would she say, how would she act when she saw him again? How did you act cool, adult, as if this sort of thing happened all the time? Grown up, and careless, and worldly-wise?

She wasn't worldly-wise. She'd been married twice and had three children and she had absolutely no idea.

Jo tiptoed to the back door and opened it. She wanted fresh air; she wanted to see the gap in the hedge, see the wall of his house, and think about what on earth she'd say when

199

she saw him again by chance, tomorrow or the next day. Had they crossed some barrier now, or was that it? Had they kissed, and now it was finished?

It had to be finished.

Marcus was just outside the door, close enough so that she bumped into him. He steadied her.

'Is it all right?' he whispered.

'She's gone to her room,' Jo said, and Marcus caught her eye, and they laughed. He fell against the wall, and she leaned on him, her head on his chest. He put his arm around her. His heart was beating hard.

'That was amazing,' he said.

'It was . . .' She breathed in his scent. Was this playing it cool? Was this finishing it? 'I didn't expect that.'

'I didn't either. And we agreed not to. But I'm glad we did.' He tilted her head up and kissed her. Once, twice, a longer third time. He was saying goodbye. She knew he was saying goodbye, he had to be.

'When can I see you again?' he whispered.

'I don't know.'

'Tomorrow?'

'I can't tomorrow.'

'Thursday?'

'I don't know. I need someone to look after the children.'

'You don't have my number.'

'I can give you mine.'

'I don't have my phone; it's in my jacket. Listen. I'll leave my light on. If you can come, come. I'll be in.'

'Waiting?'

'Marking.' His mouth quirked up. 'And waiting. Come and see me, Jo. If not Thursday, then the next day. And the next.'

He brushed her hair from her face. 'For a cup of tea, at least.'

His kiss promised more than a cup of tea. And then he was gone, running across the garden, slipping through the hedge. Jo put her hand over her mouth, as if she could trap the memory.

It was only then that she remembered the promise she'd made to Lydia.

Chapter Twenty-One

Lydia

As soon as Mum got home, Lydia ran to Avril's house. All she could think about was what Granny H had said. How she'd loved without hope or reason. How she'd never found anyone else, for forty-five years. The expression on her face when Lydia had brought down the letters, the way she had touched the envelopes as if they were a person, fragile and immeasurably precious.

They had only read one letter out of the eight, the one with the earliest postmark. It had been written the Christmas after her father had died, and the thing about it was that it sounded so *normal*. It had news about his family, his three daughters and their children, who were Lydia's cousins, now that she thought of it. Nothing about it would hint that it was the letter of a father to his son, except for the last line: *I think about you often, and hope one day to meet again.* And for the way Granny H had looked when Lydia had read it to her: greedy, drinking in every word, tears shining in her eyes.

Lydia ran faster. When she reached Avril's block of flats, she was out of breath and had to recover for a minute before she pressed the button. Avril appeared almost immediately.

'Hiya,' she said, plainly pleased, and for a minute Lydia thought that everything was back to the way it had been last week, before Harry.

'Want to go for a walk?' Lydia asked.

'Yeah, I'll get my jacket.'

Lydia waited for her outside. She didn't have her own jacket, and it was a little bit chilly, especially since she'd sweated a bit. She rubbed her hands over her arms and when Avril came down, she gave Lydia her pink hoodie. It smelled of her.

They walked around for a little while, off her estate and across the park. Lydia wasn't really sure what to say, and the longer she didn't say anything, the harder it was to start. When she'd been running, she'd had some idea of trying to persuade Avril that Harry wasn't worth it. But Avril was smiling, like she had a wonderful secret, and there was a bounce in her step.

Jealousy felt awful. It was like burning acid eating away at her insides, destroying every good bit. It made her want to strike out at Avril for being so happy. Except she didn't want to get into an argument. She didn't even want to mention Harry, because Avril would be able to tell she was jealous, but she knew that Avril was dying for her to ask about him, so she'd have an excuse to talk about him. She wanted to feel his name in her mouth, like Lydia felt Avril's name sometimes: the burr of the v on her lips, the kiss of the l on her tongue.

'How's your mum?' Lydia asked finally. 'Did she go to the parents' evening?'

It was a mistake. Avril's face closed up. 'No. And she's fine.'

'Is she out tonight?'

'She's working. Why do you keep on bringing her up?'

'Because . . . because I care about you?'

'I told you, I don't want to talk about her.'

'All right. But you know, if you do . . .'

Avril's phone went and she pulled it out of her pocket immediately, as if she'd been waiting for this very thing. She stopped walking and opened the text, and Lydia heard her sharp intake of air.

'What?'

'It's . . .' She giggled. 'Look.'

She passed over the phone. It was nearly dark outside, and the screen glowed, and Lydia could see before she even took the phone that it was the selfie of Harry's dick.

'Really?' she said.

It was the same one – the same mirror, the same underpants pulled down, the same reflection of the flash in the same spot.

'God, that is pathetic.'

Avril snatched the phone back. 'I don't think it's pathetic. I think it's sexy.'

'Av, don't you think it's a little creepy, him sending you pictures of his thing hanging out?'

'No.' She started walking again, fast.

'He's going to start asking you to send him one, now.'

'What is it with you?' Avril said. 'Why can't you just be happy that I've found a boy I like?'

'Because you deserve someone better. Harry isn't serious about you. He can't be serious about anybody.'

'And how can you possibly know that?'

'Because he . . .'

'Because he what, Lydia? Because you don't like him for

204

some reason? Because you do like him, but you blew it, and now he likes me instead?'

'Because he sent me the same picture that he just sent you.'

Avril stopped. 'When?'

'A couple of weeks ago.'

'You didn't tell me.'

'I didn't think it was important. I didn't know then that it was his go-to pic for sending to all the laydeez.'

'Show me.'

'I deleted it.'

Avril shook her head. 'I don't believe you.'

'Why would I make that up?'

'Like I said. Because you're jealous.'

Lydia was so jealous she felt like dying. 'I'm not jealous. I just don't think he's good enough for you. That's all.'

'Lydia, everyone wants Harry Carter. *Everyone*. He's the fittest boy in the whole school. In what way could he possibly be not good enough for me? Because he wasn't good enough for you? Or was he only not good enough for you as long as no one else had him?'

'I don't think you can trust him.'

'I can't trust *him*? You lied to me!'

'I didn't lie, I just—'

'Either you lied when you got the picture, or you're lying to me now.'

'Think about it,' Lydia said desperately. 'You don't know anything about him, not really. And you deserve someone who really loves you. Who you really trust. Can you picture telling Harry about your mum?'

Avril whirled around. 'I told you I don't want to talk about my mum!' she said, yelling it, practically screaming it. 'I just want to be *normal*! Just normal, like everyone else, with a real boyfriend and a normal life! Why can't you let me have that? Why can't you be happy for me?'

And then she ran off, and Lydia was so shocked that she couldn't follow her.

Chapter Twenty-Two

Honor

Honor was incandescent with rage. She fumbled under the sink for the bleach and the Cif and the cleaning rags, and found them by feel.

Right here in the kitchen. The heart of a home, the place where Jo fed her children, open to the rest of the house. Honor had heard the voices and the gasps. The panicked shuffle as the lover, whoever he was, scrambled out through the back door before being caught. Her window was open and she heard the whispered conversation afterwards. The laughter. She couldn't make out all of the words, but it was enough.

How long had it been going on? she wondered. Jo pretending to be the perfect mother, centring everything around her children and her home, even taking in her elderly mother-in-law, while all the time she was leading a double life, snatching stolen moments with her lover?

Honor began by scrubbing the table. It was covered in an oilcloth in a pretty spotted pattern. She hadn't emerged for breakfast this morning; she wouldn't have been able to face eating in this kitchen, at least not with Jo in the same room. By feel, she cleaned the entire surface of the table and then started on the work surfaces.

Jo was the type of woman who always needed a man in her life. Honor had known it from the minute she'd met her. She had no career, no interests, no intellectual pursuits. She'd been a waitress, for God's sake, until she'd found Stephen and become a housewife. She needed a man for her definition, for her direction. A limp noodle of a woman, weak and nice and pleasant and pretty, waiting for a Prince Charming to come along and rescue her. Honor had known hundreds of girls like her. Honor's parents expected her to be one of them herself, until it became clear that she was not.

Jo was a pretty blank. Too pliable, too easily swayed. Too soft with her children and with the world. It made Honor want to grit her teeth.

That spark the other day – that hint of backbone . . .

Honor shook her head, rubbing hard with the rag. No, she'd been right about Jo. She'd married Stephen, who was a decent man and who, God help him, loved her, but then when Stephen was gone, she'd married herself to that waste of space Richard, who promptly showed her what kind of man he was. And now she was leaning on another man. She'd move him in soon, or move herself and her children in with him, and the whole story would start again. It always would, with women like her. What sort of role model was she being for Lydia? How was she teaching her daughter to stand on her own two feet?

She felt her way to the sink and rinsed out the rag. The smell of lemon cleanser brought her back to reality. It was a large kitchen; much larger than Honor's. There were vast plains of surfaces to clean. Jo didn't appear to have a cleaner, or at least one hadn't shown up yet. She seemed to take care of everything herself. Most evenings, Honor could hear her scurrying around, catching up on laundry and housework, tidying the toys that seemed to multiply overnight. She had mowed the lawn the other day, first the front and then the back.

'With a new husband, she could afford a cleaner,' Honor muttered, making a vicious swipe at the toaster. Her knuckles banged against the metal, and Honor heard her own voice, and she stopped.

Had she really just said aloud that her daughter-in-law was having it off with some strange man in her kitchen, so that she would be able to *afford a cleaner*? After she, Honor, had herself spent yesterday evening telling her granddaughter about her own affair with a married man? About how she had lost control of herself, thrown herself into something passionate and hopeless, because she couldn't resist?

Who was she to condemn another woman's weaknesses or pleasures? At whom was she truly angry?

Honor cleaned the rest of the kitchen methodically, by smell and by feel, and she wrung out the rag and put it into the washing machine. By the time she had finished, she was aching at the hip, and in the shoulders too. She was becoming unfit. Unfit to exercise, unfit to judge.

Her own life had been defined by three men: Shimon, Paul and Stephen. Some feminist she was. Some role model she had been.

In her room, she put on Tchaikovsky's Violin Concerto in D Major and sat with her eyes closed to appreciate the first movement. Honor followed the thread of the violin's melody as it twisted and soared to high notes unimaginably sweet, and fluttered back down. She thought of Jo in the kitchen, the whispers and the laughter. She thought of Paul, the last time she had seen him, thirty-five years before he had written that card Lydia had read last night. That afternoon in his home, when she had done the man she loved a terrible wrong.

Chapter Twenty-Three

Jo

She couldn't see him again. It was all she could think about that night, lying in the king-sized bed alone, and in the morning, too. After breakfast she took Oscar and Iris for a walk in the opposite direction to Marcus's house so that she wouldn't be tempted to stare at it, even though it was a school day and he'd be at work.

She hadn't promised to see him again. She'd only said she didn't know.

But she had made a promise to Lydia.

'Don't do it again, Mum. Don't go with some guy just because he's good-looking and you fancy him, and because you think it might be a good idea, or because you need a man to make you feel better about yourself.'

And the pain in Lydia's voice; what she was really saying. *Don't betray my father. Again.*

Jo pushed Oscar on the roundabout and Iris on the swing and she thought about what Stephen would say. She couldn't think of anything. If Stephen were here, she wouldn't have kissed Marcus. Since Stephen wasn't here, the only way he could have an opinion about it would be if there were such a thing as an afterlife. And Jo didn't believe in that. She wanted to, but she couldn't. People lived on through their children and the memories that others had of them. If you did your best in this life, you would be remembered well. She believed in that; that was a rule she could apply to her everyday life.

She knew Stephen had never been the jealous type. She could never picture him condemning anything that made Jo happy. He would have wanted her to move on with her life. But what if that was just the way she wanted to think – the way she'd justified her decision to marry Richard?

Jo gave the roundabout an extra push, to squeals of delight from her children. Kissing Marcus wasn't a betrayal of Stephen. It was a betrayal of Lydia: of what Lydia had asked of her, of what Lydia needed her to be like as a mother. So she needed to end it with Marcus, if 'it' indeed even existed. Although her body was full of electricity, although she still tasted him on her lips, felt his body pressing against her. Even though when she closed her eyes, all she could see was the way he had looked at her.

Even though last night she had lain awake thinking of Marcus's kiss, instead of Stephen's scream.

Her phone beeped. It was a text from an unknown number.

I have been very naughty and looked up your number on L's file. My excuse is that I can't stop thinking about you. M xx

Her heart leaped and her fingers went slick on the phone. Her hand was shaking as she texted back *That IS very naughty* and sent it, and then realized that what she should have done was deleted it. And blocked his number. And written him a formal, polite note to say that this was a bad idea, that she wasn't ready for a relationship of any kind, that she had to focus on her children, but that she hoped they could be friends. And then put the letter in the post instead of putting it through his letter box, because if she went near his house, she would be tempted to knock on the door and beg him to let her in so that she could feel like that for a little while again. Like a woman. Like someone worthy of being seen.

The text came back seconds later. *I want to kiss you.*

Her children laughed and waved and went round and round. Jo's heart pounded and her fingers worked by themselves to form the words *Me too* and send them to where he was, real and solid, less than a mile away, in a classroom or a staffroom thinking about kissing her.

'Push, Mummy!'

She pushed. There were other mothers in the park: two chatting on a bench, one standing below her toddler on the monkey bars, arms upraised to catch him if he fell. She wondered if any of them had a secret like this.

She started another text. *Sorry*, it said, *I shouldn't have said that. Marcus, I think this is a bad*

Her phone beeped with another message before she could finish.

What else do you want to do with me? he asked.

She nearly staggered with desire. She steadied herself against the back of a nearby bench and glanced around at the other mothers. It was impossible any of them could feel this way, too, split between what they needed to do and what they desperately, desperately wanted.

She wanted to see Marcus naked. She wanted to touch him, taste him all over; learn his body, run her hands over his chest, push him backwards onto a bed and straddle him. She wanted him to look up into her face and see her: not the mother in the park, pushing children round and round and round again, not the housewife with her arms full of laundry and toys – but *her*. The part of her deep inside who wanted, who was still hungry to find out more, to experience everything.

Jo closed her eyes. She took deep breaths. She wasn't a reckless person. She had never thrown caution to the wind. She had always, practically from the moment she was born, put her responsibilities first. A sick mother, two husbands, children. Bills to be paid, houses to be cleaned, clothes to be washed, meals to be cooked.

But she was missing something in her life, wasn't she, something vital, something irresistible? If she could feel this way, right now, in a children's playpark at half past ten on a Thursday morning in May?

And yet her promise to Lydia.

Another text. *On second thoughts, don't tell me now. Tell me later, when I'm not at school. Bell's about to ring and I want to be able to walk down the corridor without embarrassment. M xx*

Jo laughed aloud. She pictured him, texting under his desk like a teenager, his glasses slipping down his nose, and laughed again.

'Why are you happy, Mummy?' asked Oscar as he went spinning past.

'I'm just happy,' she said to him. She put her phone back into her pocket and she pushed her children, faster and faster.

'Hello? Earth to Joanna?' Sara waved a hand in front of her face and Jo blinked.

'Sorry,' she said. 'Miles away.'

'Do you want another coffee?'

She looked at the mess that the four children had made of the café table. But Iris and Polly were colouring, Oscar was demolishing a cake, crumb by crumb, and Billy seemed happy enough with his cars. 'OK. I'll get them.'

She checked her phone at the counter, placing the order. She'd never checked her phone so much in her life as she had since this morning. For the first time, she could understand why Lydia never let her phone stray more than five inches from her right hand.

She had deleted her draft text, and then written it again over lunch. Then deleted it. She was not strong enough to delete Marcus's number. But she hadn't added it to her address book either.

She had read his text at least two dozen times. *What else do you want to do with me?*

Nine words. They were all she could think about.

'So last night,' Sara said to her, when she got back to the table with the coffees, 'I put the kids to bed early, and I put on my special lingerie. The stuff I haven't worn since Polly was born? Actually, I think I was wearing it when Polly was conceived. That's how long it's been. And I went downstairs to where Bob was watching the football, just wearing that and this slinky dressing gown I found in the back of the wardrobe. And guess what happened?'

'What?' said Jo automatically. She picked up a crayon, handed Oscar a napkin, took a sip of her coffee without tasting it.

'I stood in front of Bob and slid the dressing gown off my shoulder, like in some cheesy film. And he actually tilted his head *to look around me.* He said could I wait a few minutes, the game was going into penalties!'

'Oh.'

Sara looked outraged. Jo forced herself to remember what Sara had said.

'Really?' she tried instead.

'And the thing was, I wasn't even that disappointed. I was sort of relieved. I'd made the effort, you know? He couldn't blame me. I just went upstairs and had an early night.'

'Sleep is the most important thing, sometimes,' Jo said.

'Do you think that's how it is for everyone? It just peters out, after you've had kids?' Sara looked stricken. 'Oh wait, I'm sorry, I didn't mean to ask you that.'

'You mean because of Richard starting up with Tatiana after Iris was born?'

'It was tactless. Sorry.'

'It's all right. It's crossed my mind. Iris wasn't a good feeder. I was tired all the time.'

'Well, that wasn't your fault. It was no reason to turn to the au pair.'

'I should have made more of an effort. He'd hired the au pair so we could spend more time together. That's what he said. But I put the children first.'

'You're well shot of him. Can I have one of these?' Sara took a biscuit from the packet that Jo had opened, but not eaten, and dunked it in her coffee. 'What about with your first husband, after Lydia was born?'

'It was . . . we always made the time.' Although Lydia was not a good sleeper, and ended up in their bed five nights out of seven. He was working all hours, writing lecture notes, articles. Then there were the black hole days, when Stephen was in the house but not present, lost in his own world of pain.

But sometimes, there was an hour they could snatch on a weekend, when Lydia was napping. Sometimes they fell asleep, limbs entwined, and only woke up when their daughter crawled between them.

If she had known what was going to happen, how little time she had left with Stephen, she would have given up all of her sleep to be with him.

'It was good,' she added, feeling the need to defend Stephen. But against what?

'It must be easier with only one child.'

'Stephen was wonderful,' she said. 'There was never enough time, though. And then he was gone.'

Sara nodded. 'OK, point taken,' she said, though Jo hadn't been trying to make a point. 'I'll try again with Bob. Billy, can you not drive your cars through Oscar's cake, please? Anyway, speaking of which, have you seen the hot neighbour recently?'

Jo's face flushed. Sara leaned forward. 'What?'

'Oh, he . . .' *is sending me texts saying he is thinking about me, he wants to kiss me* '. . . it turns out he is Lydia's teacher.'

'No! What a disappointment.'

'I know.' She took a hasty drink of her coffee and scalded her mouth. 'Ow!'

Sara passed her a plastic beaker of water, smeared with child's fingerprints. 'I thought he was at the very least a hot gardener.'

'He's a Geography teacher. And also Lydia's tutor. I met him at her parents' evening.'

'Damn! Still, at least it must have made parents' evening

more interesting, to have some eye candy to look at. Did you introduce yourself as his incredibly single neighbour?'

'We . . . mostly talked about Lydia.'

Why was she lying to Sara about this?

'I have a great idea,' she said suddenly. 'Let's go lingerie shopping after this. Splash out a little. Buy something that makes us feel pretty.'

Sara laughed. 'With this lot? I don't feel like spending the next two hours untangling Billy from bras, thank you.'

'Right. Yeah. Good point.'

Secretly, she touched her phone in her pocket.

That night, after the children were in bed, when Lydia was revising in her room and Honor was listening to music in hers, Jo stood at her kitchen window looking out. His light was on, as he'd promised. The outdoor light, and a light in the top window of his house, which might be his bedroom. She watched the strip of light between the curtains, hoping to catch a glimpse of him. Hoping to catch him looking out at her.

God, she was obsessed. It had been a little less than twenty-four hours, and she'd thought of nothing but Marcus, what he was doing, whether he was thinking of her. She had deceived her friend Sara. She had still not yet sent the text ending it. She knew, to the minute, how long ago he had been in this kitchen with her.

She made herself turn away from the window and finish making the cup of tea she'd started. It was going cold already. She brought it upstairs, along with her phone. She was alone now. She'd be able to think straight. She could delete his messages, send him something cool yet friendly, and get on with her life.

The master bedroom was much too big for one person, with a king-sized bed, walk-in wardrobes that gaped half-empty. The furniture was new and one side of the bed hardly used. Jo had tried sleeping in the middle, tried sprawling out, but she always ended up on the right-hand side. She was used to taking up little space. After Richard had left she'd bought some flowered scatter cushions, with the half-formed idea of making the room seem more feminine, more *hers*. They didn't do much.

Sometimes she stayed up later than she should, doing housework, so that she would not have to come up to this room alone.

Her phone beeped as soon as she sat on the bed.

Safe now. Are the kids in bed? Did you have a good day? M xx

Her bedroom was above the kitchen. She went to the window, opened it. From this vantage point she could see the end of his bed. A blue duvet cover. Nothing else.

This has to stop, she texted, and deleted.

I promised Lydia
I hardly know you
You're young enough to

She held the button down, watching the words disappearing letter by letter. Jo swallowed, and spelled out the truth instead.

I haven't been able to stop thinking about you either, she wrote, and held her breath as she sent it off.

It didn't feel like a mistake. It felt . . . it felt the same way as she had felt in that café in Cambridge, when Stephen had put down his books and seen her for the first time.

No, not the same way. It couldn't be the same way. But she was breathless, heart pounding, stomach full of fire, feet hardly

219

tethered to the floor. Alone in her bedroom with her children asleep in the house and she wanted to dance.

It was physical. The physical symptoms of desire. It was a temporary thing, a crush, just a part of what she had felt for Stephen, but it was more powerful than she remembered. Maybe you couldn't remember something this intense, this all-encompassing, once it was gone; not in all its details. Maybe once you'd had it, like she'd had it with Stephen, it left a hole inside you and most of the time you didn't even notice something was missing, until suddenly, one day, you found someone who filled it, and you knew that you couldn't bear to be without it again.

It was more powerful than almost anything, except the pull she felt towards her own children when she held them. And even that was different. Calmer, softer, wider. Not as hungry, not as greedy or focused.

Tell me what you were thinking, texted Marcus. *Tell me what you want to do.*

Fully clothed, she slipped underneath the bedclothes. She pulled them over her head, so she was hidden, surrounded, in a warm pocket of secret air. Not seen, not heard by anyone, except for this invisible current from her phone, bounced up into space, bounced down to him. Travelling thousands of miles to travel a few metres. She licked her lips.

First, I'd unbutton your shirt, she began.

Chapter Twenty-Four

Lydia

'I don't want to fall out over a boy,' said Avril, when she came by to pick up Lydia on her way to school. Lydia had been watching for her out of the window, pretending to listen to music on her headphones.

'I don't want to either,' said Lydia.

'Good. But you can't lie to me. You can't. It does my head in, thinking that you could be hiding something from me. We're supposed to be best friends.'

'I wasn't ly—'

'Just promise not to do it, OK? Promise to always tell me the truth.'

Lydia nodded. 'I promise,' she lied.

'Sometimes I wonder if you receive these cards, since you haven't answered in so long. I suppose I can't blame you for keeping me at a distance. I'm a stranger, after all, married to a woman who's not your mother. I'm writing these cards for myself as much as for you – kidding myself that if I keep a channel of communication open, maybe one day you'll answer me. You must have given me your address for a reason, mustn't you?'

Lydia lowered the card. It was the third one she'd read; the other five sat, unopened, on Granny Honor's bed.

'What does he mean, he's a stranger? Didn't Dad spend any time with him at all?'

'To my knowledge, they only met once.'

'But why? Didn't he want to know anything about his son?'

'Until they met, Paul did not know he had a son. I never told him.'

Lydia stared at her grandmother. Her face was placid, as if she hadn't admitted something so unbelievable.

'You never told him you were pregnant? I thought . . .'

Granny Honor raised her chin. 'You thought I would place an obligation on a man who had no intention of leaving his family? I had far too much pride for that. And I had no desire to be second-best in Paul's life. That was a torture I chose not to endure.'

Lydia thought of the promise she had made to Avril this morning. 'But you *lied* to Dad.'

'I did not lie. I omitted. We never spoke of his father.'

'But didn't he ever ask?'

'When he asked, I told him that his father was not part of our lives.'

How did you criticize your own grandmother for what she'd done when your father was growing up? Lydia studied Granny Honor: the patrician nose, the stubborn chin, the steady brown eyes. She had always been a little bit scared of Granny Honor. She always felt stupid next to her. But this . . .

'I . . .' She swallowed and thought about how to say it. 'I would've been really sad not to know about my father growing up.'

222

'You think it was a mistake. You think I did wrong, not to tell either of them.'

'Well . . .'

'Your father felt that way too.'

Honor said it softly, and she looked down at her lap as she said it.

'It was a few months before he died that Stephen came to me,' she continued. 'He told me that he had met a man, a fellow academic, at a dinner. The man had stared at him all evening. He had seemed troubled. After the dinner, he approached Stephen and asked him his mother's name.

'He had worked out that Stephen was his,' Honor said. 'You see, Stephen and Paul looked very similar. To Paul, it may have been like seeing his younger self at the table with him.'

'What was it like for Dad?' Lydia asked.

'Your father . . . was very angry with me. He and I argued. It was one of the only times . . .' Honor lifted her chin again. 'I have thought of it often. Especially as Stephen died not long afterwards. I have come to think that I made a mistake. And there is nothing I can do to make it up to your father. He died with that between us.'

Granny Honor was in the armchair; Lydia was sitting on the bed, next to the unopened letters. Honor's posture was the same as it had been: proud, defiant, fierce. But something glittered in her eyes. It might be unshed tears. If they were sitting together on the sofa, Lydia might have reached out to her grandmother and hugged her. But there was a space between them. And something about Granny Honor's posture forbade her from crossing it.

'Do you think Dad ever wrote back to him?' she asked.

'I don't know. He may have, before he died.'

'I hate to think of Paul writing, and writing, and not knowing that Dad is dead. Maybe we should write back to him,' Lydia said. 'There's a return address on the back of the envelope.'

'No,' said Honor quickly.

'But he would probably want to know that Daddy is—'

'What difference can it possibly make?'

Lydia frowned. She thought it would make quite a bit of difference, personally, but Granny Honor seemed so dead set against it that she didn't pursue it.

'Paul wrote to me, too,' said Granny Honor, softly again. 'It was about the same time that Stephen and I argued. It must have been because he'd seen Stephen.'

'Don't you know why? Didn't he say in the letter?'

'I burned the letter as soon as I received it.'

Lydia couldn't imagine ever receiving something from Avril and burning it. She couldn't even leave a text un-answered for long. 'Why?'

'That chapter in my life was over.'

'But he might have been writing to tell you that he'd got a divorce. Or that his wife was dead.'

'Neither of which was true, according to the letters we're reading now,' snapped Honor. 'It was finished. We have to live with the choices we make, Lydia. Sometimes hope is too painful to contemplate.'

She stood and walked, in that shuffling way she had now, to the window. Lydia could tell when she was being dismissed. She stood too, and hesitated, looking at her grandmother's narrow back. Wondering if she should go to her and touch her shoulder. Hug her and say that she loved her anyway, even if she had kept that secret from Dad.

But Granny Honor wasn't acting as if she wanted forgiveness. And anyway, what good would Lydia's forgiveness do? Lydia had only been a little girl when all of this had happened.

She put the letter on the bed next to the others and went upstairs to her new room.

Sometimes hope is too painful to contemplate.

God, Granny Honor had lived a whole lifetime alone. She'd chosen to be by herself because she couldn't stand to hope. She'd cut herself off from the man she loved, and cut her son off, too, because she thought the pain would be less that way. Because she only wanted the man she loved if she could have him fully.

Was that what was going to happen to Lydia too?

She lay down on her bed. It was funny, but when her bedroom had been downstairs she'd been driven crazy by all the noise. But up here, she could hear nothing at all. It was almost as if she were totally alone.

Chapter Twenty-Five

Honor

Oxford, 1969

Honor has never been to Paul's house before. He invites her whenever he invites the rest of the department, for drinks or the end-of-term barbecue, but she always makes her excuses. Even before they were lovers, she hasn't wanted to see his house and the way he lives. But today is different. Today *she* is different.

Now, she stands on the doorstep, holding a bottle of wine. His house is a 1930s semi-detached in Headington, surrounded by similar houses. The stucco is painted white and the door is painted pillar-box red. It's not at all the kind of house she's imagined him in.

She hears voices through the door before it's opened by a blonde woman wearing a yellow trouser suit. She looks utterly ordinary.

His wife.

'Hello,' she says, smiling. 'You must be Honor. You're a bit early – no one else has arrived yet. You can help me put things on skewers, if you don't mind.'

'That will be fine,' says Honor automatically. She steps into Paul's house, her lover's house. Wellies and plimsolls are piled up by the door. A collection of macs hangs from pegs.

'Come through to the kitchen and I'll get you a drink. Oh, my name's Wendy, by the way.'

'I know,' says Honor. 'It's nice to meet you at last.'

She follows Wendy through carpeted rooms. There are bookshelves, wallpaper, chintz sofas, striped curtains. Flowers in vases, ashtrays on tables. A paperback novel lies open on a chair. A rag doll's feet protrude from underneath a sofa. A model of a Spitfire half-completed on a side table. The house smells of coffee and flowers and tobacco, a scent that Honor recognizes from Paul's clothes.

This could be anyone's house. Anyone's at all.

The kitchen is white and yellow, like Wendy. Children's drawings are Sellotaped to the cabinets. 'I've started on the gin already,' Wendy admits, giving Honor a perfectly ordinary smile. 'I need a cushion to get through these events. Everyone's so clever and there are so many politics, you feel you're on the verge of saying the wrong thing all the time. Can I pour you one?'

'No, thank you,' says Honor. 'Water will be fine.'

Wendy is petite, with a tidy figure and hair tied back into a ponytail. She wears hooped earrings. Wendy fills a glass from the tap and hands it to Honor, and Honor looks at the gold and diamond engagement ring that Wendy is wearing. The ring he chose. He gave it to her and asked her to marry him.

It is a perfectly ordinary ring.

'I've heard so much about you from Paul,' says Wendy. 'He says you're absolutely brilliant, one of the finest minds he's ever encountered. I've never heard such praise from him.'

Is there a meaning underneath what she's said? Honor searches Wendy's face, but can't find it. But then she doesn't know Wendy, for all her ordinariness. Wendy could mean anything.

'It's very nice of him,' says Honor. 'Paul is the brilliant one, of course. Is he in?'

'He's nipped out with the children to pick up some more food for the barbecue. Well, he's taken two of them – the littlest is upstairs with a cold. They always seem to pick up a bug when you've got plans or you're entertaining, don't they? Do you have children?'

'No,' says Honor.

That morning the doctor confirmed the test results. Ten weeks pregnant, nearly through the first trimester already. 'At thirty-five, you're a bit old to be having a first baby, Miss Levinson,' he said, and Honor had not corrected the title. 'You're what we call an elderly primigravida. But you're healthy as a horse, so I shouldn't worry.'

From counting backwards, Honor has deduced that this baby was conceived in Paul's office one lunchtime, with the blinds drawn over the windows, Honor burying her face in Paul's neck to keep herself silent. When she opened the door to leave him afterwards, her hair pinned back up, her clothes straightened, there was a student waiting outside. She couldn't know how much, if anything, he had overheard. But nothing has been said, not yet. She has not heard anything, at least, and she can't tell if the glances she is receiving from other staff are significant, or not. She has always received glances.

She will receive more, soon, when she begins to show.

'But you've got a career,' says Wendy. 'So that must be rewarding. How does it feel, though, to be in that men's club? They're all men, aren't they? Except for the secretary. I would go spare.'

'I don't mind. I like men.'

Wendy finishes her gin and tonic and looks at it ruefully. 'I'm going to be sozzled before anyone turns up at this rate. Would you mind putting some veg on these kebab skewers?'

Honor is trying to get a grip on a slippery cherry tomato when the front door opens and she hears feet running towards the kitchen. 'Mum, can we have an ice cream now?' yells a tow-headed girl in shorts, crowding up to Wendy. A second equally blonde girl follows, holding a tub of ice cream.

'Your father is such a pushover,' says Wendy. 'Did he remember the sausages as well?'

'Yeah, he—'

And then Paul is there, in the kitchen, wearing a shirt open at the collar, holding a plastic bag, saying 'Do you doubt me?'

He stops. He looks at Honor, and immediately away. Then back again, with his face prepared. He does not meet her eyes.

'Oh, hello, Honor, I didn't know you were here already.' He kisses her briefly on her cheek and Honor feels his lips, smells the tobacco and coffee and flowers. Remembers the last time they were together alone, in a B&B near Chipping Norton. How they made instant coffee and talked about Heidegger, his hand resting on her naked breast. Two weeks ago. Honor had started to suspect then, but she hadn't had a test yet.

'Has Wendy put you to work?' he asks.

'Anyone who walks into this kitchen gets put to work.'

Wendy takes the plastic bag and peers into it. 'Oh Paul, you got the wrong sausages.'

'There's such a thing as wrong sausages?'

'Yes, nobody likes this kind. And I asked for two packets. Honestly, Paul, I'm nervous as a cat already, I don't need to be worrying about the sausages.'

'I'll go back to the shop.'

'No, people will be here in a minute.'

'Mum, can I have an ice cream?'

Honor wipes her hands on a tea towel and says, 'I will just find the loo if you don't mind.'

'Upstairs, first door on the landing,' says Wendy, going to the refrigerator.

This house is full of things. Books, records, flowers, furniture, pictures. A relationship shored up with objects and history. Honor walks through the rooms and thinks, *Everything in this room has its story in their marriage, a private story not accessible to outsiders. Wendy gave Paul this; he chose this to please her; this was a wedding gift; their firstborn made this in school.*

Honor and Paul have no setting together. They meet in hotels and in his office, and once – only once – in her flat. She can't picture them with a chintz sofa, a ceramic ashtray, a cot upstairs. A narrative behind things.

She touches a photograph, framed in silver, next to the Spitfire model. It's a posed photo, taken in this room from the looks of it: Wendy, Paul, the three girls, two blonde, the youngest with dark hair like Paul's. Wendy wears pink lipstick and a flowered frock. From the length of Paul's hair and the size of the children, it was taken a few years ago. Perhaps around the time that Honor met Paul. There's no trace of it in his face in the photograph, though: no sign that he's met a

230

woman he desires. He's just smiling. An ordinary father. An ordinary house.

Honor is reflected in the glass. Her face is severe, with its prominent nose and chin, its high cheekbones. Her eyes are dark, her black hair pinned up at the back of her head. She has recently found threads of silver in it.

A sound comes from the corner of the room, and Honor starts. A third child is curled up on the sofa. The smallest girl, with the dark hair. She cuddles her doll and sucks her thumb.

'Hello,' Honor says to her. After a pause, the girl removes her thumb from her mouth.

'My mummy and daddy told me not to talk to strangers.'

'A very good policy.'

Paul enters the room; she feels it as a shift in the temperature of the air. She is sensitive to his every movement, as she has been since the moment she first saw him.

'I've got to go back to the shop,' he says, and catches Honor's wrist in his hand. 'Listen,' he begins softly, and Honor tilts her head towards the child. He drops her arm.

'Are you feeling any better, Alice?' he says to the child, going to her and sitting beside her. He puts his hand on her forehead, a gesture he has done a thousand times, and in that gesture Honor sees it all. All the minutes and hours and days and years that she has not been part of.

The tenderness that he would give their child in her womb, this same tenderness, would steal from this child on this sofa right now. It would steal from the ordinary house, the ordinary woman in the kitchen giving ice cream to her two girls.

She lays her hand on her stomach, still flat. She closes her eyes and apologizes to her future baby for stealing from him, too.

'I'll go to the shop for you,' she tells Paul. 'You stay here.'

She walks out of the door and she does not come back.

Chapter Twenty-Six

Jo

Richard didn't return her calls asking if he could have the children that weekend. Lydia was out in the evenings – she didn't say where, just that it was something to do with school – and when Jo asked her if she and Avril could stay in one evening at theirs, Lydia just shook her head and turned up her music. Even after the children were asleep, Jo couldn't leave them in the house with Honor, because she couldn't get up the stairs if anything happened.

Saturday, Lydia had gone for a run despite the pouring rain, and who knew when she would be back. Her runs seemed to go on for hours, these days; it was a good release from exam pressure. Jo stood at the kitchen sink even though the washing-up was done, looking across the garden. Was he in? Could she slip out later, when Lydia was home?

'If you want to go out,' said Honor, 'I'm capable of looking after the children for an hour or two.'

She turned around, surprised. Honor was sitting at the kitchen table; she hadn't even noticed her coming in the room.

'Oh, I couldn't.'

'Of course you could. I've been in charge of children before, you know. I can't run after them, but we can do quiet things indoors.'

'But Lydia says you don't—' Jo stopped. There was no need to remind Honor that she didn't like young children. 'I don't have to go out.'

'You never have a minute to yourself. Don't think I haven't noticed. And being a martyr doesn't make you Mother of the Year. In fact, I'm pretty sure that award has never been handed out to anyone, ever, no matter whether they sacrificed their career and social life for their children or not.'

'I haven't sacrificed,' began Jo, but then why deny it? 'I've never had a career anyway. Working in a café and then for an estate agent isn't exactly high-powered.'

'Why don't you go out for a coffee, or to do some shopping? Meet up with a friend. Take advantage of live-in childcare. I'm not going to be here for ever.'

'I didn't invite you here to be live-in childcare!'

'But I'm right about the social life, aren't I?'

Jo didn't think that Honor had looked straight at her like this since she'd moved in. 'Yes,' she admitted. 'I don't get to have much fun. But it's not a sacrifice. I don't mind.'

'Of course you don't mind. Go out anyway. We'll be fine here. Have some fun.'

Jo regarded Honor carefully. She didn't suspect anything, did she? But Honor seemed unchanged, except for this offer. Her face was still stern, frowning slightly, as if she disapproved of Jo's life even as she was trying to help with it. Then again, if Honor suddenly started grinning, Jo would know that something was wrong.

It was ten in the morning. She didn't know what Marcus would be doing; he presumably had a social life of his own.

But she could try.

She brought all of Oscar and Iris's rainy-day toys downstairs to the living room. Jigsaws, board games, blocks, cuddly animals, cars. She put a changing mat and a supply of nappies and wipes on one end of the sofa, so that Honor wouldn't have to get down on the floor to change Iris. She prepared snacks in the kitchen, made sandwiches to put under cling film, enough for the two children and Honor too.

She ran upstairs and shaved her legs and changed her underwear.

When she got back downstairs, Oscar, Iris and Honor were all on the sofa. Oscar and Iris's heads were pressed together over the tablet that Richard had bought them. They were swiping and pressing to the tinny sounds of Angry Birds squawks. She kissed the children, but they barely looked up from their screen.

'Are you sure, Honor?' she asked, hesitating by the door.

'Go, already. I'll ring if there's a problem.' Honor didn't look up either. Jo escaped out into the rain. She wanted to run, but she forced herself to walk. Just a neighbour going to visit another neighbour for a getting-to-know-you neighbourly cup of tea.

Excitement rose in her, so strong she wanted to whoop. She skipped, stopped herself from twirling, quickened her pace. She leaped up the stairs to his front door, number 36, and knocked.

He might be out. He was probably out. In which case, she would have to go back home and get an umbrella and go somewhere else, the library maybe, or for a coffee. Like Honor

235

had suggested. She could ring Sara. Or look for a new pair of shoes. Marcus and she had texted last night, late into the night, but she hadn't heard from him today, so maybe he'd gone off her. Maybe it had taken too long.

For the first time it occurred to her that though they'd communicated almost constantly for the past few days, they'd never actually rung each other. Why not? Was ringing too serious? Was it too much of a commitment to actually talk to each other? She was being presumptuous, thinking that a few kisses in her kitchen and a few days' worth of sexting gave her licence to call on him unannounced, assuming that he would want to see her.

The door opened. Marcus wore jeans and a light-blue T-shirt and his face lit up at the sight of her. She felt her body light up, too.

'Oh wow, hi,' he said.

'I've only got a little while.'

He let her in and closed the door behind him. She was breathing hard. His feet were bare. There was music playing in the other room, something with guitars. They stood in his hallway smiling at each other. He was the same person who had been on her mind constantly for the past three days, except he was real.

She had absolutely no idea what to say or do. Small talk? Greeting? Grab him and rip his clothes off?

Should she have put on more make-up? Different clothes? High heels?

Suddenly she felt the weight of his entire life that didn't involve her at all. His job, all his thoughts, his friends and family, his music, what he liked to eat, the way he spent his hours. They had hardly exchanged a hundred real words with each other. All this time she had been burning to see a stranger.

'How are you?' he asked.

'Fine. Great. I'm sorry I couldn't get over before. What . . . have you been up to?'

He shrugged. 'Work. Marking. You?'

'Kids. Cooking. Cleaning.'

'Waiting for you,' he said. He stretched out his hand and touched hers. She curled her fingers with his. His palm was warm, slightly damp.

He couldn't be as nervous as she was?

She should ask for a cup of tea. They should sit down, at his kitchen table maybe, and talk. She should get to know him better. That was the natural order of things.

But somehow they'd stepped away from the natural order.

'Where's your bedroom?' she asked him.

He drew her to him and kissed her. It wasn't as frantic as their first kiss in the kitchen, nor as lingering as their last kiss outside the house. It was slower, more thorough. Still hungry.

'It's upstairs,' he murmured against her mouth. She nodded.

She followed him upstairs. She was trembling. Ahead of her, his backside was at eye-level, his soft jeans. She looked at his back, his shoulders in his T-shirt. The way his hair curled on his neck. His feet, bare, with slender toes. He was perfect, all of him. His skin would be smooth and flawless, his body lean and strong. Not a single thread of grey in his hair. Suddenly she knew what men felt when they looked at pictures in a magazine: images translating to desire.

I will look back on this and I will wonder if it really happened, or if it was a dream.

At the top of the stairs he led her into a room. White walls, double bed, blue duvet, white sheets. It was the room she'd looked at from her own bedroom, but she felt no sense of familiarity. There was a faint scent of his shaving lotion. The bed hadn't been made. She pictured him lying in it and she shivered.

He pulled her close. 'I've been going mad thinking about you,' he said, and began to kiss her again. He put his palm on the back of her neck, under her hair.

Jo closed her eyes. Then she opened them again. She drew back a little. 'Are you certain about this?'

He raised his eyebrows. 'Are you?'

'I'm . . .'

'We don't have to,' he said quickly. 'I wouldn't want you to do anything you're not comfortable with. I just thought, after everything you said . . .'

'I'm maybe braver in texts than I am in real life.' She stepped back to get a small bit of distance, so he wasn't touching her.

'What's wrong?'

She catalogued all the reasons that it was wrong in her mind, and chose the one that was the most obvious.

'It's that I'm forty. I'm forty, Marcus, I've had three children. I've got stretch marks. I've got boobs that look better with a bra on. Cellulite, and wobbly bits. I haven't done all the pelvic-floor exercises that I should do.' She winced. 'Maybe that's too much information. But I think you should know, I'm far from perfect.'

He put his hands on her shoulders. 'I don't need you perfect,' he said to her. 'I'm happy that you're here.'

'Have you . . . have you been with older women before?'

238

'Aside from kissing you the other day?' He smiled. 'Not that I'm aware of. Jo, I'm a grown man.'

'But I'm ten years older than you.'

He shook his head. 'Our age doesn't matter. You're beautiful.'

'You haven't got a fetish? A mother complex?'

'I told you, you're nothing like my mother. You're nothing like any mother I know.' He unbuttoned the top of her dress. His fingers stroked down her chest, between her breasts. He kissed her lips, lightly, and her chin; the side of her neck. She tilted her head helplessly, her body thrumming.

'I'm probably braver in texts too,' he murmured into her ear. 'But maybe we can be brave together.'

'How?'

His smile was crooked. 'Let's do what you said you wanted to, exactly as you said you wanted to do it.'

'I don't know if I—'

'I remember every word. Why don't you start with unbuttoning my shirt?'

She laughed, nervously. 'It hasn't got buttons on it.'

'Then take it off.'

He gazed at her, with the touch of a smile still on his lips. His blue eyes sexy, a hint of stubble on his chin. His room was bare, unmarked. Anything could happen in it.

'I want you to,' he said. 'I really want you to.'

Jo swallowed, and then she grasped the hem of his T-shirt with both hands. She had undressed people before. Men before. But not so boldly, not whilst talking about it, in full daylight, her eyes open to see everything and be seen.

She pulled his T-shirt up over his head. He raised his arms to help her and she saw the dark hair under them. She didn't know what to do with his T-shirt once it was off him, so she handed it to him and he dropped it on the floor.

He wasn't smiling now. He looked very serious. 'Then you said you wanted to touch me,' he said.

She reached out a hand. Her fingers were unsteady. She touched his bare shoulder, the smooth warm skin with the bones and muscles underneath. Slowly, she slid her palm downwards. He had hardly any hair on his chest. She touched the soft jut of his nipple, the ridges of his ribs. His belly was firm, moving rapidly with his breaths. She slipped the tip of her finger into his navel.

'Then, I said I wanted to undress you.'

He did, button by button. He slipped her dress off her shoulders and let it fall next to his T-shirt. He did not kiss her, but looked at her. He unfastened her bra and eased it from her. He pushed her knickers down her legs, kneeling as he did so.

Jo could barely breathe. Her cheeks were aflame. She looked down at herself and saw the pale loose skin of her belly, the mark her bra strap had left. She saw Marcus's curly head next to her hip, felt his breath on her, wondered if he would kiss her or touch her and take what they did into his hands so she wouldn't have to think about it.

He stood. He looked her up and down and Jo had to fight to keep from apologizing. There was a mirror behind her; she had seen it when she'd come in the room. She would not look into it. She would try to see herself in his eyes.

She saw his throat working as he swallowed. 'Now,' he said, his voice hoarse, 'you wanted to push me down on the bed.'

She did. She straddled him, her palms braced against the

240

hollows of his shoulders. She felt him hard against her, and she looked down into his face. Into his eyes, which never wavered.

Later, much later, she followed him downstairs, wearing his T-shirt and her lacy knickers. Her thighs were sore, her skin rubbed into contentment. She had glimpsed her face in the mirror before she left the bedroom: her flushed cheeks, her rumpled hair.

Marcus went into the kitchen to put on the kettle and she checked her phone in her handbag, which she had dropped on the floor near the front door, and then wandered into his living room. Like all of the rest of the house, it had white walls and a neutral carpet: the default new house blank decor. He had a squashy sofa and a scarred coffee table covered with folders of marking; a television and a stereo with a record deck. The CD he'd been playing when she came in had long since finished. There was a large cardboard box near the sofa, apparently filled with newspaper. She reached for it to see what was inside, but stopped herself.

'They're photographs,' he said, coming into the room. 'I haven't had the chance to put them up yet.' He gave her one of the mugs he held. 'Your cup of tea. Finally.'

'I think I liked what we were doing even more than a cup of tea.' She curled up on the sofa and he nudged beside her, his arm around her shoulders. He was only wearing his boxer shorts. She couldn't resist running her hand up his thigh, watching how the hairs, stroked against the grain, stood up and clung to her palm.

'Where are the kids?' he asked. 'With their father? I was too distracted to ask.'

'With Honor. My mother-in-law. She hasn't rung, so I assume they're fine.' She hoped they were fine; guilt threaded into her gut. She could run back and check.

But actually, Honor was right. She did deserve some time for herself. 'What are the photographs of?'

'You're welcome to have a look.'

She knelt by the box and lifted the framed photos out, one by one, dreading the photographs of old girlfriends. But they were landscapes: bleak and rocky, ice and water. Some black and white, some colour. A blue interior of ice, a red and black lava field, a scooped-out green valley.

'You took these?'

'I've spent quite a few holidays in Iceland. I love the geology. This one.' He reached past her and took out a photo: it was white and blue curves, like the spiral of a snail shell. The scale was impossible to determine. 'I have a thing about glaciers.'

'So the teaching is a hobby?'

'The teaching is a job. The glaciers are a hobby. The mass, and how slowly they move, and how they change the environment. Mountains literally moved by water. It puts everything in perspective.' He laughed. 'All the rest of my family like to go somewhere warm on holiday. My mum calls me a penguin.'

'Penguins aren't in Iceland.'

'Well, my mum isn't always scientifically accurate.' He put the photo down. 'Anyway, there. You've discovered my dark secret.'

'That's it? Glaciers?'

'You're right, glaciers aren't a secret. My Year Sevens are sick of me banging on about them.' He grinned at her. 'You're my only secret.'

242

'I think you're mine, too.'

'That means we have a lot in common.'

No, she thought. *We have each other in common, and that is all.* She picked up the photo he'd laid down. 'You should put these up. They're beautiful.'

He gestured at the clean walls. 'It's my fear of damaging the house. Also, I haven't got a great eye. I've had them framed, but I wouldn't know where they'd look best.'

'I'll help you do it,' she said, and then blushed. Here she was, at his house for the first time, having made love with him once and exchanged some texts, and she was pushing herself forward into his life. Offering to help decorate his house, to help him become domesticated. As if she were his mother.

'Like you need more jobs to do, right?' he said. 'Come here.' She went willingly onto his lap. He slipped his hand underneath his T-shirt that she wore.

'You want to again?' she asked.

'And again, if we have time.' He nuzzled her ear. 'Tell me a secret. Something about you I don't know yet.'

'I'm only a mum,' she said, kissing his shoulder, the hollow of his collarbone. 'I'm not the kind of person who sneaks out on a Saturday to meet her lover.'

'I'm not either,' he said. 'But now we both are.' He laid her back against the cushions.

When she let herself into her house, even later than that, her body weary and singing, Oscar and Iris were in the same position, bent over the tablet.

'You're back,' said Honor. 'Did you have a good time?'

Marcus's hands on her breasts, his mouth on the curve of

243

her hip. Suddenly she was conscious of her chin and neck. They must be red from the stubble on Marcus's face.

'Yes, very nice,' she said, putting her hand over her chin in a pose she hoped looked thoughtful rather than embarrassed. 'Have you had lunch?'

'Not yet.'

Jo perched on the arm of the sofa, next to Oscar, and ruffled his hair. So fine and soft. 'You haven't been playing on these the whole time, have you?'

'The birds hate the pigs, Mummy!'

'No,' said Iris.

'We've been fine,' said Honor.

'It's just . . . normally we try to limit screen time.' She winced as she said it. She knew it was her own guilt talking.

'Why?'

'It's — you know, it's not recommended for children to spend too much time on the computer, or watching television.' *It's also not recommended for children to be abandoned whilst their mother carries on a torrid affair with the next-door neighbour.* 'I usually give them an hour a day.'

'The ability of the middle classes to punish themselves is incredible. If tablets had existed when I was their age, I would never have got off the sofa. And I hardly think that I'm intellectually disadvantaged.'

Jo rubbed her chin. 'I'll get lunch, shall I?'

Chapter Twenty-Seven

Lydia

*T*his is what love feels like.

It's a burning in your chest. A free fall through whooshing air. It's an itch in your skin which can only be soothed by touching. It's how you store up every little word and expression and hoard it for later, when you can go through it in your head and look for the coded messages. It makes you greedy and jealous and resentful and sad. It makes you hate the person you were born as – a jigsaw with a piece out of place where your heart should be.

No. I want to think about the good parts, not the bad parts.

Love gives everything another meaning, another layer on top. It means that even a wave or a smile is significant. It makes food taste better; it makes air delicious. It makes the blood pumping through your body feel like a miracle. And when you think about it, how unlikely is it that out of all the atoms in the universe, they have somehow combined to make both you and the person you love, and that chance has brought you together to be on the same patch of Earth at the same time as each other. There must be a million reasons why you should never have existed, why you should never have met. And yet you did, one morning at the school gates when neither of you had anyone but each other.

Sometimes I think about fate. If Dad hadn't died, if Mum hadn't married Richard, I would never have met Avril. Maybe I would have been happier. We would never have moved, or maybe we'd have gone back to Cambridge and maybe I would have met a girl who could have loved me back. Maybe I'd be out; maybe I would have told Dad and he would have told Mum and everything would be calm now, no scene or worries. Maybe I would feel normal, or as normal as I ever could.

But I would never have met Avril. Never seen her smiling at me across a crowd, never shared secrets and bags of crisps, never linked arms or held hands or breathed next to each other at night. And the thought of that is worse than the thought that I've missed maybe being happy, maybe in another time, another place.

Since I've met her, every April has been her month. I haven't told anyone; like so many things about Avril, it's my secret. I watch the trees and flowers bud and spring into new life and I'm always happy. It feels like the world is starting over again and that something has been renewed in me.

If I love her, if I truly love her, I want to love her no matter what. I want to understand it for the miracle it is. I want to love her without being greedy, without being jealous. In a pure way. In the best way, without any consideration of my own happiness.

Can you even love that way, in the real world? When you're itching and burning and hurting? When all you want to do is scream and kick things and rail against the fact that Avril was born without that thing that I have that makes me love her?

This is what love feels like. It feels hopeless and helpless, like holding on to a slippery rock in a churning sea. And I wouldn't give it up for anything.

I wouldn't.

★ ★ ★

'What are you writing about?' asked Bailey, and Lydia shut her notebook.

'Nothing. Just some formulae.'

The bell had gone and everyone else had left the Maths classroom, but Bailey lingered by Lydia's desk. 'It looked like words, not numbers.'

'I think better in words. Sometimes I write down the problems in words so I can understand them better.' She stood and began shovelling her books into her bag.

'I was wondering if maybe, if you'd like to come over to mine today maybe after school,' said Bailey.

Today? Seriously? Their last day before exam leave, their last day of proper school ever, before exams and the sixth form?

'I don't know. I think I'm doing something with Avril.' She was doing something with Avril: a party at Sophie's house, while her parents were working late. It had been planned weeks ago. Harry would be there.

'Avril could come too. I like Avril.'

'Everyone likes Avril,' snapped Lydia, and walked out of the classroom, Bailey tagging along with her.

'Well, just let me know,' said Bailey. 'You could stay for tea and stuff if you wanted. My mum makes this really good pizza. It's gluten free but you'd never know it.'

From the corridor behind them, a burst of laughter. It sounded like Erin's.

'Maybe,' said Lydia, and as soon as they got to the door of the Maths block, she peeled away, walking rapidly across the school yard towards Geography, even though it was break. She wanted a few minutes on her own. If worse came to worst, she could go into Mr Graham's room. He never locked it and she could pretend to be doing some extra revision.

A group of Year Sevens came chattering out and after them, Mr Graham. He was reading something on his phone and when he saw Lydia he stopped, staring at her for a minute as if he couldn't quite place her. Then he smiled, as he always did. The younger kids called him Mr Grin because everyone knew the rule that new teachers weren't supposed to smile for the entire first term they taught at a school, so that all the students would think they were mean. Mr Graham had smiled right away, in his very first tutor session with Lydia's group. He wanted to be liked. It was a weakness in a teacher, and he got some stick from some of the boys in her year because of it, but you couldn't exactly tell a teacher they should be less nice. They had to figure out those things for themselves.

'How's it going, Lydia?' he asked her and she smiled back at him, a fake smile, but he'd never know that, because it was the same fake smile she'd been giving everyone.

'Good,' she said.

'Were you coming to see me about something?' He stuffed his phone in his pocket, almost guiltily, and Lydia wondered if he'd been looking at porn on it or something. Glacier porn. Girls posed on icebergs. She and Avril had a joke about it, like they had a joke about Miss Drayton's inappropriate fixation with all the sexual metaphors in every single thing they read.

'No,' she said, 'I was just going to dump my stuff before the lesson.'

'Oh, OK. Go ahead, be my guest. I'll be back in a minute.' He smiled again, even broader than the last smile, and walked off rapidly to mainline caffeine or whatever it was that teachers did in their staff room during break time. She watched him go, and then slipped round the building past the shrubbery, to the place near the fence where sometimes people went for fags.

She didn't recognize them at first: it was just two blue jumpers and a mass of dark hair leaning against the brick building, on the blank side without any windows. Then she saw his black trainers, her long legs, his hand up her top, rucking it up so that Lydia could see a glimpse of smooth belly. The abandoned bags with the keychain Lydia had given Avril lying on the ground. Then she saw their faces, properly saw their faces: eyes closed, mouths pressed together.

The bottom fell out of her stomach. She bit her lip to stop from making any noise and backed away. Their faces hung in front of her, the little moist sounds their lips were making as they snogged. Her back hit something – at first she thought it was a tree or a post, but then it laughed and she smelled stale cigarettes and it was Winston Anthony, saying 'Watch where you're going.'

Lydia fled to the girls' cloakroom. There was a queue – there was always a queue at break time, and more girls standing at the mirrors doing their hair – but she pushed through and took the final cubicle, ignoring the protests of the other girls. She sat on the toilet with her head in her hands while they complained loudly about her. She thought she might be sick.

She knew they snogged, she knew it was happening. Why was it so bad to see it? His hand up her top, the way his legs were spread and planted on the ground as if he owned it.

She sat there until the end of break and then went to Geography, where Mr Graham said something to her that she didn't hear, and where Avril came in late, breathless and pink-cheeked. She poked Lydia on the shoulder as she passed and Lydia just looked down at the practice exam that Mr Graham had given back to her, as if she were more interested in his pencilled-in comments than in anything else.

It was the last day of proper school, the last day they were still children.

'So, can you?'

Bailey was waiting for her outside the school gates. Avril had gone to Sophie's; all the girls had gone, but Lydia had pretended she needed to talk with Mr Singh about something so she told her to go on ahead with Erin and Sophie and she'd catch up.

'Can I what?' Lydia asked.

'Can you come over to mine?'

Bailey was alone. She was still wearing those goddamn ankle socks. From the expression on her face she had been thinking of nothing except for this question since she'd asked it this morning. Did she even know about Sophie's party? No, she couldn't. She had a round face with freckles, light blue eyes and a crooked fringe, and in the inflection of her voice and the wrinkle in her forehead Lydia could see every inch of her loneliness. Imagine being so eager for a friend that you had to wait by the school gates just to have someone to talk to. Imagine if being a puppy dog was preferable to being alone.

Lydia had never been alone. Not since she'd met Avril at these same gates, going in. Since then, she'd never had to be afraid of being alone.

Until now.

'Fine,' she said to Bailey. 'I'll come over for a while. I just have to text my mum.'

Bailey nearly sagged with relief, though she had the good sense not to show it for more than a split second. 'OK, that's cool. Let's go.'

Lydia texted her mum as they walked, and Bailey got out her phone too and made as if she were checking it for messages, but there obviously wasn't anything there, so she put it back. Lydia considered texting Avril, but she couldn't think of anything natural to say, anything normal. Anyway, Avril wasn't likely to miss her if Harry was there.

'My mum will be at work,' Bailey told her. 'She works in IT and my dad is an engineer. What about your mum and dad?'

'My mum doesn't work and my dad is dead.'

'Oh,' said Bailey.

'He died ten years ago.'

'Oh, OK,' said Bailey, clearly relieved. 'What did he do before that?'

'He was a lecturer in Physics at the university.'

'We used to live in Southampton,' said Bailey. 'Before we moved here. My mum never minds if I have friends over. I used to have lots of friends over every day when I lived in Southampton.'

'Uh huh.'

'And we used to have pizza parties and sleepovers and stuff. I was really sorry to leave all my friends behind in Southampton. But we still stay in touch.'

Lydia nodded. Bailey, emboldened, continued.

'I used to have this one friend Susannah, you would have loved her. She was really sporty and clever and fun. We used to go shopping together, just hanging out and meeting other friends, for the whole day. On a Saturday. And we used to go to concerts and stuff.'

Lydia glanced at her from the corner of her eye. Did this Susannah actually exist? And if she did, was she really Bailey's friend, or just someone that Bailey wished were her friend?

'What kind of concerts?' she asked.

'Oh, you know. Everything. Susannah's dad played in a band, so he knows lots of musicians and we used to go to these local gigs for free. We were going to maybe go to Reading Festival together this summer but then we had to move. We might still go, though.'

'Uh huh.'

'Maybe you could come if you wanted.'

'Maybe.'

'You would like Susannah, I think you would be friends. And I had other friends, too. There was this one girl; Erin really reminds me of her. Do you think that Erin would think it was funny that I knew this girl in Southampton who was a lot like her?'

'How was she like her?'

'Oh you know, she was pretty like her. And popular. Always laughing. You know. Here's my house, it's this one here. It's really close to school, which is handy. That's why my mum and dad chose this one, though we looked at loads of them.'

Bailey's house was a semi-detached brick cube with diamond-paned windows, older than Lydia's and smaller, with a neatly trimmed lawn for a front garden and several inoffensive hedges near the white PVC front door. There were no cars parked in the drive and nothing to distinguish it from the other houses on Tennyson Road.

Bailey took a key out of her satchel and unlocked the door. 'Want a Coke?'

Lydia followed her through to the kitchen. Breakfast dishes were still in the sink and the refrigerator sported a large collection of novelty magnets in the shapes of pigs.

'Wow, someone likes pigs,' commented Lydia.

'Oh, I know, it's my mum, she's crazy about them. She has pigs on everything. It's pretty sad actually. Want to come up to my room?'

'OK.'

There were framed cartoons of pigs on the staircase wall. Near the top there was a large one, of three pigs, two large and one smaller. The caption read *Three Little Pigs: Alan, Charlotte, Bailey.* Lydia didn't see any particular resemblance to Bailey in the littlest pig, but she thought about Bailey posing for this picture with her mum and dad, all the time knowing that she was going to be drawn as a pig, not as herself, and she felt a wave of pity for Bailey, stronger than anything she'd felt so far.

'We can listen to music if you want,' said Bailey, pushing open the door to her bedroom with her elbow because she was holding cans of Coke in her hands. 'What do you like?'

'What do you have?'

'Oh, I can just find anything on Spotify.' She put the Cokes on the bedside table and opened up her laptop, which was on her bed. The duvet cover had pink polka-dots, like a little girl's. There was a matching shade on the bedside lamp and a pink fluffy rug on the floor, a collection of cheap make-up in front of the mirror. The walls were magnolia and there was only one poster on the wall, of Five Seconds of Summer. It was pristine.

'You like Five Seconds of Summer?' Lydia asked.

She felt Bailey gauging her quickly before the other girl replied, 'Oh, I used to, that's an old poster. I'm so over boy bands, you know?'

'Fair enough.'

'Susannah used to love them. She bought me that poster.'

'Why don't we listen to one of the bands you've seen at one of those gigs in Southampton? Did you buy the CDs?'

'Oh yeah, but the CD player on this is broken. I'll just go on Spotify. What do you like?'

'I like sixties' and seventies' stuff mostly. The Rolling Stones, the Kinks, Aretha Franklin.'

'Really?' There was a slight note of scorn in Bailey's voice. 'Nothing new?'

'My dad was crazy about all of that music and I still have all his CDs. I listen to them a lot, so it just became my favourite.'

Bailey shrugged. 'OK, that's cool. I'll make a list.' She cracked open her Coke and sat on her bed, fiddling with her laptop. 'Athena who?'

'Aretha. Aretha Franklin.' There was nowhere else to sit, so Lydia opened her own Coke and sat next to her. She looked around the room.

There weren't any CDs. Or books, or clothes littering the floor. There was nothing to show anything of Bailey's personality except for the little-girl pink things, and the one poster that you could buy off any website, nothing different from any other teenage bedroom anywhere else in the world. She wondered where Bailey's stuff was, if it was crammed into the wardrobe or hidden underneath the bed, in case someone actually came round. She wondered if Bailey had planned to invite her since this morning, and she'd prepared her room especially.

There was nothing here. Nobody. The pigs lining the rest of the house were weird, but they were at least *something*. This room reflected no personality whatsoever. She sipped her Coke and watched Bailey's profile as she chose songs online from the list that Lydia had given her. She saw all the hours that Bailey must spend in this room alone, experimenting with that make-up maybe, maybe surfing the net to keep up with people she used to know in Southampton, if they even existed.

She was lonely, and working so hard to hide . . . what?

'Those boys teasing you,' she said suddenly, though she hadn't planned to talk about it. 'You shouldn't let it show that it bothers you. If they don't get a rise out of you, they'll stop.'

'Oh, I know,' said Bailey, not looking up from her laptop, but colouring.

'Basically you just have to give them nothing to talk about,' Lydia continued. 'Either that, or just not give a shit at all.'

'I don't give a shit.'

You do, Lydia thought. *You give an enormous, colossal shit. And that's exactly what makes you their target.*

It made Lydia feel sad.

'There,' said Bailey, and the laptop started to play 'I Can't Get No Satisfaction'. She put it on the bedside table, under the lamp, and settled back on the bed next to Lydia, their backs against the wall. Their shoulders just touched. Lydia looked down at their legs: hers slim and tanned, Bailey's pale and shapeless, with those crumpled white socks.

255

'You know,' she said, 'your legs would look even longer if you folded down your socks, or didn't wear any.'

'Do you think so?'

'Definitely. And if you found black ones, they'd be even better. See what I do with mine? I fold them down over my heel so they don't show.' Lydia toed off her shoe and showed Bailey.

'Maybe I could try that, yeah.'

'And Avril showed me this thing you can do with eyeliner so it doesn't even look like you're wearing it, but it can really make your eyes look bigger. I can show you if you want.'

'Yeah, OK.'

Bailey sounded quite pleased. She took off her own shoes and tried folding her socks over her heel like Lydia did.

Lydia wasn't so foolish as to think that socks alone were going to make much of a difference to Bailey's life. But maybe if she felt more confident, if she looked like less of a victim, she would be able to resist the name-calling better. She might be able to make some of her own friends, instead of having to tag along with Lydia. Or maybe she could just relax and be herself.

'I don't think my legs are ever going to look as long as yours,' said Bailey.

'Well, that's because I run.'

'Ugh, I could never run.'

'It's not so hard, really. And after the first couple of times, it's fun. You just put on music and zone out. The girls on the cross-country team are pretty nice. You'd probably like some of them. It's an easy way to make friends.'

'Hmm. I'm not sure I could do it.'

'You can come running with me sometime. I'll help you.'

And that would not be fun, but who knew? Maybe Bailey would take to it, and she might join the team next year and make some friends.

Maybe you'll need Bailey as much as she needs you, said a little voice in Lydia's head. *If Avril keeps going out with Harry.*

'Is Erin on the team?' asked Bailey.

'Erin? God, no. She doesn't like being seen when she's sweaty.'

'I wonder if I should mention to Erin that I know this girl who is just like her. In Southampton.'

'Maybe,' said Lydia doubtfully. 'Could she be mean sometimes, like Erin?'

Bailey looked at her in confusion. 'I thought Erin was your friend?'

'Yeah. Ignore me. Do you want to try that eyeliner thing?'

Bailey nodded and got up to fetch her make-up. 'I Say A Little Prayer' came on as she sat on the bed, cross-legged, facing Lydia. 'This isn't bad. Sort of retro.'

'Yeah, it's . . . one of my favourite songs.' It was the song she played when she thought of Avril. Sometimes on her iPod, over and over and over again, as if playing it and listening to it were a prayer of its own.

Avril and Harry snogging in the bushes behind the Geography block. She swallowed hard.

'Anyway, close your eyes,' she said, picking out an eyeliner. Bailey tilted her head up so that Lydia could work on her. Lydia was slightly taller.

Bailey wasn't that bad-looking. Her face was round but her skin was good, smooth with hardly any spots. The paleness that looked pasty on her legs was more delicate on her face. Blue veins traced faint lines under her eyes. She had some freckles on her nose, and her eyelashes made fans on her cheeks. Her lips were plump, slightly open as Lydia stroked the eyeliner on her eyelids. Lydia put her left hand on the side of Bailey's face to steady it.

She'd done this same thing with Avril, her heart pounding so hard she could barely draw the eyeliner on. She'd allowed her thumb to briefly caress her cheekbone; Avril hadn't seemed to notice, but Lydia had wondered if she'd liked it.

She did the same thing with Bailey, feeling how soft her skin was. And then she felt silly. 'OK, open your eyes and look up now, I'll do the bottom.' Bailey opened her eyes and she met Lydia's gaze for a second, before she looked up. Her irises were pale blue, and her breath feathered on Lydia's wrist as she drew a fine line. Lydia was suddenly conscious of the pulse beating in Bailey's throat above her school shirt, how their knees were brushing each other as they sat close together on the bed.

'I know what it's like to feel that you don't belong,' Lydia said, keeping her voice conversational. 'I feel that sometimes, too.'

Bailey was still looking up at the ceiling.

'But you'll find someone who understands you,' said Lydia. 'You have to. There has to be *someone*. It would be too unfair if there wasn't.'

She'd finished drawing on Bailey's eyelids – she hadn't done a great job, to be honest – but Bailey was still staring up at the ceiling.

'I don't know who it is,' whispered Bailey. Her bottom lip wobbled.

Lydia dipped her head and kissed her on the mouth.

She was thinking of Avril: of sitting beside Avril as Avril

cried, of sharing a bed with Avril as Avril slept. Of the weekend at the seaside when she and Avril had sat side by side on the beach at night and made different wishes on the same shooting star. Thinking of Avril. Kissing Bailey. Her heart hammering and tears burning in her closed eyes.

Bailey's lips were slightly sticky. They were plump, softer than the lips of the boys that Lydia had kissed because she was pretending. Her skin was entirely smooth. Her breath tasted of Coke. She was the first girl that Lydia had ever kissed. Her first real kiss, with someone she didn't even love, thinking of the person she did.

Oh God, a mistake.

Her eyes snapped open and she drew away, quickly, to the end of the bed. Bailey was staring at her, wide-eyed, her mouth open.

'I'm sorry,' said Lydia. 'That was a stupid thing to do.'

'I don't—' said Bailey. 'I'm not—'

'I'm sorry. I don't know what I was thinking about.'

A tear rolled down her cheek. She wiped it away, hoping that Bailey hadn't seen it.

'Is that why . . .' said Bailey. 'Did you think that what they said was . . .'

'No! Of course not. It was a joke! But a stupid one. Anyway, I've got to go.' Lydia scrambled off the bed and grabbed her phone, nearly tipping her can of Coke over Bailey's laptop, but she caught it in time. 'Whoo! Close call,' she said cheerfully, in a voice that sounded just like her mother's to her ears. She shoved her shoes on her feet, feeling Bailey staring at her. Feeling her lips still warm. 'OK, well, see you around.'

She fled down the stairs, past the cartoon pigs, and out of the house. She ran down the street, ran in her school shoes as fast as she could with her hair whipping around her face and her bag bumping on her backside, ran until she was out of breath and rounding the corner of Shakespeare Drive into Keats Way, and only then did she realize that she hadn't told Bailey not to tell anyone what she'd done.

Chapter Twenty-Eight

Honor

Emma Bovary, arsenic.
Anna Karenina, train.
Maggie Tulliver, river.
Lucy Westenra, stake.
Tess D'Urberville, noose.
Porphyria, her own hair.
Desdemona, pillow.
Clytemnestra, son.

Fictional fallen women, a long line of them, all the way back to Eve and her apple.

For most of her life, Honor had learned about the world through reading. And in most of her reading, from a very early age, she had learned that if you were a woman, and you desired, you died.

And yet when she'd been a fallen woman herself – desiring Paul, snatching stolen moments with him – she had never felt so alive. For three years, she had been so happy she had glowed. Strangers had commented on it. She tripped lightly through life, the right words appearing on her lips, her body finally understanding why it was made. Her intellect had never been so sharp, her research never so instinctive. She had never felt she was doing wrong, never even thought of his obligations or her sins, until that evening when she visited his house and met his family.

Jo, with her secret liaisons with who knew what man, was less than subtle. She giggled over text messages and glided around the house, singing. She had a spring in her step, a sway in her hips. She whistled, picking up her children, changing nappies, scrubbing the surfaces, folding laundry. Honor could not see her clearly but she could see the glow; she could almost feel it emanating from Jo's skin.

Because the truth was this – despite Honor's reading, despite what men and a few chosen women had written for hundreds, even thousands of years: for a fallen woman, the right kind of falling was not torture. It was the best part of life.

And for most fallen women, the punishment wasn't death. It was living long after the falling was over.

They only read one Christmas card at a time. Sometimes she had Lydia read the letters twice through, and then after she was gone Honor pored over them again, the words jumping, but familiar enough, memorized. Last night Lydia had read her this:

'*I think about how precious my time with my children has been and I know that if your mother had told me of your existence, I would not have had the same time with my three girls. I would not have been able to play with them every day, or seen*

262

every small change as they grew. But I would have had time
with you. How can you choose between children? You're all
grown now, and it's too late, but I can't blame your mother. She
must have known that she could be enough for you.'

Lydia put down the letter. 'He forgave you.'

Honor reached out her hand for the letter, as if she could
absorb the words by touching them.

'I have yet to forgive myself,' she said.

'Are you certain you don't mind looking after them again,
Honor?' Jo paused in the doorway. She was nearly on tiptoe
from the force of the desire driving her out of the house.

'The physical therapist told me to stay active,' said Honor.
'It's either this or go out and join a netball team.'

Jo made a sound that was half a laugh, as if she couldn't tell
whether Honor was making a joke or not. 'Well, if you're sure.
It's a lovely day. There's a chair out in the garden if you want
to take them out there.'

'Stop fussing. Go.'

'And there are snacks in the fridge, some yoghurt. Oscar
likes the kind with no bits in, and Iris likes the kind with bits
in. And some cheese strings. And—'

'It is looking after children,' said Honor. 'Not rocket
science.'

'Well, to be honest, sometimes I think looking after
children is harder than rocket science. At least in rocket science you get to sit in a quiet room.'

'I can manage. Go.'

'I'll have my phone,' said Jo, and gave her children a last kiss
before she left them, as if she were leaving for a week, rather

than a snatched hour or two with her lover. To her surprise, Honor felt Jo swoop down and plant a kiss on her own cheek, too.

'Thank you,' she said, squeezing Honor's hand, and then she was gone.

Honor paused, taking this in. Had Jo ever kissed her before? Perhaps once in the early days, when she and Stephen were young and fresh in love. Or out of duty on their wedding day.

A little hand tugged at her sleeve. 'What are we going to do, Ganny H?' demanded Oscar.

'Honor,' she told him. 'My name is Honor.'

'OK, Ganny H. Can we play Angry Birds?'

Iris crowded up against her legs, too. Children had no sense of personal space. Their little bodies were warm against her and they smelled of milk and biscuits.

'Your mother said we shouldn't spend all our time playing video games.' But what did one do with children, how did one occupy them? 'Why don't you play with your toys for a few minutes and we'll work out what to do?'

'No!' said Iris, but both of them wandered off. Working in tandem, they pulled their toy box open and began excavating items.

It had been over forty years since Honor had been in charge of a very young child. Despite what she'd said to Jo, she had little idea of what it entailed. What she remembered best about her own early motherhood was that it had been hugely, overwhelmingly, despair-inducingly boring.

She had loved Stephen, desperately, from the moment he was born. And yet nothing in her life had prepared her for the tedium of feeds, cleans, burps, walks, sleeps. The lack of any time to herself, hardly any time to think. She was aching for Paul – even more so because Stephen looked just like him, right from the first. She wondered every minute whether she'd done the right thing in not telling Paul. She mourned the person she'd lost, even as she was caring for the person she'd gained.

And she couldn't work, of course. There were no lecture-ships available in London when she'd returned, and she couldn't bear the thought of writing to Paul to ask for a reference anyway. She'd decided to take a career break whilst she looked after Stephen. But the work had been her life, and without it, she felt invisible. Lost.

Her father was a revelation. Shimon Levinson changed nappies, prepared feeds, went for walks with the pram round and round Clissold Park. When Stephen could walk, he used to lead Shimon around by the hand. Her father brought his grandson to *shul* even though Honor protested that she was not bringing up her child in any superstitious religion – no, not even Reform. And then her father had his second heart attack, and she lost him, too.

When she'd thought about it since, she believed that she might have had a touch of post-partum depression, though it wasn't the sort of thing that was talked about then. Mostly it was the boredom, and the dark dragging time before dawn, and the days with hours and hours to fill with nothing. Waking up and thinking *Oh God, what shall I do all day?* The other mothers in the park were so young, so *married*.

She began to work when he was napping, once he was a toddler and settled into a routine. She began researching, reading, planning articles to write so she could build up her publishing history for when she was able to apply for a lecturing post again. In her head she would translate from Russian into English as they walked, as Stephen exclaimed over a bug or slipped pebbles into his pocket.

She remembered every moment, it seemed, of his life when he was older. But from those first three years, she remembered very little: sunshine in Stephen's hair, the rattle of pebbles in his pocket. She must have spent hours and hours with Stephen. She knew she had. Honor frowned and pressed herself to remember more; came up with the damp corner of a blanket that Stephen had sucked, the scent of sterilized glass bottles. The imprint of a hand on her cheek as she rocked him to sleep.

Hardly enough for three years.

She remembered better the corridors she went to in her own mind to avoid thinking about Paul, to avoid acknowledging to herself that motherhood was boring, that she was drowning in everyday tasks and lack of sleep and no conversations except for the concrete. To avoid thinking of the nights when she dreamed of that moment at the top of the staircase, looking downwards and seeing Paul standing there. To stop questioning herself about whether she was doing the right thing in not telling him.

When Stephen was three, she had taken up a part-time lectureship at University College London. Her colleagues stayed late, went to conferences, travelled for research, spent years on publications. She was passed up for promotion again and again, not because of her intellect or her academic rigour, but because her work had to fit around school hours and childminders. She was able to dedicate more hours to her work as Stephen grew, but she had lost ground. She never fulfilled the brilliant promise of her Oxford days, and

never had enough time to spend with her son, either.

Oscar and Iris were doing something complicated with wooden bricks, something that required Oscar to give his sister orders and for her to scurry back and forth with more and more bricks, fetching and carrying and dropping. Had she got down on the floor and played with Stephen, as Jo did with her children? Perhaps she had sometimes and didn't remember it now?

She hadn't. She had read with him, and talked with him, and when he was older they had gone on long walks together, to galleries, to libraries, through the cemeteries to learn names and dates.

Why hadn't she played?

A crash and a cry of dismay from Iris, and Honor hauled herself to her feet. Bricks littered the floor in every direction. If they stayed in much longer, the house was going to be a health hazard. 'We are going to the park,' she announced.

'No!' said Iris, jumping up and down and throwing a brick into the air with delight. It clattered to the floor, uncaught.

'Yes!' Honor told her, and the little girl laughed.

'Will you push me on the swings?' Oscar asked.

'Unless it kills me.' She considered the large bag that Jo took with her on all excursions with the children, and decided against it. 'Can you live with a dirty nappy for an hour, Iris?'

'No!'

No. The only power given to wilful toddlers and cantankerous old women.

'I can change nappies,' said Oscar.

Honor thought this was highly unlikely, but she nodded anyway. 'Then you will be in charge of nappies and I will be in charge of snacks.'

'Ice cream?' said Iris hopefully.

'Ice cream it is.'

'I will bring all of my trucks!' declared Oscar and he started off to get them. Honor stopped him with a hand on his tiny shoulder.

'Think this through,' she told him. 'You are small, and your sister is smaller. Your truck-carrying capability is not as large as you may think. Meanwhile I am elderly.'

'What's elderry?'

'Old. I'm old. And unable to carry every one of the dozens of trucks that you possess.'

'Not if we take your purple scooter,' suggested Oscar slyly.

She put out her hand to touch the top of his head. He was very short: sturdy, with his mother's gingery hair and his father's husky voice. He wasn't related to Honor at all, which was perhaps why she had no impulse to correct him. What she did with him and said to him was unlikely to matter. She would probably be gone by the time he was of an age to remember her.

'You,' she said, with new respect, 'will go far in life.'

'I will go to the *park*.'

'No!' yelled Iris. She jumped up and down and shook her head, her dark curls bouncing. 'No, no, *no*!'

'"No" may seem like a rational and attractive proposition when you are two,' Honor said to her, 'but when you get to my age, you will realize that you have to take the opportunities that life throws at you, before it is too late. Perhaps even after it is too late.' She clapped her hands together, and for the first time in a long time, she felt something small tickling inside her chest. Something a bit like anticipation. 'Shall we fire up the scooter?'

Oscar led them straight to it, marching across the garage like a little soldier on a mission. He put the large fire engine that he was carrying into the basket at the front of the scooter. 'Can I drive?'

She found the button to open the garage door and then turned to Iris, who was chewing on her sun hat. 'Can you get on the back of the scooter? And when I sit down, you will have to hold on to me.'

'No,' said Iris, nodding, and clambered onto the seat.

'Can I drive?' Oscar asked again.

'No,' said Honor. 'But you can do something better. Do you have sharp eyes, Oscar?'

'I have *really* sharp eyes. I can see *everything*.'

'Good. That's exactly what I need.' She stooped down as far as she could, lowering her voice confidentially. 'I need you to stand in front of me on the scooter, with your hands on the handlebars. And you need to keep a sharp eye out for things in front of us. Things we might crash into. Can you do that?'

'Yeah!'

'Well done.' She climbed onto the seat, reaching her arms either side of Oscar, perching on the edge of the seat to leave room for Iris. She found the starter switch by feel, and started the electric motor. The children squealed in excitement.

'Can we go fast?' asked Oscar.

'Fortunately, we cannot.' She positioned her hand on the throttle, ready to go. 'Now, hold on tight, children.'

'No!' cried Iris into her ear.

The scooter jerked forward. She steered towards the light. 'Now, do we go left or right to get to the park?'

'Left! No, right!'

Something occurred to her, and she slowed the scooter to a crawl. 'Do you know the difference between left and right, Oscar?'

'Umm . . .'

'Ah.' She stopped the scooter. After a moment's thought, she unbuckled her watch from her wrist and put it on Oscar's left wrist. 'So if we need to steer in the direction of the watch arm, you say "watch". And if we need to steer the other way, you say—'

'No watch!'

'Very good. So which way is the park?'

Oscar considered. 'No watch way.'

'Right it is. Tell me when we've reached the pavement, Oscar.'

His hair tickled her chin as he nodded. She started up the scooter again and proceeded forward at a crawl, listening to the gravel under the wheels, until Oscar announced, 'Now!'

She steered right and the scooter ran smoothly off the drive onto the pavement. 'Now, Oscar, it's your job to tell me if we're going to bump into anything. All right?'

'I'm *very* good at this,' said Oscar.

'I'm certain that you are.'

The park was less than a quarter of a mile away and entailed crossing two roads. Oscar guided her to the dipped kerbs, using his watch hand, and together they checked for traffic, Honor hushing the children so that she could listen. At the second crossing, Iris started bouncing on the seat and yelling, 'Park!'

'You must be quiet and calm, so that your brother and I can concentrate,' Honor told her, and Iris immediately subsided.

'Can you see any cars coming, Oscar? Look carefully.'

'No cars, Ganny H.'

'No cars!' agreed Iris.

Honor thumbed the throttle and they rolled off the kerb. 'Pa–ark,' sang Iris, in her ear, and Honor saw movement to their right. Belatedly, she heard the car coming: a low hum of engine, hardly louder than the scooter's electric whine.

Where was the brake, how did she stop? She yanked her hand from the throttle and the scooter jerked to a halt. Iris banged against her back.

'Ow!' yelled Oscar.

She heard the car pass in front of them. It was close enough so that she could feel the breeze it created, and smell its warm tyres.

'I think,' she began, and realized that she had no breath to speak with. She waited until she could breathe again, and said, 'I think this may be more dangerous than I anticipated.'

'I'm OK,' Oscar told her. 'I just bumped my arm. Can I press the button to make it go?'

'No,' said Honor. Her hands were shaking slightly as she started up the scooter again. She listened carefully and turned her head to either side several times before she crossed the road and rolled onto the pavement leading to the park. Slowly, steadily, the scooter's engine labouring against the slight incline, they made their way to the play area. Both the children jumped off the scooter.

Honor's heart was still hammering. Her palms were damp.

'I help you,' said Iris, and Honor felt a little hand creep inside hers. She let Iris assist her getting off the scooter. Oscar held the gate open for them and then the two children were off, running and shouting to each other, into the grey area where she couldn't see.

'Stay inside the play park,' she called to them, and followed the fence along counterclockwise until she found a green-painted bench to sit on. She could hear the children talking to each other.

As always, she caught the park in snatches: there was some sort of rubberized matting on the ground, presumably to make children bounce when they fell. A tracery of lines and shadow was a climbing frame; a sense of pendulum movement was the swings. She tipped her head up and felt the sunshine on her forehead and cheeks, letting it calm her. Little footfalls and chatter and laughter.

They had made it safely, and they would make it back. She would be careful. But perhaps after this, they should stay in the garden.

She laughed aloud, surprising herself. Who would have thought, at her age, that she would be embarking upon adventures? Or that those adventures would be so small and yet so important?

Someone sat beside her and she heard a conversation between two mothers about their holidays, the renovations that mother number one was doing to her house, the car that mother number two was planning to buy. This was closely followed by what both of them were planning to cook for tea tonight and a detailed exploration of what each of their toddlers would and would not eat. Allegedly Liam would not eat any food that was not white, whilst Ella would not touch anything that could not be spread with Nutella, because it rhymed with her name.

If this was the level of discourse that Jo had to tolerate on a daily basis, it was no wonder she was carrying on an affair.

'Ice cream, Ganny H,' said Iris's voice suddenly close beside her.

'Can you take me to the ice-cream van?' she asked, and was answered by Iris clasping her hand again and tugging. She stood, and her other hand was seized by Oscar.

She let them lead her, like a child, to the ice-cream van, where she bought three large 99s with Flakes, selecting the coins by feel. Then she let them lead her to another bench. The children sat on either side of her, their legs pressed against hers, their elbows bumping hers as they all ate their cornets together.

She had rarely tasted anything so delicious.

Chapter Twenty-Nine

Lydia

It was strange, having this weight of stuff to do, all the revision for the exams that would determine the rest of her life, but nothing to do right this very moment, nothing to do but think. Lydia coloured in her revision timetable with the highlighters that Mum had bought for her, took a shower, styled her hair. She rearranged her collection of Avril's cranes that sat perched on the shelf over her desk. She'd lost one or two in the move upstairs, but there were still a lot of them, all different colours and sizes. Their wings trembled as she moved them, delicate and beautiful.

She felt like she'd betrayed their friendship by kissing Bailey. How crazy was that?

This room was so quiet. You couldn't hear anything that was going on downstairs, nothing at all. All the noise used to annoy her, but now she missed it. She felt cut off from everything.

I just want to be normal, Avril had said. *Is that so wrong?*
Promise to always tell me the truth.

Lydia sighed and reached for her running clothes, but then

she thought twice about it and went downstairs to Granny H's room. 'Come in,' said Granny H to her knock, but when she entered, her grandmother was lying on her bed, fully dressed, her eyes closed.

'Are you taking a nap?'

Granny H didn't open her eyes. 'No, merely revisiting some memories.'

'Where's Mum?'

'She is outside with her friend Sara and the children.'

'Oh. I was just taking a break from my revision and I wondered if you wanted to read another letter?'

'We only have one left.'

'We can read it later, there's no hurry.' But Lydia wanted to read it now. Avril hadn't answered her texts; she was losing her. She wanted some connection, something to feel that she belonged, that she was necessary in some way. Even if it was reading letters from a man she'd never met, to a grandmother whose life was largely a mystery.

'They're in the desk.'

Lydia found them in the top drawer. If it had been her, she would have opened them all up at once and read them, but Granny H seemed to want to eke them out. She supposed that if that was all you had of someone you loved, you had to make them last. Like a collection of paper cranes.

She took out the last unopened one and drew a chair close to the bed before she opened it. 'It's another robin card,' she said. 'In fact, I think it's the same robin card as he used the year before. Maybe he had a lot left over. Don't you want to look?'

'I can imagine it. Please read it to me.'

Lydia opened the card. It was dated two years ago, and she

275

wondered again why Paul Honeywell (her grandfather, though it was hard to think of him that way) had stopped writing. Had he died, or had the letters just stopped being forwarded? Or had he got so tired of writing without a reply, so tired of trying and trying, that he'd given up?

She thought of the paper cranes again, and she had to clear her throat before she began reading the letter aloud.

'*Dear Stephen,*
'*Do you receive these letters, I wonder? Year after year I write them, and I picture you throwing them straight in the bin. I suppose I'm writing them for myself rather than for you, perhaps to assuage my guilt at never knowing you. Even choosing to write them in Christmas cards is selfish, because my family would never notice them in the outflux of post – but you're Jewish by birth and might not even celebrate Christmas. All of these letters might be nothing more than an unpleasant reminder for you of a person you never knew.*

'*Forgive me. Even though I may write these letters out of selfishness, I've tried not to be self-indulgent in them. But this has been a difficult year. Wendy died in the spring: cancer. She was a good woman, Stephen. I didn't deserve her, and I tried to be the best husband I could to her, which meant that I was no kind of father to you.*

'*In all our years together I was only unfaithful to Wendy once in either thought or deed, and that was during those years when I was with your mother. Every day I was with Honor I wished that I had met her first, before Wendy. In some ways I still wish it, though I was never brave enough to act upon it. I loved your mother more than life. I loved her more than any person except for my children. She was sharp and vibrant, in*

276

full colour compared to everyone else, and when I looked at her I saw the other half of myself.'

Lydia's voice stopped in her throat. On the bed, Granny H did not move. Lydia would have thought she had fallen asleep, except there was a fierceness about her, despite the fact that she lay on her back, eyes closed.

> *'I was the weak one in that relationship, and I was the weak one in my marriage, too. All of my love seems to be laden with guilt.*
>
> *'And now I really am being self-indulgent. I refuse to feel guilty about your existence, Stephen Levinson, or for the fact that I write to you, without any hope of return. You are one of my children, and I love you for that, and I love you for your mother's sake.*
>
> *'Your father, Paul Honeywell.'*

Granny H drew in a long breath and let it out. Lydia folded the letter. The dark writing seemed too much to look at, too naked on the white of the card. They sat, for some time, in silence, except for the sounds of Mum and Sara and the children in the garden.

'So,' said Granny H at last. 'Yes.'

Slowly, she sat up on the bed. Her eyes, now open, stared straight ahead, and seemed to be seeing someone other than Lydia, someone whom she loved and who loved her in return, so much so that they had spent nearly three of Lydia's lifetimes apart thinking of each other.

'I'm gay.' Lydia blurted it out without knowing she was going to.

Granny H blinked. She turned her head and looked Lydia up and down, in that odd sideways manner she had about her these days.

'I'm gay,' Lydia said again. 'I like girls. Not boys.'

'I know what gay means,' said Granny H, but she said it gently. 'Have you known for some time, or is this a new discovery?'

'I've always known, I think. Don't tell Mum.'

Granny H frowned. 'Why not? You don't think she would be so foolish as to disapprove, do you?'

'No – not exactly. I mean, not at all. But she'd say . . . I know what she'd say. She'd tell me that everything is all right and it's all going to be fine. That one day I'll look back on my feelings and wonder why I was so confused and hurt and it will all have just been a blip on my way to future happiness.'

'I think that is exactly what she would say. And yet it's not what you want to hear?'

'No. Because I don't want to have felt all of this for nothing. I don't want it to be a blip, part of the happy story that Mum makes up about the world. It's real.'

She sounded hoarse and frantic to her own ears. Granny H held out her hand and Lydia went to her, sat beside her, let her hold both her hands in her papery, dry, soft palms.

'It is real,' agreed Granny H. 'And it is not a happy story, not all the time. But there are compensations.'

Granny H held her hands and they both listened to OscanIrie playing outside. A high peal of giggling and the thunk of a ball against the side of the house. It sounded like another world.

'If his wife has died, you could see him again,' said Lydia.

'You mean that his wife was my blip?' Honor's voice was

dryly humorous. 'You are more like your mother than you admit.'

Lydia blushed. 'Sorry. I just . . .'

'You want a happy ending. But even though we read the stories, we are realists, you and I.'

Chapter Thirty

Jo

She couldn't believe his body. No — she could believe his body, only just; what she couldn't believe was that she was here in bed with him, not for the first time or even the second, side by side on their backs, on the bare sheet with the duvet pushed off onto the floor. They had been so eager that Marcus still had his socks on.

He pulled her over so that her head rested on his chest and she laid her hand on his flat stomach. His heart was still beating hard. She knew even from her brief experience that he would be ready to go again within half an hour. Even sooner, if she pushed the matter.

'Why are you smiling?' he asked her.

She raised her head. 'You couldn't see me smiling.'

'I felt it.' He stroked her hair back from her face. 'You're laughing at my socks, aren't you?'

'I was just thinking that the last time I slept with a man in his twenties, I was in my twenties myself.'

'I'm thirty next month. I think I want to eat cake in the rain. And then you can sleep with a man in his thirties.'

He smiled at her, then sobered. 'Was it Lydia's father?'

Jo nodded. 'Stephen.'

'How did he die? You don't have to tell me,' he added quickly.

'I don't mind. He died saving someone else's life.'

His hand had been idly playing with her hair, but it stilled. 'That's . . . amazing.'

'Stephen was like that.'

'Lydia knows?'

'Yes, of course. We're very proud of him, while at the same time missing him like crazy.'

'And your second husband . . . ?'

'Was an arsehole. Actually, I don't think I've said that aloud before. He's remarrying in July.'

'Yikes.'

She smiled at Marcus. She liked the 'yikes'. She liked that he asked about her husbands. She liked the way his hair curled on his forehead, and the laughter lines in his otherwise unlined face.

She liked him altogether more than was appropriate.

'And you?' she asked. 'Why haven't you found a nice girl and settled down yet?'

He shrugged. 'I was serious about one girl. She wasn't so serious about me.'

'Where is she now?'

'Tasmania.'

'Yikes.'

'Indeed.' He kissed her on the lips. 'My love-life history is embarrassingly brief.'

'Give it time.'

'I'm learning something new every day.' He kissed her longer, but Jo had to know, so she pulled away.

'What happened with the girl in Tasmania? If you liked her so much?'

'She wanted adventure. I wanted to stay at home and teach. I'm too nice for her, she said. Too boring.' He said it lightly, but Jo could see the pain: that he was hearing the girl's voice when he said the words. She knew they were the exact same words that his girlfriend had said when she'd left.

'I can't imagine you as too boring for anyone,' she said.

'That's what's miraculous about you, Jo. When I'm with you, I don't feel boring at all.'

'You're not. You're young and clever and ridiculously sexy.'

'And I've got a mortgage and a job and I mow the lawn every Sunday.'

'And carry on an affair with your neighbour.'

He laughed. His face was so sunny when he laughed.

'My friend Sara and her husband have been going through a bit of a dry spell,' Jo told him. 'I told her that maybe she should send him some sexy texts. Spice things up a bit.'

'Did it work?'

'He came home and demanded to know who she was having an affair with. He thought she'd sent them to him by mistake. But they had good make-up sex, so I suppose it did work.'

'You've told Sara about us, then?'

'Er . . . no.' And because he seemed to be expecting an explanation, she added, 'Not yet.'

He was watching her. She rolled onto her back to avoid his scrutiny, and caught a glimpse of the bedroom wall. She'd been too preoccupied to notice before, but he'd hung up his photographs of glaciers: six of them, across the wall of his bedroom. They were windows to other worlds. 'Oh, you hung them up.'

'It took all morning to get them straight.'

'They're beautiful.'

'You're beautiful.' He drew her closer against his naked body, and ran his fingertips lazily across her skin. 'Tell me something else about you. Not about your husbands, or about your friends – about *you*. What's your secret ambition?'

She squirmed. 'What's yours?'

'Polar explorer. Not going to happen: I'm not rich enough and too attached to my toes. I have to make do with a fortnight on a glacier every year. You can forget that humanity ever existed. I think that's why I like it so much. What's your secret ambition? Stop avoiding the question and tell me.'

'I used to want to go to university and train as a teacher.'

'You'd be good at it. You could do that, in a year or two, once the children are both at nursery. You could do it now, part-time in the evenings, and then you'd be ready to work when Oscar and Iris were in school.'

'No, it's been too long since I studied. I probably wouldn't be any good at it. Anyway, I'm always exhausted as soon as the children go to bed.'

'You don't seem exhausted to me.'

'Well, I'm sleeping these days,' she said, and was immediately surprised that she'd said it.

He propped himself on his elbow. 'What do you mean, *these days*?'

'I . . . I often get a bit of insomnia this time of year.'

'Why this time of year?'

'It's the . . .' She swallowed. 'It's the anniversary of Stephen's death, at the beginning of June. I wake up in the night and I think – Oh, this is going to sound really morbid.'

'You think of what, Jo?' he asked her quietly.

'I think of what his last moments were like. Whether he was frightened. I wasn't there, but I hear him screaming sometimes.'

His arm tightened around her.

'It wasn't perfect, our marriage,' she said. 'We had some difficult times. Honor idealizes him, and so does Lydia, and that's fine. It's wonderful actually, that they can do that. But sometimes I feel as if I'm the only one who knows the truth, and I have to keep it together for other people. And for Stephen, because he wouldn't want us to be sad. Those are . . . the kinds of things I think about late at night when I can't sleep.'

'But you said you were sleeping these days.'

'Yes.' She smiled at him. 'I'm sleeping much better. You're to thank for that.'

'I'm glad.' He sat up. 'Are you hungry? I'm starving. I was on lunch duty and I never manage to eat anything.'

'I have to get home and make the children's tea.'

'I've learned something about you by now, Jo. You've done their tea already, it's just waiting to be warmed up.'

'Yes, but Honor—'

He tilted up her chin. 'Ring her. Say you've been delayed. Come out with me for dinner.'

'Dinner?'

'Yes. You and me with our clothes on, talking to each other. Maybe a glass of wine. Like grown-ups. Fancy it?'

She fancied it so much she could taste it. 'We can't do that.'

'Why not?'

'Lydia? Your teaching position?'

'Dammit, you remembered.' A kiss. 'We could go out of town. A little country pub.'

'I don't have time.'

'I could make you dinner here? I make a mean spag bol.'

'I have to get back.' But her hand, seemingly by itself, slid down his belly, through the hair at his groin.

'But you have a little bit of time.'

'A little bit.' Her hand went lower, but she glanced at his photographs on the wall. All these places he'd been, this life he had lived, that she could never be part of. He was a stranger, still, aside from these stolen hours together.

'Do you still love her?' she couldn't help asking. 'The serious one, in Tasmania?'

'I . . . care about her. She changed me. It still hurts sometimes. I don't know. Is that love?'

'I think it is.'

'You still love Stephen. Despite the difficult times.'

'Yes,' she said. 'But I don't think about him all the time. Not . . . when we're doing this.'

His eyes closed briefly as she grasped him, but then they were looking into hers again. 'What *is* this, that we're doing?' he asked.

'I'd have thought it was self-evident.'

He caught her wrist and stopped her hand. 'I don't think it is entirely self-evident. I think you need to say.'

This, from a man ten years younger than she was, with a body and a recovery time that would put most men to shame. A man who didn't seem to realize his own power and beauty, who was nursing a bit of a broken heart, who was a good

285

listener, who travelled to glaciers so that he could be alone with their vastness.

And that smile, far too easy to like.

'I'm using you for your body,' she said. 'Haven't you noticed?'

She squeezed, and he groaned, so she did it again.

'Then go ahead and use me,' he whispered, tilting his head back and closing his eyes again.

Chapter Thirty-One

Honor

Handwriting was nearly impossible, so she had borrowed Lydia's laptop to touch-type. But the phrases that she had composed in her head felt wrong in her fingers. How could you tell a man that the son he had never known was dead? How could you explain the years of silence, the years of yearning?

She had been at it for hours and made no progress. Honor rose and went into the kitchen in search of a cup of tea. She was moving more easily, now; the pain was nearly gone, no more than a dull ache in the evenings, and she had dispensed with the cane, though she walked with an habitual shuffle in Jo's house, so as to avoid tripping over any toys. She had mapped out this house nearly as well as her own – knew how many steps to the kitchen table, how many steps to the kettle, the reaching distance to the mug cupboard. But the clutter shifted day by day.

Iris pattered over to her and hugged her leg. Honor let her hand rest on her silky curls. The kitchen was warm from the oven, and smelled of vanilla and butter.

'Ganny H, you can lick the spoon,' said Oscar, putting something wooden in her hand.

'That's all right, Oscar, you can lick it,' she said. 'My spoon-licking days are past.'

'I'm Ganny H's helper,' announced Oscar. 'Because I have good eyes.'

'Are you helping Mummy bake a cake?' Honor asked quickly.

'Two cakes!'

'Tea, Honor?' Jo's voice had a studied lightness to it. Honor nodded and sat at her seat at the kitchen table, letting the family move around her. They were glimpses of colour and shape, noises and scents, vanilla and sugar and jam, the hot mug of tea placed near her hands.

Someone knocked on the front door and it opened straight away. 'It's me!' called Jo's friend, Sara. 'Kids are in the car, can't stop, come on Oscar and Iris, we're on our way to the farm park to see the deer!'

A bustle at the door. Honor liked Sara, from what she had noticed so far. She had spirit and dark skin, which made her different from almost everyone else in this neighbourhood. 'Bye, Ganny H!' cried Oscar, running over and planting a kiss on her cheek, and then they were gone and it was quiet again.

'I'm going out as soon as the cakes are done,' said Jo, coming back to the kitchen and taking up her mixing bowl. 'And Lydia's gone to the library to revise today. So you'll have the house to yourself.'

'Are you going anywhere nice?' Honor didn't expect Jo to tell her about her lover, but she couldn't resist a little probe.

'It's . . . a friend's birthday.'

'It must be a very good friend, if you're making them two cakes.'

'One is for us. You can't make cake in this household without giving some to Oscar.'

Honor hesitated, knowing she had no right to ask, then said, 'You were awake last night.'

'Oh! You heard me? I hope I didn't disturb you.'

'I was awake. You are often up in the middle of the night.'

'I'm sorry. I try to be as quiet as I can.' Jo scraped batter into the tins. 'I . . . actually I thought it was getting better. I think I must be worried about today.'

Honor said nothing. She did not, as a habit, invite confidences from her daughter-in-law. But Jo seemed agitated as she put the cakes into the oven and washed up the bowl and spoons. Honor wondered if she was going to hear the story of Jo's affair, and she rather hoped it would not be tedious. Though it probably lacked illicit thrill, if Jo was making him a cake for his birthday.

Jo pulled out a chair and joined Honor at the table. 'Actually,' she said, sounding uncertain, 'you could come with me, if you like.'

'Come with you?'

'I'm . . . you may be angry about this.'

Honor said nothing, remembering her fury, cleaning the kitchen.

'I'm visiting Adam Akerele,' Jo said.

'Adam?' asked Honor, but as soon as she said it, the name clicked into place. 'You're not talking about Adam . . .' She had not said the name for ten years. She wasn't sure she'd even said it then. But she could see it in print, behind her eyelids, next to Stephen's. 'You visit *him*?'

'Only on his birthday. He's often lonely. I like to bring him a cake.'

The cake was not for her lover. It was for Adam Akerele. Honor clenched her teeth. 'You don't owe that man anything.'

'No, I don't, but I like to do it. I think Stephen would have liked me to. He's quite a vulnerable young man.'

'He killed Stephen.'

'Stephen died because of him. But it wasn't Adam's fault. He didn't mean to.'

'Outcomes matter. Not intentions.'

'Well, I think intentions matter as well. And it was difficult to see him at first. But then I saw how desperate he was, and how sad. And I thought: What did Stephen die for, if this young man's life is also miserable?'

'So you go to see him every year to cheer him up? Is that your mission?'

'I go to see him because it's his birthday and I think it's good to celebrate life while you've still got it.'

'You'll forgive me if I don't think that Adam Akerele's life was worth the life of my son.'

'That's not really the way it works, Honor.'

'Is this a role that comes easily to you? The saint?'

Jo stood. 'It isn't any kind of a role. My husband is dead, and it helps me feel more peaceful about it.'

'How does Lydia feel about you visiting this man?'

'I mentioned it to her once, and she became very angry. The same as you.'

'With good reason, I think.'

'Fair enough. I can't argue with you. It's been ten years, though. It's a long time to hate someone who doesn't deserve it.'

Jo left the room and Honor stayed at the table with her cold cup of tea, fuming.

Our son died, Honor typed. *You never knew him, I never allowed you to know him, and he died to save a stranger. His wife was dry-eyed at his funeral and she bakes this stranger a cake every year, and I am so angry, so angry that he did this instead of choosing to live.*

Honor deleted what she had written. She had pictured Stephen's death to herself, in dreams and in waking, many times. Sometimes it was a torture and sometimes a comfort. In her mind, Adam Akerele was hazy. A distorted blank, like the centre of her waking vision. He was a cause, a reason, a mechanism, a curse.

In the kitchen, Jo was placing an iced cake into a tin.

'All right,' Honor said to her. 'All right, I will come with you. But don't expect me to say anything to him. I don't like him. But I'm curious. I want to see what my son lost his life to save.'

Jo put on Radio 4 as they drove, which obviated the need for talking, but Honor was too preoccupied to say much anyway. She did not want to find an explanation for her son's death, because that would mean that she had accepted it. And she could not accept, would never accept, that her beautiful, brilliant boy, so full of potential and intelligence and love, could be gone.

Ten years. He was not the sort of person whom time erased. Honor's feelings did not tarnish and fade. She loved rarely, but she loved fully and for ever.

'So you should know about Adam,' said Jo, as they drove through the centre of Brickham and out the other side. 'I only see him once a year – he doesn't want to see me any more than that — but sometimes he's better than others. He has some mental health issues. I'm not sure what, exactly, because he's not comfortable talking about it, but I do know that things can get bad if he's not taking his medication.'

This is the life that Stephen sacrificed his for?

'Last year, he'd found a job, so I'm hoping that everything's gone well for him. He's not very good at keeping in touch.'

'What do you get out of this visit?' Honor couldn't help asking.

'It isn't for sainthood. The first time I saw him, I wanted some answers. I wanted to know what had happened. And he was able to give me some details, though not quite enough.' She was silent for a moment. 'I keep going because I feel connected to Adam. In Stephen's last moments, they shared something. He's alive because my husband was a good man. And I like knowing that.'

Honor frowned. 'I'm not sure I need reminding.'

'And also, I like him.' Jo signalled left, and parked the car outside a block of flats made of yellow brick. 'And he enjoys my cake, which is always gratifying.'

They made slow progress around the tower block to the entrance. There was a wheelchair ramp, and they walked up that. Graffiti spattered the side of the building, the desperate, incoherent communication of those with too much time on their hands. Jo buzzed at the door and held it open for Honor to come through.

The corridor was cramped and had a definite whiff of mildew and urine. On the fourth door along, someone had Sellotaped a single green balloon. Honor's fingers brushed it.

'Looks like he's having a party,' said Jo cheerfully, and she knocked. The door was opened by a woman. Honor took in hooped earrings and part of an elaborate hairstyle. 'Hi, I'm Jo, and this is my mother-in-law, Honor Levinson. We've come to wish Adam a Happy Birthday.'

'Come in,' said the woman, and led them through another narrow corridor into what was presumably the living room. Honor stopped short in the door, assailed by the scent of old paper. A library. She reached out and encountered a stack of paperback books lining the wall. All around her vision, she could see books. They appeared to line the walls, floor to ceiling, stacked on top of each other, three deep, tottering. If there had been any bookcases, they were long since buried. The room was dim, and there were other scents as well: cooking oil, coffee, something familiar that niggled at the back of her memory.

'Happy Birthday, Adam!' said Jo, going straight to someone sitting in a chair in the corner. She hugged him and gave him the cake tin.

'My favourite again?' he asked her.

'Of course.'

Honor stepped further into the library room and surveyed the details that she could snatch of Adam Akerele. He wore a blue and white football top. His skin was glossy, dark, unlined. Honor stood as straight as she could, defying anyone to offer her a seat.

'I'll get some plates,' said the young woman who had let them in.

'That's my girlfriend, Ellie,' Adam told Jo. 'We've been seeing each other since October.'

'That's really fantastic, Adam. I'm so pleased for you.'

'She's a good woman. Puts up with me. How are your little ones?'

293

'They're great. Both growing like crazy. And Lydia is about to do her GCSEs; we're incredibly proud of her. Adam, this is my mother-in-law, Dr Honor Levinson. She's Stephen's mother.'

The young man jumped to his feet. 'Oh wow, Stephen's mum? Oh wow, please, sit down, sit down here, Ellie will be back with cake, she'll make tea as well, or would you rather have a coffee?'

'No, thank you.' But Adam had grabbed Honor's hand in both of his before she could recoil, and was shaking it as if he could pull it off. His hands were large and warm and slightly damp.

'Mum,' Adam said, 'this is Stephen's mum. Stephen's.'

A seismic move in the corner of the room and a large woman bore down on her. She was not as tall as Honor, but at least three times as broad. Honor caught a glimpse of her hair, straightened like poker irons and sticking out from her round head.

She seized Honor and hugged her hard. Honor squeaked as the air was squeezed out of her, pressed up against the woman's massive bosom.

'Thank you so much,' the woman boomed in her ear. 'Thank you, I cannot thank you enough.' She leaned back, still holding Honor, but looking up into her face. She was an indistinct brown, too close to see. Honor breathed, stunned, smelling wool and Anaïs Anaïs perfume. That was the scent she had smelled with the books, the scent she'd recognized. The same scent Stephen had bought her for her birthday, when he was what? Eleven? Twelve? Flowery, too sweet, too girlish for Honor. She had worn it every day until the bottle was empty.

'Thank you for your son,' Adam's mother said. The woman was all softness, all-enveloping warmth and flowers. A rich full voice. 'Thank you for giving me mine. My only son. As you are a mother, you will know how I feel.'

'Yes,' Honor found herself saying. 'I think that I do.'

They sang Happy Birthday and someone put music on the CD player that nestled in a bower of paperbacks. Adam danced with everyone: Jo, his mother, the social worker who had turned up after they had, even Honor. She sat in a chair, but he took her hands in his large moist ones and swayed back and forth, smiling down at her.

As far as she was aware, she hadn't met many people with mental illness and she had no idea whether this was normal for Adam or not. But when he danced with Ellie, awkwardly, knocking books off the piles as they moved so that they pooled like petals at their feet, he seemed happy.

Jo clapped along to the music, as if it were the birthday party of one of her own children.

When they cut the cake and put it on paper plates, Adam sat beside her, close enough so that she could hear the soft sounds his mouth made when he ate. 'I think of your son every day,' he told her.

She was not able to eat much of the cake. It was too sweet. She was trying to reconcile this corporeal and solid young man with the indistinct person she had always imagined.

'He was clever, wasn't he?' Adam asked. 'I found out later that he was a scientist.'

'A physicist.'

'I could tell he was clever just from the way he spoke to me.'

'How . . .' Honor swallowed, cloying sweetness.

She had thought about Stephen's last words, late at night, alone, and in dreams. But they were unclear; speculation only, as indistinct as her picture of Adam Akerele. More often, she had heard his voice raised in anger against her, as it had been during their last argument.

Perhaps one set of words could supplant the other.

'What did he say to you?' she asked.

Adam settled deeper into his chair. 'I was on the bridge, going to jump off. I was waiting for a train, so it would hit me. I wanted to be sure, you know? I really wanted to top myself. And then there was this man in running clothes, climbing over the railing. I thought he wanted to jump, too, and I remember thinking, Isn't it funny that there are two crazies at the same place at the same time?'

He spoke in the manner of a person who had told this story many times: his party piece, perhaps. No; he would have spoken of it in therapy. And to Jo.

'But then he told me not to jump. He asked me my name, and he told me that I shouldn't jump. So I knew he was trying to save me. And then he asked me if I knew what gravity was, what caused it.'

Honor had never heard Stephen in a lecture theatre, but she had heard him speak to Lydia when she was small. He was always patient, gentle, never spoke to her as if she were too young for rational thought. She thought that Stephen would have spoken to Adam like this.

'So I said, "Well, sort of," because at the moment I wasn't really thinking about gravity or whatever, I was more interested in when the train was coming. And then he told me this. I'll never forget it. He told me that gravity was the force between two objects, and that everything in the universe, no matter how big or small, had gravity. That everything was pulling on everything else.'

Honor closed her eyes. The room had gone quiet around them. Adam's voice was soft, a bit reedy. In her mind it became Stephen's deeper voice, the hint of North London accent he had never quite lost. He had always been so good at explaining.

'Even people,' said Adam.

Said Stephen, in her mind.

'Gravity makes stars burn and worlds turn but it's in people, too. Any two people, close to each other, exert a force on each other commensurate with their distance. The closer they are, the stronger it is.'

Honor's mouth formed the words. They came out of her as a whisper.

The closer they are, the stronger it is.

'And then,' Adam continued, 'I heard a siren behind us, and I sort of went to turn around and look, and I lost my balance for a minute. The ledge was pretty narrow. And he reached out to help me — but we weren't that close, not actually close enough to touch. Just close enough to talk. And I didn't even see him slip, I just saw his arm and his face. I did put my hand out to grab him but I missed. I wasn't quick enough. I remember him looking me in the face, though. It seemed like a really long time, but it couldn't have been a second, even. We just looked at each other. Like we . . . like we knew each other. Like we understood.'

Adam shifted. She could hear the chair creak beneath him.

'And then he fell,' Adam said.

★ ★ ★

On the drive back, Honor turned over the book that Adam had pressed upon her before they left. It was entirely familiar: *A Treasury of English Verse*, a paperback with a cover soft from handling.

'I didn't expect him to be so young,' she said.

'He's twenty-six. He was sixteen when he tried to jump. The same age that Lydia is now.' Jo shook her head. 'I have a lot of reasons to count my blessings.'

'I also did not expect . . .' Honor couldn't work out exactly which word to choose. She did not like Adam, precisely. Her sympathy for him was limited. But she felt something for him, an emotion that had perhaps not yet been named.

'I did not know what to expect,' she finished.

'You were angry,' said Jo. 'Maybe you're not so angry any more?'

'No. Not angry. It is difficult to be angry with someone so . . .' Again, the term eluded her. She meant something like *real*, but that was not precise enough. 'It is difficult to be angry with someone who remembers Stephen's words so well.'

'The gravity,' agreed Jo. 'I haven't heard that in a while. Yes. It's such a Stephen thing to say, isn't it?'

'He used to drop stones and feathers and leaves from the bridge in the park, into the pond. He was always doing experiments, even as a child.'

'I'm glad you came today,' said Jo.

Honor nodded. She was not glad. But she was . . .

Thankful?

'When I first met Adam – he wasn't in such good shape then; he was actually in hospital because they sectioned him after his suicide attempt – I realized that if Stephen hadn't been there, then Adam would be dead. And I couldn't wish that on anyone.'

Honor thought about this. It was very probable that Jo was a better person than she was. As sincere as this young man had been, as grateful as his mother was, whatever connection she had felt in that strange stuffy room lined obsessively with words, Honor knew that if she were given a choice, she would not choose Adam Akerele's life over Stephen Levinson's.

But she hadn't been given that choice. She was given this reality.

Was it time to learn to accept it?

'When the hospital rang,' Jo said, in a very quiet voice, so quiet it could barely be heard over the motor of the car, 'and I found out that Stephen had fallen from a bridge, I thought at first that he had jumped.'

'You thought that *he*—'

'He used to get these depressions. Not often, and not always, but sometimes. He called them black holes. They were times when he felt that all the joy had been sucked out of his life. And there wasn't anything I could do to help him, then; I just had to be there and ride it out with him, let him know that Lydia and I would be there when he emerged again. He said that running helped. And he was out running, that day.'

Honor did not know what to say. Her Stephen, the person she knew better than any other. She thought back to those long dark days when he had been a baby. What he might have imbibed with the milk he sucked from her body.

'He didn't want to tell you,' Jo added. 'He didn't want you to worry. And they weren't frequent, Honor. He was all right most of the time. He was better than all right. We were happy together.'

Honor thought of Stephen and Jo's wedding day, at the register office in Cambridge. She thought of how she had sat in the front row and wilfully ignored the way they looked at each other. Smiled at each other. That moment when her son had slipped the ring onto his bride's finger. She had abandoned Judaism a long time before, but she was seething at the civil ceremony.

She thought of invitations she had refused, the burning jealousy in her gut, masked as contempt. The height she had assumed to look down on her daughter-in-law.

She had thought sometimes that Jo reminded her of Paul's wife, Wendy: pretty and domesticated. She had used that sometimes to justify her jealous dislike. But the truth was simpler, and worse: in her eyes, no one would have been good enough for Stephen.

Ironically, she was seeing more clearly now.

'I have not been very kind to you, Jo,' she said.

'Oh. Well.' Jo was clearly embarrassed. 'It's all in the past, anyway.'

Honor laid her head against the car window. The vibrations of the engine buzzed against her skull, down her spine, into her hips.

For ten years, Honor had thought that since Stephen, her centre of gravity, was gone, everything and everyone was gone. She had wanted the world to collapse around her, to burn away like the letter with its Californian postmark and its air-mail stickers, into ashes and dust. She had thought the tragedy was that it had not collapsed, not burned away. That she had gone on living when everything that she had to live for was being erased, removed from the centre of her life, leaving her with nothing but the periphery.

Incredibly, it seemed that she was moving on. She was discovering other forces of gravity. However late.

When they returned to Jo's house, she switched on the laptop and typed for a long time, without thinking. It helped, not being able to see the words.

Chapter Thirty-Two

Lydia

Lydia's first exam was French and it was weird to come into school in the afternoon, in her uniform but without anything but her crib sheet, a pencil case and a bottle of water, and to wait outside near the door to the hall while all the other students in the other years were sitting in lessons. It felt as if she hadn't been in school for ages, even though it had been only a week. A week of nearly constant revision, most of it alone, some of it with Avril. Their conversation was stilted, but Avril didn't seem to notice.

Lydia hadn't thought she would be really nervous for her exams – especially not for French, as French was easy – but there was something gnawing at her stomach, and she was sweating under her school jumper. Mrs Fowler was near the entrance to the hall, directing the students where to wait in the corridor, checking their pencil cases and water bottles, reminding everyone they'd have to throw away their crib sheets before they went in. 'You're taking AS?' she asked Lydia, checking her clipboard. 'Wait with the sixth form, please, instead of with Year Eleven. Quiet outside the examination hall, please.'

At first Lydia had felt silly in French lessons, as the only one wearing school uniform, but she'd got over that by October. Now, though, standing with a handful of students in jeans and T-shirts or summer dresses, separated by several metres from the other people in her year who were taking French GCSE, she felt silly again. Avril wasn't taking French and didn't have any exams till tomorrow, but Lydia knew most of the students waiting to take their exams, and it was odd not to be standing with them.

Bailey stood across the corridor, clutching a bottle of water. Lydia hadn't seen her since that day before study leave. She noticed that Bailey was wearing black socks. She was also talking in a low voice with Erin, who wasn't actually rolling her eyes or curling her lip. In fact, the two of them seemed to be quite friendly.

Well, Bailey must be pleased, anyway. She'd seemed to want to impress Erin.

Just then, the two of them glanced up and caught Lydia looking at them. Bailey blushed and an enormous grin grew slowly on Erin's face.

'Good luck,' Lydia mouthed to them.

Erin blew her a kiss, and giggled.

The sight hit Lydia like a cold weight in her stomach.

A kiss? What did that mean? Had Bailey said something?

Bailey's head ducked and Erin turned to Olivia, standing beside her, and said something Lydia couldn't hear.

'Stop the talking,' called Mrs Fowler, 'and sixth form, you may enter the hall. Remember, no talking, no noise whatsoever in the examination room.'

'Don't be nervous,' said the person behind Lydia in the queue, a lower sixth boy called Paolo. 'It'll be fine. That said, I'm shit scared.'

He smiled at her and then they were through the door. Lydia found her seat, with her name card on it, scratch paper already laid out waiting for her. She watched as the GCSE group filed into the room, but none of them glanced at her. They were all intent on finding their own places.

It was nothing, she told herself. It was nothing. It was Erin being flamboyant, blowing her a kiss for luck. She was sitting quite near the front of the room and couldn't see anyone she knew around her. She looked over her shoulder, and was tapped sharply on the other shoulder.

'Keep your face forward,' said Mr Singh, and he put an exam booklet on her desk.

Lydia drew in a deep breath and concentrated on writing her name and student number on the booklet. Concentrated on keeping her heart-rate down, on thinking in French. Erin had probably blown sixteen million kisses today. She was a big kiss-blower.

'You may begin,' said Mr Singh.

Erin caught up with her at the end of the corridor. She had Olivia and Sophie with her, though no sign of Bailey. 'How'd the A level go?'

Lydia nearly sagged with relief. 'It was all right, I think. How was yours?'

'It didn't go so well. I think I could have used a *kiss* for luck.'

Sophie giggled and Lydia nearly stumbled. Erin was smiling, that mean smile that she often had.

'*Un baiser,*' said Olivia. 'Isn't that how you say it at A level? *Très romantique.*'

'Where are you going now?' Erin asked her. 'Going to find Bailey? Or Avril?'

'I've got another exam,' Lydia managed.

'All right, see you later, darling. Ta ta.' Erin wiggled her fingers at Lydia, and both Sophie and Olivia giggled this time.

Chapter Thirty-Three

Jo

'Hey, neighbour.'

Jo looked up from her rose bush. Marcus was standing on the other side of the hedge. Her heart leaped and she lowered her secateurs.

Oscar beat her to it, though. He ran over to the hedge, clutching the bunch of dandelions he'd been picking. 'I have super eyes!' he told Marcus. 'I am a superhero!'

'Well, that is fantastic,' said Marcus. 'Who are the flowers for? Your mummy?'

'Lyddie. She has exams.'

Iris toddled up behind him, waving two more dandelions clenched in her chubby fist. 'I pick too!'

'They look great. First exams today, eh?' Marcus looked over at Jo. 'How'd they go? I haven't seen her since before half-term.'

'She's not home yet; she's probably gone for a coffee with Avril. I'm making a bouquet for her room, and cooking her favourite for dinner.'

'And I'm helping,' said Oscar.

'Oscar is really into helping at the moment,' said Jo. She came up closer to the hedge, close enough so that she could touch Marcus through the gap, if she dared. 'He's been fetching and carrying stuff for Honor all week. Iris, too, when she can. They've been a real help to her, and to me.'

'You have a bit of pollen on your cheek.' Marcus reached over and brushed it off, his thumb lingering on her face. 'It looks lovely.'

Jo held out her roses so that he could smell them. 'You've got a bit of pollen, too,' she said, and took off her gardening glove so she could run her finger over his lower lip. He touched it with his tongue, and she whispered, 'Naughty.'

'I've been waiting for days to be naughty,' he whispered back. 'But someone hasn't been free.'

'I'm going to be a flower girl,' said Oscar.

'No,' said Jo, 'Iris is going to be a flower girl. You're going to be a page boy. For my ex's wedding,' she added to Marcus. 'His fiancée is coming over in a bit to measure the children for their outfits.'

'This is the famous au pair?'

'The famous au pair.'

'You let her in the house?' he said in a low voice.

She shrugged. 'I don't have much choice. It's all very civilized.'

'I wouldn't find it easy to be civilized in that situation, I must admit.'

'He's their father, and she'll be their stepmother.'

'I suppose I'm protective.' He leaned over the hedge and said to Iris, 'Want to come over here for a minute? I'll give you something to help you be a flower girl.'

'No,' said Iris, raising her arms to him. He hesitated, clearly

307

not certain whether to go with her words or her actions.

'She's going through a "no" phase,' said Jo.

'No!' Iris repeated, waving her arms at him and jumping to be picked up, until he gave in and lifted her over the hedge to his garden.

Oscar raised his arms too, saying 'Me! Me!' until Marcus also lifted him over.

Jo watched her lover set her son down, a little bit concerned that both of her children went so easily with a stranger. Then again, Marcus wasn't a stranger, not to Jo . . .

But neither was her relationship with Marcus something you could tell the children about. She thought about how angry she'd been when Richard had announced that Tatiana was moving in with him and would be spending weekends with the children. How humiliated she'd been, how wrong it felt that her children were part of this illicit relationship. It was hardly any different, was it, letting her children spend time with the man she was having sex with in secret?

'We probably need to be a little bit careful,' she said quietly.

'Don't worry, I'm safe with children, I've been CRB checked for my job,' he said, his head turned away towards the children. For the first time since she'd known him, his voice had an edge to it.

'I didn't mean—'

'I know what you meant. I'll only have them for a minute.'

They disappeared from sight behind the hedge, and Jo heard them whispering. She shot a look back at the house, to see if Honor was peering out of the window or if Tatiana had turned up yet, but she didn't see anyone. Putting her glove back on, she began trimming the thorns off the early roses she'd cut for Lydia's room.

How would people view her, if they knew? Would she be the object of attention and gossip again, this time for something that she'd done herself? She remembered those horrible days after Richard had left, alone in the park, struggling to carry on as normal when she knew that everyone was talking about her. This time, would the whispers be about not Poor Jo, Left For The Au Pair, but Pervy Jo, Shagging The Young Neighbour? Cougar Jo, Carrying On With Her Daughter's Teacher, And In Front Of Her Young Children?

It was like an episode of one of those staged reality shows that Jo watched sometimes, guiltily knowing she should be doing something else.

Oscar laughed.

'Shhh,' she heard Marcus whisper. 'Do you remember what to say?'

'No!' declared Iris.

She couldn't see Marcus, who was hiding behind the high bit of the hedge, but she could see his arms as he lifted her little daughter over and deposited her carefully on the ground. She held an enormous bouquet of sweet peas and ferns. Iris toddled a few solemn steps towards Jo, and then held up her bouquet.

'For Mummy,' she said, and put it into Jo's hands.

Oscar was lifted over too, holding a small bouquet of violas added to his bunch of dandelions. He ran to her instead of copying Iris's flower-girl gait. 'These ones are for Lydia!' he cried. 'Marcus said I could have them and give them to her from me.'

Marcus appeared in the gap, a bit of fern on his collar. Jo, her hands full of flowers, sorry for her thoughts about cougars and reality television, said 'Thank you.'

'You don't have to give them to Lydia if you don't think it's appropriate. I won't be offended.'

'I . . . I might say Oscar picked them.'

'And so he did. But I hope you'll keep the ones from Iris.'

She nodded, sniffing their perfume. She had accepted a thousand bouquets from her children, buttercups and daisies and dandelions in yellow or blowsy fluff, but when was the last time a man had given her flowers?

'I'm sorry,' she said.

'It frustrates me to be on the margins of your life,' he said to her. 'I can get tired of feeling like a dirty secret.'

Tatiana came round the side of the house. 'Hello, my darlinks!' she called to the children. 'I'm here!'

'Is that her?' Marcus asked.

Jo nodded. 'I have to go. I'm sorry. Thanks for the flowers.'

'Meet me later. I'll be here.' His gaze flickered to Tatiana, waiting by the side of the house, and back to Jo. 'She doesn't look like much competition. Your ex is crazy.'

'I'll text you,' she murmured, and gathered up Oscar and Iris to shepherd them back to the house.

Tatiana was waiting for them by the back door. 'Oh, flowers?' she asked Oscar, holding out her hands. 'So pretty.'

'They're Lyddie's,' he said, going past her through the door on his sturdy legs.

'Hello, Tatiana,' said Jo, looking behind her for Richard.

'I'm here alone,' said Tatiana. 'Richard is at work. I knocked, but no one answered.'

'I was in the garden, and Lydia is out. I would have thought Honor would answer, though?' Jo went inside. Her mother-in-law was sitting on the sofa, hands folded, gazing serenely into the middle distance. 'Honor, didn't you hear the door?'

'I thought it was a nuisance caller,' said Honor.

Jo frowned at Honor, who appeared unfazed, and then shrugged at Tatiana. 'Would you like some tea? A cold drink?'

'Oh, I can get.' Tatiana took a glass out of the cabinet and filled it with cold water from the filter in the fridge.

Jo, her hands full of flowers, opened a cupboard door with her foot and peered inside. 'Now where are those vases?'

'Let me do it,' said Tatiana. Stretching her long body, she reached for the cupboard over the fridge. 'Do you want the big one?'

'Er . . . actually the big one and a little one. Please.'

Tatiana took down a glass vase and a smaller porcelain one that had come from Jo's mother's house. Without checking with Jo, she took them to the sink and began to fill them with water. Jo watched her, suddenly remembering how there had always been arrangements of flowers in the house when Tatiana lived with them. She had always assumed that Tatiana had bought them, that it had been a little nice touch. What if they had actually been presents for Tatiana, from Richard?

'These are for Lydia,' Jo said, arranging the roses she had cut along with Oscar's bouquet of dandelions and violas in the porcelain vase. 'She did her first exams today.'

'Oh, how exciting,' said Tatiana, taking a tape measure out of the pocket of her slim cream-coloured trousers. 'Iris, darlink, come here, I will measure you for pretty dress. It will be pink and sparkly.'

'No,' said Iris.

'You do not like pink?' Tatiana shot Jo a look. 'I thought she liked pink.'

'She's going through a—'

'Are you the au pair?'

The two of them froze at Honor's voice. It was clear and commanding. Honor still sat on the sofa, gazing into the middle distance. Oscar had sat beside her.

'I used to be au pair,' said Tatiana. 'Now I will marry Richard next month. Are you the grandmother?' She went to Honor, and held out her hand for Honor to shake.

Honor did not take it. '*Poshla von otsyuda, blyad, kotoraya spit s chuzhimi muzhyami,*' she said.

Tatiana turned pale. 'I—'

Oscar twisted up to look at her. 'What were those funny words, Ganny?'

Honor turned her head to look directly at Tatiana. She raised her eyebrows expectantly.

'*Nu?*' Honor said.

'I – yes. I mean, no. I mean . . . I will go.'

Tatiana shoved her tape measure back into her trousers and hurried out of the door. It swung closed behind her and Jo heard the engine of her car starting up outside.

'What did you say to her?' Jo asked, wide-eyed.

'It was Russian,' Honor said to Oscar, and to Jo she said, 'I told her to get out of your house because she was a husband-stealing whore.'

Jo stared. Oscar blinked.

'What's a whore?' he asked.

The door opened again with a bang, and Jo jumped, ready for Tatiana to come back into the house, yelling at Honor in Russian. But it was Lydia. She threw her bag down next to

312

the door and started for the stairs without acknowledging anyone.

Jo hurried to her. 'How were your exams, sweetheart?'

'Fine.' She thumped up the stairs and Jo heard her bedroom door slam.

'It doesn't sound as if they were fine,' said Honor. Her voice was entirely calm.

'Why did you say that to Tatiana?'

'Because it is true, and also because it galls me to see you welcoming someone like that and letting them make themselves at home. You are too accommodating for your own good, Jo.'

Jo bristled. 'Are you saying that I let her come in here and steal my husband?'

'No; he made his foolish choices all by himself. I am saying that now that she has done it, you have no reason to let her assume that she is in control here, where you live.'

'Well, I . . .' She thought of how Tatiana had known where the glasses were, and where the vases were kept. 'I'm trying to be nice.'

'There's niceness, and then there's insanity. Do you think that Lydia is upset about something?'

'I'll go and check.' Jo put her sweet peas in water, picked up the porcelain vase with Lydia's flowers and went upstairs with it. Faintly from the living room she could hear Oscar asking again, 'What's a whore?'

Oh God. She'd deal with that later. She knocked on Lydia's closed bedroom door. 'Sweetheart? Are you all right?'

No answer.

'Did your exams go OK?'

Stomping feet, and the door opened a bare inch. 'My exams were fine, there's nothing wrong with my *exams*, don't worry. Can I get a little privacy for like five minutes, please?'

'OK,' said Jo. 'But Oscar picked these for you, to say congratulations.'

Lydia's hand came out and took the flowers. She made to shut the door again, but Jo put her hand out.

'I'm making chicken cacciatore,' she said quickly. 'And you don't have any exams tomorrow morning, do you? Do you want to ring Avril and ask her if she wants to come for tea, as a celebration?'

'Avril didn't have exams today.'

'Well, that's fine, she can come anyway.'

'Avril has a boyfriend.'

Jo bit her lip. 'Oh. I . . . I understand.'

'You don't understand anything.'

'But I do, sweetheart. I thought we hadn't seen her around very much. Lydia, don't worry. Avril's not the type to forget who her friends are.'

'Isn't she?'

'No,' said Jo with conviction. 'She's a nice girl, and you've been inseparable for ages. It's bound to feel strange when she starts seeing someone. But you can still have good times together, the two of you.'

'Can we?'

'Of course you can! Why don't you ring her anyway and see if she's free? She probably needs a break from revision, too. You don't want to work all the time, sweetheart, you'll just burn yourself out. You need to have a little bit of fun every now and then, you know.'

'A little bit of fun?' Lydia's face was half cut off by the door, but she was regarding Jo incredulously. 'You think this is fun? You think *any* of this is *fun*?'

'I can see that it's very stressful, but it's only the beginning. You've got weeks of exams yet. Be a little bit easier on yourself, darling.'

'I'll be easier on myself when you stop nagging me to have fun!'

Lydia slammed the door. Considering it had only been open an inch or two, the noise was surprising. Jo gazed at it for a few moments, then heaved a sigh and went back downstairs to send Marcus a sneaky text, and also to make up an innocuous meaning for the word 'whore'.

Chapter Thirty-Four

Lydia

Mum was ridiculous. How could someone always try to see the bright side? How could she think that everything could be solved by making someone's favourite dinner? Offering her sympathy and pats on the back as if she was five years old, empty platitudes promising that she and Avril would still have good times together when she didn't have a clue about how Lydia felt about Avril?

Lydia was aware that she was being unfair; her mother didn't know how she felt because she hadn't told her. But there was a certain wild freedom about striking out at her mother when she'd been worrying about veiled threats from her friends. And besides, she'd left her phone at home during her exam, and she needed to check whether Avril had rung. All the way home she'd been picturing scenarios about Erin ringing Avril and telling her that Lydia had kissed Bailey. Imagining Erin's vicious grin and Avril's eyes widening in horror. Trying to work out how she'd explain it, whether she could blame Bailey – which seemed unfair, but still, Bailey had been the one to talk, hadn't she? Or another story she could make up. They were acting out a film scene? She was actually just applying lipstick? She slipped and her lips met Bailey's?

She couldn't make up a story. She would have to tell the truth.

She should have told the truth ages ago, then she wouldn't be facing this now. Should have told the truth from the start. And given up the intimacy with Avril, the easy trust, the stolen touches and glances, all of which were precious, and all of which were based on a lie.

Feeling sick, Lydia picked up her phone from her bed. There were no missed calls and no messages.

Avril didn't know then. She sagged onto the bed in relief. She would still have to tell her, but she could do it in her own way. She'd say that she was lonely, and experimenting. She'd say she'd suspected for a while. She'd say she'd never had any feelings about Avril. Of course not. They were just best friends.

It would be horrible. It would be another lie. But at least things could carry on, not so different from usual. Things might even be better.

Her phone beeped, and she looked more carefully at the screen. There were over fifty Facebook notifications. As she watched, it turned to fifty-two.

Her hands were cold. She clicked up her profile. The first thing she saw was a comment from Darren Raymond.

Hey LL I hear your a lezza now is that how you know what pussy tastes like

Darren Raymond. Stupid joke. Nobody paid any attention to him. Except there were comments underneath Darren's.

OMG is she? That explains alot.

I always thought there was something between her and A

OMFG i never knew she is in athletics with me guys i get changed in front of her all the time this is gross

'Gross?' Lydia spat out. 'It's your fat arse that's gross, Becky.'

She didn't want to scroll down — fifty-two notifications, now fifty-three — but she did. There were pictures. Someone had posted the pic of her and Avril at Monica's party, their arms around each other's shoulders, identical cans of Strongbow in their hands, tongues stuck out at the camera. They'd put a thought bubble coming out of Lydia's head.

Nice tits.

Lydia scrolled down, helpless, taking in the malice and the doctored photos, the gleeful outrage and hysterical disgust.

i dont mind people being gay this is the 21st century after all but they should say so and not make us believe there normal people

guys do you think her and Avril have been doing it all this time, thats hot!

She read every single one of them. Every single one, except that more were coming in. Then she dropped her phone on her bed and stood there, staring at it as if it were the problem, as if it were a venomous snake she was trying to work out how to kill.

She understood how the internet worked. She couldn't reply in any way without making it worse. She had to see Avril, but could she? Should she really? Avril had been tagged over and over again in the conversation. She hadn't said anything yet. Maybe that was because of shock, or because she was being loyal to Lydia, but then again, she hadn't rung Lydia either.

Maybe she was too busy snogging Harry. For the first time,

Lydia found herself fervently wishing that Avril was in a park somewhere, behind a building, under a tree, with Harry Carter's hand up her top. She snatched up her phone again and rang her, but it went to voicemail. 'Call me right away, OK?' she said. 'Don't look online, just call me.'

She sent a text, too, to be sure, and then she pictured Avril not snogging Harry, but instead sitting with him and reading her phone. Not answering because she was too disgusted. Telling Harry about all the times she'd got changed in front of Lydia, all the times they'd shared a bed, the time they'd gone swimming naked together in the Rylances' pool at midnight, how they'd borrowed each other's clothes including bras and knickers.

She stuffed her phone in her back pocket and ran out of the house again, towards Avril's.

Her school shoes were rubbish for running but Lydia hardly noticed the clomp. She crossed a road in front of a car and only dimly heard the brakes squeal and the horn sound. At Avril's block, she leaned on the bell until the door buzzed open.

The door to the flat was ajar and Lydia knocked and went inside. 'Avril?' Mrs Toller was sitting on the sofa, remote in her hand. She still had her work uniform on, or maybe she was about to start another shift. 'Hi, Mrs Toller, is Avril here?'

Avril's mum squinted up at her. 'She said she was spending the afternoon revising at your house.'

'Oh. I – yeah, she popped out to get a book and I thought she'd come back here. Maybe she left it at school instead.'

'Don't you have exams? Should you be gallivanting all over town?'

'Just on a break. I'll probably meet her on the way back to my house. Thanks, see you later!'

Lydia checked the park and the shopping precinct. She checked the place by the river where they went sometimes, the playpark at the back of the end of Avril's estate. At Starbucks she caught a glimpse of a group of people wearing blue school uniforms, spread over the sofas at the back, and she left quickly before anyone from her school could spot her. She checked her phone again and there were no new messages but there were twenty-eight new Facebook notifications and she had nine new Snapchats. She didn't check any of them.

Her feet brought her reluctantly back home. She wasn't stupid, she knew what she had to do. She had to close down her Facebook, delete Snapchat. No, she had to keep them, so she had evidence. But evidence for what?

She had to tell her mum.

The thought brought a certain relief. She'd tell Mum. And Mum would be surprised, but she'd be on her side. Mum would help her figure out what to do.

Inside the house, Granny H was on the sofa with OscanIrie. Oscar was pretending to read them a book. 'Are you all right, Lydia?' said Honor without looking up.

She could tell Granny H, too. Granny H would be furious on her behalf. Honor couldn't do anything – Lydia wasn't even sure that Granny H knew what Facebook was – but she'd be righteously angry. She'd call Darren Raymond extraordinary names.

If she told Granny H and Mum, Lydia could be at home and relax into the truth. Not always on guard, not always hiding behind a mask.

She tried to imagine it: all that honesty.

'Where's Mum?'

'She's in the garden, I think.'

Lydia nodded and headed for the back door. She knew what she would do. She would find her mum, probably weeding, her hands in gloves and soil. She'd kneel down beside her and she would hug her and her mother would envelop her in her arms. Just like she used to do when she was a little girl, when Lydia believed that she could make everything all right. She would tell her everything, out there in the garden near the roses. Her mother would give Lydia her full attention, like she used to. That time before she married Richard, when they used to talk about her father, when it felt like it was just the two of them against the world, when it felt like it was going to be that way for ever. And it hadn't been; her mum had chosen Richard instead. But maybe this time, it could be.

Lydia had it all planned out in her head by the time she stepped out of the back door and onto the grass. And then she stopped, because her mother wasn't by the rose bush. She was by the back hedge, near that part that was gappy, with a man. They stood close to each other, talking. His hand was on her elbow; hers was on his shoulder.

The man was Mr Graham. From school.

As she watched, Mr Graham inclined his head and kissed her mother on her lips. Mum wrapped her arms around his neck and he pulled her closer.

For the first time, a sob rose in Lydia's throat. She choked it back and turned and ran. Not into the house: around the side and down the street again, in the opposite direction. Within ten minutes she was pounding on Bailey's door.

Bailey opened it. As soon as she saw Lydia she looked down and to the side, half a smirk on her face.

'Why did you tell them?' Lydia was out of breath, more from emotion than from sprinting.

Bailey didn't answer; she just kept on looking to the side. She had eyeliner on.

'Who did you tell first – Erin? And then the others? Why? Did you want to make friends? Is that it? You offered them a juicy bit of information about me so that they'd like you?'

'I don't see why you're so upset,' said Bailey. '*I'm* not the one who's been keeping secrets about who I really am.'

'I tried to help you! I stood up for you. I was nice to you when nobody else was.'

'Yeah, because you wanted to *attack* me. In my own *bedroom*. It's gross.'

'Because I felt sorry for you.'

'Because you thought I was perverted like you, and you thought I didn't know anybody so I would lie for you, too.' Bailey met Lydia's eyes now, and her face was twisted and pink with righteous disgust. 'All I did was tell the truth. If you have to face the consequences now, it's your own fault. Not my problem.'

'But Darren Raymond. Becky Alderman. Everyone knows. You told *everyone*. All those filthy things they said about you, and now they're saying them about me. Don't you even care?' She reached out to Bailey, not sure if she wanted to grab her or shake her or hit her, anything to remind Bailey that she was real, she was a person.

Bailey flinched back. 'Don't touch me!' she yelled. 'Don't touch me, I don't like it!'

She slammed the door in Lydia's face.

Chapter Thirty-Five

Lydia

They were ranged against her outside the school building the next morning. A wall of blue jumpers, grey skirts and trousers, sitting, standing in clumps, leaning against the wall. All of Year Eleven was taking the English Language exam. Lydia passed through the school gates alone, her shoulders self-consciously straight, her chin high.

She had texted her mother, invented supper at Avril's, wandered for hours around the streets of dead poets until dark, her thoughts going round and round and finding no home. She tried Avril's flat again, but she wasn't in. Every few seconds her phone beeped with a new Facebook notification until she turned it off and went home, straight up the stairs to her bedroom where she didn't sleep, imagining what people were saying.

And here they were, outside the school waiting for their morning exam.

Her eyes went immediately to Avril – as always Avril had a gravitational force, something that meant that Lydia looked for her first, found her in a crowd. She was with Harry. His arm was around her shoulders. But they were looking at her, like everyone was looking at her. She felt the weight of dozens of eyes.

She could not keep the mask in place. After years, it had deserted her. She had thought, walking here, dizzy from not having eaten or slept, that she might be able to face it out. Be breezy, nonchalant, all 'oh, you never knew?' That was the best way. She knew it was the best way.

Instead in the silence that surrounded her, she stared at Avril and she knew that the hunger in her own face was so naked and raw that everyone could see it.

Someone sniggered. It was the sound of over a hundred Facebook posts and comments and texts and images, the sound of all the whispers, electronic and real.

'Lezzy Lyddie,' said someone, probably Darren Raymond, but she was too busy looking at Avril, trying to read Avril's expression, to listen.

'Shut up,' said Avril, and she ducked under Harry's arm. She walked up to Avril. 'Lyds, we have to talk.'

'Can we watch?' called someone else, and there was laughter.

Avril turned to the crowd and showed them her middle finger.

'Go on, snog her!'

Lydia was rooted to the spot, hot and cold all at once, her mouth dry. Avril put her hands on her hips.

'Shut the hell up,' Avril said to the others. 'It's a stupid rumour. We're *best friends*, I would know if she was gay.' She faced Lydia. 'Right, Lyds? If you were gay, you would tell me.'

Avril, angry, was magnificent. Her eyes flashed and her head was tilted, full of attitude, full of defiance. *It's the two of us against the world,* said her stance. It had always been the two of them against the world.

'You'd tell me,' Avril said again. 'I'd know. Right? Tell them.'

Lydia could not speak.

No one was jeering now. No one was saying anything. They were watching, avid. Every person in her year, people she had laughed with, studied with, eaten lunch with, waiting for her to say something. There were words in her mouth but she couldn't get them out. They were blocked there like stones.

Lydia saw the exact moment when Avril realized the truth, because the colour drained out of her face. For a split second, Lydia thought she was going to faint. She reached out for her, to catch her or help her, and Avril stepped quickly back. She stepped back, just in the same way that Bailey had stepped back. There was a noise, like a collective inhalation from the crowd, and the other students crept closer to them, surrounding them in a circle.

'You are,' whispered Avril. 'Oh my God, it's true.'

Nudges. Whispers. Someone laughed.

'I couldn't — I was going to —' Lydia had no idea what she was saying. 'It doesn't make any difference.'

'You *lied* to me. All this time, you've been lying to me.'

'I didn't — it wasn't lying, I—'

'It was lying. You never told me. I trusted you with everything, I told you *everything*, and you never said. Never.'

There were tears in Avril's eyes.

'Avril, I . . .'

She shook her head. 'I thought you were my best friend.'

325

'I am.'

'You promised never to lie to me, Lydia! *You promised!* What else have you been lying to me about?'

I love you.

The circle around them, tight and close.

'Nothing,' said Lydia. 'I swear it, nothing.'

'I can't deal with this. I feel like I don't know you at all.'

Avril looked the same way she had when Lydia had helped her pick her mother off the bathroom floor. Sick and scared and exhausted, unshed tears in her eyes.

'Avril,' Lydia said, helpless.

'Girls!' Madame Fournier, the French teacher, pushed her way into the circle. She made hurrying movements with her small hands. 'What are you doing? The exam is starting, it's time to go inside. Get into your places.'

The crowd dispersed instantly. Avril turned her back on Lydia and hurried to her place in the queue. Lydia watched her go. She watched the other students stand back to give her a wide berth. Avril did not glance in Lydia's direction.

'Go, you'll be late,' Madame Fournier told Lydia. 'Foundation tier in the back, Higher tier at the front. You're Higher, aren't you? It's important that we begin exams in an orderly fashion. Quietly now, quickly. What is the matter with you, did you not hear me? Quickly!'

How was it possible that she was still holding her pencil case, her bottle of water? Lydia walked to her place in the queue, in between Marie Lavelle and Zachary Linton. They both shifted quickly so that there was a large gap between them. She looked at her shoes, feeling the eyes of everyone on her.

'Right, we will proceed into the building,' announced Madame Fournier. 'Silently, now.'

Lydia's face flamed and her head was almost too heavy to lift. In the silence she felt them watching, heard them breathing. She could almost hear the thoughts flinging around in the air, the significance in the coughs and fidgets. Shuffling forward with the others, row by row, to her seat with her name and her number and her examination booklet, sheafs of lined paper waiting for answers.

Her desk was near the front of the room. There were only two people ahead of her in the row, but she could feel the weight of every single person behind her where she couldn't see them, but where they could see the back of her head, the vulnerable skin of her neck. They could examine her and find her wanting, wrong, incorrect. She got out a pencil, a pen, a highlighter, and noticed that her hands were shaking and damp.

An examination paper was placed on her desk. She glanced up to see Mr Graham, and a wave of cold engulfed her. He smiled at her and moved on to give out more papers.

'You may begin,' said a voice, and Lydia opened her paper. It was full of words, black shapes on white.

All this time you've been lying to me?

I thought you were my best friend.

Behind her, the scratching of biros on paper. Someone cleared their throat. Someone uncapped their water bottle. A page was turned, then another. She saw her hands on the desk as if they belonged to someone else. Rubber-soled shoes walked between desks, spelling out a soft rhythm, voicing all the thoughts in this closed and airless room. *Liar. Liar. Lezza. Pervert. These examinations will determine your future. I feel like I don't know you at all.*

Lydia jumped up, scraping her chair back. She stumbled

out of her seat, up the aisle, out through the door and out of the building. Towards the morning light, away from the thoughts and stares and words, to somewhere she could run.

'Lydia!' A voice behind her, a male voice, deep and adult, not unlike how she remembered her father's. She didn't stop, but he caught up with her a few metres from the building. A hand on her elbow.

Mr Graham. She shuddered away from his touch.

'Lydia,' he said, slightly out of breath, his glasses halfway down his nose. 'What's the matter?'

'I need to get out of here.'

'Are you ill? Calm down, tell me what's wrong. You can have a break and come back, it's OK, you'll be all right.'

'I won't be all right. I won't be. It's all ruined.'

He frowned with concern and compassion. Fake, of course. 'I understand, there's a lot of pressure. But you can do this – I have faith in you. Can you tell me what's wrong?'

All the messages, all the laughter, Avril's eyes brimming with tears. If she told Mr Graham, he'd tell her mother. Whisper it to her in their lovers' time.

'Lydia?' he said. 'Please, tell me what's happening.'

'You want me to tell *you* what's wrong?' she spat out. 'Why would *you* understand?'

'Well, I am your tutor, but if you'd rather speak to—'

'You're also fucking my mother.'

She'd thrown it out, not really believing it was true but saying it to shock, to hurt, to drive him away so he'd leave her alone. But the way he went completely still, his hand at his face about to push up his glasses, frozen, told her that she'd been right. The realization drove the blood from her face, dropped the earth out from under her.

'Oh my God,' she gasped. 'You really have. You've been fucking my mother.'

'Lydia. I don't— I never meant to—'

'You fucked her *by mistake*?'

'Calm down, please.' He was looking around quickly, to see if anyone had heard them, and she felt sick.

'That's all you care about – keeping your secret. You don't care about me, you don't care about anything, either of you!'

A part of her, a part that was somehow still rational, wondered if they could hear her through the open windows of the hall. They were standing in almost exactly the same place where she had just stood with Avril. The same place they had stood all those years ago, on that first day, when they walked into school together.

'Lydia, tell me why you ran out of your exam.' Mr Graham's voice was steady. Trying to be reasonable. At least she'd wiped the smile off his face. 'If it's because of me and Jo, that doesn't have to—'

She recoiled when he said her mother's name. 'Leave me alone. Just leave me the fuck alone.'

She wheeled away from him and off, out of the school gates and down the street, running clumsily, her hands both pressed to her chest as if she had been struck there.

Chapter Thirty-Six

Jo

It was incredible how lovely and peaceful the house could be without the children in it. Radio 4 played quietly on the kitchen windowsill, and Jo could hear a blackbird singing outside, probably on the apple tree. It was warm enough for all the doors and windows to be open, sending a green-scented breeze through the house. Honor was out for a walk, and it was Iris's first morning at nursery with Oscar: a trial run, and just for two hours, three days a week, nine till eleven. When the children were with Richard the house felt empty to Jo, but two hours was perfect. Their scents lingered, their games only paused, not abandoned. Iris had been happy to go, toddling in after her older brother with barely a single cheerful 'No!'

Honor might have offered to look after them – she seemed to be developing a bond with the children, which was more than Jo had ever hoped for. And Honor and Jo seemed to have come to some new understanding since they had been to see Adam together. Honor had softened, somehow. She had said, *I have not been very kind to you, Jo.* And though Jo would have thought that it would take a lot more after all these years of enmity, she found that actually, that one sentence of apology, of acknowledgement, was enough.

Still, Honor wouldn't be with them for ever. Probably not for very much longer at all; she was walking without a limp now and would be well enough to go home soon. Besides, Jo wasn't ready to tell anyone, let alone Honor, what she was thinking of doing with her six hours of freedom a week.

She perched on a kitchen island stool and opened the laptop, which she hardly ever used except for occasionally doing the weekly shop online or getting tips about potty training. She'd bookmarked the Open University webpage already.

She couldn't afford the tuition; she couldn't really afford the extra hours for Iris in nursery. But surely she could do something to save the money: sell the car and get a more economical one, switch supermarkets, not use the tumble dryer at all. With Richard remarrying, he might be amenable to selling this house, and she could find somewhere smaller for them to live – maybe even somewhere that would be all theirs, where she would feel at ease to decorate. Where she could put up a shelf for her teacups.

She was only investigating now. She wasn't committing to anything, not yet. They had to see how Iris got on at nursery, get through Lydia's exams, work out a budget and a timetable.

It was just that there was something about the way that Marcus had looked at her when she'd confessed she wanted to get that degree she'd never earned, maybe even teach. He'd looked at her as if she could do it. As if she were a person who had more possibilities than she knew.

331

Jo was clicking through to the courses, not wanting to look at the tuition fees yet, when her phone rang. As always, she got a warm thrill when she saw it was from Marcus.

'I was just thinking of you,' she answered. 'Isn't it risky to ring during school hours?'

'It's about Lydia,' said Marcus, and Jo sat upright on her stool. 'She's walked out of her exam. She seems really upset. I thought she was ill, so I went after her, and she ...' He lowered his voice. 'She knows about us.'

'Oh no.' Jo's hand flew to her mouth. 'Oh God, that's dreadful.'

She tried to think of how Lydia could have found out. Had she glimpsed them through a not-closed curtain, had she snooped on Jo's phone? Jo thought she had been so careful, but how many other people might know, too, while she had been blissfully carrying on?

'Yes,' said Marcus flatly. 'Dreadful.'

'I need to go,' she said. 'I need to find her.'

'All right,' said Marcus, and she hung up.

She grabbed her keys, planning the route that would make her most likely to intercept Lydia on her way home from school, trying to think of what she could possibly say, when the door opened. But it wasn't Lydia; it was Honor. She was walking without her cane, and she shut the door carefully behind her, wiping her feet although it was dry outside.

'Have you seen Lydia?' Jo asked wildly. 'Did she walk past you?'

'I haven't,' said Honor. 'Doesn't she have an exam this morning?'

'I've just had a call from ... from school to say she walked out. I need to find her and make sure she's OK.'

The door opened a second time and Lydia came in. Her hair swung loose from her elastic; her eyes were rimmed with red. 'Lyddie,' said Jo, holding out her arms.

Lydia stepped around her as if she were a stone in her path, and headed for the staircase.

'Lydia. What's wrong? Please tell me.'

'Why do you care?'

'I'm your mother. Of course I care.'

'No,' said Lydia, without turning around. 'No, you lost the right to ask me about my personal problems when you broke your promise to me.'

She began to climb the stairs. Jo followed her. 'Lydia, it's not like that.'

'What's it like then? Are you *in love?*' She sneered the words. 'Did you want revenge on Richard, or was it just because shagging a younger man made you feel better about yourself?'

Jo fought not to argue or to crumple in shame. 'I'm an adult. I can make my own choices. But let's talk about—'

'*You promised me.*' Lydia stopped on the stairs, turning around so quickly that Jo put out her hands, certain her daughter was going to fall. But Lydia held on to the banister. Her knuckles were white.

'Did you leave your exam because of this?' Jo asked.

'It's not about the exams, so you can stop harping on about them. Don't you ever think that anything might be more important?'

'Lydia, honey—'

'You disgust me,' Lydia spat. 'You make me sick. You talk about love and how wonderful it is, and then you do this, and it pollutes it. It's . . . everything is dirty and wrong.'

The last word was on a sob. Lydia ran up the stairs, one flight then another, her feet banging on the treads, and they heard her door crashing shut at the top of the house.

'Oh God,' said Jo again, her hands over her mouth. She sat on the stairs, her mind racing. The promise she had made her daughter, and almost immediately broken. This was all her fault, because she hadn't been able to control herself. Lydia had somehow found out, and it had upset her so much that she was messing up her exams. Messing up her future.

And the contempt in her eyes . . .

'Excuse me,' said Honor. Jo blinked and looked up; Honor was standing on the step beneath her. She must have heard everything. Jo swallowed down hot shame.

'Do you mind letting me past?' Honor asked.

'You can't climb—'

'I've been climbing these stairs for practice for the past three weeks. I'd like to try to talk to my granddaughter, see if I can help.'

'It's my fault,' said Jo. Her voice broke.

Honor put a hand on Jo's shoulder. 'Don't I keep telling you that the world isn't your responsibility? You were right. You're a grown-up. I don't know what kind of foolish promise you made to Lydia, mind.'

'She's disgusted with me. My little girl.'

'You're not the only one in this family with secrets.' Honor put her foot on the step where Jo was sitting, and Jo moved over to let her past. Her mother-in-law climbed up steadily but slowly, grasping the handrail. Jo listened to each step and heard the brisk rap, finally, on her daughter's door.

She could hear Honor's voice, but not the words she said; she seemed to be talking for a long time. But she couldn't hear Lydia replying, and the door never opened. Eventually Honor descended. 'She won't speak with me. She says she doesn't want to speak to anyone. She just wants to be left alone. Perhaps she'll feel better when she's calmed down.'

'Maybe I should call Avril. She might be able to talk to her.'

'Isn't she in her exam?'

Maybe Marcus would know what to say, Jo thought, and then knew she was being ridiculous.

Stephen would know. Stephen and Lydia had always been so close. Even when she was a toddler, he could talk her out of tantrums. Jo put her head between her knees, squeezing back tears.

Honor's hand on her shoulder again. 'Let's have a nice cup of tea,' she said, apparently without irony.

Chapter Thirty-Seven

Lydia

*T*he messages just keep on coming. One after another, relentless.
I shouldn't look, I shouldn't turn on my phone, but I keep on
hoping for something from Avril. Anything. Even more angry words
would be better than silence.

But she hasn't got in touch. Instead I've had the Facebook
posts, the texts, the emails. I've read every one. I shouldn't. But
I can't look away. There's the name-calling and the filth, some
of it from people I have never even heard of, trolls and weirdos,
but there are also some messages of support. Whitney, who has
never spoken to me in her life, seems determined to defend me to
all and sundry, and educate everyone about What It's Like To Be
Gay.

Somehow, the messages of support are even worse than the filthy
stuff. It's like I've become an issue, a cause, rather than a person. As if
I've done something or am someone that has to be defended. It all
underlines that from now on, I will be the girl who came out by
snogging the least popular girl in the school, the girl who That
happened to. I'll be a label, a focus, a stereotype, someone people will
whisper about when I've passed in the corridor. My name will be

shorthand for a bullied lesbian. Nothing else I've ever done or felt or thought about will matter.

All these people looking at me.

I'm also the girl who freaked out in her exam. Who ran out, didn't take it, will fail English because of it, totally fucking up my chance to go to Cambridge, which was one of the only two things I've ever really wanted.

The other thing is Avril.

I haven't rung her. She doesn't want me to. She wants nothing to do with me. I saw the revulsion in her face, not because of who I am but because I lied to her. I lied to her. Every day, every minute, from the first time we met. I lied to her because I am a fucking coward and because I didn't trust her heart to be big enough to keep on being friends with me even if she couldn't love me, too. I chose a hopeless dream instead of a real relationship. I betrayed her and everything I feel about her, and I'll never get her back. Never.

That's why I look at every single message online: as penance. Because I deserve it.

Mum and Granny H keep on knocking at my door. Mum left a tray outside with lunch, and then, when I didn't eat that, she left another outside with dinner. I could smell the food through the door and it made me feel sick. Mum has started pleading with me to come out, to talk. She's said over and over and over again how sorry she is for shagging my teacher. She thinks that's what this is all about, and I'll admit it felt good to be angry at her for it, but now I think it's so small, so desperate, so sad. Like the kiss I gave to Bailey, when I wanted to be kissing Avril.

Granny H came up too. Forty-five years, she's been lonely. Is this what I have to look forward to? Being needy like Mum, or being alone like Granny H?

Mostly, I've been sitting on my bed looking out through the

337

skylight. Watching the clouds gather and the rain begin to fall. It hits the glass in burst circles. It's a cliché to say it looks like tears.

I've been thinking a lot about Dad. How everything changed for him in a moment, too. Everything gone for ever.

OscanIrie went to bed, and after some more pleading and knocking, Mum went to bed, too. I thought she'd camp outside my room to be honest, but eventually I heard her go downstairs, heard the water running faintly. And then everything was quiet, and it was dark outside, and my phone was silent for minutes at a time. It had stopped raining. I opened my bathroom window wide and I gathered up all of my paper cranes. They weighed hardly anything. I put them in the bathtub and then, with a cigarette lighter, I burned them, one by one. The smoke lifted out of the window and away.

I didn't understand why Granny H burned that letter she got from my grandfather, all those years ago, without opening it. But I understand now.

I know what I have to do to make this stop.

Chapter Thirty-Eight

Honor

The house came to life, as it did every morning, with high-pitched voices and the scamper of little feet. Honor was sitting on her bed, fully dressed. She had been up since four, when she'd given up on sleep. Every time she closed her eyes she saw what Jo had spoken to her about, in the car, on the way home from Adam Akerele's flat. She'd seen it every night since then: Stephen running away from his black holes. Running and running in those worn trainers, the shorts with the unravelling hem. All that sadness he had carried inside his tall body, and she had never seen it.

An imperious banging on the door, and it opened. 'Morning, Ganny H!' cried Oscar and she felt him taking her hand. 'Breakfast time! Mummy says I can put the toast in myself.'

She squeezed his small damp hand and let him lead her to the table, although she could do it now with her eyes closed. 'Morning, Honor,' said Jo, among the clatter of plates and the crinkle of the bread wrapper. 'Tea will be ready in a tick.'

'You sound tired.'

'I didn't sleep much,' Jo admitted. 'I was too worried.'

'She hasn't emerged, then?' Honor asked, although she would have heard it if she had.

'She hasn't made a peep. I even rang her mobile, but she didn't pick up. I don't know what to do. She's got an exam at nine thirty this morning, but I've got to take Oscar and Iris to nursery. I could let them stay at home, but Iris has only just started, and the routine . . .'

'I'll be here,' said Honor. 'I'll try to talk with her again.'

'I'll be back by quarter past.' Jo sighed, and her spoon made a musical sound against the side of the mug. 'Thank you. With any luck, she'll . . .'

'I'm making toast, Ganny H! I'm spreading them with jam myself!'

'Iris, try to get the porridge in your mouth, please, instead of on your top.' Jo put tea in front of Honor. 'Listen,' she said quietly. 'You know what Lydia was talking about yesterday, about me and—'

'I know about it,' said Honor. 'It's fine.'

'You do? It is?'

'Here you are! Toast!'

It smelled distinctly burned. Honor picked up a slice and bit into it. 'Delicious.'

'The other piece is for me,' said Oscar happily and climbed up into his chair at Honor's right side.

'You don't . . .' Jo was nearly whispering. 'You don't think it's a betrayal of Stephen?'

'Stephen is dead, and you're alive. I don't know who it is, of course, though I fully approve of the younger man part.'

Then Iris started flinging her porridge, and Jo was too busy to talk. Honor ate up her toast, every blackened dry bit of it, whilst Jo bustled around getting the children fed and ready to

340

go. 'I'll only be a quarter of an hour,' she said, and then: 'Iris! Please don't take your shoes off again! Ring me if she comes out, will you, Honor?'

The door shut behind them. Minutes later, Honor heard Lydia's footsteps on the stairs.

'Have you been waiting until the coast is clear?' called Honor. The footsteps hesitated, and then came down the rest of the staircase and approached. 'You've been worrying your mother silly.'

'I know,' said Lydia. She stood behind Honor, her hands on the back of Honor's chair. Honor could hear her breathing, soft and steady. She twisted her neck but she couldn't see her face, just her blue school jumper.

'Are you off?'

'Yes.' Suddenly she wrapped her arms around Honor. She hugged her, fiercely and hard enough to squeeze the breath from Honor's chest, her hair like silk on the side of Honor's face, surrounding her with the familiar little-girl smell of strawberries and something scorched, like the toast.

'I'm sorry,' she whispered, her words warm on Honor's skin. Honor raised her hands to hold Lydia's arms, feeling her youth, her slender strength. Thinking of all those years when she'd been afraid to hold her granddaughter, afraid of loving her too much, and now the girl was almost grown.

'I'm sorry, too,' said Honor.

Lydia kissed Honor's cheek. And then she was gone.

Chapter Thirty-Nine

Jo

Marcus had rung twice last night, and once this morning before breakfast. Jo hadn't answered. It was the first time she hadn't listened to his messages right away in a fever of anticipation; instead, his name on the screen only brought a wave of guilt. Honor had been nice to say that she was fine with Jo having an affair, with a younger man especially, but Jo knew she had broken a promise to Lydia. She knew that the silence and the recriminations were her punishment. If Lydia ruined her future by mucking up her exams, Jo would never forgive herself.

The ladies at the nursery were lovely as always, welcoming her children with smiles and open arms, but Jo was jumpy as a cat. Her phone rang just as she was leaving and she snatched it up. 'She's left just now,' Honor told her, and Jo breathed a sigh of relief.

She drove to Waitrose. Lydia mocked her for thinking that food could solve everything, but they had a lot to talk about today, and in her experience, talking went much better with chocolate cake. Half an hour later, while she was juggling a cake box, a plastic bag full of milk and bread, and her car keys, her phone rang again. She leaned the cake box on her hip to answer.

'Mrs Merrifield? This is Tina Hutchinson at Woodley Grove School. I'm ringing about Lydia's attendance at examinations.'

Mrs Hutchinson, the head teacher. She was a terrifying woman, though Jo had never had any cause to be terrified of her until now. She put the cake box on the bonnet of her car. 'Yes, Mrs Hutchinson, thanks for calling. We're so sorry about what happened yesterday. Lydia and I have to sit down and have a proper chat about it, and I hope that we can work it out. Can I make an appointment to come in to talk about re-sitting the exam she missed?'

'Of course, but we're obviously concerned about today's exam as well. And for Lydia's welfare, of course.'

'Today's?'

'Yes. It would be helpful if you would ring us if you knew she was going to miss an exam, so the other students don't suffer unnecessary delays.'

'She . . .' Jo leaned against the car. 'She hasn't turned up for this morning's exam?'

'No.'

'But she . . .' Jo swallowed. 'I have to go.'

'Mrs Merrifield—'

Jo rang off and immediately rang Lydia. The phone went straight to voicemail. She'd started the car and disengaged the handbrake before noticing that the cake box was still on the bonnet.

Her route home took her past the school. She searched the pavements as she drove, looking for Lydia, and when she

343

arrived at home she jumped out of the car and ran inside. 'Is Lydia here?' she asked Honor, who was wiping down the breakfast table.

'She left,' said Honor, a frown beginning.

'But where did she go? Did she say she was going to her exams?'

'I don't think so, she—'

Jo ran up the two flights of stairs to Lydia's room. The door was open and the room was empty: bed made, clothes hung up, books and pens arranged neatly on the desk. A smell of burning hung in the air. Even though she knew Lydia wasn't here, Jo stepped into the room, as if it could tell her where her daughter had gone. On the purple bedspread lay a notebook: a blue composition book, the kind she used to use in school. It had a yellow Post-it note attached to the cover, one of the ones Jo had bought her to help with her revision.

Sorry, it said in Lydia's rounded handwriting. Cold flooded Jo's body.

Nearly all the pages were full of Lydia's writing. She skimmed the first page – *It started with yoghurt* – but it was too much of a violation to read any more. She shoved it under her arm and hurried back down the stairs, to Honor.

'What did she tell you?' she demanded, her voice too high. 'What did she tell you this morning, before she left?'

She had never seen Honor flustered. 'She . . . she just said she was off. And then she kissed me. And said she was sorry.'

'Sorry. Like this?' Jo shoved the book with its Post-it message into Honor's hands.

She ran her thumbs over the cover. 'What is it?'

'I think it's a diary. She left it in the middle of her bed. Honor – she didn't turn up for her exam this morning.'

344

'Where would she go?'

'Will you read it?' Jo asked her. 'I don't want to read her diary. I don't want – it's her private thing, and I don't want to make her any more angry at me than she already is. But if you read it, she wouldn't mind so much. Please. Just tell me if it says where she's gone.'

Honor put the diary back into Jo's hands.

'You will have to read it,' she said calmly. 'I am blind.'

Jo stared at her. Her unwavering gaze. 'You're—'

'Read it. Time may be of the essence.'

There was page after page, undated, but if there were any clues, they would probably be near the end. Jo flipped through the pages of writing, catching a word here and there – *Avril*, but also *Harry*, *Bailey*, *Darren*, who were these people? – before she settled on the last entries. It was written in biro, the handwriting messier than Lydia's normally was, so much so that Jo had to work to decipher some of the words.

The messages just keep on coming. One after another, relentless.

She couldn't take it in. Avril, lying, Facebook. *I deserve it.* Burning the paper cranes.

I know what I have to do to make it stop.

And then the last part, on a separate page, written carefully, the biro pressing the words into the paper like embossing. *I think about it all the time,* Lydia had written. Deliberately, as if she had made up her mind. As if she were just marking time, doing this one last thing. *I wasn't there, but I know this was how it happened.*

'She's written about Stephen,' gasped Jo. 'The last thing she's written, she's written about Stephen. Oh my God. I know where she is.'

She dropped the book and turned for the door, but Honor grasped her arm. 'I'm coming with you,' she said.

'But you're—'

'I'm blind and I'm useless. I'm coming with you. You may need some help.'

'We'll go in the car,' said Jo. 'It's not far, it will be faster.'

Her hands shook on the keys and were slick on the wheel. She backed out of the drive, spraying gravel.

'What did you learn?' Honor asked, buckling her seatbelt – by feel, how had Jo not noticed that she did everything by feel? 'In the diary? What had she written?'

Jo floored the accelerator. 'She's fallen out with Avril. And she's being bullied. At school and online, for being gay. She's gay. Why didn't she tell me?'

'She wasn't ready for you to know.'

A turn, taken too quickly, sliding both Jo and Honor on their seats. 'How do you know that?'

'Because she told me. And before you say anything about that, no, I did not tell you, because I respected her secrets. Just as I did not tell Lydia about your secret.'

'Or any of us about yours,' said Jo bitterly. 'How long have you been blind?'

'For some months. Before my fall.'

Another turn, and then straight past houses and fences, mothers walking with children, an elderly man with two terriers. A car going the other way sounded its horn, warning them of their speed.

She never drove down this road. She would go miles out of her way to avoid it. Yet she knew the exact place where the road turned, and the houses stopped, and the trees began, forming a shield from the noise and the drop. The branches bent over the road, making a tunnel of green, and then the car was on the bridge.

Jo saw Lydia right away: just her head and shoulders, her hair gleaming coppery against the green leaves. She was near the middle of the bridge, and she was on the wrong side of the railing. The falling side. The jumping side.

Jo cried out and braked the car with a squealing of tyres. 'Stay here,' she gasped to Honor; 'call 999. My phone's in my bag.' She leaped out of the car, engine still running, and ran to Lydia, arms outstretched. Before she could reach her, she had a sudden thought and stopped. She didn't want to frighten her, to make her lose her footing on whatever ledge was on the other side. Slowly, not taking her eyes off her daughter, she crept forward until she was at the railing. She put her hands on it; her left hand rested on the plaque in Stephen's memory. The words pressed against her palm.

'Lydia?' she said softly, carefully, using the tone she had used when she tucked Lydia into bed, the tenderness she had used when her little girl came to her in the middle of the night from a bad dream. 'Lydia, it's Mum.'

Lydia didn't appear to hear her. She gazed out, not downwards into the railway cutting: out towards the bridge about half a mile away, which was a twin to this one, but her eyes seemed unfocused, as if she were looking at blank air. Her face had no expression. She wore her school jumper and her hair was pulled back into that messy bun, tendrils escaping. But her body was trembling as if she were cold or afraid, trembling hard when everything else was so still.

Someone had to come. Someone had to be here soon. Honor was ringing 999, and someone must have noticed what was happening, seen the girl standing ready to jump off the bridge. Jo looked around and saw no one. Just the Range Rover, skewed, with its door open. No houses were visible

347

from here. All she could see was her daughter and the bridges and the trees and the drop, with the railway tracks an impossible distance below.

Jo hardly dared to look away from Lydia's face, but she risked a glance over the railing at the ledge where she stood. It was about five inches wide, not quite the length of a full brick. Lydia was wearing her running shoes, she saw. Not her school shoes. They had better grips, thank God. She wasn't holding on to anything; her back was against the railing. Her body shook violently. She was so slender, colt-legged in her short school skirt. A breeze could blow her off. The railing was over waist-height. Jo could grab her and try to haul her over, but would Lydia anticipate what she was doing and jump?

Jo didn't pause to think. She stood on tiptoe, raised her leg and swung herself over the wall. Her toes touched the narrow ledge and she let herself down onto it, first one leg and then the other. She wore rubber-soled flats, sensible shoes for running after children. And for climbing bridges. Hanging on to the railing, never taking her gaze from Lydia, she said again, 'Lydia. Lyddie. It's Mum.'

Lydia's eyes focused. 'You shouldn't be here,' she said. Her teeth chattered as she said it, and Jo had to fight not to reach out and grab her. Steady her.

'Sweetheart,' said Jo right away, 'I am so, so sorry. I never meant to hurt you, or to not be there for you.'

'This isn't about you, Mum. This has nothing to do with you.'

'I know. I read your diary, sweetheart. I'm sorry but I found it on your bed and I was worried about you. I know what's been going on with you, and it breaks my heart that people

348

can be so cruel. But it's not worth this, Lydia. It's not worth jumping.'

'Daddy didn't jump,' said Lydia.

'He was trying to save someone else,' said Jo. 'I don't want you to fall. I don't want to lose you, too.'

'I don't want to cope with it any more, Mum.' Lydia's voice was high and weak, almost the voice of a little girl. 'I've been pretending for so long, and I'm tired. Maybe if I hadn't pretended, this would all be all right, but I don't think it would be. Avril never would have loved me. That's all I can think of, over and over.'

Lydia hung her head. A tear welled up in her eye and fell into the void below.

'Even if I hadn't lied,' she said, 'I still would have lost her. I was always going to lose her, except this way, I've lost her in every way, for ever.'

'Lydia—'

'Don't say it,' said Lydia, turning her head so suddenly towards Jo that Jo reached out with her left hand, afraid that her daughter would lurch off the ledge. 'Don't say it's all going to be all right. Because it isn't. I've fucked it up! You don't understand. It isn't ever going to be all right again.'

'I was going to say,' said Jo softly, 'that I've lost a person I loved. I've lost a few. And I understand. I might not feel it exactly the same way you do, but I understand. You feel . . . especially at first, you feel that there's nothing left. No good things in this world.'

'You're going to say to me that there *are* good things. It's what you always say.'

Yes, good things like you. Jo bit it back. Lydia had told her not to say everything was going to be all right. Her daughter

349

didn't want optimism, now. She didn't want to be looking on the bright side, or soldiering on. She wanted a reason to live. And that was quite different.

'You always tell me how to feel,' said Lydia. 'You're always trying to make me feel better. But I'm not you, Mum, I'm myself, and I'm not the same as you. I never have been.'

Lydia's hands were in fists, holding on to nothing. The knuckles were white. Her knees were trembling. Jo shouldn't be looking at her knees, she should be keeping eye contact, but Lydia's knees were naked, pale. There were goosebumps on her legs. They looked like the legs of a child.

She remembered that whole autumn when Lydia was four – a skinny, flyaway four – and insisted on wearing her favourite summer dress every day, without tights, even in the frost.

She looked back up into Lydia's face, saw the faint mascara trails under her eyes. Saw the shadow of her little girl's face overlaid on the face of this young desperate woman.

'It doesn't matter how different we are,' Jo said. 'I love you, Lydia. I love nothing and nobody more than I love you.'

Lydia shook her head. 'It doesn't matter.'

'It might not matter to you. But it matters to me. And to Oscar, and to Iris, and—'

'And to me,' said Honor. Jo glanced over her shoulder just long enough to see that Honor had left the car and was standing behind them. 'Even though I can't climb over this damn rail and risk my life, like your foolish mother. I love you, Lydia. You're the only relative I have left in this world, did you know that? The only one. And I very much hope you're not going to leave me the last of the Levinson line. Especially as I have only just begun to get to know you.'

'I just want it to be over,' said Lydia. 'I want it all to be *over*, don't you understand? I don't want to feel this way any more!'

'Lyddie—'

'And don't tell me it won't last, that things will get better! That I'll look back on this and laugh. You don't come to a fucking bridge about to jump off it and look back on it and laugh. You do it. You *do* it! You jump.'

Lydia lifted her foot and Jo's heart stopped.

'I met a young man who came to a bridge to jump off it,' said Honor, suddenly, 'a *fucking* bridge as you say, and he looks back on it and is grateful that he didn't.'

Lydia's hair fluttered around her face. A breeze blew from the railway cutting, bringing the scent of leaves and grease. She was so beautiful, Jo's daughter.

'I remember when you were born,' Jo told her, hardly knowing what she was saying. 'It was the middle of the night, did I tell you that? And the ward was quiet, even though they say a maternity ward never is. I'd been in labour for hours. Your father was there, holding my hand and singing to me. He was a lot of things, your father, a lot of wonderful things, but he was a horrible singer. I was in between pushes and I was so tired, I didn't think I could make it. I was ready to call it off, just tell the midwife that you could stay inside me, don't bother, I needed to sleep, and Stephen started singing "Isn't She Lovely". He did a Stevie Wonder impression and it was awful. *Awful*. I started laughing, and then the contraction came, and there you were. Born in laughter. Your eyes were wide open and you were the most beautiful, beautiful thing I had ever seen.'

'This is how you know she loves you,' added Honor. 'Because babies are universally ugly. Except for your father.'

Lydia's lips tightened. It wasn't a smile, but it was something, an emotion other than fear.

'When people ask me who I am,' said Jo, 'I tell them I'm just a mother. And that's true, but you know what? It's not true, too. I'm not just a mother. I'm *your* mother, and I'm Oscar's and Iris's mother. And having you, and loving you, has been the most important and wonderful thing in my life. You are so precious to me, Lydia. Nothing and nobody could ever replace you. Never. And you might think that isn't much to be, but to me, you are my everything.'

She was entirely focused on Lydia. Lydia's hair as it blew, light as gossamer. Lydia's skirt ruffling, the rapid pulse that beat in Lydia's neck. Lydia's eyes, hazel, the same as Stephen's, with the long lashes, staring out over the void. *Look at me*, Jo thought with every fibre of her being. *Look at me, see how much I love you, see how precious you are. Look at me, and leave this bridge and come home.*

'Daddy was right here when he fell,' said Lydia. 'Right here where we're standing now. I always thought that Daddy could fly.'

'Don't fall,' said Jo. She wanted to reach out for Lydia, to take her hand, to hold her, but she didn't dare. 'Don't fall, Lydia. We would miss you.'

Lydia closed her eyes. Jo tensed, certain she was about to jump, ready to try to catch her, grab her hand, snag her jumper, anything. She would jump with her if she had to, tangle their bodies together to try to get underneath her to break her fall. Because she could not watch her child die.

She could carry on after anything else, but not that.

'Lydia,' she whispered and the name was blown away from her.

Lydia opened her eyes. She looked at Jo.

'OK,' she said. 'OK. I won't do it. I love you, too.'

She reached out her hand to Jo and Jo leaned over and hugged her, one-armed, their foreheads together.

'I love you so much,' whispered Jo. 'Please, let's get off this bridge.'

Lydia nodded. Jo helped her turn around and she saw Lydia's damp palms slipping on the railing. Her grip looked fragile, and she was still shaking, breathing hard in little sobs. Jo steadied her as she lifted her leg to climb over. Lydia on tiptoe on the ledge, impossibly slender, poised above the drop, for a moment held there only by the thinnest pull of gravity.

Then Lydia swung herself over and into her grandmother's arms.

Jo breathed out a shuddering sigh of relief. She closed her eyes, tried to process it, to believe it. Her daughter was safe.

Oh, *Stephen*, she thought, balanced above where Stephen had died. *I've saved her. She's all right.*

Out of nothing the train came.

An explosion below them, a wind and a rush, a streak of black and yellow shaking the bridge. Jo started, her foot slipped on the ledge, her hand scrabbled for the railing and missed it. And then Jo fell.

Chapter Forty

Lydia

I think about it all the time. I wasn't there, but I know this was how it happened.

Dad could run for ever and ever, and nothing could stop him. He had long strides, a beautiful rhythm. You only had to look at him to know that he could do anything.

When he stood on that bridge next to that man, near the place where they later put that plaque to his memory, he didn't feel any fear. He stood on the ledge – it's a little ledge, I've seen it, about four or five inches wide – and he looked out into clear air. From that high, you must feel as if you could take off and fly: spread your arms and soar, like a paper crane.

He wasn't afraid. He was confident, sure-footed, full of power and grace. He was saving someone's life, a stranger's life. And when he stepped off that ledge, running in air, he must have known what it felt like to be free.

Chapter Forty-One

Lydia

The train passed below like a scream. Lydia grabbed for her mother and her hand closed around some material – Mum's sleeve. Mum was falling.

Her body slid down and Lydia got a grip on her arm; Mum's hand grabbed her wrist, the two of them holding on to each other. Mum's feet kicked in the air. Her face looked up into Lydia's, green eyes wide, mouth in an O of shock.

'Mum,' Lydia gasped, or maybe she didn't have time to gasp but thought it, and felt herself tipping over, pulled over the railing by gravity and her mother's body. Her feet off the pavement, her body tilted, the railing digging into her stomach.

She wasn't strong enough. They were both going over, together, daughter and wife in the same place where Stephen Levinson had died, just seconds after Lydia had decided not to jump, after all.

The train thundered below them.

Then arms went around Lydia's waist from behind, thin but strong as bone. 'No,' muttered Granny Honor in her ear and

Lydia knew that she was trying to hold her back. But Lydia's hand was sweating, it was slippery. She could feel her grip giving way on her mother's arm, felt her weight teetering forward. And Granny H was so old . . .

'Let me go.' She couldn't hear her mother, but she could see her lips moving. Saw and felt her hand open so that she wasn't pulling Lydia down. Lydia shook her head and she held on tighter, pulling back as hard as she could into her grandmother's arms.

A blur of fluorescent yellow beside her. Arms, more arms reaching over her and around her. A man leaned his entire body almost over the wall, part of some human chain, seizing Mum under her arms and hauling her upwards. Hands pulled Lydia, too. She heard shouting, suddenly loud in the silence left behind by the train passing.

'Let go!' someone yelled in her ear. 'She's safe, let her go!'

Lydia didn't let Mum go.

The railing scraped hard against her elbow, tearing her skin, and then she was on the pavement on the bridge, and Mum was, too. Shaking, sobbing, unable to catch her breath, in the flashing lights from the police cars and ambulance and surrounded by people, she finally let go of her mother's arm, her hand screaming with pain. She knelt there on the ground and fell into her mother, crying into her neck, hearing her breathing, feeling her stroking her hair, just like she used to when she was a little girl.

'It's all right,' Mum whispered. 'It's all right.'

Chapter Forty-Two

Honor

Honor had broken her wrist. She had felt it happening – felt the snap when she was holding on to Lydia – but she didn't feel any pain until she got to the hospital. One of the paramedics put a splint on it at the scene. 'Which one was trying to jump, then?' he asked her conversationally.

'None of your business,' Honor told him.

In the ambulance she sat beside Lydia and Jo. She held Lydia's hand with her good one. No one said anything.

For Honor, it had been a confusion of sound. She'd heard Lydia agree not to jump, as the train approached. She hadn't seen Jo slip, but she had felt it somehow, through the skin of the bridge or the way Lydia suddenly lurched next to her. She had thrown her arms around Lydia and heard her struggling, the panting of her breath. She'd heard the cars pulling up behind them, the shouts of the police and paramedics.

The train, she had seen: a streak of black and sunshine yellow in the bottom of her vision, travelling oblivious onward.

When they reached A&E, Lydia was taken off almost

immediately, and Jo went with her. Honor's pocket buzzed and beeped, and she pulled out Jo's phone, forgotten in her pocket since she had rung 999.

'Excuse me,' she said to the man sitting in the waiting room next to her, who appeared to have a swathe of white bandages wrapped round his head, 'can you see whom this message is from?'

He took the phone in his rough hand. 'Marcus,' he said. 'There are a few of them. Want me to read them to you?'

'No. Would you please find Richard in the contacts? And ring him for me?' The man swiped the screen a few times and gave the phone back to her. Richard picked up on the ninth ring.

'Jo?' he said. 'I'm in the middle of something, what is it?'

'It's not Jo. It's Honor Levinson.'

'Honor.' Richard had never liked her; he probably liked her even less now if his fiancée had told him what she'd said to her. Honor did not care.

'You will need to extricate yourself from the middle of whatever it is you are doing, because you have to pick up your children from nursery.'

'What? Why? Jo's got them today.'

'Jo has had an accident. She's fine, but she needs you to act on your responsibilities.' *For once*, she didn't add.

'An accident? What? Where is she?'

'In hospital. She won't be in for long. But the children are only in nursery until noon. You need to pick them up and take them to your house. It's the Little Bear Nursery.'

'But— I'm . . .'

Honor did not reply. Richard seemed to sense her frown

358

even down the phone, because when he spoke again, he sounded bewildered rather than aggrieved.

'Where's the Little Bear Nursery?'

'You're their father, you've got Google, you figure it out,' said Honor, and rang off.

A nurse brought her through to a curtained cubicle with a narrow bed; Honor accepted painkillers. 'It's probably broken,' said the nurse cheerfully, 'but it might just be sprained.'

'It's broken,' Honor told her. 'I heard it. I've got a touch of osteoporosis.'

'Have you got a touch of AMD as well?'

'AMD?'

'Age-related macular degeneration? Bit of poor eyesight, especially in the middle? My mum's got it – she looks out of the corner of her eyes like you. My brother's an optometrist; there are things you can do to slow it down, you know. It's irreversible but there are lots of ways to help. There's a leaflet around here somewhere. I'll find it for you.'

'Thank you,' said Honor. 'You are very observant.'

'Mum finds that she notices sounds more, and smells, too. Sometimes I swear she has a sixth sense now that her eyesight has started to go. She rings me, when I've had a rotten day. It's as if she knows.'

'I don't believe in sixth senses.'

'Maybe it's just a mother thing, then. Anyway, Dr Levinson, I'll find someone to take you up to X-ray.'

Honor leaned her head back against the paper-covered pillow and closed her eyes. In the darkness, she saw Stephen, as clear as he had ever been in life.

'We saved her,' she whispered to him, and she didn't believe in sixth senses, but she saw him nodding. She saw him smile.

Chapter Forty-Three

Jo

Jo sat in a hard chair outside the consulting room, holding a plastic cup full of tea that she did not want. Her shoulder throbbed and her whole body ached, despite the painkillers she'd taken. Inside, someone from Child and Adolescent Mental Health Services was talking with Lydia. They had asked Jo to wait outside, maybe go for a cup of tea in the canteen, and whilst Jo understood the reason, understood it was to make sure that Lydia wasn't hampered in discussing anything by the presence of her family, it brought home to her the weight of what had happened. In the emotion, in the adrenaline rush of trying to save Lydia, and then being saved herself, she had been able to forget that this crisis wasn't the work of a day or two. It was months – *years* – during which Lydia had been suffering and she had been looking the other way.

Lydia had tried to commit suicide. The people in that room with her were trying to determine whether she was likely to do it again, and whether she would be allowed to go home. The fate of her own child was utterly out of her hands.

They'd been in hospital for hours. Jo had sent Honor home in a cab, her arm in a cast. Apparently she had arranged for Richard to pick up Oscar and Iris; a phone call had confirmed it. Richard had wanted to know what was happening, but Jo had said she'd explain later. It was difficult enough for her to deal with everything that was in her head without subjecting it to Richard's scrutiny. Honor would have told him all he needed to know. And probably added a few choice words in Russian for his girlfriend.

Jo smiled despite herself. They had saved Lydia, she and Honor together. And then Lydia and Honor had saved her. Whatever happened, that was something. *Where there's life, there's hope*, her mother used to say, crippled with MS.

Yet with her body aching, her daughter behind yet another closed door, she couldn't convince herself that everything was going to be all right. Or that it wasn't all her own fault that Child and Adolescent Mental Health Services were interviewing Lydia right now.

She'd never even noticed that her own daughter was gay. Or that she was in love with her best friend – the same best friend who spent huge amounts of time under Jo's roof. She'd known nothing about the bullying.

She got up and put the full cup of tea in the bin. Lydia had shut her out, yes. But she had been too busy to notice the reasons why. Too busy looking on the bright side, getting remarried, having children. Having an affair. She'd thought she'd been trying her best as a mother, doing everything she could for her children, but from Lydia's point of view, she was needy. Small and desperate.

What had she thought she was doing?

'Jo,' said someone, and even before she consciously

recognized who it was, her heart made a great thump of gladness and relief. Marcus was standing there in the corridor, in shirt sleeves and a tie, car keys in his hand. He opened his arms to her and she went straight into them, resting her head against his chest, and as he held her tight she realized for the first time what she had been doing.

She had been falling in love. That was what she had been busy doing while her daughter was going through hell. Not having an affair. Not carrying on with the neighbour. Not using a younger man for his body.

Falling in love.

Marcus tilted up her chin. 'Are you all right?'

'How did you know we were here?'

'We heard that something happened with Lydia at the bridge. Is she hurt? Are you hurt? Why do you have your arm in a sling?'

'Lydia was . . . she thought she wanted to jump off. It's the same place where her father died.'

He tightened his hold on her. 'But she's OK?'

'She's all right. I mean, physically. She's all right.'

His scent, the grey-blue of his eyes, the way his hair curled against his neck. The way her body fitted into his. The way he was looking at her. Why hadn't she noticed the meaning of this, either?

'What's the sling for?'

'I was on the bridge with her. On the ledge. I fell off, but she caught me.'

Marcus's face went white. 'You fell?'

'She caught me. And Honor caught her. And then the police were there.' She touched his cheek: he looked frightened to death. 'We're all alive. Honor broke her wrist. I

362

dislocated my shoulder and tore some tendons. Lydia's got a few bruises and scrapes, that's all. She's with the consultant now. Talking to her about why she did it.'

'My God,' whispered Marcus. He kissed her forehead, her cheek. He stared at her face, as if he couldn't believe she was there.

What had *he* been doing all this time they were together?

'I knew she hadn't turned up for her exam,' Marcus was saying, 'but I didn't think that she'd . . . I came right here as soon as I heard.' He smoothed her hair back. 'Why did she do it, Jo?'

A nurse walked by. She didn't pay any attention to Jo and Marcus, but Jo extricated herself gently from Marcus's arms.

'She's broken up with her best friend,' she said. 'And she's being bullied because she's gay.'

Marcus was still pale. 'How did I miss this?'

'I missed it too. She said it was on Facebook.' Jo took her phone from her pocket and called up Facebook. 'She's such a sensible girl that I haven't checked this for a long time. I should have . . .' Lydia's page came up and Jo gasped. The comments, over and over. Some from children that Jo recognized. Instinctively she went to press the button to get rid of the website but Marcus took the phone gently from her hands. He swore, and dug his own phone out of his pocket and dialled a number.

'Ahmed?' he said into it. 'I need you to go to Lydia Levinson's Facebook page and take a screenshot of it. Yes, in Year Eleven. There are some comments that are going to be deleted soon and we need to have a record of them. Thanks.'

Jo's hands were shaking and she was cold. 'I know those kids. They're children.'

'We'll delete the page,' Marcus told her. 'But not till we've collected the evidence. Come here.' He led her to the hard chair, and pulled up another beside it, lacing his fingers with hers on her uninjured side. 'The school will get involved. Those kids will be punished. I'll make sure it happens, Jo. I promise you.'

'She never told me,' Jo said, and all the tears that had stayed away while she'd been trying to save Lydia, while she'd been in the hospital trying to make sure everything was all right, welled up in her eyes.

Marcus gave her a handkerchief. Because he carried a clean handkerchief in the pocket of his trousers. Because that was the sort of man who made her heart melt, the sort of man who she could fall in love with.

He put his arm around her, being careful not to hurt her shoulder, as she cried. She didn't let herself cry for long, because her daughter was behind that door and she might come out at any time, with a doctor who had the power to decide whether Lydia was able to come back home or had to be admitted for psychiatric help; a doctor who might not approve of Jo having a younger boyfriend, who might point out that it was bad for Lydia's mental health. Just two minutes, tops, where the tears flowed from her eyes and she allowed herself to lean against Marcus, hear his breathing and feel the cotton of his shirt, the strong arm embracing her. Then she sat up and wiped her eyes and nose with his handkerchief and folded it. She looked upwards, at the Styrofoam tiles of the ceiling, taking deep breaths to calm herself.

'It's my fault,' said Marcus.

'What?'

He'd got some colour back, but his hair was messier than

usual. He hadn't shaved. His shirt had a scorch mark near the collar.

'I should have known. I saw her every day, and those kids too. I saw all of them. I saw her run out of an exam yesterday. I'm her tutor. It's my job to notice, and I didn't.'

'No,' she said. 'It's my job to notice. I'm her mother. I've been . . . too busy.'

'You've got two other children,' said Marcus. 'But I've been too distracted. Every time I saw Lydia, I couldn't help thinking about . . . so I never really pressed her. Never really talked. And then yesterday, when she accused me, I was shocked. I had no idea she knew about us. If I'd been paying more attention—'

'We shouldn't have done it. We should have stayed away from each other.'

'I know. It would have been wiser to wait, maybe.' He squeezed her hand, and ran his thumb over the back of it.

'We shouldn't have done it at all.'

His thumb stilled. 'Jo?'

'I can't do this.' She swallowed, tasting the tears that she hadn't yet shed. 'I can't be so selfish. I can't think of myself instead of my children. I was too busy having an affair with you to notice what was happening with Lydia. I can't do it, Marcus. I have to stop now.'

'You don't mean—'

'It was fun,' she said firmly, 'but it has to be over now.'

She attempted a smile.

He took his hand away from hers. 'It was fun,' he repeated. 'After this. All that's just happened. That's what you think it's been between us?'

No, I'm in love with you, and that's even worse. Because if I'm in love with you, and you're in love with me, we have to change

365

everything about our lives to be together. And I've got enough changes to deal with right now. I have to concentrate on my children.

She nodded. 'It's what we were both after, wasn't it? We knew it couldn't be anything else.'

Marcus stood up. 'So why am I here?'

'Because you're a nice person? A good neighbour. Lydia's tutor.'

'And someone you had fun with.' He wasn't disguising the anger in his voice. 'This is why you haven't been returning my calls.'

'I haven't been returning your calls because I've been worrying about Lydia.'

'So have I.'

'But you're—'

'Not part of your life. A bit of fun. Nothing compared to your first husband, the hero. I get it. I get it loud and clear. I should have been listening before.' He shoved his hands into his pockets. 'I'll be off, then. Ring me if you need anything. I'll help you in any way I can. But I won't hold my breath.'

The door of the consulting room opened and the doctor stepped out. 'Mrs . . . er . . . Levinson?'

'Merrifield,' said Jo. 'Yes.' She stood up, peering past the doctor's shoulder to where Lydia sat in a chair, her hands clasped between her knees.

Marcus hesitated, and then he turned and left. Jo fought not to glance at him.

Inside the consulting room, Lydia reached her hand out to her mother. Jo sat close to her, in an echo of the pose she'd just sat in with Marcus.

'I've had a good chat with Lydia,' said the doctor, sitting in her own chair, 'and I'm satisfied that she knows exactly how serious this attempt was. However, she tells me that she had decided not to go through with it, before the police intervened.'

'Yes,' said Jo. She searched Lydia's face. 'Yes?'

Lydia nodded.

'She tells me this is at least partly in response to bullying at school and online.'

'The school knows about it. They've promised to help.' She felt Lydia scrutinizing her, the same way Jo had just scrutinized Lydia, and she turned to her and smiled. Incredible how she could smile now, here. 'We're all going to help. I'm not going to get distracted, Lydia. I'm going to be there.'

'My experience is that she'll need significant support at home.'

'And she'll get it. You'll get it, Lydia. Your grandmother and I will give you everything you need. We love you and we want you to come home.'

'I want to come home,' said Lydia, and her voice was so small and vulnerable that Jo gathered her up in her arms, ignoring the pain from her shoulder.

'Nothing,' she whispered fiercely. 'Nothing is more important than you.'

Chapter Forty-Four

Lydia

Being home was weird. She felt like she'd been away for much longer than a few hours. She kept on walking around touching things: OscanIrie's toys, the vase of flowers on the kitchen island, the soft face of her childhood teddy bear. Thinking that she might not have been able to touch any of this again. She might have been gone, nothing more than an absence.

OscanIrie were at their dad's for a few days, but it felt as if they were going to be back any minute. Oscar's wellies had toppled over by the front door, and Iris's beaker sat on the draining board. Lydia ran her finger over the marks Iris had made in indelible marker on the tablecloth. If she'd jumped, would it have felt this way for the people she left behind? As if she were about to come back? She remembered it feeling that way when Dad had died. It was the reason she'd waited for the post and spirited away the letters. She'd been angry, as a child, at Jo for clearing Dad's stuff away: getting rid of his clothes, his books, his shoes by the door. But picturing herself in her father's place, she started to understand the reason for it. That brief moment of hope when you saw something that belonged to your dead loved one, that split second of believing they were still there, must be the worst torture in the world.

She wore pyjamas and slippers, as if she were ill. She kept on hugging her mum, all the time, even when her mum was in the middle of something – making tea or whatever. She was taller than her mother – she'd never even noticed it happening, growing taller than her mother – but she ducked her head under Jo's chin as if she were still a little girl and inhaled her scent of rose perfume. She kept curling up on the sofa with Honor as well. Honor was bony and you had to be careful of her broken wrist, but she touched Lydia's face and hair and hands in a way that made Lydia feel understood. It was Honor's way of seeing.

'Why didn't you tell us you were blind?' she asked her grandmother.

Her fingers trailed over Lydia's mouth and chin. 'I was afraid that admitting it would change everything. I would no longer be allowed to remain in my home; I would be seen as useless and vulnerable. And I was ashamed.'

She tilted Lydia's face towards hers. Lydia could see now, that Granny H's eyes moved too much; that she was looking out of the sides rather than the centre, looking at parts of things instead of wholes. She'd thought it was diffidence, before. It was sort of amazing how knowing one simple fact about a person could change your entire perspective of what they were like.

'Did you feel that way,' Granny H asked her, 'about how you are? Ashamed? Afraid?'

'Sometimes.'

'But now it's the truth that's important.' Honor lowered her voice. 'Except about those flapjacks your mother made this morning. I had to hide mine under a cushion before it broke all my teeth.'

'Mostly I felt alone,' confessed Lydia. 'All alone, even when I was with other people.'

'Yes. Loneliness is powerful and terrible.'

She nodded against her grandmother's meagre shoulder, feeling her fingers seeing her. Said, 'I'll read to you. You must miss reading.'

'We shall have to teach you Russian.'

Now that she was without the mask she'd worn for so many years, she felt raw and delicate, like newly formed skin. But clean, in a way. She thought of the things that had been said to her and they still hurt, but it was at a distance almost. It was like the idea of exams going on without her: something that belonged to a different girl, a different life, somewhere far away from this house with her mother and her grandmother and her. Those moments on the bridge had been more real.

She would have to go out into the world without her mask soon. Not yet. But soon. She'd stand up straight, like Granny Honor did. She'd believe that things would get better, like Mum did.

And yet the ache for Avril didn't go away. It stayed with her all the time. Sometimes it melted into the background, but mostly it was a sharp knife in her middle. The person she had lost; the person she was never getting back.

Chapter Forty-Five

Jo

Two days passed in the sort of slow-and-fast-motion that Jo remembered from having a newborn in the house. Lydia seemed to be sleeping a lot, mostly on the sofa under a blanket. Honor and Jo crept around her when she slept, and when she was awake, they held her and talked with her – about everyday things, normal things, but sometimes about things that mattered. Sometimes they just watched television.

Sara came round the first afternoon with an enormous takeaway curry and two bottles of white wine, which she put straight into Jo's fridge. 'I can't cook for shit, not compared with you,' she said, 'but I can use a telephone, and you need to eat.'

'Sara,' Jo began, and then she faltered. 'I . . . haven't told you everything.'

'OK,' said Sara. 'You will. Later. Right now, look after your daughter, and yourself. And don't forget to eat.'

She hugged Jo before she left, and sent Bob round after work to cut Jo's lawn.

When Jo held Lydia, she felt calm, with a sense of purpose. At other times, she drifted around the house and tried not to think. She missed Oscar and Iris, even though their absence was only temporary; her body craved their little bodies, their wriggling and their scent and their high voices. She missed Marcus. She found herself standing at her kitchen sink, looking over at his house through the gap in the hedge. She tended the sweet peas he had given her, removing dead heads, trimming the stems, replacing the water. They would fade very soon and so would this feeling. So would the memory of his hands on her, his clothes discarded on the floor, the cups of tea he had brought her in bed, every one of which he made sure she would drink right to the bottom. The way he looked at her and made her heart sing.

'You'll stay with us,' she said to Honor in a hushed voice when Lydia had drifted off whilst watching *EastEnders*. 'As long as you like. And that's an order, not a request. I know you love your own house, but you always have a home with us here.'

Honor nodded curtly, but a compression of her lips revealed that she understood what Jo was saying and how much she meant it.

'How long are you going to torture yourself?' she asked, instead of replying to Jo.

'I'm not torturing myself.' Jo got up and went to put on the kettle. Honor followed her.

'She needs a mother, not a martyr or a saint.'

'I'm pretty far from a saint.' Jo turned, folding her arms. 'Is that why you suddenly offered to babysit, by the way? Because you knew I was seeing someone?'

'At first that's why I offered. Then I started to enjoy it.'

'And you weren't concerned about being in charge of children without being able to see?'

'I was concerned. Especially after our trip on the scooter.'

'You drove them on the *scooter*?'

'Only once.'

'This is what I mean. I didn't even notice that I was leaving my children with a blind woman. Which by the way, Honor, was not a good idea at all.'

'I know. It was a mistake. I make them on occasion.'

'You are a piece of work, Honor Levinson.' Jo couldn't help smiling when she said it.

'And you are making yourself needlessly unhappy, Joanna Merrifield. You can be a mother and be a woman as well. Though I never seemed to achieve it, myself.'

'No. Not now. My children need me.'

'Talk to me again when you haven't had sex in forty-five years,' said Honor, 'and tell me then whether you think you've made the right decision.'

She coaxed Lydia out for a walk on Saturday morning. In some ways, it was lovely, having Lydia so dependent, but she knew it couldn't last. She watched as Lydia tilted her head up to soak in the sun and she thought about her daughter going back to school, facing all those people. Lydia coming out as gay to everyone. Lydia living the rest of her life, fighting her battles, moving away, becoming an adult.

Lydia would do it, because she was clever and beautiful and brave. And then Oscar would do it, fighting his own particular battles, and then Iris. They would all leave home, leave Jo behind, and that was exactly what should happen. The normal order of things. Jo would have to open her hands and let them fly.

And what would she be left with then?

Instead of following this line of thought, she walked with Lydia and asked her, 'How long have you known?'

'I always knew I was different,' said Lydia. 'And I knew I was in love with Avril from the moment I met her.'

'Like me with your father.' *And like Marcus and me.* Retrospectively, she could recognize that jolt she'd felt on first meeting him, that afternoon over the hedge. The way she'd been drawn to him in her kitchen. When she'd been twenty she'd called it love, and when she was forty she called it desire. But it was the same feeling. Different, in a million little ways, but also the same.

'Except it won't have a happy ending,' said Lydia. 'She's really angry with me, Mum. She thinks I lied to her.'

'Maybe she's ashamed that she never noticed. I know that I am.'

'I didn't want you to know. I mean, I did want you to know, and I got angry that you didn't guess, but it wasn't really your fault. I was working very hard to hide it.'

Keats Way was bathed in sunlight: the neat hedges, the gravel drives, the mowed lawns – all a perfect façade for the secrets that they had each hidden, all three women in that too-new, blank and cluttered house. 'We have to tell the truth now,' Jo said. 'Even if it hurts. We have to trust each other.'

Lydia nodded. 'That's why I left my diary for you to read. It might even be why I kept it in the first place. I wanted people to read it, and understand me. But it was easier to write it than to say it. Mum?'

'Yes, darling?'

'That last bit I wrote. The bit about Dad.'

'I read it. It's the anniversary tomorrow. Ten years. It was beautiful, what you wrote. I could see the love for your father shining through.' Jo took Lydia's hand. 'He suffered from depression. He never let you see it when he was alive, and I never told you about it after he was gone. It wasn't his fault, and it didn't mean he loved us any less. In fact, I think it meant that he loved us even more.'

'I didn't know.'

'I should have told you. I only shared the good parts, but you deserve to know the bad parts, too.'

'I think what I wrote was wrong. That's one thing I was thinking about when I was up on the bridge, before you came. I said that he wasn't afraid, because I needed him not to have been afraid. But he must have been.'

'He was afraid for the other man. For Adam. Not for himself.'

'But when he fell, he must have been scared. Weren't you scared? When you almost fell?'

Jo stopped walking and closed her eyes. For ten years she had been trying not to think of that moment of terror: Stephen's last moment, the moment of falling. In daylight hours she had thought, instead, of moving on, of loving him and remembering him, of celebrating the life he had saved. She baked cakes for Adam every year, raised Lydia every day. She saw Stephen's features on his daughter.

But at night, she thought of the scream he must have birthed, the air torn from his throat, the rush of the ground, the knowledge that this was over, his life was over. His black hole claiming him at last.

When she had nearly fallen, she had looked up, not down. She had thought of Lydia and of Oscar and of Iris. She had thought of Marcus – yes, him, too. She had thought of Stephen and Honor. Not the ending, not the life over, but the love that was for ever.

'I knew that you would catch me,' she said to her daughter.

Chapter Forty-Six

Lydia

They were on their way back from their walk, laughing about something that Oscar had said on the phone the night before, his sudden obsession with giant space ants, when Lydia saw her walking towards them. She was in shorts and a sweatshirt, sunglasses pushed up onto her head, and she was carrying a plastic cup with a straw in it. Lydia's heart made a great thump and she stopped walking.

Avril walked faster until she met them. 'Hi, Lyds,' she said, her cheeks flushed. 'I just . . . I just came from your house. Your gran said you weren't home. Hi, Mrs M. Gosh, did you hurt your arm?'

'Hi, Avril,' said Mum, and she touched Lydia on the elbow. 'I'll go in and get that banana bread started.' And she left the two of them together, on the pavement in the sunshine, looking at each other, almost as if they'd just met for the first time.

'She's been baking like crazy,' Lydia told Avril. 'And her friend brought round all this curry. If I don't start running again soon I'm going to need that stupid calorie-counting app.'

'I brought you a Frappuccino,' said Avril, holding out the cup. 'I didn't know what else . . . did you really try to throw yourself off that bridge? Really, the same one where your dad fell?'

Lydia shrugged. 'Yeah. I didn't, though.' She took the cup from Avril, being careful not to touch her fingers, and sipped through the straw. It was mocha, her favourite. 'Do you want to go to the park?'

The two of them walked side by side around the corner and into the park. Without needing to speak, they turned left and walked up the slight hill, ignoring the winding path and going straight to the top. Lydia dropped onto the bench and Avril sat beside her. This was the spot where you could see nearly the whole park: the football pitch, the playpark, the pond where the little kids liked to feed the ducks. It was where they had always sat on a Saturday afternoon, and sometimes after school.

'I'm sorry,' Avril said. 'I'm so sorry. I was angry with you, but not about— I don't care if you're gay, I don't care who you fancy. I was just angry because you didn't tell me. I didn't think you would . . . I didn't know it would get so bad.'

'We go to school with some real dickheads.'

'Lyds, they are awful. I told everyone who I saw to shut up, and Harry is doing it, too. School have been calling people's parents. Erin's, and Sophie's. Darren's already been suspended, though there doesn't seem much point seeing as we're only going in for exams. What are you going to do about exams?'

'We're not sure yet. My mum's going in to talk with them on Monday. Maybe I can take them somewhere else, and make the rest up in January.'

'I miss you,' said Avril. 'I miss you a lot. I've been trying to ring you for days.'

'My phone's turned off.'

'Yes. I should have come before, but . . .'

'You didn't know what to say to your friend who had tried to pitch herself off a bridge. It's OK, I don't think I'd know what to say either.'

'Why'd you do it, Lydia? Was it them? Was it me? Was it because I was so angry with you? Because me and Harry were spending so much time together and you were lonely? Was it because Bailey didn't fancy you?'

'It was a lot of things. It wasn't Bailey; Bailey is a cow. I don't want to jump off a bridge any more.'

'Good.'

Lydia drank her mocha. Usually Avril would have asked her for a sip by now, and ended up drinking half of it. She wasn't sure if she was letting Lydia have it all because it had been a peace-offering, or because of what Avril now knew about Lydia. Like it was too close to kissing to share the same straw.

She thought of all the guilty times when she had savoured this kind of kiss by proxy. All the stolen glances and touches, all the secret feelings. That precious part of herself that she had been hiding from the person she loved most in the world.

'So we're friends again?' asked Avril.

'Yeah.'

'And if you find a girlfriend who's not a cow maybe we can have double dates together?'

'Maybe. Though probably not. There's not much choice around here.'

'If you want to go to college instead of staying at school for A levels, I'll do that with you. I asked my mum and she said I could.'

'What about Harry?'

'Harry might anyway.' Avril blushed. 'I know you don't like him, but he did stand up for you, Lyds, afterwards. He really did, and I didn't even ask him.'

Lydia nodded. She pulled her knees up to her chest on the bench and rested her chin on one of them. There was a group of boys playing football on the pitch, and some girls chatting near the pond. They were too far away to recognize; they were just normal people, doing normal things. Sitting up here, she could almost picture herself rejoining them one day.

'It'll be good not to hide,' she said. 'It was pretty tiring.'

'Do you . . .' Avril bit her lip. 'OK, I'm only going to ask you this once, because it's sort of weird, and you don't even have to answer me if you don't want to. But you're my best friend so I have to know.'

But after that Avril just sat there, watching the boys playing football. They could hear them shouting good-natured abuse to each other. Lydia felt a burning in her chest. She knew why Avril couldn't say it.

This was the moment, the moment she'd been thinking about for almost as long as she'd known Avril. The moment where she was supposed to open her heart and let the truth shine out. Where she was supposed to be brave enough not to care about the consequences, where she was supposed to wait, holding her breath and hoping for the answer that would make her happy rather than the answer that she knew was the truth.

Her mother had said: it was the time to trust. The time to

be truthful to each other, and let love sort everything out.

But there were all those other moments with Avril. Not the ones where Lydia was silently wanting, where she yearned to touch but couldn't. There were the moments of laughing together, or watching a television programme in separate houses while they were texting to each other, throwing Maltesers into each other's mouths and missing. The moment where Avril had asked Lydia to walk into school with her that first day because both of them were invisible and visible in the wrong sort of ways, because both of them wanted to be normal and be liked.

Those moments were truth, too. And they were precious enough not to be lost to another kind of truth.

'No, you're not my type,' she said to Avril. And when she smiled at her, it was mostly a real smile. One that would become more real as time went on. Because she was beginning to discover that there was a sort of freedom in hopelessness. It let you look for other, new things to hope for.

Chapter Forty-Seven

Lydia

After Avril had gone home to revise, Lydia walked around the corner to her house. She sped up when she saw the postman, out of instinct almost, and intercepted him before he turned into her drive. He gave her a small bundle of post, circulars and bills. 'Nice day for it,' he said to her, and walked off on the rest of his round. Lydia put the bundle under her arm. Mum was on her knees in the flower bed near the front door, weeding with her good hand. She glanced up and Lydia knew that she'd been watching out for her.

'You shouldn't be doing that with your shoulder,' Lydia said. She held out the post and her mother shook her head.

'Dirty hands. Anyway, I wanted to get this done before Richard brings Oscar and Iris back tomorrow. How did it go with Avril?' She wiped hair away from her forehead, leaving a smear of soil.

'Yeah. We're friends.' Her mother studied her. 'It's OK,' Lydia said. 'I mean, it's not OK, but I'd rather have her as a friend than not having her at all.'

'Are you sure she isn't . . . ?'

'No, Mum, she isn't. You really have no gaydar whatsoever, do you?'

Mum laughed, but then she caught sight of something behind Lydia and she stopped. A violent blush rose on her cheeks.

'Mum?' Lydia turned. She should have guessed: it was Mr Graham, at the end of their drive.

Mum scrambled to her feet. There were dark dirt patches on the knees of her jeans. Lydia looked back at Mr Graham and he was flushed, too. God, like a couple of teenagers. How embarrassing.

He hesitated. 'I . . . er, wondered if I could talk with Lydia?'

'Of course,' said Mum, obviously trying really hard to be calm, and she went into the house, shutting the door a bit too firmly behind her. Lydia watched Mr Graham watching her go. He had on a T-shirt and jeans. It was sort of weird to see him in normal person clothes. Also weird to see him looking at her mother that way.

He cleared his throat and came up the drive. 'It's partly an unofficial school visit. I wanted to see how you were doing, and talk with you a bit about what you think you might want to do about your exams.'

'I haven't had much time to think about them.' Lydia sat on the grass, laying the post beside her, and Mr Graham joined her. He wasn't wearing his glasses, which made him look even less teacherish.

'And that's absolutely fine. Your health is the most important thing. I thought you'd like to know that the school did have a look at the cache of your Facebook page before it was deleted, and several students have been suspended as a result. The ones in Year Eleven will be taking their exams, but in a different part of the building. They'll be completely isolated from the rest of the school.'

Lydia nodded. As when Avril had told her, it didn't really give her any pleasure to know that people were being punished because of her. They deserved it, but she'd rather it hadn't happened at all. 'I might go to the college next year.'

'Good idea. We can arrange for you to do some exams at the college now, if you're up for it. But we can sort all that out on Monday when you come in with your mum. The thing that I wanted to tell you is that this isn't make or break, Lydia. You can catch up on all of these exams. And it is my personal priority to ensure that your future isn't affected because of this. I know you want to go to Oxbridge after A levels, and though it might take a little more time for that to happen, I'll do everything I can to give you the best possible shot.'

She knew it was at least partly his guilt talking, but she could also tell that he meant what he said.

'It happened to me,' he added, in a lower voice. 'Though I was younger than you and I was bullied for a different reason. And it was boys who were picking on me, for being smaller than them, so it was a little bit more . . . straightforward. But it was similar enough.'

'Oh.'

'I should have noticed what was happening with you. I'm very sorry that I didn't. If it helps . . . it does get better, Lydia. Though you never forget it. If you're lucky, it can make you stronger.'

'Thanks,' she said. Not prepared for this shift of perspective from seeing Mr Grin, the teacher who smiled too much, to a person who'd suffered, who maybe wanted to be liked because he had spent too long without friends.

What if everyone had something like this – a similar twist inside, a reason, a fear? Even Erin, Darren, Bailey? What if it was all done, every bit of it, to connect, to be liked, not to fall through emptiness, alone?

She sat very still on the grass, feeling a bit dizzy with the thought of it. An entire universe inside every person, too huge to comprehend, except in glimpses. The world so much larger than she had ever imagined, so much bigger than she had thought it could be when she balanced on the ledge of the bridge.

Mr Graham cleared his throat, bringing her back to here, in front of her house, sitting with her teacher who was suddenly a human being.

'I also ...' He took a deep breath. 'I also wanted to apologize for keeping secrets from you. And if I missed seeing something important because of the way I feel about your mother, I am truly sorry.'

'OK.'

'What happened between your mother and me has absolutely nothing to do with you. Nothing at all.'

'God, I hope not.'

'And I like her a lot. I don't know if she feels the same way about me.'

Lydia grimaced. There were glimpses inside a person, and then there were *glimpses*. 'That's sort of gross, actually.'

'Because you don't like me, or because you don't think I'm good for her, or ... ?'

'Because she's my mum. Would you like to think about your mum shagging the neighbour?'

'My mum lives next door to two gay men and a goat. But I take your point.' He sighed. 'I probably shouldn't tell you this, but I don't think I can live up to your dad.'

'Nobody can,' said Lydia. 'But the thing is, he's dead.'

'That makes it even harder to live up to him. Lydia, this might be a bit unusual, but I wanted to ask your permission to invite your mother out on a date.'

'You don't need my permission,' she said, surprised.

'I think I do. You're the most important thing to your mum right now, and that's the way it should be. I want to be part of her life, but I can't – I don't want to be – unless you're OK with it.' He held out his hands. 'It would be all above board, no secrets. Dinner, a movie. Boring stuff.' He smiled wryly.

Lydia considered him. He was all right. He tried too hard, but you couldn't hold that against him, especially once you knew why. He was better than Richard by a long shot. And the way her mother had actually blushed when she saw him . . . it was sort of sweet . . . and a little disgusting. But sweet. And didn't her mother have more inside her, too – more than Lydia would have ever thought?

'Knock yourself out,' she said. 'She's inside now. Probably taking a cake out of the oven. It might be a good time to ask. If she says no she might feel obliged to feed you in compensation.'

She watched him go inside the house, and listened hard for any sounds of pots and pans being flung about. But there was nothing like that. All she could hear was a wood pigeon sighing, and the distant sound of crows, and the buzz of a hedge-trimmer. Maybe, far away, a train.

She turned over the envelopes that the postman had given her, remembering how she had used to wait for the post when she was a little girl, hoping for something exciting, or something she could put away and save for the day when she might be able to give it to her daddy. She remembered how she'd longed to read his letters aloud to him, and see the pleasure and surprise when he listened.

It had been a magical wish, a wish that would never come true. But today had been a day of second chances. You never knew.

Gas bill, credit-card bill, a clothing catalogue, money off online shopping. At the bottom, made of tissue-y thin paper, was a blue airmail envelope with a US stamp and a California postmark, addressed in a handwriting that she recognized. It was the same handwriting that had been on eight carefully saved Christmas cards full of words of regret and love, which had been written to her father but read aloud, years later, by his daughter to her grandmother.

It was addressed to *Dr Honor Levinson*.

Lydia let the rest of the post fall onto the grass. Holding the letter to her heart, she ran into the house to deliver it.

Acknowledgements

Thank you to my agent Teresa Chris and my editor Harriet Bourton – you are absolutely my dream team. Also thanks to Francesca Best, Bella Bosworth, Sarah Harwood and Alice Murphy-Pyle, and everyone at Transworld who are so brilliant. Thank you to Alicia Clancy and the St Martin's team in the United States, and to Patricia Moosbrugger, for making a big dream come true. I have owed my copy-editor Joan Deitch very many thanks for a very long time now: thank you, Joan, for your keen eyes and understanding.

Thank you to Dr Linda Cameron OD for advice on AMD, including giving me funky glasses that replicated Honor's view of the world. Thanks to Dr Joanna Cannon for advice on mental health services for young people, and Clare Mackintosh for insight into police response to attempted suicide. Thanks to Dr Iris Kwok, Caroline Stewart and my brother Dr Matthew Cohen for medical advice on what to do with an eighty-year-old woman with a broken hip, and to my cousin Sara Kass for advice about physical therapy and really unwise ways to use a mobility scooter. Thanks too to my cousins Olivia and Lewis Kass for advice and demonstrations on how teenagers use social media. Thank you to Irina Hernon for providing Russian translation of insults during our children's Sports Day, and to Kirsty Jane McCluskey for discussing the nuances of said insults. Thanks to young Oliver Frankland for going through a 'No!' phase.

Thank you to my running buddies Harriet Greaves and Claudia Spence for listening to my plot problems while we covered the miles. Thank you to Rowan Coleman for sharing and encouraging certain unhealthy obsessions, and to Brigid Coady, Miranda Dickinson, Tamsyn Murray, Cally Taylor, Kate Harrison, Natasha Onwu, Anna Scamans and Ruth Ng for constant support.

Thanks as always to my husband, my son, and my parents, all of whom have taught me everything and who put up with me.

Last, but certainly not least, thank you to Stonewall (www.stonewall.org.uk) and the It Gets Better Project (www.itgetsbetter.org) for helping young people facing homophobic and transphobic bullying.

Julie Cohen grew up in the western mountains of Maine. Her house was just up the hill from the library and she spent many hours walking back and forth, her nose in a book. She studied English literature at Brown University and Cambridge University and is a popular speaker and teacher of creative writing, including classes for *The Guardian* and Literature Wales. Her books have been translated into fifteen languages and have sold nearly a million copies. Julie lives in Berkshire with her husband, son, and a terrier of dubious origin. She is also the author of *Dear Thing* and *Where Love Lies*. Visit her online at www.julie-cohen.com.

1. Which of the three protagonists—Honor, Jo, or Lydia—
   do you think is the true heroine of this novel?

2. All three women feel that they are different from each
   other . . . but how are they alike?

3. The book begins with Honor's fall, and there are
   many types of falling in this novel, both literal and
   metaphorical. What others can you find, and why do
   you think falling is important in the book?

*Discussion
Questions*

4. Honor, Jo, and Lydia all fall in love with the wrong
   people. How do they each deal with this problem in
   different ways?

5. In Lydia's school, there are openly homosexual
   students who are accepted. Why do you think Lydia is
   afraid to tell the truth about her sexuality, and why do
   you think she's bullied for it?

6. The novel has a fairly open ending: what do you think
   happens next?

7. Honor says: "Sometimes hope is too painful to
   contemplate." And later, Lydia thinks: "There was
   a sort of freedom in hopelessness." What do you
   think the novel is saying about hope, and about
   second chances?

St. Martin's
Griffin

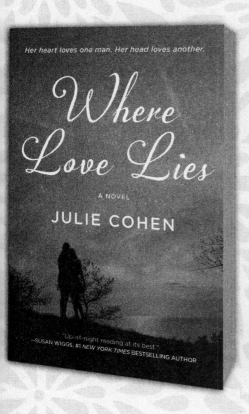
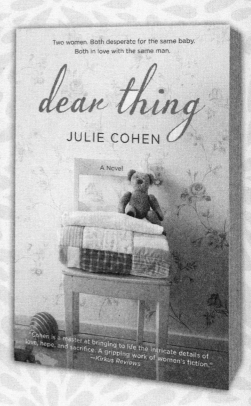
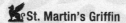